Greatest Horse Stories

BLACK BEAUTY by Anna Sewell

UNBROKEN by Jessie Haas

NATIONAL VELVET by Enid Bagnold

D0124124

■ HARPERCOLLINS*PUBLISHERS*

ANNA SEWELL

Black Beauty

HarperTrophy®
A Division of HarperCollins*Publishers*

Black Beauty was first published in 1877.

Harper Trophy® is a registered trademark
of HarperCollins Publishers Inc.

Black Beauty
Library of Congress Cataloging-in-Publication Data
Sewell, Anna, 1820–1878.
   Black Beauty / Anna Sewell.
       p.   cm.
   Summary: A horse in nineteenth-century England recounts his experiences with both
good and bad masters.
   ISBN 0-694-01243-2
   1. Horses—Juvenile Fiction.   [1. Horses—Fiction.]   I. Title.
PZ10.3.S38Bl   1998   98-22607
[Fic]—dc21   CIP
                                                                                    AC

Typography by Alicia Mikles
5   6   7   8   9   10
❖
First Harper Trophy edition, 1998

Visit us on the World Wide Web!
http://www.harperchildrens.com

Contents

Part One

1

My Early Home

THE FIRST PLACE that I can well remember was a large pleasant meadow with a pond of clear water in it. Some shady trees leaned over it, and rushes and water-lilies grew at the deep end. Over the hedge on one side we looked into a plowed field, and on the other we looked over a gate at our master's house, which stood by the roadside; at the top of the meadow was a plantation of fir trees, and at the bottom a running brook overhung by a steep bank.

While I was young I lived upon my mother's milk, as I could not eat grass. In the daytime I ran by her side, and at night I lay down close by her. When it was hot we used to stand by the pond in the shade of the trees, and when it was cold, we had a nice warm shed near the plantation.

As soon as I was old enough to eat grass, my mother used to go out to work in the daytime, and come back in the evening.

There were six young colts in the meadow besides me; they were older than I was; some were nearly as large as grown-up horses. I used to run with them, and had great fun; we used to gallop all together round and round the field, as hard as we could go. Sometimes we had rather rough play, for they would frequently bite and kick as well as gallop.

One day, when there was a good deal of kicking, my mother whinnied to me to come to her, and then she said:

"I wish you to pay attention to what I am going to say to you. The colts who live here are very good colts, but they are cart-horse colts, and, of course, they have not learned manners. You have been well bred and well born; your father has a great name in these parts, and your grandfather won the cup two years at the Newmarket races; your grandmother had the sweetest temper of any horse I ever knew, and I think you have never seen me kick or bite. I hope you will grow up gentle and good, and never learn bad ways; do your work with a good will, lift your feet up well when you trot, and never bite or kick even in play."

I have never forgotten my mother's advice; I knew she was a wise old horse, and our master thought a great deal of her. Her name was Duchess, but he often called her Pet.

Our master was a good, kind man. He gave us good food, good lodging, and kind words; he spoke as kindly to us as he did to his little children. We were all fond of him, and my mother loved him very much. When she saw him at the gate, she would neigh with joy, and trot up to him. He would pat and stroke her and say, "Well, old Pet, and how is your little Darkie?" I was a dull black, so he called me Darkie; then he would give me a piece of bread, which was very good, and sometimes he brought a carrot for my mother. All the horses would come to him, but I think we were his favorites. My mother always took him to the town on a market day in a light gig.

There was a plowboy, Dick, who sometimes came into our field to pluck blackberries from the hedge. When he had eaten all he wanted, he would have what he called fun with the colts, throwing stones and sticks at them to make them gallop. We did not much mind him, for we could gallop off; but sometimes a stone would hit and hurt us.

One day he was at this game, and did not know that the master was in the next field; but he was there, watching what was going on. Over the hedge he jumped in a snap, and catching Dick by the arm, he gave him such a box on the ear as made him roar with the pain and surprise. As soon as we saw the master, we trotted up nearer to see what went on.

"Bad boy!" he said. "Bad boy to chase the colts. This is not the first time, nor the second, but it shall be the last. There—take your money and go home. I shall not want you on my farm again." So we never saw Dick any more. Old Daniel, the man who looked after the horses, was just as gentle as our master, so we were well off.

2

The Hunt

BEFORE I WAS two years old a circumstance happened which I have never forgotten. It was early in the spring; there had been a little frost in the night, and a light mist still hung over the plantations and meadows. I and the other colts were feeding at the lower part of the field when we heard, quite in the distance, what sounded like the cry of dogs. The oldest of the colts raised his head, pricked his ears, and said, "There are the hounds!" and immediately cantered off, followed by the rest of us to the upper part of the field, where we could look over the hedge and see several fields beyond. My mother and an old riding horse of our master's were also standing near, and seemed to know all about it.

"They have found a hare," said my mother, "and if they come this way we shall see the hunt."

And soon the dogs were all tearing down the field of young wheat next to ours. I never heard such a noise as they made. They did not bark, nor howl, nor whine, but kept on a "yo! yo, o, o! yo! yo, o, o!" at the top of their voices. After them came a number of men

on horseback, some of them in green coats, all galloping as fast as they could. The old horse snorted
and looked eagerly after them, and we young colts
wanted to be galloping with them, but they were soon
away into the fields lower down; here it seemed as
if they had come to a stand; the dogs left off barking, and ran about every way with their noses to the
ground.

"They have lost the scent," said the old horse;
"perhaps the hare will get off."

"What hare?" I said.

"Oh! I don't know *what* hare; likely enough it may
be one of our own hares out of the plantation; any
hare they can find will do for the dogs and men to run
after." And before long the dogs began their "yo! yo,
o, o!" again, and back they came all together at full
speed, making straight for our meadow at the part
where the high bank and hedge overhang the brook.

"Now we shall see the hare," said my mother; and
just then a hare wild with fright rushed by and made
for the plantation. On came the dogs. They burst over
the bank, leaped the stream, and came dashing across
the field, followed by the huntsmen. Six or eight men
leaped their horses clean over, close upon the dogs.
The hare tried to get through the fence; it was too
thick, and she turned sharp round to make for the

road, but it was too late; the dogs were upon her with their wild cries; we heard one shriek, and that was the end of her. One of the huntsmen rode up and whipped off the dogs, who would soon have torn her to pieces. He held her up by the leg, torn and bleeding, and all the gentlemen seemed well pleased.

As for me, I was so astonished that I did not at first see what was going on by the brook; but when I did look, there was a sad sight; two fine horses were down, one was struggling in the stream, and the other was groaning on the grass. One of the riders was getting out of the water covered with mud, the other lay quite still.

"His neck is broken," said my mother.

"And serve him right, too," said one of the colts.

I thought the same, but my mother did not join with us.

"Well, no," she said, "you must not say that; but though I am an old horse, and have seen and heard a great deal, I never yet could make out why men are so fond of this sport; they often hurt themselves, often spoil good horses, and tear up the fields, and all for a hare or a fox, or a stag, that they could get more easily some other way; but we are only horses, and don't know."

While my mother was saying this, we stood and

looked on. Many of the riders had gone to the young man; but my master, who had been watching what was going on, was the first to raise him. His head fell back and his arms hung down, and everyone looked very serious. There was no noise now; even the dogs were quiet, and seemed to know that something was wrong. They carried him to our master's house. I heard afterward that it was young George Gordon, the squire's only son, a fine, tall young man, and the pride of his family.

There was now riding off in all directions to the doctor's, to the farrier's, and no doubt to Squire Gordon's, to let him know about his son. When Mr. Bond, the farrier, came to look at the black horse that lay groaning on the grass, he felt him all over, and shook his head; one of his legs was broken. Then some one ran to our master's house and came back with a gun; presently there was a loud bang and a dreadful shriek, and then all was still; the black horse moved no more.

My mother seemed much troubled; she said she had known that horse for years, and that his name was "Rob Roy"; he was a good bold horse, and there was no vice in him. She never would go to that part of the field afterward.

Not many days after, we heard the church bell

tolling for a long time; and looking over the gate we saw a long, strange black coach that was covered with black cloth and was drawn by black horses; after that came another and another and another, and all were black, while the bell kept tolling, tolling. They were carrying young Gordon to the churchyard to bury him. He would never ride again. What they did with Rob Roy I never knew; but 'twas all for one little hare.

3
My Breaking In

I WAS NOW beginning to grow handsome; my coat had grown fine and soft, and was bright black. I had one white foot, and a pretty white star on my forehead. I was thought very handsome; my master would not sell me till I was four years old; he said lads ought not to work like men, and colts ought not to work like horses till they were quite grown up.

When I was four years old, Squire Gordon came to look at me. He examined my eyes, my mouth, and my legs; he felt them all down; and then I had to walk and trot and gallop before him. He seemed to like me, and said, "When he has been well broken in, he will do very well." My master said he would break me in himself, as he should not like me to be frightened or hurt, and he lost no time about it, for the next day he began.

Every one may not know what breaking in is, therefore I will describe it. It means to teach a horse to wear a saddle and bridle and to carry on his back a man, woman, or child; to go just the way they wish, and to go quietly. Besides this, he has to learn to wear a collar, a crupper, and a breeching, and to stand still while they are put on; then to have a cart or a chaise fixed behind him, so that he cannot walk or trot without dragging it after him. And he must go fast or slow, just as his driver wishes. He must never start at what he sees, nor speak to other horses, nor bite, nor kick, nor have any will of his own; but always do his master's will, even though he may be very tired or hungry; but the worst of all is, when his harness is once on, he may neither jump for joy nor lie down for weariness. So you see this breaking in is a great thing.

I had of course long been used to a halter and a headstall, and to be led about in the field and lanes quietly, but now I was to have a bit and bridle; my master gave me some oats as usual, and after a good deal of coaxing, he got the bit into my mouth, and the bridle fixed, but it was a nasty thing! Those who have never had a bit in their mouths cannot think how bad it feels; a great piece of cold hard steel as thick as a man's finger to be pushed into your mouth, between your teeth and over your tongue, with the ends coming out at the corner of your mouth, and held fast there by straps over your head, under your throat, round your nose, and under your chin; so that no way in the world can you get rid of the nasty hard thing. It is very bad! Yes, very bad! At least I thought so; but

I knew my mother always wore one when she went out, and all horses did when they were grown up; and so, what with the nice oats, and what with my master's pats, kind words, and gentle ways, I got to wear my bit and bridle.

Next came the saddle, but that was not half so bad; my master put it on my back very gently, while old Daniel held my head; he then made the girths fast under my body, patting and talking to me all the time; then I had a few oats, then a little leading about; and this he did every day till I began to look for the oats and the saddle. At length, one morning, my master got on my back and rode me round the meadow on the soft grass. It certainly did feel queer; but I must say I felt rather proud to carry my master, and as he continued to ride me a little every day I soon became accustomed to it.

The next unpleasant business was putting on the iron shoes; that too was very hard at first. My master went with me to the smith's forge, to see that I was not hurt or got any fright. The blacksmith took my feet in his hands, one after the other, and cut away some of the hoof. It did not pain me, so I stood still on three legs till he had done them all. Then he took a piece of iron the shape of my foot, and clapped it on, and drove some nails through the shoe quite into my hoof, so that the shoe was firmly on. My feet felt very stiff and heavy, but in time I got used to it.

And now having got so far, my master went on to break me to harness; there were more new things to wear. First, a stiff heavy collar just on my neck, and a bridle with great side-pieces against my eyes called blinkers, and blinkers indeed they were, for I could not see on either side, but only straight in front of me. Next there was a small saddle with a nasty stiff strap that went right under my tail; that was the crupper: I hated the crupper—to have my long tail doubled up and poked through that strap was almost as bad as the bit. I never felt more like kicking, but of course I could not kick such a good master, and so in time I got used to everything, and could do my work as well as my mother.

I must not forget to mention one part of my training, which I have always considered a very great advantage. My master sent me for a fortnight to a neighboring farmer's, who had a meadow which was skirted on one side by the railway. Here were some sheep and cows, and I was turned in among them.

I shall never forget the first train that ran by. I was feeding quietly near the pales which separated the meadow from the railway, when I heard a strange sound at a distance, and before I knew whence it came—with a rush and a clatter, and a puffing out of smoke—a long black train of something flew by, and was gone almost before I could draw my breath. I turned and galloped to the further side of the meadow as fast as I could go, and there I stood snorting with astonishment and fear. In the course of the day many other trains went by, some more slowly. These drew up at the station close by, and sometimes made an awful shriek and groan before they stopped. I thought it very dreadful, but the cows went on eating very quietly, and hardly raised their heads as the black frightful thing came puffing and grinding past.

For the first few days I could not feed in peace; but as I found that this terrible creature never came into the field, or did me any harm, I began to disregard it, and very soon I cared as little about the passing of a train as the cows and sheep did.

Since then I have seen many horses much alarmed and restive at the sight or sound of a steam engine; but thanks to my good master's care, I am as fearless at railway stations as in my own stable. Now if any one wants to break in a young horse well, that is the way.

My master often drove me in double harness with my mother because she was steady and could teach me how to go better than a strange horse. She told me the better I behaved, the better I should be treated, and that it was wisest always to do my best to please my master. "But," said she, "there are a great many kinds of men; there are good, thoughtful men like our master, that any horse may be proud to serve; but there are bad, cruel men, who never ought to have a horse or dog to call their own. Besides, there are a great many foolish men, vain, ignorant, and careless, who never trouble themselves to think. These spoil more horses than all, just for want of sense; they don't mean it, but they do it for all that. I hope you will fall into good hands; but a horse never knows who may buy him, or who may drive him. It is all a chance for us, but still I say, do your best wherever it is, and keep up your good name."

4

Birtwick Park

AT THIS TIME I used to stand in the stable, and my coat was brushed every day till it shone like a rook's wing. It was early in May, when there came a man from Squire Gordon's, who took me away to the Hall. My master said, "Good-bye, Darkie. Be a good horse, and always do your best." I could not say good-bye, so I put my nose into his hand. He patted me kindly, and I left my first home. As I lived some years with Squire Gordon, I may as well tell something about the place.

Squire Gordon's Park skirted the village of Birtwick. It was entered by a large iron gate, at which stood the first lodge, and then you trotted along on a smooth road between clumps of large old trees; then another lodge and another gate, which brought you to the house and the gardens. Beyond this lay the home paddock, the old orchard, and the stables. There was accommodation for many horses and carriages; but I need only describe the stable into which I was taken; this was very roomy, with four good stalls; a large swinging window opened into the yard, which made it pleasant and airy.

The first stall was a large square one, shut in behind with a wooden gate; the others were common stalls, good stalls, but not nearly so large; it had a low rack for hay and a low manger for corn; it was called a loose box, because the horse that was put into it was not tied up, but left loose, to do as he liked. It is a great thing to have a loose box.

Into this fine box the groom put me; it was clean, sweet, and airy. I never was in a better box than that, and the sides were not so high but that I could see all that went on through the iron rails that were at the top.

He gave me some very nice oats, he patted me, spoke kindly, and then went away.

When I had eaten my corn, I looked round. In the stall next to mine stood a little fat gray pony, with a thick mane and tail, a very pretty head, and a pert little nose.

I put my head up to the iron rails at the top of my box and said, "How do you do? What is your name?"

He turned round as far as his halter would allow, held up his head, and said, "My name is Merrylegs. I am very handsome, I carry the young ladies on my back, and sometimes I take our mistress out in the low chair. They think a great deal of me, and so does James.

Are you going to live next door to me in the box?"

I said, "Yes."

"Well, then," he said, "I hope you are good-tempered; I do not like any one next door who bites."

Just then a horse's head looked over from the stall beyond; the ears were laid back, and the eye looked rather ill-tempered. This was a tall chestnut mare, with a long handsome neck. She looked across to me and said:

"So it is you who have turned me out of my box. It is a very strange thing for a colt like you, to come and turn a lady out of her own home."

"I beg your pardon," I said, "I have turned no one out. The man who brought me put me here, and I had nothing to do with it; and as to my being a colt, I am turned four years old and am a grown-up horse. I never had words yet with horse or mare, and it is my wish to live at peace."

"Well," she said, "we shall see. Of course I do not want to have words with a young thing like you." I said no more.

In the afternoon, when she went out, Merrylegs told me all about it.

"The thing is this," said Merrylegs, "Ginger has a bad habit of biting and snapping; that is why they call her Ginger, and when she was in the loose box, she used to snap very much. One day she bit James in the arm and made it bleed, and so Miss Flora and Miss Jessie, who are very fond of me, were afraid to come into the stable. They used to bring me nice things to eat, an apple or a carrot, or a piece of bread, but after Ginger stood in that box they dared not come, and I missed them very much. I hope they will now come again, if you do not bite or snap."

I told him I never bit anything but grass, hay, and corn, and could not think what pleasure Ginger found it.

"Well, I don't think she does find pleasure," said Merrylegs; "it is just a bad habit. She says no one was ever kind to her, and why should she not bite? Of course, it is a very bad habit; but I am sure, if all she says be true, she must have been very ill-used before she came here. John does all he can to please her, and James does all he can, and our master never uses a whip if a horse acts right; so I think she might be good-tempered here. You see," he said, with a wise look, "I am twelve years old; I know a great deal, and I can tell you there is not a better place for a horse all round the country than this. John is the best groom that ever was, he has been here fourteen years; and you never saw such a kind boy as James is, so that it is all Ginger's own fault that she did not stay in that box."

19

5
A Fair Start

THE NAME OF the coachman WAS John Manly; he had a wife and one little child, and they lived in the coachman's cottage, very near the stables.

The next morning he took me into the yard and gave me a good grooming, and just as I was going into my box, with my coat soft and bright, the Squire came in to look at me, and seemed pleased. "John," he said, "I meant to have tried the new horse this morning, but I have other business. You may as well take him around after breakfast; go by the common and the Highwood, and back by the water mill and the river. That will show his paces."

"I will, sir," said John. After breakfast he came and fitted me with a bridle. He was very particular in letting out and taking in the straps, to fit my head comfortably; then he brought the saddle, but it was not broad enough for my back; he saw it in a minute and went for another, which fitted nicely. He rode me first slowly, then a trot, then a canter, and when we were on the common he gave me a light touch with his whip, and we had a splendid gallop.

"Ho, ho! my boy," he said, as he pulled me up, "you would like to follow the hounds, I think."

As we came back through the Park we met the Squire and Mrs. Gordon walking; they stopped, and John jumped off.

"Well, John, how does he go?"

"First-rate, sir," answered John. "He is as fleet as a deer, and has a fine spirit too; but the lightest touch of the rein will guide him. Down at the end of the common we met one of those traveling carts hung all over with baskets, rugs, and such like; you know, sir, many horses will not pass those carts quietly; he just took a good look at it, and then went on as quiet and pleasant as could be. They were shooting rabbits near the Highwood, and a gun went off close by; he pulled up a little and looked, but did not stir a step to right or left. I just held the rein steady and did not hurry him, and it's my opinion he has not been frightened or ill-used while he was young."

"That's well," said the Squire, "I will try him myself tomorrow."

The next day I was brought up for my master. I remembered my mother's counsel and my good old master's, and I tried to do exactly what he wanted me to do. I found he was a very good rider, and thoughtful for his horse too. When he came home the lady was at the hall door as he rode up.

"Well, my dear," she said, "how do you like him?"

"He is exactly what John said," he replied; "a pleasanter creature I never wish to mount. What shall we call him?"

"Would you like Ebony?" said she. "He is as black as ebony."

"No, not Ebony."

"Will you call him Blackbird, like your uncle's old horse?"

"No, he is far handsomer than old Blackbird ever was."

"Yes," she said, "he is really quite a beauty, and he has such a sweet, good-tempered face and such a fine, intelligent eye—what do you say to calling him Black Beauty?"

"Black Beauty—why, yes, I think that is a very good name. If you like it shall be his name." And so it was.

When John went into the stable, he told James that master and mistress had chosen a good, sensible English name for me, that meant something, not like Marengo, or Pegasus, or Abdallah. They both laughed, and James said, "If it was not for bringing back the past, I should have named him Rob Roy, for

I never saw two horses more alike."

"That's no wonder," said John. "Didn't you know that Farmer Grey's old Duchess was the mother of them both?"

I had never heard that before; and so poor Rob Roy who was killed at that hunt was my brother! I did not wonder that my mother was so troubled. It seems that horses have no relations; at least, they never know each other after they are sold.

John seemed very proud of me: he used to make my mane and tail almost as smooth as a lady's hair, and he would talk to me a great deal; of course I did not understand all he said, but I learned more and more to know what he *meant*, and what he wanted me to do. I grew very fond of him, he was so gentle and kind. He seemed to know just how a horse feels, and when he cleaned me, he knew the tender places, and the ticklish places; when he brushed my head, he went as carefully over my eyes as if they were his own, and never stirred up any ill-temper.

James Howard, the stable boy, was just as gentle and pleasant in his way, so I thought myself well off. There was another man who helped in the yard, but he had very little to do with Ginger and me.

A few days after this I had to go out with Ginger in the carriage. I wondered how we should get on together; but except laying her ears back when I was led up to her, she behaved very well. She did her work honestly, and did her full share, and I never wish to have a better partner in double harness. When we came to a hill, instead of slackening her pace, she would throw her weight right into the collar, and pull away straight up. We had both the same sort of courage at our work, and John had oftener to hold us in than to urge us forward; he never had to use the whip with either of us; then our paces were much the same, and I found it very easy to keep step with her when trotting, which made it pleasant, and master always liked it when we kept step well, and so did John. After we had been out two or three times together we grew quite friendly and sociable, which made me feel very much at home.

As for Merrylegs, he and I soon became great friends; he was such a cheerful, plucky, good-tempered little fellow that he was a favorite with everyone, and especially with Miss Jessie and Flora, who used to ride him about in the orchard, and have fine games with him and their little dog Frisky.

Our master had two other horses that stood in another stable. One was Justice, a roan cob, used for riding or for the luggage cart; the other was an old brown hunter, named Sir Oliver; he was past work now, but was a great favorite with the master, who gave him the run of the Park; he sometimes did a little light carting on the estate, or carried one of the young ladies when they rode out with their father, for he was very gentle and could be trusted with a child as well as Merrylegs. The cob was a strong, well-made, good-tempered horse, and we sometimes had a little chat in the paddock, but of course I could not be so intimate with him as with Ginger, who stood in the same stable.

6

Liberty

I WAS QUITE happy in my new place, and if there was one thing that I missed, it must not be thought I was discontented; all who had to do with me were good, and I had a light airy stable and the best of food. What more could I want? Why, liberty! For three years and a half of my life I had had all the liberty I could wish for; but now, week after week, month after month, and no doubt year after year, I must stand up in a stable night and day except when I am wanted, and then I must be just as steady and quiet as any old horse who has worked twenty years. Straps here and straps there, a bit in my mouth, and blinkers over my eyes. Now, I am not complaining, for I know it must be so. I only mean to say that for a young horse full of strength and spirits who has been used to some large field or plain, where he can fling up his head and toss up his tail and gallop away at full speed, then round and back again with a snort to his companions—I say it is hard never to have a bit more liberty to do as you like. Sometimes, when I have had less exercise than usual, I have felt so full of life and spring that when John has taken me out to exercise I really could not keep quiet. Do what I would, it seemed as if I must jump, or dance, or prance, and many a good shake I know I must have given him, especially at the first; but he was always good and patient.

"Steady, steady, my boy," he would say. "Wait a bit, and we will have a good swing, and soon get the tickle out of your feet." Then as soon as we were out of the village, he would give me a few miles at a spanking trot, and then bring me back as fresh as before, only clear of the fidgets, as he called them. Spirited horses, when not enough exercised, are often called skittish, when it is only play; and some grooms will punish them, but our John did not, he knew it was only high spirits. Still, he had his own ways of making me understand by the tone of his voice or the touch of the rein. If he was very serious and quite determined, I always knew it by his voice, and that had more power with me than anything else, for I was very fond of him.

I ought to say that sometimes we had our liberty for a few hours; this used to be on fine Sundays in the summertime. The carriage never went out on Sundays, because the church was not far off.

It was a great treat to us to be turned out into the

home paddock or the old orchard. The grass was so cool and soft to our feet, the air so sweet, and the freedom to do as we liked was so pleasant—to gallop, to lie down, and roll over on our backs, or to nibble the sweet grass. Then it was a very good time for talking, as we stood together under the shade of the large chestnut tree.

7

Ginger

ONE DAY WHEN Ginger and I were standing alone in the shade we had a great deal of talk; she wanted to know all about my bringing up and breaking in, and I told her.

"Well," said she, "if I had had your bringing up I might have had as good a temper as you, but now I don't believe I ever shall."

"Why not?" I said.

"Because it has been all so different with me," she replied. "I never had any one, horse or man, that was kind to me, or that I cared to please; for in the first place I was taken from my mother as soon as I was weaned, and put with a lot of other young colts. None of them cared for me, and I cared for none of them. There was no kind master like yours to look after me, and talk to me, and bring me nice things to eat. The man that had the care of us never gave me a kind word in my life. I do not mean that he ill-used me, but he did not care for us one bit further than to see that we had plenty to eat and shelter in the winter.

"A footpath ran through our field, and very often

the great boys passing through would fling stones to make us gallop. I was never hit, but one fine young colt was badly cut in the face, and I should think it would be a scar for life. We did not care for them, but of course it made us more wild, and we settled it in our minds that boys were our enemies.

"We had very good fun in the free meadows, galloping up and down and chasing each other round and round the field; then standing still under the shade of the trees. But when it came to breaking in, that was a bad time for me; several men came to catch me, and when at last they closed me in at one corner of the field, one caught me by the forelock, another caught me by the nose and held it so tight I could hardly draw my breath; then another took my under jaw in his hard hand and wrenched my mouth open, and so by force they got on the halter and the bar into my mouth; then one dragged me along by the halter, another flogging behind, and this was the first experience I had of men's kindness; it was all force. They did not give me a chance to know what they wanted. I was high bred and had a great deal of spirit, and was very wild, no doubt, and gave them, I dare say, plenty of trouble, but then it was dreadful to be shut up in a stall day after day instead of having my liberty, and I fretted and pined and wanted to get loose. You know yourself it's bad enough when you have a kind master and plenty of coaxing, but there was nothing of that sort for me.

"There was one—the old master, Mr. Ryder—who, I think, could soon have brought me round, and could have done anything with me, but he had given up all the hard part of the trade to his son and to another experienced man, and he only came at times to oversee. His son was a strong, tall, bold man; they called him Samson, and he used to boast that he had never found a horse that could throw him. There was no gentleness in him as there was in his father, but only hardness, a hard voice, a hard eye, a hard hand, and I felt from the first that what he wanted was to wear all the spirit out of me, and just make me into a quiet, humble, obedient piece of horseflesh. 'Horseflesh!' Yes, that is all that he thought about," and Ginger stamped her foot as if the very thought of him made her angry.

She went on: "If I did not do exactly what he wanted, he would get put out, and make me run round with that long rein in the training field till he had tired me out. I think he drank a good deal, and I am quite sure that the oftener he drank the worse it was for me. One day he had worked me hard in every way he could, and when I lay down I was tired and miserable and angry; it all seemed so hard. The next morning he came for me early, and ran me round again for a long time. I had scarcely had an hour's rest, when he came again for me with a saddle and bridle and a new kind of bit. I could never quite tell how it came about; he had only just mounted me on the training ground, when something I did put him out of temper, and he chucked me hard with the rein. The new bit was very painful, and I reared up suddenly, which angered him still more, and he began to flog me. I felt my whole spirit set against him, and I began to kick and plunge, and rear as I had never done before, and we had a regular fight. For a long time he stuck to the saddle and punished me cruelly with his whip and spurs, but my blood was thoroughly up, and I cared for nothing he could do if only I could get him off. At last, after a terrible struggle, I threw him off backward. I heard him fall heavily on the turf, and without looking behind me, I galloped off to the other end of the field; there I turned round and saw my persecutor slowly rising from the ground and going into the stable. I stood under an oak tree and watched, but no one came to catch me. The time went on, the sun was very hot, the flies swarmed round me, and settled on my bleeding flanks where the spurs had dug in. I felt hungry, for I had not eaten since the early morning, but there was not enough grass in that meadow for a goose to live on. I wanted to lie down and rest, but with the saddle strapped tightly on there was no comfort, and there was not a drop of water to drink. The afternoon wore on, and the sun got low. I saw the other colts led in, and I knew they were having a good feed.

"At last, just as the sun went down, I saw the old master come out with a sieve in his hand. He was a very fine old gentleman with quite white hair, but his voice was what I should know him by among a thousand. It was not high, nor yet low, but full, and clear, and kind, and when he gave orders it was so steady and decided that every one knew, both horses and men, that he expected to be obeyed. He came quietly along, now and then shaking the oats about that he had in the sieve, and speaking cheerfully and gently to me, 'Come along, lassie, come along, lassie; come along, come along.' I stood still and let him come up. He held the oats to me and I began to eat without fear; his voice took all my fear away. He stood by, patting and stroking me while I was eating, and seeing the clots of blood on my side he seemed very vexed. 'Poor lassie! It was a bad business, a bad business!' Then he quietly took the rein and led me to the stable; just at the door stood Samson. I laid my ears back and snapped at him. 'Stand back,' said the master, 'and keep out of her way; you've done a bad day's work for this filly.' He growled out something about a vicious brute. 'Hark ye,' said the father, 'a bad-tempered man will never make a good-tempered horse. You've not learned your trade yet, Samson.' Then he led me into my box, took off the saddle and bridle with his own hands, and tied me up; then he called for a pail of warm water and a sponge, took off his coat, and while the stable man held the pail, he sponged my sides a good while, so tenderly that I was sure he knew how sore and bruised they were. 'Whoa! my pretty one,' he said, 'stand still, stand still.' His very voice did me good, and the bathing was very comfortable. The skin was so broken at the corners of my mouth that I could not eat the hay, the stalks hurt me. He looked closely at it, shook his head, and told the man to fetch a good bran mash and put some meal into it. How good that mash was, and so soft and healing to my mouth. He stood by all the time I was eating, stroking me and talking to the man. 'If a high-mettled creature like this,' said he, 'can't be broken by fair means, she will never be good for anything.'

"After that he often came to see me, and when my mouth was healed, the other breaker, Job they called him, went on training me; he was steady and thoughtful, and I soon learned what he wanted."

8

Ginger's Story Continued

THE NEXT TIME that Ginger and I were together in the paddock, she told me about her first place.

"After my breaking in," she said, "I was bought by a dealer to match another chestnut horse. For some weeks he drove us together, and then we were sold to a fashionable gentleman, and were sent up to London. I had been driven with a bearing rein by the dealer, and I hated it worse than anything else; but in this place we were reined far tighter; the coachman and his master thinking we looked more stylish so. We were often driven about in the Park and other fashionable places. You who never had a bearing rein on, don't know what it is, but I can tell you it is dreadful.

"I like to toss my head about and hold it as high as any horse; but fancy now yourself, if you tossed your head up high and were obliged to hold it there, and that for hours together, not able to move it at all, except with a jerk still higher, your neck aching till you did not know how to bear it. Besides that, to have two bits instead of one; and mine was a sharp one, it hurt my tongue and my jaw, and the blood from my tongue colored the froth that kept flying from my lips as I chafed and fretted at the bits and rein. It was worst when we had to stand by the hour waiting for our mistress at some grand party or entertainment, and if I fretted or stamped with impatience the whip was laid on. It was enough to drive one mad."

"Did not your master take any thought for you?" I said.

"No," said she, "he only cared to have a stylish turnout, as they call it; I think he knew very little about horses. He left that to his coachman, who told him I had an irritable temper; that I had not been well broken to the bearing rein, but I should soon get used to it; but *he* was not the man to do it, for when I was in the stable, miserable and angry, instead of being smoothed and quieted by kindness, I got only a surly word or a blow. If he had been civil, I would have tried to bear it. I was willing to work, and ready to work hard too; but to be tormented for nothing but their fancies angered me. What right had they to make me suffer like that? Besides the soreness in my mouth and the pain in my neck, it always made my windpipe feel bad, and if I had stopped there long, I know it would have spoiled my breathing; but I grew more and more restless and irritable, I could not help it; and I began to snap and kick when any one came to harness me; for this the groom beat me, and one day, as they had just buckled us into the carriage, and were straining my head up with that rein, I began to plunge and kick with all my might. I soon broke a lot of harness, and kicked myself clear; so that was an end of that place.

"After this, I was sent to Tattersall's to be sold; of course I could not be warranted free from vice, so nothing was said about that. My handsome appearance and good paces soon brought a gentleman to bid for me, and I was bought by another dealer; he tried me in all kinds of ways and with different bits, and he soon found out what I could bear. At last he drove me quite without a bearing rein, and then sold me as a perfectly quiet horse to a gentleman in the country; he was a good master, and I was getting on very well, but his old groom left him and a new one came. This man was as hard-tempered and hard-handed as Samson; he always spoke in a rough, impatient voice, and if I did not move in the stall the moment he wanted me, he would hit me above the hocks with his stable broom or the fork, whichever he might have in his hand. Everything he did was rough, and I began to hate him; he wanted to make me afraid of him, but I was too high-mettled for that; and one day when he had aggravated me more than usual,

I bit him, which of course put him in a great rage, and he began to hit me about the head with a riding whip. After that, he never dared to come into my stall again, either my heels or my teeth were ready for him, and he knew it. I was quite quiet with my master, but of course he listened to what the man said, and so I was sold again.

"The same dealer heard of me, and said he thought he knew one place where I should do well. ''Twas a pity,' he said, 'that such a fine horse should go to the bad for want of a real good chance,' and the end of it was that I came here not long before you did; but I had then made up my mind that men were my natural enemies and that I must defend myself. Of course it is very different here, but who knows how long it will last? I wish I could think about things as you do; but I can't after all I have gone through."

"Well," I said, "I think it would be a real shame if you were to bite or kick John or James."

"I don't mean to," she said, "while they are good to me. I did bite James once pretty sharp, but John said, 'Try her with kindness,' and instead of punishing me as I expected, James came to me with his arm bound up, and brought me a bran mash and stroked me; and I have never snapped at him since, and I won't either."

I was sorry for Ginger, but of course I knew very little then, and I thought most likely she made the worst of it. However, I found that as the weeks went on she grew much more gentle and cheerful, and had lost the watchful, defiant look that she used to turn on any strange person who came near her; and one day James said, "I do believe that mare is getting fond of me, she quite whinnied after me this morning when I had been rubbing her forehead."

"Aye, aye, Jim, 'tis the Birtwick balls," said John, "she'll be as good as Black Beauty by and by; kindness is all the physic she wants, poor thing!" Master noticed the change too, and one day when he got out of the carriage and came to speak to us as he often did, he stroked her beautiful neck. "Well, my pretty one, well, how do things go with you now? You are a good bit happier than when you came to us, I think."

She put her nose up to him in a friendly, trustful way, while he rubbed it gently.

"We shall make a cure of her, John," he said.

"Yes, sir, she's wonderfully improved; she's not the same creature that she was. It's the Birtwick balls, sir," said John, laughing.

This was a little joke of John's; he used to say that a regular course of the Birtwick horse balls would cure almost any vicious horse; these balls, he said, were made up of patience and gentleness, firmness and petting, one pound of each to be mixed up with half-a-pint of common sense, and given to the horse every day.

9

Merrylegs

MR. BLOMEFIELD, THE Vicar, had a large family of boys and girls; sometimes they used to come and play with Miss Jessie and Flora. One of the girls was as old as Miss Jessie; two of the boys were older, and there were several little ones. When they came, there was plenty of work for Merrylegs, for nothing pleased them so much as getting on him by turns and riding him all about the orchard and the home paddock, and this they would do by the hour together.

One afternoon he had been out with them a long time, and when James brought him in and put on his halter, he said:

"There, you rogue, mind how you behave yourself, or we shall get into trouble."

"What have you been doing, Merrylegs?" I asked.

"Oh!" said he, tossing his little head, "I have only been giving those young people a lesson. They did not know when they had had enough, nor when I had had enough, so I just pitched them off backward; that was the only thing they could understand."

"What!" said I, "you threw the children off? I

thought you did know better than that! Did you throw Miss Jessie or Miss Flora?"

He looked very much offended, and said:

"Of course not, I would not do such a thing for the best oats that ever came into the stable; why, I am as careful of our young ladies as the master could be, and as for the little ones, it is I who teach them to ride. When they seem frightened or a little unsteady on my back, I go as smooth and as quiet as old pussy when she is after a bird; and when they are all right, I go on again faster, you see, just to use them to it; so don't you trouble yourself preaching to me; I am the best friend and the best riding master those children have. It is not them, it is the boys; boys," said he, shaking his mane, "are quite different; they must be broken in as we were broken in when we were colts, and just be taught what's what. The other children had ridden me about for nearly two hours, and then the boys thought it was their turn, and so it was, and I was quite agreeable. They rode me by turns, and I galloped them about up and down the fields and all about the orchard for a good hour. They had each cut a great hazel stick for a riding whip, and laid it on a little too hard; but I took it in good part, till at last I thought we had had enough, so I stopped two or three times by way of a hint. Boys, you see, think a horse or pony is like a steam engine or a thrashing machine, and can go on as long and as fast as they please; they never think that a pony can get tired, or have any feelings; so as the one who was whipping me could not understand, I just rose up on my hind legs and let him slip off behind—that was all. He mounted me again, and I did the same. Then the other boy got up, and as soon as he began to use his stick I laid him on the grass, and so on, till they were able to understand—that was all. They are not bad boys; they don't wish to be cruel. I like them very well; but you see I had to give them a lesson. When they brought me to James and told him, I think he was very angry to see such big sticks. He said they were only fit for drovers or gypsies, and not for young gentlemen."

"If I had been you," said Ginger, "I would have given those boys a good kick, and that would have given them a lesson."

"No doubt you would," said Merrylegs, "but then I am not quite such a fool (begging your pardon) as to anger our master or make James ashamed of me. Besides, those children are under my charge when they are riding; I tell you they are entrusted to me. Why, only the other day I heard our master say to Mrs. Blomefield, 'My dear madam, you need not be anxious about the children, my old Merrylegs will take as much care of them as you or I could. I assure you I would not sell that pony for any money, he is so perfectly good-tempered and trustworthy.' And do you think I am such an ungrateful brute as to forget all the kind treatment I have had here for five years, and all the trust they place in me, and turn vicious because a couple of ignorant boys used me badly? No! No! You never had a good place where they were kind to you; and so you don't know, and I'm sorry for you, but I can tell you good places make good horses. I wouldn't vex our people for anything; I love them, I do," said Merrylegs, and he gave a low "ho, ho, ho" through his nose, as he used to do in the morning when he heard James's footstep at the door.

"Besides," he went on, "if I took to kicking, where should I be? Why, sold off in a jiffy, and no character, and I might find myself slaved about under a butcher's boy, or worked to death at some seaside place where no one cared for me, except to find out how fast I could go, or be flogged along in some cart with three or four great men in it going out for a Sunday spree, as I have often seen in the place I lived in before I came here. "No," said he, shaking his head, "I hope I shall never come to that."

10

A Talk in the Orchard

GINGER AND I were not of the regular tall carriage horse breed, we had more of the racing blood in us. We stood about fifteen and a half hands high; we were therefore just as good for riding as we were for driving, and our master used to say that he disliked either horse or man that could do but one thing; and as he did not want to show off in London parks, he preferred a more active and useful kind of horse. As for us, our greatest pleasure was when we were saddled for a riding party; the master on Ginger, the mistress on me, and the young ladies on Sir Oliver and Merrylegs. It was so cheerful to be trotting and cantering all together that it always put us in high spirits. I had the best of it, for I always carried the mistress; her weight was little, her voice was sweet, and her hand was so light on the rein that I was guided almost without feeling it.

Oh! If people knew what a comfort to horses a light hand is, and how it keeps a good mouth and a good temper, they surely would not chuck, and drag, and pull at the rein as they often do. Our mouths are so tender that where they have not been spoiled or hardened with bad or ignorant treatment, they feel the slightest movement of the driver's hand, and we know in an instant what is required of us. My mouth had never been spoiled, and I believe that was why the mistress preferred me to Ginger, although her paces were certainly quite as good. She used often to envy me, and said it was all the fault of breaking in, and the gag bit in London, that her mouth was not so perfect as mine; and then old Sir Oliver would say, "There, there! Don't vex yourself; you have the greatest honor; a mare that can carry a tall man of our master's weight, with all your spring and sprightly action, does not need to hold her head down because she does not carry the lady. We horses must take things as they come, and always be contented and willing so long as we are kindly used."

I had often wondered how it was that Sir Oliver had such a very short tail; it really was only six or seven inches long, with a tassel of hair hanging from it; and on one of our holidays in the orchard I ventured to ask him by what accident it was that he had lost his tail. "Accident!" he snorted with a fierce look. "It was no accident! It was a cruel, shameful, cold-blooded act! When I was young I was taken to a place where these cruel things were done; I was tied up, and made fast so that I could not stir, and then they came and cut off my long and beautiful tail, through the flesh and through the bone, and took it away."

"How dreadful!" I exclaimed.

"Dreadful! Ah! It was dreadful; but it was not only the pain, though that was terrible and lasted a long time; it was not only the indignity of having my best ornament taken from me, though that was bad; but it was this, how could I ever brush the flies off my sides and my hind legs any more? You who have tails just whisk the flies off without thinking about it, and you can't tell what a torment it is to have them settle upon you and sting and sting, and have nothing in the world to lash them off with. I tell you it is a lifelong wrong, and a lifelong loss; but thank Heaven, they don't do it now."

"What did they do it for then?" said Ginger.

"For fashion!" said the old horse, with a stamp of his foot. "For fashion! If you know what that means; there was not a well-bred young horse in my time that had not his tail docked in that shameful way, just as if the good God that made us did not know what we wanted and what looked best."

"I suppose it is fashion that makes them strap our heads up with those horrid bits that I was tortured with in London," said Ginger.

"Of course it is," said he. "To my mind, fashion is one of the wickedest things in the world. Now look, for instance, at the way they serve dogs, cutting off their tails to make them look plucky, and shearing up their pretty little ears to a point to make them both look sharp, forsooth. I had a dear friend once, a brown terrier—'Skye,' they called her. She was so fond of me that she never would sleep out of my stall; she made her bed under the manger, and there she had a litter of five as pretty little puppies as need be; none were drowned, for they were a valuable kind, and how pleased she was with them! And when they got their eyes open and crawled about, it was a real pretty sight; but one day the man came and took them all away; I thought he might be afraid I should tread upon them. But it was not so; in the evening poor Skye brought them back again, one by one in her mouth; not the happy little things that they were, but bleeding and crying pitifully; they had all had a piece of their tails cut off, and the soft flap of their pretty little ears was cut quite off. How their mother licked them, and how troubled she was, poor thing! I never forgot it. They healed in time, and they forgot the pain, but the nice soft flap that of course was intended to protect the delicate part of their ears from dust and injury, was gone forever. Why don't they cut their own children's ears into points to make them look sharp? Why don't they cut the end off their noses to make them look plucky? One would be just as sensible as the other. What right have they to torment and disfigure God's creatures?"

Sir Oliver, though he was so gentle, was a fiery old fellow, and what he said was all so new to me and so dreadful that I found a bitter feeling toward men rise up in my mind that I never had before. Of course Ginger was very much excited; she flung up her head with flashing eyes and distended nostrils, declaring that men were both brutes and blockheads.

"Who talks about blockheads?" said Merrylegs, who just came up from the old apple tree, where he had been rubbing himself against the low branch. "Who talks about blockheads? I believe that is a bad word."

"Bad words were made for bad things," said Ginger, and she told him what Sir Oliver had said.

"It is all true," said Merrylegs sadly, "and I've seen that about the dogs over and over again where I lived first; but we won't talk about it here. You know that master, and John, and James are always good to us, and talking against men in such a place as this doesn't seem fair or grateful, and you know there are good masters and good grooms beside ours, though of course ours are the best."

This wise speech of good little Merrylegs, which we knew was quite true, cooled us all down, especially Sir Oliver, who was dearly fond of his master; and to turn the subject I said, "Can any one tell me the use of blinkers?"

"No!" said Sir Oliver shortly. "Because they are no use."

"They are supposed," said Justice, the roan cob, in his calm way, "to prevent horses from shying and starting and getting so frightened as to cause accidents."

"Then what is the reason they do not put them on riding horses; especially on ladies' horses?" said I.

"There is no reason at all," said he quietly, "except the fashion; they say that a horse would be so frightened to see the wheels of his own cart or carriage coming behind him that he would be sure to run away, although of course when he is ridden he sees them all about him if the streets are crowded. I admit they do sometimes come too close to be pleasant, but we don't run away; we are used to it, and understand it, and if we never had blinkers put on, we should never want them; we should see what was there, and know what was what, and be much less frightened than by only seeing bits of things that we can't understand."

Of course there may be some nervous horses who have been hurt or frightened when they were young, and may be the better for them, but as I never was nervous, I can't judge.

"I consider," said Sir Oliver, "that blinkers are dangerous things in the night; we horses can see much better in the dark than men can, and many an accident would never have happened if horses might have had the full use of their eyes. Some years ago, I remember, there was a hearse with two horses return- ing one dark night, and just by Farmer Sparrow's house, where the pond is close to the road, the wheels went too near the edge, and the hearse was over- turned into the water; both the horses were drowned, and the driver hardly escaped. Of course after this accident a stout white rail was put up that might be easily seen, but if those horses had not been partly blinded, they would of themselves have kept farther from the edge, and no accident would have hap- pened. When our master's carriage was overturned, before you came here, it was said that if the lamp on the left side had not gone out, John would have seen the great hole that the road makers had left; and so he might, but if old Colin had not had blinkers on he would have seen it, lamp or no lamp, for he was far too knowing an old horse to run into danger. As it was, he was very much hurt, the carriage was broken, and how John escaped nobody knew."

"I should say," said Ginger, curling her nostril, "that these men, who are so wise, had better give orders that in the future all foals should be born with their eyes set just in the middle of their foreheads, instead of on the side; they always think they can improve upon Nature and mend what God has made."

Things were getting rather sore again, when Merrylegs held up his knowing little face and said, "I'll tell you a secret: I believe John does not approve of blinkers; I heard him talking with master about it one day. The master said that 'if horses had been used to them, it might be dangerous in some cases to leave them off,' and John said he thought it would be a good thing if all colts were broken in without blinkers, as was the case in some foreign countries. So let us cheer up, and have a run to the other end of the orchard; I believe the wind has blown down some apples, and we might just as well eat them as the slugs."

Merrylegs could not be resisted, so we broke off our long conversation, and got up our spirits by munching some very sweet apples which lay scattered on the grass.

11

Plain Speaking

THE LONGER I lived at Birtwick, the more proud and happy I felt at having such a place. Our master and mistress were respected and beloved by all who knew them; they were good and kind to everybody and everything; not only men and women, but horses and donkeys, dogs and cats, cattle and birds; there was no oppressed or ill-used creature that had not a friend in them, and their servants took the same tone. If any of the village children were known to treat any creature cruelly, they soon heard about it from the Hall.

The squire and Farmer Grey had worked together, as they said, for more than twenty years, to get bearing reins on the cart horses done away with, and in our parts we seldom saw them; but sometimes if mistress met a heavily-laden horse with his head strained up, she would stop the carriage and get out, and reason with the driver in her sweet serious voice, and try to show him how foolish and cruel it was.

I don't think any man could withstand our mistress. I wish all ladies were like her. Our master, too, used to come down very heavy sometimes. I remember he was riding me toward home one morning, when we saw a powerful man driving toward us in a light pony chaise, with a beautiful little bay pony, with slender legs and a high-bred sensitive head and face. Just as he came to the Park gates, the little thing turned toward them; the man, without word or warning, wrenched the creature's head round with such a force and suddenness that he nearly threw it on its haunches. Recovering itself, it was going on, when he began to lash it furiously. The pony plunged forward, but the strong, heavy hand held the pretty creature back with force almost enough to break its jaw, while the whip still cut into him. It was a dreadful sight to me, for I knew what fearful pain it gave that delicate little mouth; but master gave me the word, and we were up with him in a second.

"Sawyer," he cried in a stern voice, "is that pony made of flesh and blood?"

"Flesh and blood and temper," he said; "he's too fond of his own will, and that won't suit me." He spoke as if he was in a strong passion. He was a builder who had often been to the Park on business.

"And do you think," said master sternly, "that treatment like this will make him fond of your will?"

"He had no business to make that turn; his road

was straight on!" said the man roughly.

"You have often driven that pony up to my place," said master. "It only shows the creature's memory and intelligence; how did he know that you were not going there again? But that has little to do with it. I must say, Mr. Sawyer, that more unmanly, brutal treatment of a little pony it was never my painful lot to witness; and by giving way to such passions you injure your own character as much, nay more, than you injure your horse, and remember, we shall all have to be judged according to our works, whether they be towards man or towards beast."

Master rode me home slowly, and I could tell by his voice how the thing had grieved him. He was just as free to speak to gentlemen of his own rank as to those below him; for another day, when we were out, we met a Captain Langley, a friend of our master's; he was driving a splendid pair of grays in a kind of break. After a little conversation the Captain said:

"What do you think of my new team, Mr. Gordon? You know, you are the judge of horses in these parts, and I should like your opinion."

The master backed me a little, so as to get a good view of them. "They are an uncommonly handsome pair," he said, "and if they are as good as they look, I am sure you need not wish for anything better; but I see you still hold that pet scheme of yours for worrying your horses and lessening their power."

"What do you mean," said the other, "the bearing reins? Oh, ah! I know that's a hobby of yours; well, the fact is, I like to see my horses hold their heads up."

"So do I," said master, "as well as any man, but I don't like to see them *held up*; that takes all the shine out of it. Now, you are a military man, Langley, and no doubt like to see your regiment look well on parade, 'Heads up,' and all that; but you would not take much credit for your drill if all your men had their heads tied to a backboard! It might not be much harm on parade, except to worry and fatigue them, but how would it be in a bayonet charge against the enemy, when they want the free use of every muscle, and all their strength thrown forward? I would not give much for their chance of victory. And it is just the same with horses: you fret and worry their tempers, and decrease their power; you will not let them throw their weight against their work, and so they have to do too much with their joints and muscles, and of course it wears them up faster. You may depend upon it, horses were intended to have their heads free, as free as men's are; and if we could act a little more according to common sense, and a good deal less according to fashion, we should find many things work easier; besides, you know as well as I that if a horse makes a false step, he has much less chance of recovering himself if his head and neck are fastened back. And now," said the master, laughing, "I have given my hobby a good trot out, can't you make up your mind to mount him too, Captain? Your example would go a long way."

"I believe you are right in theory," said the other, "and that's rather a hard hit about the soldiers, but—well—I'll think about it," and so they parted.

12

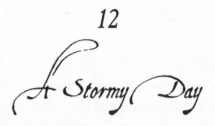

A Stormy Day

ONE DAY LATE in the autumn, my master had a long journey to go on business. I was put into the dogcart, and John went with his master. I always liked to go in the dogcart, it was so light, and the high wheels ran along so pleasantly. There had been a great deal of rain, and now the wind was very high, and blew the dry leaves across the road in a shower. We went along merrily till we came to the toll bar and the low wooden bridge. The river banks were rather high, and the bridge, instead of rising, went across just level, so that in the middle, if the river was full, the water would be nearly up to the woodwork and planks; but as there were good substantial rails on each side, people did not mind it.

The man at the gate said the river was rising fast, and he feared it would be a bad night. Many of the meadows were under water, and in one low part of the road the water was halfway up to my knees; the bottom was good, and master drove gently, so it was no matter.

When we got to the town, of course, I had a good wait, but as the master's business engaged him a long time, we did not start for home till rather late in the afternoon. The wind was then much higher, and I heard the master say to John, he had never been out in such a storm; and so I thought, as we went along the skirts of a wood, where the great branches were swaying about like twigs, and the rushing sound was terrible.

"I wish we were well out of this wood," said my master.

"Yes, sir," said John, "it would be rather awkward if one of these branches came down upon us."

The words were scarcely out of his mouth when there was a groan, and a crack, and a splitting sound, and tearing, crashing down among the other trees came an oak, torn up by the roots, and it fell right across the road just before us. I will never say I was not frightened, for I was. I stopped still, and I believe I trembled; of course I did not turn round or run away; I was not brought up to that. John jumped out and was in a moment at my head.

"That was a very near touch," said my master. "What's to be done now?"

"Well, sir, we can't drive over that tree, nor yet get round it; there will be nothing for it but to go back to the four crossways, and that will be a good six miles before we get round to the wooden bridge again; it will make us late, but the horse is fresh."

So back we went and round by the crossroads, but by the time we got to the bridge it was very nearly dark. We could just see that the water was over the middle of it; but as that happened sometimes when the floods were out, master did not stop. We were going along at a good pace, but the moment my feet touched the first part of the bridge, I felt sure there was something wrong. I dare not go forward, and I made a dead stop. "Go on, Beauty," said my master, and he gave me a touch with the whip, but I dare not stir; he gave me a sharp cut, I jumped, but I dare not go forward.

"There's something wrong, sir," said John, and he sprang out of the dogcart and came to my head and looked all about. He tried to lead me forward. "Come on, Beauty, what's the matter?" Of course I could not tell him, but I knew very well that the bridge was not safe.

Just then the man at the tollgate on the other side ran out of the house, tossing a torch about like one mad.

"Hoy, hoy, hoy! Halloo! Stop!" he cried.

"What's the matter?" shouted my master.

"The bridge is broken in the middle, and part of it is carried away; if you come on you'll be into the river."

"Thank God!" said my master.

"You Beauty!" said John, and took the bridle and gently turned me round to the right-hand road by the river side. The sun had set some time ago, the wind seemed to have lulled off after that furious blast which tore up the tree. It grew darker and darker, stiller and stiller. I trotted quietly along, the wheels hardly making a sound on the soft road. For a good while neither master nor John spoke, and then master began in a serious voice. I could not understand much of what they said, but I found they thought, if I had gone on as the master wanted me, most likely the bridge would have given way under us, and horse, chaise, master, and man would have fallen into the river; and as the current was flowing very strongly, and there was no light and no help at hand, it was more than likely we should all have been drowned. Master said, God had given men reason, by which they could find out things for themselves, but He had given animals knowledge which did not depend on reason, and which was much more prompt and perfect in its way, and by which they had often saved the lives of men. John had many stories to tell of dogs and horses, and the wonderful things they had done; he thought people did not value their animals half enough, nor make friends of them as they ought to do. I am sure he makes friends of them if ever a man did.

At last we came to the Park gates and found the gardener looking out for us. He said that mistress had been in a dreadful way ever since dark, fearing some accident had happened, and that she had sent James off on Justice, the roan cob, toward the wooden bridge to make inquiry after us.

We saw a light at the hall door and at the upper windows, and as we came up mistress ran out, saying, "Are you really safe, my dear? Oh! I have been so anxious, fancying all sorts of things. Have you had no accident?"

"No, my dear; but if your Black Beauty had not been wiser than we were, we should all have been carried down the river at the wooden bridge." I heard no more, as they went into the house, and John took me to the stable. Oh, what a good supper he gave me that night, a good bran mash and some crushed beans with my oats, and such a thick bed of straw, and I was glad of it, for I was tired.

13
The Devil's Trademark

ONE DAY WHEN John and I had been out on some business of our master's, and were returning gently on a long, straight road, at some distance we saw a boy trying to leap a pony over a gate; the pony would not take the leap, and the boy cut him with the whip, but he only turned off on one side. He whipped him again, but the pony turned off on the other side. Then the boy got off and gave him a hard thrashing, and knocked him about the head; then he got up again and tried to make him leap the gate, kicking him all the time shamefully, but still the pony refused. When we were nearly at the spot, the pony put down his head and threw up his heels and sent the boy neatly over into a broad quickset hedge, and with the rein dangling from his head, he set off home at a full gallop. John laughed out quite loud. "Served him right," he said.

"Oh! Oh! Oh!" cried the boy, as he struggled about among the thorns. "I say, come and help me out."

"Thank ye," said John, "I think you are quite in the right place, and maybe a little scratching will teach you not to leap a pony over a gate that is too high for him." And so with that John rode off. "It may be," said he to himself, "that young fellow is a liar as well as a cruel one; we'll just go home by Farmer Bushby's, Beauty, and then if anybody wants to know, you and I can tell 'em, ye see." So we turned off to the right, and soon came up to the stack yard and within sight of the house. The farmer was hurrying out into the road, and his wife was standing at the gate, looking very frightened.

"Have you seen my boy?" said Mr. Bushby as we came up. "He went out an hour ago on my black pony, and the creature is just come back without a rider."

"I should think, sir," said John, "he had better be without a rider, unless he can be ridden properly."

"What do you mean?" said the farmer.

"Well, sir, I saw your son whipping, and kicking, and knocking that good little pony about shamefully because he would not leap a gate that was too high for him. The pony behaved well, sir, and showed no vice; but at last he just threw up his heels and tipped the young gentleman into the thorn hedge. He wanted me to help him out; but I hope you will excuse me, sir, I did not feel inclined to do so. There's no bones broken, sir, he'll only get a few scratches. I love horses, and it riles me to see them badly used; it is a bad plan to aggravate an animal till he uses his heels; the first time is not always the last."

During this time the mother began to cry, "Oh, my poor Bill, I must go and meet him; he must be hurt."

"You had better go into the house, wife," said the farmer. "Bill wants a lesson about this, and I must see that he gets it; this is not the first time nor the second that he has ill-used that pony, and I shall stop it. I am much obliged to you, Manly. Good evening."

So we went on, John chuckling all the way home; then he told James about it, who laughed and said, "Serve him right. I knew that boy at school; he took great airs on himself because he was a farmer's son; he used to swagger about and bully the little boys. Of course we elder ones would not have any of that non-sense, and let him know that in the school and the playground farmers' sons and laborers' sons were all alike. I well remember one day, just before afternoon school, I found him at the large window catching flies and pulling off their wings. He did not see me, and I gave him a box on the ears that laid him sprawling on the floor. Well, angry as I was, I was almost fright-ened, he roared and bellowed in such a style. The boys rushed in from the playground, and the master ran in from the road to see who was being murdered. Of course I said fair and square at once what I had done, and why; then I showed the master the flies, some crushed and some crawling about helpless, and I showed him the wings on the windowsill. I never saw him so angry before; but as Bill was still howling and whining, like the coward that he was, he did not give him any more punishment of that kind, but set him up on a stool for the rest of the afternoon, and said that he should not go out to play for that week. Then he talked to all the boys very seriously about cruelty, and said how hard-hearted and cowardly it was to hurt the weak and the helpless; but what stuck in my mind was this, he said that cruelty was the devil's own trademark, and if we saw any one who took pleasure in cruelty, we might know who he belonged to, for the devil was a murderer from the beginning, and a tormentor to the end. On the other hand, where we saw people who loved their neighbors, and were kind to man and beast, we might know that was God's mark, for 'God is Love.'"

"Your master never taught you a truer thing," said John; "there is no religion without love, and people may talk as much as they like about their religion, but if it does not teach them to be good and kind to man and beast, it is all a sham—all a sham, James, and it won't stand when things come to be turned inside out and put down for what they are."

14

James Howard

ONE MORNING EARLY in December, John had just
led me into my box after my daily exercise, and was
strapping my cloth on, and James was coming in from
the corn chamber with some oats, when the master
came into the stable. He looked rather serious, and
held an open letter in his hand. John fastened the
door of my box, touched his cap, and waited for
orders.

"Good morning, John," said the master. "I want
to know if you have any complaint to make of James?"

"Complaint, sir? No, sir."

"Is he industrious at his work and respectful to
you?"

"Yes, sir, always."

"You never find he slights his work when your
back is turned?"

"Never, sir."

"That's well; but I must put another question.
Have you no reason to suspect that when he goes
out with the horses to exercise them, or to take a message, that he stops about talking to his acquaintances,

or goes into houses where he has no business, leaving the horses outside?"

"No, sir, certainly not, and if anybody has been saying that about James, I don't believe it, and I don't mean to believe it unless I have it fairly proved before witnesses; it's not for me to say who has been trying to take away James's character, but I will say this, sir, that a steadier, pleasanter, honester, smarter young fellow I never had in this stable. I can trust his word and I can trust his work; he is gentle and clever with the horses, and I would rather have them in his charge than with half the young fellows I know of in laced hats and liveries; and whoever wants a character of James Howard," said John, with a decided jerk of his head, "let them come to John Manly."

The master stood all this time grave and attentive, but as John finished his speech a broad smile spread over his face, and looking kindly across at James, who all this time had stood still at the door, he said, "James, my lad, set down the oats and come here; I am very glad to find that John's opinion of your character agrees so exactly with my own. John is a cautious man," he said, with a droll smile, "and it is not always easy to get his opinion about people, so I thought if I beat the bush on this side, the birds would fly out, and I should learn what I wanted to know quickly; so now we will come to business. I have a letter from my brother-in-law, Sir Clifford Williams, of Clifford Hall. He wants me to find him a trustworthy young groom, about twenty or twenty-one, who knows his business. His old coachman, who has lived with him twenty years, is getting feeble, and he wants a man to work with him and get into his ways, who would be able, when the old man was pensioned off, to step into his place. He would have eighteen shillings a week at first, a stable suit, a driving suit, a bedroom over the coach house, and a boy under him. Sir Clifford is a good master, and if you could get the place, it would be a good start for you. I don't want to part with you, and if you left us I know John would lose his right hand."

"That I should, sir," said John, "but I would not stand in his light for the world."

"How old are you, James?" said master.

"Nineteen next May, sir."

"That's young; what do you think, John?"

"Well, sir, it is young; but he is as steady as a man, and is strong, and well grown, and though he has not had much experience in driving, he has a light firm hand and a quick eye, and he is very careful, and I am quite sure no horse of his will be ruined for want of having his feet and shoes looked after."

"Your word will go the furthest, John," said the master, "for Sir Clifford adds in a postscript, 'If I could find a man trained by your John I should like him better than any other.' So, James, lad, think it over, talk to your mother at dinner time, and then let me know what you wish."

In a few days after this conversation it was fully settled that James should go to Clifford Hall in a month or six weeks, as it suited his master, and in the meantime he was to get all the practice in driving that could be given to him. I never knew the carriage to go out so often before: when the mistress did not go out, the master drove himself in the two-wheeled chaise; but now, whether it was master or the young ladies, or only an errand, Ginger and I were put into the carriage and James drove us. At the first John rode with him on the box, telling him this and that, and after that James drove alone.

Then it was wonderful what a number of places the master would go to in the city on Saturday, and what queer streets we were driven through. He was sure to go to the railway station just as the train was coming in, and cabs and carriages, carts and omnibuses were all trying to get over the bridge together; that bridge wanted good horses and good drivers when the railway bell was ringing, for it was narrow, and there was a very sharp turn up to the station, where it would not have been at all difficult for people to run into each other, if they did not look sharp and keep their wits about them.

15

The Old Hostler

AFTER THIS, IT was decided by my master and mistress to pay a visit to some friends who lived about forty-six miles from our home, and James was to drive them. The first day we traveled thirty-two miles. There were some long, heavy hills, but James drove so carefully and thoughtfully that we were not at all harassed. He never forgot to put on the drag as we went downhill, nor to take it off at the right place. He kept our feet on the smoothest part of the road, and if the uphill was very long, he set the carriage wheels a little across the road, so as not to run back, and gave us a breathing. All these little things help a horse very much, particularly if he gets kind words into the bargain.

We stopped once or twice on the road, and just as the sun was going down we reached the town where we were to spend the night. We stopped at the principal hotel, which was in the marketplace; it was a very large one; we drove under an archway into a long yard, at the further end of which were the stables and coach houses. Two hostlers came to take us out. The head hostler was a pleasant, active little man, with a crooked leg, and a yellow striped waistcoat. I never saw a man unbuckle harness so quickly as he did, and with a pat and a good word he led me to a long stable, with six or eight stalls in it, and two or three horses. The other man brought Ginger; James stood by while we were rubbed down and cleaned.

I never was cleaned so lightly and quickly as by that little old man. When he had done, James stepped up and felt me over, as if he thought I could not be thoroughly done, but he found my coat as clean and smooth as silk.

"Well," he said, "I thought I was pretty quick, and our John quicker still, but you do beat all I ever saw for being quick and thorough at the same time."

"Practice makes perfect," said the crooked little hostler, "and 'twould be a pity if it didn't; forty years' practice, and not perfect! Ha, ha! That would be a pity; and as to being quick, why, bless you! That is only a matter of habit; if you get into the habit of being quick, it is just as easy as being slow; easier, I should say; in fact, it don't agree with my health to be hulking about over a job twice as long as it need take. Bless you! I couldn't whistle if I crawled over my work as some folks do! You see, I have been about horses ever since I was twelve years old, in hunting stables, and racing stables; and being small, ye see, I was jockey for several years; but at the Goodwood, ye see, the turf was very slippery and my poor Larkspur got a fall, and I broke my knee, and so of course I was of no more use there. But I could not live without horses, of course I couldn't, so I took to the hotels. And I can tell ye it is a downright pleasure to handle an animal like this, well-bred, well-mannered, well-cared-for; bless ye! I can tell how a horse is treated. Give me the handling of a horse for twenty minutes, and I'll tell you what sort of a groom he has had. Look at this one, pleasant, quiet, turns about just as you want him, holds up his feet to be cleaned out, or anything else you please to wish; then you'll find another fidgety, fretty, won't move the right way, or starts across the stall, tosses up his head as soon as you come near him, lays his ears, and seems afraid of you; or else squares about at you with his heels. Poor things! I know what sort of treatment they have had. If they are timid, it makes them start or shy; if they are high-mettled, it makes them vicious or dangerous; their tempers are mostly made when they are young. Bless you! They are like children, train 'em up in the way they should go, as the good book says, and when they are old they will not depart from it, if they have a chance, that is."

"I like to hear you talk," said James. "That's the

way we lay it down at home, at our master's."

"Who is your master, young man, if it be a proper question? I should judge he is a good one, from what I see."

"He is Squire Gordon, of Birtwick Park, the other side the Beacon Hills," said James.

"Ah, so, so, I have heard tell of him; fine judge of horses, ain't he? The best rider in the county?"

"I believe he is," said James, "but he rides very little now, since the poor young master was killed."

"Ah, poor gentleman; I read all about it in the paper at the time. A fine horse killed too, wasn't there?"

"Yes," said James, "he was a splendid creature, brother to this one, and just like him."

"Pity, pity!" said the old man. "'Twas a bad place to leap, if I remember; a thin fence at top, a steep bank down to the stream, wasn't it? No chance for a horse to see where he is going. Now, I am for bold riding as much as any man, but still there are some leaps that only a very knowing old huntsman has any right to take. A man's life and a horse's life are worth more than a fox's tail, at least I should say they ought to be."

During this time the other man had finished Ginger and had brought our corn, and James and the old man left the stable together.

16

The Fire

LATER ON IN the evening, a traveler's horse was brought in by the second hostler, and while he was cleaning him, a young man with a pipe in his mouth lounged into the stable to gossip.

"I say, Towler," said the hostler, "just run up the ladder into the loft and put some hay down into this horse's rack, will you? Only lay down your pipe."

"All right," said the other, and went up through the trap door; and I heard him step across the floor overhead and put down the hay. James came in to look at us the last thing, and then the door was locked.

I cannot say how long I had slept, nor what time in the night it was, but I woke up very uncomfortable, though I hardly knew why. I got up, the air seemed all thick and choking. I heard Ginger coughing and one of the other horses moved about restlessly; it was quite dark, and I could see nothing, but the stable was very full of smoke, and I hardly knew how to breathe.

The trap door had been left open, and I thought that was the place it came through. I listened and heard a soft rushing sort of noise, and a low crackling and snapping. I did not know what it was, but there was something in the sound so strange that it made me tremble all over. The other horses were now all awake; some were pulling at their halters, others were stamping.

At last I heard steps outside, and the hostler who had put up the traveler's horse burst into the stable with a lantern, and began to untie the horses, and try to lead them out; but he seemed in such a hurry and so frightened himself that he frightened me still more. The first horse would not go with him; he tried the second and third, and they too would not stir. He came to me next and tried to drag me out of the stall by force; of course that was no use. He tried us all by turns and then left the stable.

No doubt we were very foolish, but danger seemed to be all round, and there was nobody we knew to trust in, and all was strange and uncertain. The fresh air that had come in through the open door made it easier to breathe, but the rushing sound overhead grew louder, and as I looked upward through the bars of my empty rack, I saw a red light flickering on the wall. Then I heard a cry of "Fire" outside, and the old hostler quietly and quickly came in; he got one horse out, and went to another, but the flames were playing round the trap door, and the roaring overhead was dreadful.

The next thing I heard was James's voice, quiet and cheery, as it always was.

"Come, my beauties, it is time for us to be off, so wake up and come along." I stood nearest the door, so he came to me first, patting me as he came in.

"Come, Beauty, on with your bridle, my boy, we'll soon be out of this smother." It was on in no time; then he took the scarf off his neck, and tied it lightly over my eyes, and patting and coaxing he led me out of the stable. Safe in the yard, he slipped the scarf off my eyes, and shouted, "Here somebody! Take this horse while I go back for the other."

A tall, broad man stepped forward and took me, and James darted back into the stable. I set up a shrill whinny as I saw him go. Ginger told me afterward that whinny was the best thing I could have done for her, for had she not heard me outside, she would never have had courage to come out.

There was much confusion in the yard; the horses being got out of other stables, and the carriages and gigs being pulled out of houses and sheds, lest the flames should spread further. On the other side the yard, windows were thrown up, and people were shouting all sorts of things; but I kept my eye fixed on the stable door, where the smoke poured out thicker than ever, and I could see flashes of red light; presently I heard above all the stir and din a loud, clear voice, which I knew was master's:

"James Howard! James Howard! Are you there?" There was no answer, but I heard a crash of something falling in the stable, and the next moment I gave a loud, joyful neigh, for I saw James coming through the smoke leading Ginger with him; she was coughing violently and he was not able to speak.

"My brave lad!" said master, laying his hand on his shoulder. "Are you hurt?"

James shook his head, for he could not yet speak.

"Aye," said the big man who held me, "he is a brave lad, and no mistake."

"And now," said master, "when you have got your breath, James, we'll get out of this place as quickly as we can." And we were moving toward the entry, when from the marketplace there came a sound of galloping feet and loud rumbling wheels.

"'Tis the fire engine! The fire engine!" shouted two or three voices, "Stand back, make way!" and clattering and thundering over the stones two horses dashed into the yard with a heavy engine behind them. The firemen leaped to the ground; there was no need to ask where the fire was—it was rolling up in a great blaze from the roof.

We got out as fast as we could into the broad quiet

marketplace; the stars were shining, and except the noise behind us, all was still. Master led the way to a large hotel on the other side, and as soon as the hostler came, he said, "James, I must now hasten to your mistress; I trust the horses entirely to you, order whatever you think is needed," and with that he was gone. The master did not run, but I never saw mortal man walk so fast as he did that night.

There was a dreadful sound before we got into our stalls—the shrieks of those poor horses that were left burning to death in the stable—it was very terrible and made both Ginger and me feel very bad. We, however, were taken in and well done by.

The next morning the master came to see how we were and to speak to James. I did not hear much, for the hostler was rubbing me down, but I could see that James looked very happy, and I thought the master was proud of him. Our mistress had been so much alarmed in the night that the journey was put off till the afternoon, so James had the morning on hand, and went first to the inn to see about our harness and the carriage, and then to hear more about the fire. When he came back we heard him tell the hostler about it. At first no one could guess how the fire had been caused, but at last a man said he saw Dick Towler go into the stable with a pipe in his mouth, and when he came out he had not one, and went to the tap for another. Then the under hostler said he had asked Dick to go up the ladder to put down some hay, but told him to lay down his pipe first. Dick denied taking the pipe with him, but no one believed him. I remember our John Manly's rule, never to allow a pipe in the stable, and thought it ought to be the rule everywhere.

James said the roof and floor had all fallen in, and that only the black walls were standing; the two poor horses that could not be got out were buried under the burnt rafters and tiles.

17
John Manly's Talk

THE REST OF our journey was very easy, and a little after sunset we reached the house of my master's friend. We were taken into a clean, snug stable; there was a kind coachman, who made us very comfortable, and who seemed to think a good deal of James when he heard about the fire.

"There is one thing quite clear, young man," he said, "your horses know who they can trust; it is one of the hardest things in the world to get horses out of a stable when there is either fire or flood. I don't know why they won't come out, but they won't—not one in twenty."

We stopped two or three days at this place and then returned home. All went well on the journey; we were glad to be in our own stable again, and John was equally glad to see us.

Before he and James left us for the night, James said, "I wonder who is coming in my place."

"Little Joe Green at the Lodge," said John.

"Little Joe Green! Why, he's a child!"

"He is fourteen and a half," said John.

"But he is such a little chap!"

"Yes, he is small, but he is quick and willing, and kind-hearted, too, and then he wishes very much to come, and his father would like it; and I know the master would like to give him the chance. He said if I thought he would not do, he would look out for a bigger boy; but I said I was quite agreeable to try him for six weeks."

"Six weeks!" said James. "Why, it will be six months before he can be of much use! It will make you a deal of work, John."

"Well," said John with a laugh, "work and I are very good friends; I never was afraid of work yet."

"You are a very good man," said James. "I wish I may ever be like you."

"I don't often speak of myself," said John, "but as you are going away from us out into the world, to shift for yourself, I'll just tell you how I look on these things. I was just as old as Joseph when my father and mother died of the fever, within ten days of each other, and left me and my cripple sister Nelly alone in the world, without a relation that we could look to for help. I was a farmer's boy, not earning enough to keep myself, much less both of us, and she must have gone to the workhouse but for our mistress (Nelly calls her her angel, and she has good right to do so).

She went and hired a room for her with old Widow Mallet, and she gave her knitting and needlework when she was able to do it; and when she was ill she sent her dinners and many nice, comfortable things, and was like a mother to her. Then the master, he took me into the stable under old Norman, the coachman that was then. I had my food at the house, and my bed in the loft, and a suit of clothes and three shillings a week, so that I could help Nelly. Then there was Norman; he might have turned round and said at his age he could not be troubled with a raw boy from the plowtail, but he was rather like a father to me, and took no end of pains with me. When the old man died some years after, I stepped into his place, and now of course I have top wages, and can lay by for a rainy day or a sunny day, as it may happen, and Nelly is as happy as a bird. So you see, James, I am not the man that should turn up his nose at a little boy and vex a good, kind master. No, no! I shall miss you very much, James, but we shall pull through, and there's nothing like doing a kindness when 'tis put in your way, and I am glad I can do it."

"Then," said James, "you don't hold with that saying, 'Everybody look after himself, and take care of number one'?"

"No, indeed," said John, "where should I and

Nelly have been if master and mistress and old Norman had only taken care of number one? Why— she in the workhouse and I hoeing turnips! Where would Black Beauty and Ginger have been if you had only thought of number one? Why, roasted to death! No, Jim, no! That is a selfish, heathenish saying, whoever uses it, and any man who thinks he has nothing to do but take care of number one, why, it's a pity but what he had been drowned like a puppy or a kitten, before he got his eyes open, that's what I think," said John, with a very decided jerk of his head.

James laughed at this; but there was a thickness in his voice when he said, "You have been my best friend except my mother. I hope you won't forget me."

"No, lad, no!" said John. "And if ever I can do you a good turn I hope you won't forget me."

The next day Joe came to the stables to learn all he could before James left. He learned to sweep the stable, to bring in the straw and hay; he began to clean the harness, and helped to wash the carriage. As he was quite too short to do anything in the way of grooming Ginger and me, James taught him upon Merrylegs, for he was to have full charge of him, under John. He was a nice little bright fellow, and always came whistling to his work.

Merrylegs was a good deal put out at being "mauled about," as he said, "by a boy who knew nothing," but toward the end of the second week he told me confidentially that he thought the boy would turn out well.

At last the day came when James had to leave us; cheerful as he always was, he looked quite down-hearted that morning.

"You see," he said to John, "I am leaving a great deal behind; my mother and Betsy, and you, and a good master and mistress, and then the horses, and my old Merrylegs. At the new place there will not be a soul that I shall know. If it were not that I shall get a higher place, and be able to help my mother better, I don't think I should have made up my mind to it. It is a real pinch, John."

"Aye, James, lad, so it is, but I should not think much of you if you could leave your home for the first time and not feel it. Cheer up, you'll make friends there and if you get on well—as I am sure you will, it will be a fine thing for your mother, and she will be proud enough that you have got into such a good place as that."

So John cheered him up, but every one was sorry to lose James; as for Merrylegs, he pined after him for several days, and went quite off his appetite. So John took him out several mornings with a leading rein when he exercised me, and trotting and galloping by my side got up the little fellow's spirits again, and he was soon all right.

Joe's father would often come in and give a little help, as he understood the work and Joe took a great deal of pains to learn, and John was quite encouraged about him.

18

Going for the Doctor

ONE NIGHT, A few days after James had left, I had eaten my hay and was lying down in my straw fast asleep, when I was suddenly roused by the stable bell ringing very loud. I heard the door of John's house open, and his feet running up to the Hall. He was back again in no time; he unlocked the stable door, and came in, calling out, "Wake up, Beauty! You must go well now, if ever you did." And almost before I could think, he had got the saddle on my back and the bridle on my head. He just ran round for his coat, and then took me at a quick trot up to the Hall door. The Squire stood there with a lamp in his hand.

"Now, John," he said, "ride for your life—that is, for your mistress's life; there is not a moment to lose. Give this note to Doctor White; give your horse a rest at the inn, and be back as soon as you can."

John said, "Yes, sir," and was on my back in a minute. The gardener who lived at the lodge had heard the bell ring, and was ready with the gate open, and away we went through the Park and through the village, and down the hill till we came to the tollgate.

John called very loud and thumped upon the door; the man was soon out and flung open the gate.

"Now," said John, "do you keep the gate open for the Doctor; here's the money," And off we went again.

There was before us a long piece of level road by the river side; John said to me, "Now Beauty, do your best," and so I did; I wanted no whip nor spur, and for two miles I galloped as fast as I could lay my feet to the ground; I don't believe that my old grandfather who won the race at Newmarket could have gone faster. When we came to the bridge, John pulled me up a little and patted my neck. "Well done, Beauty, good old fellow," he said. He would have let me go slower, but my spirit was up, and I was off again as fast as before. The air was frosty, the moon was bright, it was very pleasant. We came through a village, then through a dark wood, then uphill, then downhill, till after an eight-mile run we came to the town, through the streets and into the marketplace. It was all quite still except the clatter of my feet on the stones—everybody was asleep. The church clock struck three as we drew up at Doctor White's door. John rang the bell twice, and then knocked at the door like thunder. A window was thrown up, and Doctor White, in his nightcap, put his head out and said, "What do you want?"

"Mrs. Gordon is very ill, sir. Master wants you to go at once; he thinks she will die if you cannot get there. Here is a note."

"Wait," he said, "I will come."

He shut the window, and was soon at the door.

"The worst of it is," he said, "that my horse has been out all day and is quite done up; my son has just been sent for, and he has taken the other. What is to be done? Can I have your horse?"

"He has come at a gallop nearly all the way, sir, and I was to give him a rest here; but I think my master would not be against it if you think fit, sir."

"All right," he said, "I will soon be ready."

John stood by me and stroked my neck; I was very hot. The doctor came out with his riding whip.

"You need not take that, sir," said John. "Black Beauty will go till he drops. Take care of him, sir, if you can; I should not like any harm to come to him."

"No, no, John," said the doctor, "I hope not." And in a minute we had left John far behind.

I will not tell about our way back. The doctor was a heavier man than John, and not so good a rider; however, I did my very best. The man at the tollgate had it open. When we came to the hill, the doctor drew me up. "Now, my good fellow," he said, "take some breath." I was glad he did, for I was nearly spent, but that breathing helped me on, and soon we were in the Park. Joe was at the lodge gate; my master was at the Hall door, for he had heard us coming. He spoke not a word; the doctor went into the house with him, and Joe led me to the stable. I was glad to get home, my legs shook under me, and I could only stand and pant. I had not a dry hair on my body, the water ran down my legs, and I steamed all over—Joe used to say, like a pot on the fire.

Poor Joe! He was young and small, and as yet he knew very little, and his father, who would have helped him, had been sent to the next village; but I am sure he did the very best he knew. He rubbed my legs and my chest, but he did not put my warm cloth on me; he thought I was so hot I should not like it. Then he gave me a pailful of water to drink; it was cold and very good, and I drank it all; then he gave me some hay and some corn, and thinking he had done right, he went away.

Soon I began to shake and tremble, and turned deadly cold; my legs ached, my loins ached, and my chest ached, and I felt sore all over. Oh, how I wished for my warm, thick cloth as I stood and trembled. I wished for John, but he had eight miles to walk, so I lay down in my straw and tried to go to sleep. After a long while I heard John at the door; I gave a low

moan, for I was in great pain. He was at my side in a
moment, stooping down by me. I could not tell him
how I felt, but he seemed to know it all; he covered me
up with two or three warm cloths, and then ran to the
house for some hot water; he made me some warm
gruel, which I drank, and then I think I went to sleep.

John seemed to be very much put out. I heard
him say to himself over and over again, "Stupid boy!
Stupid boy! No cloth put on, and I dare say the water
was cold too; boys are no good." But Joe was a good
boy after all.

I was now very ill; a strong inflammation had
attacked my lungs, and I could not draw my breath
without pain. John nursed me night and day; he
would get up two or three times in the night to come
to me. My master, too, often came to see me.

"My poor Beauty," he said one day, "my good
horse, you saved your mistress's life, Beauty. Yes,
you saved her life." I was very glad to hear that, for it
seems the doctor had said if we had been a little longer
it would have been too late. John told my master he
never saw a horse go so fast in his life. It seemed as if
the horse knew what was the matter. Of course I did,
though John thought not; at least I knew as much as
this, that John and I must go at the top of our speed,
and that it was for the sake of the mistress.

19

Only Ignorance

I DO NOT know how long I was ill. Mr. Bond, the horse doctor, came every day. One day he bled me; John held a pail for the blood. I felt very faint after it, and thought I should die, and I believe they all thought so too.

Ginger and Merrylegs had been moved into the other stable, so that I might be quiet, for the fever made me very quick of hearing; any little noise seemed quite loud, and I could tell every one's foot-step going to and from the house. I knew all that was going on. One night John had to give me a draught; Thomas Green came in to help him. After I had taken it and John had made me as comfortable as he could, he said he should stay half-an-hour to see how the medicine settled. Thomas said he would stay with him, so they went and sat down on a bench that had been brought into Merrylegs's stall, and put down the lantern at their feet, that I might not be disturbed with the light.

For a while both men sat silent, and then Tom Green said in a low voice:

"I wish, John, you'd say a bit of a kind word to Joe. The boy is quite broken-hearted; he can't eat his meals, and he can't smile. He says he knows it was all his fault, though he is sure he did the best he knew, and he says, if Beauty dies, no one will ever speak to him again. It goes to my heart to hear him. I think you might give him just a word; he is not a bad boy."

After a short pause John said slowly, "You must not be too hard upon me, Tom. I know he meant no harm, I never said he did; I know he is not a bad boy. But you see, I am sore myself; that horse is the pride of my heart, to say nothing of his being such a favorite with the master and mistress; and to think that his life may be flung away in this manner is more than I can bear. But if you think I am hard on the boy, I will try to give him a good word tomorrow—that is, I mean if Beauty is better."

"Well, John, thank you. I knew you did not wish to be too hard, and I am glad you see it was only ignorance."

John's voice almost startled me as he answered, "*Only* ignorance! Only *ignorance!* How can you talk about *only* ignorance? Don't you know that it is the worst thing in the world, next to wickedness?—and which does the most mischief, heaven only knows. If people can say, 'Oh! I did not know, I did not mean any harm,' they think it is all right. I suppose Martha Mulwash did not mean to kill that baby when she dosed it with Dalby and soothing syrups; but she did kill it, and was tried for manslaughter."

"And serve her right, too," said Tom. "A woman should not undertake to nurse a tender little child without knowing what is good and what is bad for it."

"Bill Starkey," continued John, "did not mean to frighten his brother into fits when he dressed up like a ghost and ran after him in the moonlight; but he did; and that bright, handsome little fellow, that might have been the pride of any mother's heart, is just no better than an idiot, and never will be, if he lives to be eighty years old. You were a good deal cut up yourself, Tom, two weeks ago, when those young ladies left your hothouse door open, with a frosty east wind blowing right in; you said it killed a good many of your plants."

"A good many!" said Tom. "There was not one of the tender cuttings that was not nipped off. I shall have to strike all over again, and the worst of it is that I don't know where to go to get fresh ones. I was nearly mad when I came in and saw what was done."

"And yet," said John, "I am sure the young ladies did not mean it; it was only ignorance!"

I heard no more of this conversation, for the medicine did well and sent me to sleep, and in the morning I felt much better; but I often thought of John's
words when I came to know more of the world.

20

Joe Green

JOE GREEN WENT on very well; he learned quickly, and was so attentive and careful that John began to trust him in many things. But, as I have said, he was small for his age, and it was seldom that he was allowed to exercise either Ginger or me; but it so happened one morning that John was out with Justice in the luggage cart, and the master wanted a note to be taken immediately to a gentleman's house, about three miles distant, and sent his orders for Joe to saddle me and take it, adding the caution that he was to ride steadily.

The note was delivered, and we were quietly returning till we came to the brick field. Here we saw a cart heavily laden with bricks; the wheels had stuck fast in the stiff mud of some deep ruts, and the carter was shouting and flogging the two horses unmercifully. Joe pulled up. It was a sad sight. There were the two horses straining and struggling with all their might to drag the cart out, but they could not move it; the sweat streamed from their legs and flanks, their sides heaved, and every muscle was strained, while the man, fiercely pulling at the head of the forehorse, swore and lashed most brutally.

"Hold hard," said Joe. "Don't go on flogging the horses like that; the wheels are so stuck that they cannot move the cart." The man took no heed, but went on lashing.

"Stop! Pray stop!" said Joe. "I'll help you to lighten the cart; they can't move it now."

"Mind your own business, you impudent young rascal, and I'll mind mine." The man was in a towering passion and the worse for drink, and laid on the whip again. Joe turned my head, and the next moment we were going at a round gallop toward the house of the master brick maker. I cannot say if John would have approved of our pace, but Joe and I were both of one mind, and so angry that we could not have gone slower.

The house stood close by the roadside. Joe knocked at the door and shouted, "Halloa! Is Mr. Clay at home?" The door was opened, and Mr. Clay himself came out.

"Halloa, young man! You seem in a hurry; any orders from the squire this morning?"

"No, Mr. Clay, but there's a fellow in your brickyard flogging two horses to death. I told him to stop and he wouldn't; I said I'd help him to lighten the cart, and he wouldn't; so I have come to tell you. Pray, sir, go." Joe's voice shook with excitement.

"Thank ye, my lad," said the man, running in for his hat; then pausing for a moment—"Will you give evidence of what you saw if I should bring the fellow up before a magistrate?"

"That I will," said Joe, "and glad too." The man was gone, and we were on our way home at a smart trot.

"Why, what's the matter with you, Joe? You look angry all over," said John, as the boy flung himself from the saddle.

"I am angry all over, I can tell you," said the boy, and then in hurried, excited words he told all that had happened. Joe was usually such a quiet, gentle little fellow that it was wonderful to see him so roused.

"Right, Joe! You did right, my boy, whether the fellow gets a summons or not. Many folks would have ridden by and said 'twas not their business to inter-fere. Now, I say that with cruelty and oppression it is everybody's business to interfere when they see it; you did right, my boy."

Joe was quite calm by this time, and proud that John approved of him, and cleaned out my feet and rubbed me down with a firmer hand than usual.

They were just going home to dinner when the

footman came down to the stable to say that Joe was wanted directly in master's private room; there was a man brought up for ill-using horses, and Joe's evidence was wanted. The boy flushed up to his forehead, and his eyes sparkled. "They shall have it," said he.

"Put yourself a bit straight," said John. Joe gave a pull at his necktie and a twitch at his jacket, and was off in a moment. Our master being one of the county magistrates, cases were often brought to him to settle, or say what should be done. In the stable we heard no more for some time, as it was the men's dinner hour, but when Joe came next into the stable I saw he was in high spirits; he gave me a good-natured slap, and said, "We won't see such things done, will we, old fellow?" We heard afterward that he had given his evidence so clearly, and the horses were in such an exhausted state, bearing marks of such brutal usage, that the carter was committed to take his trial, and might possibly be sentenced to two or three months in prison.

It was wonderful what a change had come over Joe. John laughed, and said he had grown an inch taller in that week, and I believe he had. He was just as kind and gentle as before, but there was more purpose and determination in all that he did—as if he had jumped at once from a boy into a man.

21

The Parting

I NOW HAD lived in this happy place three years, but sad changes were about to come over us. We heard from time to time that our mistress was ill. The doctor was often at the house, and the master looked grave and anxious. Then we heard that she must leave her home at once, and go to a warm country for two or three years. The news fell upon the household like the tolling of a death bell. Everybody was sorry; but the master began directly to make arrangements for breaking up his establishment and leaving England. We used to hear it talked about in our stable; indeed, nothing else was talked about.

John went about his work silent and sad, and Joe scarcely whistled. There was a great deal of coming and going; Ginger and I had full work.

The first of the party who went were Miss Jessie and Flora, with their governess. They came to bid us good-bye. They hugged poor Merrylegs like an old friend, and so indeed he was. Then we heard what had been arranged for us. Master had sold

Ginger and me to his old friend, the Earl of W——,
for he thought we should have a good place there.
Merrylegs he had given to the Vicar, who was wanting a pony for Mrs. Blomefield, but it was on the
condition that he should never be sold, and that
when he was past work he should be shot and
buried.

Joe was engaged to take care of him and to help
in the house, so I thought that Merrylegs was well off.
John had the offer of several good places, but he said
he should wait a little and look round.

The evening before they left, the master came
into the stable to give some directions, and to give his
horses the last pat. He seemed very low-spirited; I
knew that by his voice. I believe we horses can tell
more by the voice than many men can.

"Have you decided what to do, John?" he said. "I
find you have not accepted any of those offers."

"No, sir; I have made up my mind that if I could
get a situation with some first-rate colt breaker and
horse trainer, it would be the right thing for me.
Many young animals are frightened and spoiled by
wrong treatment, which need not be, if the right man
took them in hand. I always get on well with horses,
and if I could help some of them to a fair start, I

should feel as if I was doing some good. What do you think of it, sir?"

"I don't know a man anywhere," said master, "that I should think so suitable for it as yourself. You understand horses, and somehow they understand you, and in time you might set up for yourself; I think you could not do better. If in any way I can help you, write to me. I shall speak to my agent in London, and leave your character with him."

Master gave John the name and address, and then he thanked him for his long and faithful service; but that was too much for John. "Pray, don't, sir, I can't bear it; you and my dear mistress have done so much for me that I could never repay it. But we shall never forget you, sir, and please God we may some day see mistress back again like herself; we must keep up hope, sir." Master gave John his hand, but he did not speak, and they both left the stable.

The last sad day had come; the footman and the heavy luggage had gone off the day before, and there were only master and mistress and her maid. Ginger and I brought the carriage up to the Hall door for the last time. The servants brought out cushions and rugs and many other things, and when all were arranged, master came down the steps carrying the mistress in his arms (I was on the side next to the house, and could see all that went on); he placed her carefully in the carriage, while the house servants stood round crying.

"Good-bye, again," he said, "we shall not forget any of you," and he got in. "Drive on, John."

Joe jumped up, and we trotted slowly through the Park and through the village, where the people were standing at their doors to have a last look and to say, "God bless them."

When we reached the railway station, I think mistress walked from the carriage to the waiting room. I heard her say in her own sweet voice, "Good-bye, John. God bless you." I felt the rein twitch, but John made no answer; perhaps he could not speak. As soon as Joe had taken the things out of the carriage, John called him to stand by the horses, while he went on the platform. Poor Joe! He stood close up to our heads to hide his tears. Very soon the train came puffing up into the station; then two or three minutes, and the doors were slammed to, the guard whistled, and the train glided away, leaving behind it only clouds of white smoke and some very heavy hearts.

When it was quite out of sight, John came back. "We shall never see her again," he said— "never." He took the reins, mounted the box, and with Joe drove slowly home; but it was not our home now.

Part Two

22
Earlshall

THE NEXT MORNING after breakfast Joe put Merrylegs into the mistress's low chaise to take him to the vicarage; he came first and said good-bye to us, and Merrylegs neighed to us from the yard. Then John put the saddle on Ginger and the leading rein on me, and rode us across the country about fifteen miles to Earlshall Park, where the Earl of W—— lived. There was a very fine house and a great deal of stabling. We went into the yard through a stone gateway, and John asked for Mr. York. It was some time before he came. He was a fine-looking, middle-aged man, and his voice said at once that he expected to be obeyed. He was very friendly and polite to John, and after giving us a slight look, he called a groom to take us to our boxes, and invited John to take some refreshment.

We were taken to a light, airy stable, and placed in boxes adjoining each other, where we were rubbed down and fed. In about half-an-hour John and Mr. York, who was to be our new coachman, came in to see us.

"Now, Mr. Manly," he said, after carefully looking at us both, "I can see no fault in these horses, but we all know that horses have their peculiarities as well as men, and that sometimes they need different treatment. I should like to know if there is anything particular in either of these that you would like to mention."

"Well," said John, "I don't believe there is a better pair of horses in the country, and right grieved I am to part with them, but they are not alike. The black one is the most perfect temper I ever knew; I suppose he has never known a hard word or a blow since he was foaled, and all his pleasure seems to be to do what you wish; but the chestnut, I fancy, must have had bad treatment; we heard as much from the dealer. She came to us snappish and suspicious, but when she found what sort of place ours was, it all went off by degrees; for three years I have never seen the smallest sign of temper, and if she is well treated there is not a better, more willing animal than she is. But she is naturally a more irritable constitution than the black horse; flies tease her more; anything wrong in the harness frets her more; and if she were ill-used or unfairly treated, she would not be unlikely to give tit for tat. You know that many high-mettled horses will do so."

"Of course," said York, "I quite understand, but you know it is not easy in stables like these to have all the grooms just what they should be. I do my best, and there I must leave it. I'll remember what you have said about the mare."

They were going out of the stable when John stopped and said, "I had better mention that we have never used the "bearing rein" with either of them; the black horse never had one on, and the dealer said it was the gag bit that spoiled the other's temper."

"Well," said York, "if they come here they must wear the bearing rein. I prefer a loose rein myself, and his lordship is always very reasonable about horses; but my lady—that's another thing; she will have style, and if her carriage horses are not reined up tight she wouldn't look at them. I always stand out against the gag bit, and shall do so, but it must be tight up when my lady rides!"

"I am sorry for it, very sorry," said John; "but I must go now, or I shall lose the train."

He came round to each of us to pat and speak to us for the last time; his voice sounded very sad.

I held my face close to him, that was all I could do to say good-bye; and then he was gone, and I have never seen him since.

The next day Lord W—— came to look at us; he

seemed pleased with our appearance.

"I have great confidence in these horses," he said, "from the character my friend Mr. Gordon has given me of them. Of course they are not a match in color, but my idea is that they will do very well for the carriage while we are in the country. Before we go to London I must try to match Baron; the black horse, I believe, is perfect for riding."

York then told him what John had said about us.

"Well," said he, "you must keep an eye to the mare, and put the bearing rein easy; I dare say they will do very well with a little humoring at first. I'll mention it to her ladyship."

In the afternoon we were harnessed and put in the carriage, and as the stable clock struck three we were led round to the front of the house. It was all very grand, and three or four times as large as the old house at Birtwick, but not half so pleasant, if a horse may have an opinion. Two footmen were standing ready, dressed in drab livery, with scarlet breeches and white stockings. Presently we heard the rustling sound of silk as my lady came down the flight of stone steps. She stepped round to look at us; she was a tall, proud-looking woman, and did not seem pleased about something, but she said nothing, and got into the carriage. This was the first time of wearing a

bearing rein, and I must say, though it certainly was
a nuisance not to be able to get my head down now
and then, it did not pull my head higher than I was
accustomed to carry it. I felt anxious about Ginger,
but she seemed to be quiet and content.

The next day at three o'clock we were again at the
door, and the footmen as before; we heard the silk
dress rustle, and the lady came down the steps, and
in an imperious voice she said, "York, you must put
those horses' heads higher; they are not fit to be
seen."

York got down, and said very respectfully, "I beg
your pardon, my lady, but these horses have not been
reined up for three years, and my lord said it would
be safer to bring them to it by degrees; but if your
ladyship pleases, I can take them up a little more."

"Do so," she said.

York came round to our heads and shortened the
rein himself, one hole, I think; every little makes a difference, be it for better or worse, and that day we had
a steep hill to go up. Then I began to understand
what I had heard of. Of course I wanted to put my
head forward and take the carriage up with a will, as
we had been used to do; but no, I had to pull with my
head up now, and that took all the spirit out of me,
and the strain came on my back and legs. When we

came in, Ginger said, "Now you see what it is like, but this is not bad, and if it does not get much worse than this I shall say nothing about it, for we are very well treated here; but if they strain me up tight, why, let 'em look out! I can't bear it, and I won't."

Day by day, hole by hole, our bearing reins were shortened, and instead of looking forward with pleasure to having my harness put on as I used to do, I began to dread it. Ginger, too, seemed restless, though she said very little. At last I thought the worst was over; for several days there was no more shortening, and I determined to make the best of it and do my duty, though it was now a constant harass instead of a pleasure; but the worst was not come.

23

A Strike for Liberty

ONE DAY MY lady came down later than usual, and the silk rustled more than ever.

"Drive to the Duchess of B——'s," she said, and then after a pause, "Are you never going to get those horses' heads up, York? Raise them at once, and let us have no more of this humoring and nonsense."

York came to me first, while the groom stood at Ginger's head. He drew my head back and fixed the rein so tight that it was almost intolerable; then he went to Ginger, who was impatiently jerking her head up and down against the bit, as was her way now. She had a good idea of what was coming, and the moment York took the rein off the terret in order to shorten it, she took her opportunity and reared up so suddenly that York had his nose roughly hit and his hat knocked off; the groom was nearly thrown off his legs. At once they both flew to her head, but she was a match for them, and went on plunging, rearing, and kicking in a most desperate manner. At last she kicked right over the carriage pole and fell down, after giving me a severe blow on my near quarter. There is no knowing what further mischief she might have done had not York promptly sat himself down flat on her head to prevent her struggling, at the same time calling out, "Unbuckle the black horse! Run for the winch and unscrew the carriage pole! Cut the trace here, somebody, if you can't unhitch it." One of the footmen ran for the winch, and another brought a knife from the house.

The groom soon set me free from Ginger and the carriage, and led me to my box. He just turned me in as I was and ran back to York. I was much excited by what had happened, and if I had ever been used to kick or rear, I am sure I should have done it then; but I never had, and there I stood angry, sore in my leg, my head still strained up to the terret on the saddle, and no power to get it down. I was very miserable, and felt much inclined to kick the first person who came near me.

Before long, however, Ginger was led in by two grooms, a good deal knocked about and bruised. York came with her and gave his orders, and then came to look at me. In a moment he let down my head.

"Confound these bearing reins!" he said to himself; "I thought we should have some mischief soon.

Master will be sorely vexed. But there—if a woman's husband can't rule her, of course a servant can't; so I wash my hands of it, and if she can't get to the Duchess's garden party I can't help it."

York did not say this before the men; he always spoke respectfully when they were by. Now he felt me all over, and soon found the place above my hock where I had been kicked. It was swelled and painful; he ordered it to be sponged with hot water, and then some lotion was put on.

Lord W—— was much put out when he learned what had happened; he blamed York for giving way to his mistress, to which he replied that in future he would much prefer to receive his orders only from his lordship; but I think nothing came of it, for things went on the same as before. I thought York might have stood up better for his horses, but perhaps I am no judge.

Ginger was never put into the carriage again, but when she was well of her bruises, one of Lord W——'s younger sons said he should like to have her; he was sure she would make a good hunter. As for me, I was obliged still to go in the carriage, and had a fresh partner called Max; he had always been used to the tight rein. I asked him how it was he bore it.

"Well," he said, "I bear it because I must, but

it is shortening my life, and it will shorten yours too if you have to stick to it."

"Do you think," I said, "that our masters know how bad it is for us?"

"I can't say," he replied, "but the dealers and the horse doctors know it very well. I was at a dealer's once, who was training me and another horse to go as a pair; he was getting our heads up, as he said, a little higher and a little higher every day. A gentleman who was there asked him why he did so. 'Because,' said he, 'people won't buy them unless we do. The London people always want their horses to carry their heads high and to step high. Of course it is very bad for the horses, but then it is good for trade. The horses soon wear up, or get diseased, and they come for another pair.' That," said Max, "is what he said in my hearing, and you can judge for yourself."

What I suffered with that rein for four long months in my lady's carriage it would be hard to describe; but I am quite sure that, had it lasted much longer, either my health or my temper would have given way. Before that, I never knew what it was to foam at the mouth, but now the action of the sharp bit on my tongue and jaw, and the constrained position of my head and throat always caused me to froth at the mouth more or less. Some people think it very

fine to see this, and say, "What fine, spirited creatures!" But it is just as unnatural for horses as for
men to foam at the mouth; it is a sure sign of some
discomfort, and should be attended to. Besides this,
there was a pressure on my windpipe, which often
made my breathing very uncomfortable; when I returned from my work, my neck and chest were
strained and painful, my mouth and tongue tender,
and I felt worn and depressed.

In my old home I always knew that John and my
master were my friends; but here, although in many
ways I was well treated, I had no friend. York might
have known, and very likely did know, how that rein
harassed me; but I suppose he took it as a matter
of course that could not be helped; at any rate, nothing was done to relieve me.

24

The Lady Anne

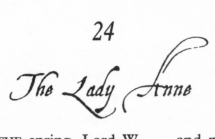

EARLY IN THE spring, Lord W—— and part of his family went up to London, and took York with them. I and Ginger and some other horses were left at home for use, and the head groom was left in charge.

The Lady Harriet, who remained at the Hall, was a great invalid, and never went out in the carriage, and the Lady Anne preferred riding on horseback with her brother, or cousins. She was a perfect horse-woman, and as gay and gentle as she was beautiful. She chose me for her horse, and named me "Black Auster." I enjoyed these rides very much in the clear cold air, sometimes with Ginger, sometimes with Lizzie. This Lizzie was a bright bay mare, almost thoroughbred, and a great favorite with the gentle-men, on account of her fine action and lively spirit; but Ginger, who knew more of her than I did, told me she was rather nervous.

There was a gentleman of the name of Blantyre staying at the Hall; he always rode Lizzie, and praised her so much that one day Lady Anne ordered the sidesaddle to be put on her, and the other saddle on me. When we came to the door, the gentleman seemed very uneasy.

"How is this?" he said. "Are you tired of your good Black Auster?"

"Oh, no, not at all," she replied, "but I am amiable enough to let you ride him for once, and I will try your charming Lizzie. You must confess that in size and appearance she is far more like a lady's horse than my own favorite."

"Do let me advise you not to mount her," he said. "She is a charming creature, but she is too nervous for a lady. I assure you she is not perfectly safe; let me beg you to have the saddles changed."

"My dear cousin," said Lady Anne, laughing, "pray do not trouble your good careful head about me. I have been a horsewoman ever since I was a baby, and I have followed the hounds a great many times, though I know you do not approve of ladies hunting; but still that is the fact, and I intend to try this Lizzie that you gentlemen are all so fond of; so please help me to mount like a good friend as you are."

There was no more to be said; he placed her carefully on the saddle, looked to the bit and curb, gave the reins gently into her hand, and then mounted me. Just as we were moving off, a footman came out with a slip of paper and message from the Lady Harriet. "Would they ask this question for her at Doctor Ashley's, and bring the answer?"

The village was about a mile off, and the Doctor's house was the last in it. We went along gaily enough till we came to his gate. There was a short drive up to the house between tall evergreens. Blantyre alighted at the gate, and was going to open it for Lady Anne, but she said, "I will wait for you here, and you can hang Auster's rein on the gate."

He looked at her doubtfully—"I will not be five minutes," he said.

"Oh, do not hurry yourself; Lizzie and I shall not run away from you."

He hung my rein on one of the iron spikes, and was soon hidden among the trees. Lizzie was standing quietly by the side of the road a few paces off with her back to me. My young mistress was sitting easily with a loose rein, humming a little song. I listened to my rider's footsteps until they reached the house, and heard him knock at the door. There was a meadow on the opposite side of the road, the gate of which stood open; just then some cart horses and several young colts came trotting out in a very disorderly manner, while a boy behind was cracking a great whip. The colts were wild and frolicsome, and one of them bolted across the road and blundered up against Lizzie's hind legs; and whether it was the stupid colt, or the loud cracking of the whip, or both together, I cannot say, but she gave a violent kick, and dashed off into a headlong gallop. It was so sudden that Lady Anne was nearly unseated, but she soon recovered herself. I gave a loud, shrill neigh for help; again and again I neighed, pawing the ground impatiently, and tossing my head to get the rein loose. I had not long to wait. Blantyre came running to the gate; he looked anxiously about, and just caught sight of the flying figure, now far away on the road. In an instant he sprang into the saddle. I needed no whip, no spur, for I was as eager as my rider; he saw it, and giving me a free rein, and leaning a little forward, we dashed after them.

For about a mile and a half the road ran straight, and then bent to the right, after which it divided into two roads. Long before we came to the bend, she was out of sight. Which way had she turned? A woman was standing at her garden gate, shading her eyes with her hand, and looking eagerly up the road. Scarcely drawing the rein, Blantyre shouted, "Which way?" "To the right!" cried the woman, pointing with her hand, and away we went up the right-hand road; then for a moment we caught sight of her;

another bend and she was hidden again. Several times we caught glimpses, and then lost them. We scarcely seemed to gain ground upon them at all. An old road mender was standing near a heap of stones—his shovel dropped and his hands raised. As we came near he made a sign to speak. Blantyre drew the rein a little. "To the common, to the common, sir; she has turned off there." I knew this common very well; it was for the most part very uneven ground, covered with heather and dark green furze bushes, with here and there a scrubby old thorn tree; there were also open spaces of fine short grass, with anthills and mole turns everywhere; the worst place I ever knew for a headlong gallop.

We had hardly turned on the common, when we caught sight again of the green habit flying on before us. My lady's hat was gone, and her long brown hair was streaming behind her. Her head and body were thrown back, as if she were pulling with all her remaining strength, and as if that strength were nearly exhausted. It was clear that the roughness of the ground had very much lessened Lizzie's speed, and there seemed a chance that we might overtake her.

While we were on the highroad, Blantyre had given me my head; but now, with a light hand and a practiced eye, he guided me over the ground in such a masterly manner that my pace was scarcely slackened, and we were decidedly gaining on them.

About halfway across the heath there had been a wide dyke recently cut, and the earth from the cutting was cast up roughly on the other side. Surely this would stop them! But no; with scarcely a pause Lizzie took the leap, stumbled among the rough clods, and fell. Blantyre groaned, "Now, Auster, do your best!" He gave me a steady rein. I gathered myself well together and with one determined leap cleared both dyke and bank.

Motionless among the heather, with her face to the earth, lay my poor young mistress. Blantyre kneeled down and called her name—there was no sound. Gently he turned her face upward; it was ghastly white, and the eyes were closed. "Annie, dear Annie, do speak!" But there was no answer. He unbuttoned her habit, loosened her collar, felt her hands and wrists, then started up and looked wildly round him for help.

At no great distance there were two men cutting turf, who, seeing Lizzie running wild without a rider, had left their work to catch her.

Blantyre's halloo soon brought them to the spot. The foremost man seemed much troubled at the sight, and asked what he could do.

"Can you ride?"

"Well, sir, I bean't much of a horseman, but I'd risk my neck for the Lady Anne; she was uncommon good to my wife in the winter."

"Then mount this horse, my friend—your neck will be quite safe—and ride to the doctor's and ask him to come instantly—then on to the Hall—tell them all that you know, and bid them send me the carriage with Lady Anne's maid and help. I shall stay here."

"All right, sir, I'll do my best, and I pray God the dear young lady may open her eyes soon." Then, seeing the other man, he called out, "Here, Joe, run for some water, and tell my missis to come as quick as she can to the Lady Anne."

He then somehow scrambled into the saddle, and with a "Gee up" and a clap on my sides with both his legs, he started on his journey, making a little circuit to avoid the dyke. He had no whip, which seemed to trouble him, but my pace soon cured that difficulty, and he found the best thing he could do was to stick to the saddle and hold me in, which he did manfully. I shook him as little as I could help, but once or twice on the rough ground he called out, "Steady! Woah! Steady!" On the highroad we were all right; and at the doctor's and the Hall he did his errand like a good man and true. They asked him in to take a drop of something. "No, no," he said; "I'll be back to 'em again by a short cut through the fields, and be there afore the carriage."

There was a great deal of hurry and excitement after the news became known. I was just turned into my box, the saddle and bridle were taken off, and a cloth thrown over me.

Ginger was saddled and sent off in great haste for Lord George, and I soon heard the carriage roll out of the yard.

It seemed a long time before Ginger came back and before we were left alone; and then she told me all that she had seen.

"I can't tell much," she said. "We went a gallop nearly all the way, and got there just as the doctor rode up. There was a woman sitting on the ground with the lady's head in her lap. The doctor poured something into her mouth, but all that I heard was, 'She is not dead.' Then I was led off by a man to a little distance. After a while she was taken to the carriage, and we came home together. I heard my master say to a gentleman who stopped him to inquire, that he hoped no bones were broken, but that she had not spoken yet."

When Lord George took Ginger for hunting, York shook his head; he said it ought to be a steady hand to train a horse for the first season, and not a random rider like Lord George.

Ginger used to like it very much, but sometimes when she came back I could see that she had been very much strained, and now and then she gave a short cough. She had too much spirit to complain, but I could not help feeling anxious about her.

Two days after the accident, Blantyre paid me a visit; he patted me and praised me very much, he told Lord George that he was sure the horse knew of Annie's danger as well as he did. "I could not have held him in if I would," said he. "She ought never to ride any other horse." I found by their conversation that my young mistress was now out of danger, and would soon be able to ride again. This was good news to me, and I looked forward to a happy life.

25
Reuben Smith

NOW I MUST say a little about Reuben Smith, who was left in charge of the stables when York went to London. No one more thoroughly understood his business than he did, and when he was all right there could not be a more faithful or valuable man. He was gentle and very clever in his management of horses, and could doctor them almost as well as a farrier, for he had lived two years with a veterinary surgeon. He was a first-rate driver; he could take a four-in-hand or a tandem as easily as a pair. He was a handsome man, a good scholar, and had very pleasant manners. I believe everybody liked him; certainly the horses did.

The only wonder was that he should be in an under situation, and not in the place of a head coachman like York; but he had one great fault, and that was the love of drink. He was not like some men, always at it; he used to keep steady for weeks or months together, and then he would break out and have a "bout" of it, as York called it, and be a disgrace to himself, a terror to his wife, and a nuisance to all that had to do with him. He was, however, so useful that two or three times York had hushed the matter up, and kept it from the Earl's knowledge; but one night, when Reuben had to drive a party home from a ball, he was so drunk that he could not hold the reins, and a gentleman of the party had to mount the box and drive the ladies home. Of course, this could not be hidden, and Reuben was at once dismissed; his poor wife and little children had to turn out of the pretty cottage by the Park gate and go where they could. Old Max told me all this, for it happened a good while ago; but shortly before Ginger and I came Smith had been taken back again. York had interceded for him with the Earl, who is very kindhearted, and the man had promised faithfully that he would never taste another drop as long as he lived there. He had kept his promise so well that York thought he might be safely trusted to fill his place while he was away, and he was so clever and honest that no one else seemed so well fitted for it.

It was now early in April, and the family was expected home some time in May. The light brougham was to be fresh done up, and as Colonel Blantyre was obliged to return to his regiment, it was arranged that Smith should drive him to the town in it, and ride back; for this purpose he took the saddle with him, and I was chosen for the journey. At the station the Colonel put some money into Smith's hand and bid him good-bye, saying, "Take care of your young mistress, Reuben, and don't let Black Auster be hacked about by any random young prig that wants to ride him—keep him for the lady."

We left the carriage at the maker's, and Smith rode me to the White Lion, and ordered the hostler to feed me well and have me ready for him at four o'clock. A nail in one of my front shoes had started as I came along, but the hostler did not notice it till just about four o'clock. Smith did not come into the yard till five, and then he said he should not leave till six, as he had met with some old friends. The man then told him of the nail, and asked if he should have the shoe looked to.

"No," said Smith, "that will be all right till we get home."

He spoke in a very loud, offhand way, and I thought it very unlike him not to see about the shoe, as he was generally wonderfully particular about loose nails in our shoes. He did not come at six, nor seven, nor eight, and it was nearly nine o'clock before he called for me, and then it was in a loud, rough voice. He seemed in a very bad temper, and abused the hostler, though I could not tell what for.

The landlord stood at the door and said, "Have a

care, Mr. Smith!" but he answered angrily with an oath; and almost before he was out of the town he began to gallop, frequently giving me a sharp cut with his whip, though I was going at full speed. The moon had not yet risen, and it was very dark. The roads were stony, having been recently mended; going over them at this pace, my shoe became looser, and as we neared the turnpike gate it came off.

If Smith had been in his right senses, he would have been sensible of something wrong in my pace, but he was too drunk to notice anything.

Beyond the turnpike was a long piece of road, upon which fresh stones had just been laid—large sharp stones, over which no horse could be driven quickly without risk of danger. Over this road, with one shoe gone, I was forced to gallop at my utmost speed, my rider meanwhile cutting into me with his whip, and with wild curses urging me to go still faster. Of course my shoeless foot suffered dreadfully; the hoof was broken and split down to the very quick, and the inside was terribly cut by the sharpness of the stones.

This could not go on; no horse could keep his footing under such circumstances, the pain was too great. I stumbled, and fell with violence on both my knees. Smith was flung off by my fall, and owing to the speed I was going at, he must have fallen with great force.

I soon recovered my feet and limped to the side of the road, where it was free from stones. The moon had just risen above the hedge, and by its light I could see Smith lying a few yards beyond me. He did not rise; he made one slight effort to do so, and then there was a heavy groan. I could have groaned too, for I was suffering intense pain both from my foot and knees; but horses are used to bearing their pain in silence. I uttered no sound, but I stood there and listened. One more heavy groan from Smith; but though he now lay in the full moonlight I could see no motion. I could do nothing for him nor myself, but, oh, how I listened for the sound of horse, or wheels, or footsteps. The road was not much frequented, and at this time of the night we might stay for hours before help came to us. I stood watching and listening. It was a calm, sweet April night; there were no sounds but a few low notes of a nightingale, and nothing moved but the white clouds near the moon and a brown owl that flitted over the hedge. It made me think of the summer nights long ago, when I used to lie beside my mother in the green pleasant meadow at Farmer Grey's.

26
How it Ended

IT MUST HAVE been nearly midnight when I heard at a great distance the sound of a horse's feet. Sometimes the sound died away, then it grew clearer again and nearer. The road to Earlshall led through plantations that belonged to the Earl; the sound came in that direction, and I hoped it might be someone coming in search of us. As the sound came nearer and nearer, I was almost sure I could distinguish Ginger's step; a little nearer still, and I could tell she was in the dogcart. I neighed loudly, and was overjoyed to hear an answering neigh from Ginger, and men's voices. They came slowly over the stones, and stopped at the dark figure that lay upon the ground.

One of the men jumped out, and stooped down over it. "It is Reuben," he said, "and he does not stir!"

The other man followed and bent over him. "He's dead," he said. "Feel how cold his hands are."

They raised him up, but there was no life, and his hair was soaked with blood. They laid him down again, and came and looked at me. They soon saw my cut knees.

"Why, the horse has been down and thrown him! Who would have thought the black horse would have done that? Nobody thought he could fall. Reuben must have been lying here for hours! Odd, too, that the horse has not moved from the place."

Robert then attempted to lead me forward. I made a step, but almost fell again.

"Halloo! He's bad in his foot as well as his knees. Look here—his hoof is cut all to pieces; he might well come down, poor fellow! I tell you what, Ned, I'm afraid it hasn't been all right with Reuben. Just think of him riding a horse over these stones without a shoe! Why, if he had been in his right senses he would just as soon have tried to ride him over the moon. I'm afraid it has been the old thing over again. Poor Susan! She looked awfully pale when she came to my house to ask if he had not come home. She made believe she was not a bit anxious, and talked of a lot of things that might have kept him. But for all that she begged me to go and meet him. But what must we do? There's the horse to get home as well as the body—and that will be no easy matter."

Then followed a conversation between them, till it was agreed that Robert, as the groom, should lead me, and that Ned must take the body. It was a hard job to get it into the dogcart, for there was no one to hold Ginger; but she knew as well as I did what was going on, and stood as still as a stone. I noticed that, because, if she had a fault, it was that she was impatient in standing.

Ned started off very slowly with his sad load, and Robert came and looked at my foot again; then he took his handkerchief and bound it closely round, and so he led me home. I shall never forget that night walk; it was more than three miles. Robert led me on very slowly, and I limped and hobbled on as well as I could with great pain. I am sure he was sorry for me, for he often patted and encouraged me, talking to me in a pleasant voice.

At last I reached my own box, and had some corn; and after Robert had wrapped up my knees in wet cloths, he tied up my foot in a bran poultice, to draw out the heat and cleanse it before the horse doctor saw it in the morning, and I managed to get myself down on the straw, and slept in spite of the pain.

The next day, after the farrier had examined my wounds, he said he hoped the joint was not injured, and if so, I should not be spoiled for work, but I should never lose the blemish. I believe they did the best to make a good cure, but it was a long and painful one. Proud flesh, as they called it, came up in my knees, and was burned out with caustic; and when at last it was healed, they put a blistering fluid over the front of both knees to bring all the hair off; they had some reason for this, and I suppose it was all right.

As Smith's death had been so sudden, and no one was there to see it, there was an inquest held. The landlord and hostler at the White Lion, with several other people, gave evidence that he was intoxicated when he started from the inn. The keeper of the toll-gate said he rode at a hard gallop through the gate; and my shoe was picked up among the stones, so that the case was quite plain to them, and I was cleared of all blame.

Everybody pitied Susan. She was nearly out of her mind; she kept saying over and over again, "Oh! He was so good—so good! It was all that cursed drink; why will they sell that cursed drink? Oh, Reuben, Reuben!" So she went on till after he was buried, and then, as she had no home or relations, she, with her six little children, was obliged once more to leave the pleasant home by the tall oak trees, and go into that great gloomy Union House.

27

Ruined, and Going Downhill

As SOON AS my knees were sufficiently healed, I was turned into a small meadow for a month or two; no other creature was there, and though I enjoyed the liberty and the sweet grass, yet I had been so long used to society that I felt very lonely. Ginger and I had become fast friends, and now I missed her company extremely. I often neighed when I heard horses' feet passing in the road, but I seldom got an answer; till one morning the gate was opened, and who should come in but dear old Ginger. The man slipped off her halter and left her there. With a joyful whinny I trotted up to her; we were both glad to meet, but I soon found that it was not for our pleasure that she was brought to be with me. Her story would be too long to tell, but the end of it was that she had been ruined by hard riding, and was now turned off to see what rest would do.

Lord George was young and would take no warning; he was a hard rider, and would hunt whenever he could get the chance, quite careless of his horse. Soon after I left the stable there was a steeplechase, and he determined to ride. Though the groom told him she was a little strained, and was not fit for the race, he did not believe it, and on the day of the race urged Ginger to keep up with the foremost riders. With her high spirit, she strained herself to the utmost; she came in with the first three horses, but her wind was touched, besides which he was too heavy for her, and her back was strained. "And so," she said, "here we are, ruined in the prime of our youth and strength— you by a drunkard, and I by a fool; it is very hard." We both felt in ourselves that we were not what we had been. However, that did not spoil the pleasure we had in each other's company; we did not gallop about as we once did, but we used to feed, and lie down together, and stand for hours under one of the shady lime trees with our heads close to each other; and so we passed our time till the family returned from town.

One day we saw the Earl come into the meadow, and York was with him. Seeing who it was, we stood still under our lime tree, and let them come up to us. They examined us carefully. The Earl seemed much annoyed.

"There is three hundred pounds flung away for no earthly use," said he; "but what I care most for is that these horses of my old friend, who thought they would find a good home with me, are ruined. The mare shall have a twelve-month's run, and we shall see what that will do for her; but the black one, he must be sold; 'tis a great pity, but I could not have knees like these in my stables."

"No, my lord, of course not," said York; "but he might get a place where appearance is not of much consequence, and still be well treated. I know a man in Bath, the master of some livery stables, who often wants a good horse at a low figure; I know he looks well after his horses. The inquest cleared the horse's character, and your lordship's recommendation, or mine, would be sufficient warrant for him."

"You had better write to him, York. I should be more particular about the place than the money he would fetch."

After this they left us.

"They'll soon take you away," said Ginger, "and I shall lose the only friend I have, and most likely we shall never see each other again. 'Tis a hard world!"

About a week after this, Robert came into the field with a halter, which he slipped over my head, and led me away. There was no leave-taking of Ginger; we neighed to each other as I was led off, and she trotted anxiously along by the hedge, calling to me as long as she could hear the sound of my feet.

Through the recommendation of York, I was bought by the master of the livery stables. I had to go by train, which was new to me, and required a good deal of courage the first time; but as I found the puffing, rushing, whistling, and, more than all, the trembling of the horse box in which I stood did me no real harm, I soon took it quietly.

When I reached the end of my journey, I found myself in a tolerably comfortable stable, and well attended to. These stables were not so airy and pleasant as those I had been used to. The stalls were laid on a slope instead of being level, and as my head was kept tied to the manger, I was obliged always to stand on the slope, which was very fatiguing. Men do not seem to know yet that horses can do more work if they can stand comfortably and can turn about; however, I was well fed and well cleaned, and, on the whole, I think our master took as much care of us as he could. He kept a good many horses and carriages of different kinds for hire. Sometimes his own men drove them; at others, the horse and chaise were let to gentlemen or ladies who drove themselves.

28

A Job Horse and His Drivers

HITHERTO I HAD always been driven by people who at least knew how to drive; but in this place I was to get my experience of all the different kinds of bad and ignorant driving to which we horses are subjected; for I was a "job horse," and was let out to all sorts of people who wished to hire me; and as I was good-tempered and gentle, I think I was oftener let out to the ignorant drivers than some of the other horses, because I could be depended upon. It would take a long time to tell of all the different styles in which I was driven, but I will mention a few of them.

First, there were the tight-rein drivers—men who seemed to think that all depended on holding the reins as hard as they could, never relaxing the pull on the horse's mouth, or giving him the least liberty of movement. They are always talking about "keeping the horse well in hand," and "holding a horse up," just as if a horse was not made to hold himself up.

Some poor, broken-down horses, whose mouths have been made hard and insensible by just such drivers as these, may, perhaps, find some support in it; but for a horse who can depend upon its own legs, and who has a tender mouth, and is easily guided, it is not only tormenting, but it is stupid.

Then there are the loose-rein drivers, who let the reins lie easily on our backs, and their own hand rest lazily on their knees. Of course, such gentlemen have no control over a horse, if anything happens suddenly. If a horse shies, or starts, or stumbles, they are nowhere, and cannot help the horse or themselves till the mischief is done. Of course, for myself, I had no objection to it, as I was not in the habit either of starting or stumbling, and had only been used to depend on my driver for guidance and encouragement. Still, one likes to feel the rein a little in going downhill, and likes to know that one's driver is not gone to sleep.

Besides, a slovenly way of driving gets a horse into bad and often lazy habits, and when he changes hands he has to be whipped out of them with more or less pain and trouble. Squire Gordon always kept us to our best paces and our best manners. He said that spoiling a horse and letting him get into bad habits was just as cruel as spoiling a child, and both had to suffer for it afterward.

Besides, these drivers are often careless altogether, and will attend to anything else rather than their horses. I went out in the phaeton one day with one of them; he had a lady and two children behind. He flopped the reins about as we started, and of course gave me several unmeaning cuts with the whip, though I was fairly off. There had been a good deal of road mending going on, and even where the stones were not freshly laid down there were a great many loose ones about. My driver was laughing and joking with the lady and the children, and talking about the country to the right and the left; but he never thought it worth while to keep an eye on his horse or to drive on the smoothest parts of the road; and so it easily happened that I got a stone in one of my fore feet.

Now, if Mr. Gordon or John, or in fact any good driver had been there, he would have seen that something was wrong before I had gone three paces. Or even if it had been dark, a practiced hand would have felt by the rein that there was something wrong in the step, and they would have got down and picked out the stone. But this man went on laughing and talking, while at every step the stone became more firmly wedged between my shoe and the frog of my foot. The stone was sharp on the inside and round on the outside, which, as every one knows, is the most dangerous kind that a horse can pick up, at the same time cutting his foot and making him most liable to stumble and fall.

Whether the man was partly blind, or only very careless, I can't say, but he drove me with that stone in my foot for a good half-mile before he saw anything. By that time I was going so lame with the pain that at last he saw it and called out, "Well, here's a go! Why, they have sent us out with a lame horse! What a shame!"

He then chucked the reins and flipped about with the whip, saying, "Now, then, it's no use playing the old soldier with me; there's the journey to go, and it's no use turning lame and lazy."

Just at this time a farmer came riding up on a brown cob. He lifted his hat and pulled up.

"I beg your pardon, sir," he said, "but I think there is something the matter with your horse; he goes very much as if he had a stone in his shoe. If you will allow me, I will look at his feet; these loose scattered stones are confounded dangerous things for the horses."

"He's a hired horse," said my driver. "I don't know what's the matter with him, but it is a great shame to send out a lame beast like this."

The farmer dismounted, and slipping his rein over his arm, at once took up my near foot.

"Bless me, there's a stone! Lame! I should think so!"

At first he tried to dislodge it with his hand, but as it was now very tightly wedged, he drew a stone-pick out of his pocket, and very carefully, and with some trouble, got it out. Then holding it up, he said, "There, that's the stone your horse had picked up. It is a wonder he did not fall down and break his knees into the bargain!"

"Well, to be sure!" said my driver. "That is a queer thing! I never knew that horses picked up stones before."

"Didn't you?" said the farmer, rather contemptuously. "But they do, though, and the best of them will do it, and can't help it sometimes on such roads as these. And if you don't want to lame your horse, you must look sharp and get them out quickly. This foot is very much bruised," he said, setting it gently down and patting me. "If I might advise, sir, you had better drive him gently for a while; the foot is a good deal hurt, and the lameness will not go off directly."

Then, mounting his cob and raising his hat to the lady, he trotted off.

When he was gone, my driver began to flop the reins about and whip the harness, by which I understood that I was to go on, which of course I did, glad that the stone was gone, but still in a good deal of pain.

This was the sort of experience we job horses often came in for.

29

Cockneys

THEN THERE IS the steam-engine style of driving; these drivers were mostly people from towns, who never had a horse of their own, and generally traveled by rail.

They always seemed to think that a horse was something like a steam engine, only smaller. At any rate, they think that if only they pay for it, a horse is bound to go just as far, and just as fast, and with just as heavy a load as they please. And be the roads heavy and muddy, or dry and good; be they stony or smooth, uphill or downhill, it is all the same—on, on, on, one must go at the same pace, with no relief and no consideration.

These people never think of getting out to walk up a steep hill. Oh, no, they have paid to ride, and ride they will! The horse? Oh, he's used to it! What were horses made for, if not to drag people uphill? Walk! A good joke indeed! And so the whip is plied and the rein is chucked, and often a rough, scolding voice cries out, "Go along, you lazy beast!" And then another slash of the whip, when all the time we are doing our very best to get along, uncomplaining and obedient, though often sorely harassed and downhearted.

This steam-engine style of driving wears us up faster than any other kind. I would far rather go twenty miles with a good considerate driver than I would go ten with some of these; it would take less out of me.

Another thing—they scarcely ever put on the drag, however steep the downhill may be, and thus bad accidents sometimes happen; or if they do put it on, they often forget to take it off at the bottom of the hill, and more than once I have had to pull halfway up the next hill, with one of the wheels lodged fast in the drag shoe, before my driver chose to think about it; and that is a terrible strain on a horse.

Then these cockneys, instead of starting at an easy pace as a gentleman would do, generally set off at full speed from the very stable yard; and when they want to stop, they first whip us and then pull up so suddenly that we are nearly thrown on our haunches, and our mouths jagged with the bit—they call that pulling up with a dash! And when they turn a corner, they do it as sharply as if there were no right side or wrong side of the road.

I well remember one spring evening I and Rory had been out for the day. (Rory was the horse that mostly went with me when a pair was ordered, and a good honest fellow he was.) We had our own driver, and as he was always considerate and gentle with us, we had a very pleasant day. We were coming home at a good smart pace about twilight. Our road turned sharp to the left; but as we were close to the hedge on our own side, and there was plenty of room to pass, our driver did not pull us in. As we neared the corner I heard a horse and two wheels coming rapidly down the hill toward us. The hedge was high and I could see nothing, but the next moment we were upon each other. Happily for me, I was on the side next the hedge. Rory was on the left side of the pole, and had not even a shaft to protect him. The man who was driving was making straight for the corner, and when he came in sight of us he had no time to pull over to his own side. The whole shock came upon Rory. The gig shaft ran right into the chest, making him stagger back with a cry that I shall never forget. The other horse was thrown upon his haunches, and one shaft broken. It turned out that it was a horse from our own stables, with the high-wheeled gig that the young men were so fond of.

The driver was one of those random, ignorant fellows, who don't even know which is their own side of the road, or, if they know, don't care. And there was poor Rory with his flesh torn open and bleeding, and the blood streaming down. They said if it had been a little more to one side it would have killed him; and a good thing for him, poor fellow, if it had.

As it was, it was a long time before the wound healed, and then he was sold for coal carting; and what that is, up and down those steep hills, only horses know. Some of the sights I saw there, where a horse had to come downhill with a heavily loaded two-wheel cart behind him, on which no drag could be placed, make me sad even now to think of.

After Rory was disabled, I often went in the carriage with a mare named Peggy, who stood in the next stall to mine. She was a strong, well-made animal, of a bright dun color, beautifully dappled, and with a dark-brown mane and tail. There was no high breeding about her, but she was very pretty and remarkably sweet-tempered and willing. Still, there was an anxious look about her eye, by which I knew that she had some trouble. The first time we went out together I thought she had a very odd pace; she seemed to go partly in a trot, partly in a canter—three or four paces, and then to make a little jump forward.

It was very unpleasant for any horse who pulled with her, and made me quite fidgety. When we got home I asked her what made her go in that odd, awkward way.

"Ah," she said in a troubled manner, "I know my paces are very bad, but what can I do? It really is not my fault; it is just because my legs are so short. I stand nearly as high as you, but your legs are a good three inches longer above your knees than mine, and of course you can take a much longer step, and go much faster. You see, I did not make myself. I wish I could have done so; I would have had long legs then. All my troubles come from my short legs," said Peggy, in a desponding tone.

"But how is it," I said, "when you are so strong and good-tempered and willing?"

"Why, you see," said she, "men will go so fast, and if one can't keep up to other horses, it is nothing but whip, whip, whip, all the time. And so I have had to keep up as I could, and have got into this ugly shuffling pace. It was not always so; when I lived with my first master I always went a good regular trot, but then he was not in such a hurry. He was a young clergyman in the country, and a good, kind master he was. He had two churches a good way apart, and a great deal of work, but he never scolded or whipped me for not going faster. He was very fond of me. I only wish I was with him now; but he had to leave and go to a large town, and then I was sold to a farmer.

"Some farmers, you know, are capital masters; but I think this one was a low sort of man. He cared nothing about good horses or good driving; he only cared for going fast. I went as fast as I could, but that would not do, and he was always whipping; so I got into this way of making a spring forward to keep up. On market nights he used to stay very late at the inn, and then drive home at a gallop.

"One dark night he was galloping home as usual, when all of a sudden the wheel came against some great heavy thing in the road, and turned the gig over in a minute. He was thrown out and his arm broken, and some of his ribs, I think. At any rate, it was the end of my living with him, and I was not sorry. But you see it will be the same everywhere for me, if men *must* go so fast. I wish my legs were longer!"

Poor Peggy! I was very sorry for her, and I could not comfort her, for I knew how hard it was upon slow-paced horses to be put with fast ones; all the whipping comes to their share, and they can't help it.

She was often used in the phaeton, and was very much liked by some of the ladies, because she was so gentle; and some time after this she was sold to two ladies who drove themselves, and wanted a safe, good horse.

I met her several times out in the country, going a
good steady pace, and looking as gay and contented
as a horse could be. I was very glad to see her, for she
deserved a good place.

After she left us, another horse came in her stead.
He was young, and had a bad name for shying and
starting, by which he had lost a good place. I asked
him what made him shy.

"Well, I hardly know," he said. "I was timid when
I was young, and was a good deal frightened several
times, and if I saw anything strange I used to turn and
look at it—you see, with our blinkers one can't see or
understand what a thing is unless one looks round—
and then my master always gave me a whipping,
which of course made me start on, and did not make
me less afraid. I think if he would have let me just
look at things quietly, and see that there was nothing
to hurt me, it would have been all right, and I should
have got used to them. One day an old gentleman
was riding with him, and a large piece of white paper
or rag blew across just on one side of me. I shied and
started forward. My master as usual whipped me
smartly, but the old man cried out, 'You're wrong!
you're wrong! You should never whip a horse for shying; he shies because he is frightened, and you only
frighten him more and make the habit worse.' So I

suppose all men don't do so. I am sure I don't want to shy for the sake of it; but how should one know what is dangerous and what is not, if one is never allowed to get used to anything? I am never afraid of what I know. Now I was brought up in a park where there were deer; of course, I knew them as well as I did a sheep or a cow, but they are not common, and I know many sensible horses who are frightened at them, and who kick up quite a shindy before they will pass a paddock where there are deer."

I knew what my companion said was true, and I wished that every young horse had as good masters as Farmer Grey and Squire Gordon.

Of course we sometimes came in for good driving here. I remember one morning I was put into the light gig, and taken to a house in Pulteney Street. Two gentlemen came out; the taller of them came round to my head; he looked at the bit and bridle, and just shifted the collar with his hand, to see if it fitted comfortably.

"Do you consider this horse wants a curb?" he said to the hostler.

"Well," said the man, "I should say he would go just as well without; he has an uncommon good mouth, and though he has a fine spirit he has no vice; but we generally find people like the curb."

"I don't like it," said the gentleman. "Be so good as to take it off, and put the rein in at the cheek. An easy mouth is a great thing on a long journey, is it not, old fellow?" he said, patting my neck.

Then he took the reins, and they both got up. I can remember now how quietly he turned me round, and then with a light feel of the rein, and drawing the whip gently across my back, we were off.

I arched my neck and set off at my best pace. I found I had some one behind me who knew how a good horse ought to be driven. It seemed like old times again, and made me feel quite gay.

This gentleman took a great liking to me, and after trying me several times with the saddle he prevailed upon my master to sell me to a friend of his, who wanted a safe, pleasant horse for riding. And so it came to pass that in the summer I was sold to Mr. Barry.

30

A Thief

MY NEW MASTER was an unmarried man. He lived at
Bath, and was much engaged in business. His doctor
advised him to take horse exercise, and for this purpose he bought me. He hired a stable a short distance
from his lodgings, and engaged a man named Filcher
as groom. My master knew very little about horses,
but he treated me well, and I should have had a good
and easy place but for circumstances of which he was
ignorant. He ordered the best hay with plenty of oats,
crushed beans, and bran, with vetches, or rye grass,
as the man might think needful. I heard the master
give the order, so I knew there was plenty of good
food, and I thought I was well off.

For a few days all went on well. I found that my
groom understood his business. He kept the stable
clean and airy, and he groomed me thoroughly; and
was never otherwise than gentle. He had been an
hostler in one of the great hotels in Bath. He had
given that up, and now cultivated fruit and vegetables

for the market, and his wife bred and fattened poultry and rabbits for sale. After a while it seemed to me that my oats came very short; I had the beans, but bran was mixed with them instead of oats, of which there were very few; certainly not more than a quarter of what there should have been. In two or three weeks this began to tell upon my strength and spirits. The grass food, though very good, was not the thing to keep up my condition without corn. However, I could not complain, nor make known my wants. So it went on for about two months; and I wondered my master did not see that something was the matter. However, one afternoon he rode out into the country to see a friend of his, a gentleman farmer, who lived on the road to Wells. This gentleman had a very quick eye for horses; and after he had welcomed his friend, he said, casting his eye over me:

"It seems to me, Barry, that your horse does not look so well as he did when you first had him; has he been well?"

"Yes, I believe so," said my master, "but he is not nearly so lively as he was; my groom tells me that horses are always dull and weak in the autumn, and that I must expect it."

"Autumn, fiddlesticks!" said the farmer. "Why, this is only August; and with your light work and good food he ought not to go down like this, even if it was autumn. How do you feed him?"

My master told him. The other shook his head slowly, and began to feel me over.

"I can't say who eats your corn, my dear fellow, but I am much mistaken if your horse gets it. Have you ridden very fast?"

"No, very gently."

"Then just put your hand here," said he, passing his hand over my neck and shoulder; "he is as warm and damp as a horse just come up from grass. I advise you to look into your stable a little more. I hate to be suspicious, and, thank heaven, I have no cause to be, for I can trust my men, present or absent; but there are mean scoundrels, wicked enough to rob a dumb beast of his food. You must look into it." And turning to his man, who had come to take me: "Give this horse a right good feed of bruised oats, and don't stint him."

Dumb beasts! Yes, we are; but if I could have spoken I could have told my master where his oats went to. My groom used to come every morning about six o'clock, and with him a little boy, who always had a covered basket with him. He used to go with his father into the harness room where the corn was kept, and I could see them, when the door stood ajar, fill a little bag with oats out of the bin, and then he used to be off.

Five or six mornings after this, just as the boy had left the stable, the door was pushed open, and a policeman walked in, holding the child tight by the arm; another policeman followed, and locked the door on the inside, saying, "Show me the place where your father keeps his rabbits' food."

The boy looked very frightened and began to cry; but there was no escape, and he led the way to the corn bin. Here the policeman found another empty bag like that which was found full of oats in the boy's basket.

Filcher was cleaning my feet at the time, but they soon saw him, and though he blustered a good deal, they walked him off to the "lock-up," and his boy with him. I heard afterward that the boy was not held to be guilty, but the man was sentenced to prison for two months.

31

A Humbug

MY MASTER WAS not immediately suited, but in a few days my new groom came. He was a tall, good-looking fellow enough; but if ever there was a humbug in the shape of a groom, Alfred Smirk was the man. He was very civil to me, and never used me ill; in fact, he did a great deal of stroking and patting, when his master was there to see it. He always brushed my mane and tail with water, and my hoofs with oil before he brought me to the door, to make me look smart; but as to cleaning my feet, or looking to my shoes, or grooming me thoroughly, he thought no more of that than if I had been a cow. He left my bit rusty, my saddle damp, and my crupper stiff.

Alfred Smirk considered himself very handsome; he spent a great deal of time about his hair, whiskers, and necktie, before a little looking glass in the harness room. When his master was speaking to him, it was always, "Yes, sir; yes, sir"; touching his hat at every word; and every one thought he was a very nice young man, and that Mr. Barry was very fortunate to meet with him. I should say he was the laziest, most conceited fellow I ever came near. Of course it was a great thing not to be ill-used, but then a horse wants more than that. I had a loose box, and might have been very comfortable if he had not been too indolent to clean it out. He never took all the straw away, and the smell from what lay underneath was very bad; while the strong vapors that rose made my eyes smart and inflame, and I did not feel the same appetite for my food.

One day his master came in and said, "Alfred, the stable smells rather strong; should not you give that stall a good scrub, and throw down plenty of water?"

"Well, sir," he said, touching his cap, "I'll do so if you please, sir; but it is rather dangerous, sir, throwing down water in a horse's box; they are very apt to take cold, sir. I should not like to do him an injury, but I'll do it if you please, sir."

"Well," said his master, "I should not like him to take cold; but I don't like the smell of this stable. Do you think the drains are all right?"

"Well, sir, now you mention it, I think the drain does sometimes send back a smell; there may be something wrong, sir."

"Then send for the bricklayer and have it seen to," said his master.

"Yes, sir, I will."

The bricklayer came and pulled up a great many bricks, but found nothing amiss; so he put down some lime and charged the master five shillings, and the smell in my box was as bad as ever. But that was not all—standing as I did on a quantity of moist straw, my feet grew unhealthy and tender, and the master used to say:

"I don't know what is the matter with this horse; he goes very fumble-footed. I am sometimes afraid he will stumble."

"Yes, sir," said Alfred, "I have noticed the same myself, when I have exercised him."

Now the fact was that he hardly ever did exercise me, and when the master was busy, I often stood for days together without stretching my legs at all, and yet being fed just as high as if I were at hard work. This often disordered my health, and made me sometimes heavy and dull, but more often restless and feverish. He never even gave me a meal of green meat, or a bran mash, which would have cooled me, for he was altogether as ignorant as he was conceited; and then, instead of exercise or change of food, I had to take horse balls and draughts; which, beside the nuisance of having them poured down my throat, used to make me feel ill and uncomfortable.

One day my feet were so tender, that trotting over some fresh stones with my master on my back, I made two such serious stumbles, that as he came down Lansdown into the city, he stopped at the farrier's and asked him to see what was the matter with me. The man took up my feet one by one and examined them; then standing up and dusting his hands one against the other, he said:

"Your horse has got the 'thrush,' and badly too; his feet are very tender; it is fortunate that he has not been down. I wonder your groom has not seen to it before. This is the sort of thing we find in foul stables, where the litter is never properly cleaned out. If you will send him here tomorrow, I will attend to the hoof, and I will direct your man how to apply the liniment which I will give him."

The next day I had my feet thoroughly cleansed and stuffed with tow, soaked in some strong lotion; and an unpleasant business it was.

The farrier ordered all the litter to be taken out of my box day by day, and the floor kept very clean. Then I was to have bran mashes, a little green meat, and not so much corn, till my feet were well again. With this treatment I soon regained my spirits, but Mr. Barry was so much disgusted at being twice deceived by his grooms that he determined to give up keeping a horse, and to hire when he wanted one. I was therefore kept till my feet were quite sound, and was then sold again.

Part Three

32

A Horse Fair

No doubt a horse fair is a very amusing place to those who have nothing to lose; at any rate, there is plenty to see.

Long strings of young horses out of the country, fresh from the marshes; and droves of shaggy little Welsh ponies, no higher than Merrylegs; and hundreds of cart horses of all sorts, some of them with their long tails braided up and tied with scarlet cord; and a good many like myself, handsome and high-bred, but fallen into the middle class, through some accident or blemish, unsoundness of wind, or some other complaint. There were some splendid animals quite in their prime, and fit for anything; they were throwing out their legs and showing off their paces in high style, as they were trotted out with a leading rein, the groom running by the side. But round in the background there were a number of poor things, sadly broken down with hard work, with their knees knuckling over and their hind legs swinging out at every step. And there were some very dejected-looking old horses, with the under lip hanging down and the ears lying back heavily, as if there was no more pleasure in life, and no more hope; there were some so thin you might see all their ribs, and some with old sores on their backs and hips. These were sad sights for a horse to look upon, who knows not but he may come to the same state.

There was a great deal of bargaining, of running up and beating down; and if a horse may speak his mind so far as he understands, I should say there were more lies told and more trickery at that horse fair than a clever man could give an account of. I was put with two or three other strong, useful-looking horses, and a good many people came to look at us. The gentlemen always turned from me when they saw my broken knees; though the man who had me swore it was only a slip in the stall.

The first thing was to pull my mouth open, then to look at my eyes, then feel all the way down my legs, and give me a hard feel of the skin and flesh, and then try my paces. It was wonderful what a difference there was in the way these things were done. Some did it in a rough, offhand way, as if one was only a piece of wood; while others would take their hands gently over one's body, with a pat now and then, as much as to say, "By your leave." Of course I judged a good deal of the buyers by their manners to myself.

There was one man, I thought, if he would buy me, I should be happy. He was not a gentleman, nor yet one of the loud, flashy sort that call themselves so. He was rather a small man, but well made, and quick in all his motions. I knew in a moment by the way he handled me, that he was used to horses; he spoke gently, and his gray eye had a kindly, cheery look in it. It may seem strange to say—but it is true all the same—that the clean, fresh smell there was about him made me take to him; no smell of old beer and tobacco, which I hated, but a fresh smell as if he had come out of a hayloft. He offered twenty-three pounds for me, but that was refused, and he walked away. I looked after him, but he was gone, and a very hard-looking, loud-voiced man came. I was dreadfully afraid he would have me; but he walked off. One or two more came who did not mean business. Then the hard-faced man came back again and offered twenty-three pounds. A very close bargain was being driven, for my salesman began to think he should not get all he asked, and must come down; but just then the gray-eyed man came back again. I could not help reaching out my head toward him. He stroked my face kindly.

171

"Well, old chap," he said, "I think we should suit each other. I'll give twenty-four for him."

"Say twenty-five and you shall have him."

"Twenty-four ten," said my friend, in a very decided tone, "and not another sixpence—yes or no?"

"Done," said the salesman; "and you may depend upon it there's a monstrous deal of quality in that horse, and if you want him for cab work, he's a bargain."

The money was paid on the spot, and my new master took my halter, and led me out of the fair to an inn, where he had a saddle and bridle ready. He gave me a good feed of oats and stood by while I ate it, talking to himself and talking to me. Half an hour after, we were on our way to London, through pleasant lanes and country roads, until we came into the great London thoroughfare, on which we traveled steadily, till in the twilight we reached the great city. The gas lamps were already lighted; there were streets to the right, and streets to the left, and streets crossing each other for mile upon mile. I thought we should never come to the end of them. At last, in passing through one, we came to a long cab stand, when my rider called out in a cheery voice, "Good-night, Governor!"

"Halloo!" cried a voice. "Have you got a good one?"

"I think so," replied my owner.

"I wish you luck with him."

"Thank ye, Governor," and he rode on. We soon turned up one of the side streets, and about halfway up that we turned into a very narrow street, with rather poor-looking houses on one side, and what seemed to be coach houses and stables on the other.

My owner pulled up at one of the houses and whistled. The door flew open, and a young woman, followed by a little girl and boy, ran out. There was a very lively greeting as my rider dismounted.

"Now, then, Harry, my boy, open the gates, and mother will bring us the lantern."

The next minute they were all standing round me in a small stable yard.

"Is he gentle, father?"

"Yes, Dolly, as gentle as your own kitten; come and pat him."

At once the little hand was patting about all over my shoulder without fear. How good it felt!

"Let me get him a bran mash while you rub him down," said the mother.

"Do, Polly, it's just what he wants, and I know you've got a beautiful mash ready for me."

"Sausage dumpling and apple turnover!" shouted the boy, which set them all laughing. I was led into a comfortable, clean-smelling stall, with plenty of dry straw, and after a capital supper I lay down, thinking I was going to be happy.

33

A London Cab Horse

MY NEW MASTER'S name was Jeremiah Barker, but as every one called him Jerry, I shall do the same. Polly, his wife, was just as good a match as a man could have. She was a plump, trim, tidy little woman, with smooth, dark hair, dark eyes, and a merry little mouth. The boy was nearly twelve years old, a tall, frank, good-tempered lad; and little Dorothy (Dolly they called her) was her mother over again, at eight years old. They were all wonderfully fond of each other; I never knew such a happy, merry family before, or since. Jerry had a cab of his own, and two horses, which he drove and attended to himself. His other horse was a tall, white, rather large-boned animal, called Captain. He was old now, but when he was young he must have been splendid; he had still a proud way of holding his head and arching his neck; in fact, he was a high-bred, fine-mannered, noble old horse, every inch of him. He told me that in his early youth he went to the Crimean War; he belonged to an

officer in the cavalry, and used to lead the regiment.
I will tell more of that hereafter.

The next morning, when I was well groomed,
Polly and Dolly came into the yard to see me and
make friends. Harry had been helping his father since
the early morning, and had stated his opinion that I
should turn out a "regular brick." Polly brought me a
slice of apple, and Dolly a piece of bread, and made
as much of me as if I had been the "Black Beauty" of
olden time. It was a great treat to be petted again and
talked to in a gentle voice, and I let them see as well
as I could that I wished to be friendly. Polly thought
I was very handsome, and a great deal too good for a
cab, if it was not for the broken knees.

"Of course there's no one to tell us whose fault
that was," said Jerry, "and as long as I don't know, I
shall give him the benefit of the doubt; for a firmer,
neater stepper I never rode. We'll call him 'Jack,' after
the old one—shall we, Polly?"

"Do," she said, "for I like to keep a good name
going."

Captain went out in the cab all the morning.
Harry came in after school to feed me and give me
water. In the afternoon I was put into the cab. Jerry
took as much pains to see if the collar and bridle
fitted comfortably as if he had been John Manly over

again. When the crupper was let out a hole or two, it all fitted well. There was no bearing rein—no curb—nothing but a plain ring snaffle. What a blessing that was!

After driving through the side street we came to the large cab stand where Jerry had said "Good night." On one side of this wide street were high houses with wonderful shop fronts, and on the other was an old church and churchyard, surrounded by iron palisades. Alongside these iron rails a number of cabs were drawn up, waiting for passengers; bits of hay were lying about on the ground; some of the men were standing together talking; some were sitting on their boxes reading the newspaper; and one or two were feeding their horses with bits of hay and a drink of water. We pulled up in the rank at the back of the last cab. Two or three men came round and began to look at me and pass their remarks.

"Very good for a funeral," said one.

"Too smart-looking," said another, shaking his head in a very wise way; "you'll find out something wrong one of these fine mornings, or my name isn't Jones."

"Well," said Jerry pleasantly, "I suppose I need not find it out till it finds me out, eh? And if so, I'll keep up my spirits a little longer."

177

Then came up a broad-faced man, dressed in a great gray coat with great gray cape, and great white buttons, a gray hat, and a blue comforter loosely tied round his neck; his hair was gray, too; but he was a jolly-looking fellow, and the other men made way for him. He looked me all over, as if he had been going to buy me; and then straightening himself up with a grunt, he said, "He's the right sort for you, Jerry; I don't care what you gave for him, he'll be worth it." Thus my character was established on the stand.

This man's name was Grant, but he was called "Gray Grant," or "Governor Grant." He had been the longest on that stand of any of the men, and he took it upon himself to settle matters and stop disputes. He was generally a good-humored, sensible man; but if his temper was a little out, as it was sometimes, when he had drunk too much, nobody liked to come too near his fist, for he could deal a very heavy blow.

The first week of my life as a cab horse was very trying. I had never been used to London, and the noise, the hurry, the crowds of horses, carts, and carriages that I had to make my way through made me feel anxious and harassed; but I soon found that I could perfectly trust my driver, and then I made myself easy, and got used to it.

Jerry was as good a driver as I had ever known,

and what was better, he took as much thought for his horses as he did for himself. He soon found out that I was willing to work and do my best, and he never laid the whip on me, unless it was gently drawing the end of it over my back when I was to go on; but generally I knew this quite well by the way in which he took up the reins, and I believe his whip was more frequently stuck up by his side than in his hand.

In a short time I and my master understood each other as well as horse and man can do. In the stable, too, he did all that he could for our comfort. The stalls were the old-fashioned style, too much on the slope; but he had two movable bars fixed across the back of our stalls, so that at night, and when we were resting, he just took off our halters and put up the bars, and thus we could turn about and stand whichever way we pleased, which is a great comfort.

Jerry kept us very clean, and gave us as much change of food as he could, and always plenty of it; and not only that, but he always gave us plenty of clean fresh water, which he allowed to stand by us both night and day, except of course when we came in warm. Some people say that a horse ought not to drink all he likes; but I know if we are allowed to drink when we want it, we drink only a little at a time, and it does us a great deal more good than swallowing

down half a bucketful at a time, because we have
been left without till we are thirsty and miserable.
Some grooms will go home to their beer and leave
us for hours with our dry hay and oats and nothing
to moisten them; then of course we gulp down too
much at once, which helps to spoil our breathing and
sometimes chills our stomachs.

But the best thing we had here was our Sundays
for rest; we worked so hard in the week that I do
not think we could have kept up to it but for that
day; besides, we had then time to enjoy each other's
company. It was on these days that I learned my companion's history.

34

An Old War Horse

CAPTAIN HAD BEEN broken in and trained for an army horse; his first owner was an officer of cavalry going out to the Crimean War. He said he quite enjoyed the training with all the other horses, trotting together, turning together, to the right hand or to the left, halting at the word of command, or dashing forward at full speed at the sound of the trumpet, or signal of the officer. He was, when young, a dark, dappled iron-gray, and considered very handsome. His master, a young, high-spirited gentleman, was very fond of him and treated him from the first with the greatest care and kindness. He told me he thought the life of an army horse was very pleasant; but when it came to being sent abroad, over the sea in a great ship, he almost changed his mind.

"That part of it," said he, "was dreadful! Of course we could not walk off the land into the ship; so they were obliged to put strong straps under our bodies, and then we were lifted off our legs in spite

of our struggles, and were swung through the air over
the water, to the deck of the great vessel. There we
were placed in small close stalls, and never for a long
time saw the sky, or were able to stretch our legs. The
ship sometimes rolled about in high winds, and we
were knocked about, and felt bad enough. However,
at last it came to an end, and we were hauled up, and
swung over again to the land; we were very glad, and
snorted and neighed for joy, when we once more felt
firm ground under our feet.

"We soon found that the country we had come to
was very different from our own and that we had
many hardships to endure besides the fighting; but
many of the men were so fond of their horses that
they did everything they could to make them comfortable, in spite of snow, wet, and all things out of
order."

"But what about the fighting?" said I. "Was not
that worse than anything else?"

"Well," said he, "I hardly know; we always liked
to hear the trumpet sound, and to be called out, and
were impatient to start off, though sometimes we
had to stand for hours, waiting for the word of command; and when the word was given, we used to
spring forward as gaily and eagerly as if there were no
cannon balls, bayonets, or bullets. I believe so long

as we felt our rider firm in the saddle, and his hand steady on the bridle, not one of us gave way to fear, not even when the terrible bombshells whirled through the air and burst into a thousand pieces.

"I, with my noble master, went into many actions together without a wound; and though I saw horses shot down with bullets, pierced through with lances, and gashed with fearful saber cuts; though we left them dead on the field, or dying in the agony of their wounds, I don't think I feared for myself. My master's cheery voice, as he encouraged his men, made me feel as if he and I could not be killed. I had such perfect trust in him that while he was guiding me, I was ready to charge up to the very cannon's mouth. I saw many brave men cut down, many fall mortally wounded from their saddles. I had heard the cries and groans of the dying, I had cantered over ground slippery with blood, and frequently had to turn aside to avoid trampling on wounded man or horse, but, until one dreadful day, I had never felt terror; that day I shall never forget."

Here old Captain paused for a while and drew a long breath; I waited, and he went on.

"It was one autumn morning, and as usual, an hour before daybreak our cavalry had turned out, ready caparisoned for the day's work, whether it might be fighting or waiting. The men stood by their horses waiting, ready for orders. As the light increased there seemed to be some excitement among the officers; and before the day was well begun, we heard the firing of the enemy's guns.

"Then one of the officers rode up and gave the word for the men to mount, and in a second every man was in his saddle, and every horse stood expecting the touch of the rein, or the pressure of his rider's heels, all animated, all eager; but still we had been trained so well that, except by the champing of our bits, and the restive tossing of our heads from time to time, it could not be said that we stirred.

"My dear master and I were at the head of the line, and as all sat motionless and watchful, he took a little stray lock of my mane which had turned over on the wrong side, laid it over on the right, and smoothed it down with his hand; then patting my neck, he said, 'We shall have a day of it today, Bayard, my beauty; but we'll do our duty as we have done.' He stroked my neck that morning more, I think, than he had ever done before; quietly on and on, as if he were thinking of something else. I loved to feel his hand on my neck, and arched my crest proudly and happily; but I stood very still, for I knew all his moods, and when he liked me to be quiet, and when gay.

"I cannot tell all that happened on that day, but I will tell of the last charge that we made together; it was across a valley right in front of the enemy's cannon. By this time we were well used to the roar of heavy guns, the rattle of musket fire, and the flying of shot near us; but never had I been under such a fire as we rode through on that day. From the right, from the left, and from the front, shot and shell poured in upon us. Many a brave man went down, many a horse fell, flinging his rider to the earth; many a horse without a rider ran wildly out of the ranks; then terrified at being alone, with no hand to guide him, came pressing in among his old companions, to gallop with them to the charge.

"Fearful as it was, no one stopped, no one turned back. Every moment the ranks were thinned, but as our comrades fell, we closed in to keep them together; and instead of being shaken or staggered in our pace, our gallop became faster and faster as we neared the cannon, all clouded in white smoke, while the red fire flashed through it.

"My master, my dear master, was cheering on his comrades with his right arm raised on high, when one of the balls, whizzing close to my head, struck him. I felt him stagger with the shock, though he uttered no cry; I tried to check my speed, but the sword dropped

from his right hand, the rein fell loose from the left,
and sinking backward from the saddle he fell to the
earth; the other riders swept past us, and by the force
of their charge I was driven from the spot where he
fell.

"I wanted to keep my place by his side, and not
leave him under that rush of horses' feet, but it was
in vain; and now, without a master or a friend, I was
alone on that great slaughter ground. Then fear took
hold of me, and I trembled as I had never trembled
before; and I too, as I had seen other horses do, tried
to join in the ranks and gallop with them; but I was
beaten off by the swords of the soldiers. Just then, a
soldier whose horse had been killed under him caught
at my bridle and mounted me; and with this new
master I was again going forward; but our gallant
company was cruelly overpowered, and those who
remained alive after the fierce fight for the guns came
galloping back over the same ground. Some of the
horses had been so badly wounded that they could
scarcely move from the loss of blood; other noble
creatures were trying on three legs to drag themselves
along, and others were struggling to rise on their fore
feet, when their hind legs had been shattered by shot.
Their groans were piteous to hear, and the beseeching look in their eyes as those who escaped passed by

and left them to their fate, I shall never forget. After the battle the wounded men were brought in, and the dead were buried."

"And what about the wounded horses?" I said. "Were they left to die?"

"No, the army farriers went over the field with their pistols and shot all that were ruined; some that had only slight wounds were brought back and attended to, but the greater part of the noble, willing creatures that went out that morning never came back! In our stables there was only about one in four that returned.

"I never saw my dear master again. I believe he fell dead from the saddle. I never loved any other master so well. I went into many other engagements, but was only once wounded, and then not seriously; and when the war was over I came back again to England, as sound and strong as when I went out."

I said, "I have heard people talk about war as if it was a very fine thing."

"Ah," said he, "I should think they never saw it. No doubt it is very fine when there is no enemy, when it is just exercise and parade and sham fight. Yes, it is very fine then; but when thousands of good brave men and horses are killed, or crippled for life, it has a very different look."

"Do you know what they fought about?" said I.

"No," he said, "that is more than a horse can understand, but the enemy must have been awfully wicked people, if it was right to go all that way over the sea on purpose to kill them."

35

Jerry Barker

I NEVER KNEW a better man than my new master. He was kind and good, and as strong for the right as John Manly; and so good-tempered and merry that very few people could pick a quarrel with him. He was very fond of making little songs, and singing them to himself. One he was very fond of was this:

"Come, father and mother,
And sister and brother,
Come, all of you, turn to
And help one another."

And so they did; Harry was as clever at stable work as a much older boy, and always wanted to do what he could. Then Polly and Dolly used to come in the morning to help with the cab—to brush and beat the cushions, and rub the glass, while Jerry was giving us a cleaning in the yard, and Harry was rubbing the harness. There used to be a great deal of laughing and fun between them, and it put Captain and me in much better spirits than if we had heard scolding and hard words. They were always early in the morning, for Jerry would say:

> *"If you in the morning*
> *Throw minutes away,*
> *You can't pick them up*
> *In the course of the day.*
> *You may hurry and scurry,*
> *And flurry and worry,*
> *You've lost them forever,*
> *Forever and aye. "*

He could not bear any careless loitering and waste of time; and nothing was so near making him angry as to find people who were always late, wanting a cab horse to be driven hard, to make up for their idleness.

One day, two wild-looking young men came out of a tavern close by the stand, and called Jerry.

"Here, cabby! Look sharp, we are rather late; put on the steam, will you, and take us to the Victoria in time for the one o'clock train? You shall have a shilling extra."

"I will take you at the regular pace, gentlemen; shillings don't pay for putting on the steam like that."

Larry's cab was standing next to ours; he flung open the door, and said, "I'm your man, gentlemen!

Take my cab, my horse will get you there all right," and as he shut them in, with a wink toward Jerry, said, "It's against his conscience to go beyond a jog trot." Then slashing his jaded horse, he set off as hard as he could. Jerry patted me on the neck. "No, Jack, a shilling would not pay for that sort of thing, would it, old boy?"

Although Jerry was determinedly set against hard driving to please careless people, he always went a good fair pace, and was not against putting on the steam, as he said, if only he knew *why*.

I well remember one morning, as we were on the stand waiting for a fare, a young man, carrying a heavy portmanteau, trod on a piece of orange peel which lay on the pavement, and fell down with great force.

Jerry was the first to run and lift him up. He seemed much stunned, and as they led him into a shop, he walked as if he were in great pain. Jerry of course came back to the stand, but in about ten minutes one of the shopmen called him, so we drew up to the pavement.

"Can you take me to the South-Eastern Railway?" said the young man. "This unlucky fall has made me late, I fear; but it is of great importance that I should not lose the twelve o'clock train. I should be most thankful if you could get me there in time, and will gladly pay you an extra fare."

"I'll do my very best," said Jerry heartily, "if you think you are well enough, sir," for he looked dreadfully white and ill.

"I *must* go," he said earnestly. "Please open the door, and let us lose no time."

The next minute Jerry was on the box, with a cheery chirrup to me, and a twitch of the rein that I well understood.

"Now then, Jack, my boy," said he, "spin along, we'll show them how we can get over the ground, if we only know why."

It is always difficult to drive fast in the city in the middle of the day, when the streets are full of traffic, but we did what could be done; and when a good driver and a good horse, who understand each other, are of one mind, it is wonderful what they can do. I had a very good mouth—that is, I could be guided by the slightest touch of the rein; and that is a great thing in London, among carriages, omnibuses, carts, vans, trucks, cabs, and great wagons creeping along at a walking pace; some going one way, some another, some going slowly, others wanting to pass them; omnibuses stopping short every few minutes to take up a passenger, obliging the horse that is coming behind to

pull up too, or to pass, and get before them; perhaps
you try to pass, but just then something else comes
dashing in through the narrow opening, and you have
to keep in behind the omnibus again; presently you
think you see a chance, and manage to get to the
front, going so near the wheels on each side that half
an inch nearer and they would scrape.

Well—you get along for a bit, but soon find yourself in a long train of carts and carriages all obliged to
go at a walk; perhaps you come to a regular block-up,
and have to stand still for minutes together, till something clears out into a side street, or the policeman
interferes; you have to be ready for any chance—to
dash forward if there be an opening, and be quick as
a rat dog to see if there be room, and if there be time,
lest you get your own wheels locked or smashed, or
the shaft of some other vehicle run into your chest or
shoulder. All this is what you have to be ready for. If
you want to get through London fast in the middle of
the day, it wants a deal of practice.

Jerry and I were used to it, and no one could beat
us at getting through when we were set upon it. I was
quick and bold, and could always trust my driver;
Jerry was quick and patient at the same time, and
could trust his horse, which was a great thing too. He
very seldom used the whip; I knew by his voice, and

his "click click," when he wanted to get on fast, and by the rein where I was to go; so there was no need for whipping; but I must go back to my story.

The streets were very full that day, but we got on pretty well as far as the bottom of Cheapside, where there was a block for three or four minutes. The young man put his head out and said anxiously, "I think I had better get out and walk; I shall never get there if this goes on."

"I'll do all that can be done, sir," said Jerry. "I think we shall be in time. This block-up cannot last much longer, and your luggage is very heavy for you to carry, sir."

Just then the cart in front of us began to move on, and then we had a good turn. In and out, in and out we went, as fast as horseflesh could do it, and for a wonder had a good clear time on London Bridge, for there was a whole train of cabs and carriages all going our way at a quick trot—perhaps wanting to catch that very train. At any rate, we whirled into the station with many more, just as the great clock pointed to eight minutes to twelve o'clock.

"Thank God! We are in time," said the young man, "and thank you, too, my friend, and your good horse. You have saved me more than money can ever pay for. Take this extra half crown."

"No, sir, no, thank you all the same; so glad we
hit the time, sir; but don't stay now, sir, the bell is
ringing. Here, porter! Take this gentleman's luggage—Dover line—twelve o'clock train—that's it,"
and without waiting for another word, Jerry wheeled
me round to make room for other cabs that were
dashing up at the last minute, and drew up on one
side till the crush was past.

"'So glad!' he said. 'So glad!' Poor young fellow!
I wonder what it was that made him so anxious!"

Jerry often talked to himself quite loud enough for
me to hear, when we were not moving.

On Jerry's return to the rank, there was a good
deal of laughing and chaffing at him for driving hard
to the train for an extra fare, as they said, all against
his principles, and they wanted to know how much he
had pocketed.

"A good deal more than I generally get," said he,
nodding slyly. "What he gave me will keep me in little comforts for several days."

"Gammon!" said one.

"He's a humbug," said another, "preaching to us,
and then doing the same himself."

"Look here, mates," said Jerry, "the gentleman
offered me half a crown extra, but I didn't take it;
'twas quite pay enough for me to see how glad he was

to catch that train; and if Jack and I choose to have a quick run now and then, to please ourselves, that's our business and not yours."

"Well," said Larry, "*you'll* never be a rich man."

"Most likely not," said Jerry, "but I don't know that I shall be the less happy for that. I have heard the commandments read a great many times and I never noticed that any of them said, 'Thou shalt be rich'; and there are a good many curious things said in the New Testament about rich men that I think would make me feel rather queer if I was one of them."

"If you ever do get rich," said Governor Grant, looking over his shoulder across the top of his cab, "you'll deserve it, Jerry, and you won't find a curse come with your wealth. As for you, Larry, you'll die poor; you spend too much in whipcord."

"Well," said Larry, "what is a fellow to do if his horse won't go without it?"

"You never take the trouble to see if he will go without it; your whip is always going as if you had the St. Vitus' dance in your arm, and if it does not wear you out, it wears your horse out; you know you are always changing your horses, and why? Because you never give them any peace or encouragement."

"Well, I have not had good luck," said Larry, "that's where it is."

"And you never will," said the Governor. "Good Luck is rather particular who she rides with, and mostly prefers those who have got common sense and a good heart; at least that is my experience."

Governor Grant turned round again to his newspaper, and the other men went to their cabs.

36
The Sunday Cab

ONE MORNING, AS Jerry had just put me into the shafts and was fastening the traces, a gentleman walked into the yard. "Your servant, sir," said Jerry.

"Good morning, Mr. Barker," said the gentleman. "I should be glad to make some arrangements with you for taking Mrs. Briggs regularly to church on Sunday mornings. We go to the New Church now, and that is rather further than she can walk."

"Thank you, sir," said Jerry, "but I have only taken out a six-day license,* and therefore I could not take a fare on a Sunday; it would not be legal."

"Oh!" said the other, "I did not know yours was a six-day cab; but of course it would be very easy to alter your license. I would see that you did not lose by it; the fact is, Mrs. Briggs very much prefers you to drive her."

"I should be glad to oblige the lady, sir, but I had a seven-day license once, and the work was too hard

---

* AUTHOR'S NOTE.—*Six-day license.* A few years since the annual charge for a cab license was very much reduced and the difference between the six- and seven-day cabs was abolished.

for me, and too hard for my horses. Year in and year out, not a day's rest, and never a Sunday with my wife and children, and never able to go to a place of worship, which I had always been used to do before I took to the driving box. So for the last five years I have only taken a six-day license, and I find it better all the way round."

"Well, of course," replied Mr. Briggs, "it is very proper that every person should have rest, and be able to go to church on Sundays, but I should have thought you would not have minded such a short distance for the horse, and only once a day; you would have all the afternoon and evening for yourself, and we are very good customers, you know."

"Yes, sir, that is true, and I am grateful for all favors, I am sure, and anything that I could do to oblige you, or the lady, I should be proud and happy to do; but I can't give up my Sundays, sir, indeed I can't. I read that God made man, and He made horses and all the other beasts, and as soon as He had made them, He made a day of rest, and bade that all should rest one day in seven; and I think, sir, He must have known what was good for them, and I am sure it is good for me; I am stronger and healthier altogether, now that I have a day of rest; the horses are fresh too, and do not wear up nearly so fast. The six-day drivers all tell me the same, and I have laid by more money in the savings bank than ever I did before; and as for the wife and children, sir—why, heart alive! They would not go back to the seven days for all they could see."

"Oh, very well," said the gentleman. "Don't trouble yourself, Mr. Barker, any further. I will inquire somewhere else." And he walked away.

"Well," says Jerry to me, "we can't help it, Jack, old boy; we must have our Sundays."

"Polly!" he shouted, "Polly, come here."

She was there in a minute.

"What is it all about, Jerry?"

"Why, my dear, Mr. Briggs wants me to take Mrs. Briggs to church every Sunday morning. I say I have only a six-day license. He says, 'Get a seven-day license, and I'll make it worth your while.' And you know, Polly, they are very good customers to us. Mrs. Briggs often goes out shopping for hours, or making calls, and then she pays down fair and honorable like a lady; there's no beating down, or making three hours into two hours and a half, as some folks do; and it is easy work for the horses; not like tearing along to catch trains for people that are always a quarter of an hour too late; and if I don't oblige her in this matter, it is very likely we shall lose them altogether.

What do you say, little woman?"

"I say, Jerry," says she, speaking very slowly, "I say, if Mrs. Briggs would give you a sovereign every Sunday morning, I would not have you a seven-day cabman again. We have known what it was to have no Sundays, and now we know what it is to call them our own. Thank God, you earn enough to keep us, though it is sometimes close work to pay for all the oats and hay, the license, and the rent besides; but Harry will soon be earning something, and I would rather struggle on harder than we do than go back to those horrid times when you hardly had a minute to look at your own children, and we never could go to a place of worship together, or have a happy, quiet day. God forbid that we should ever turn back to those times; that's what I say, Jerry."

"And that is just what I told Mr. Briggs, my dear," said Jerry, "and what I mean to stick to. So don't go and fret yourself, Polly (for she had begun to cry); I would not go back to the old times if I earned twice as much, so that is settled, little woman. Now cheer up, and I'll be off to the stand."

Three weeks had passed away after this conversation, and no order had come from Mrs. Briggs; so there was nothing but taking jobs from the stand. Jerry took it to heart a good deal, for of course the work was harder for horse and man. But Polly would always cheer him up, and say, "Never mind, father, never mind:

> *"Do your best,*
> *And leave the rest,*
> *'Twill all come right*
> *Some day or night."*

It soon became known that Jerry had lost his best customer, and for what reason. Most of the men said he was a fool, but two or three took his part.

"If workingmen don't stick to their Sunday," said Truman, "they'll soon have none left; it is every man's right and every beast's right. By God's law we have a day of rest, and by the law of England we have a day of rest; and I say we ought to hold to the rights these laws give us, and keep them for our children."

"All very well for you religious chaps to talk so," said Larry, "but I'll turn a shilling when I can. I don't believe in religion, for I don't see that your religious people are any better than the rest."

"If they are not better," put in Jerry, "it is because they are *not* religious. You might as well say that our country's laws are not good because some people break them. If a man gives way to his temper, and speaks evil of his neighbor, and does not pay his debts, he is *not* religious. I don't care how much he goes to church. If some men are shams and humbugs, that does not make religion untrue. Real religion is the best and truest thing in the world; and the only thing that can make a man really happy, or make the world any better."

"If religion was good for anything," said Jones, "it would prevent your religious people from making us work on Sundays, as you know many of them do, and that's why I say religion is nothing but a sham—why, if it was not for the church- and chapelgoers it would be hardly worth while our coming out on a Sunday. But they have their privileges, as they call them, and I go without. I shall expect them to answer for my soul, if I can't get a chance of saving it."

Several of the men applauded this, till Jerry said:

"That may sound well enough, but it won't do; every man must look after his own soul; you can't lay it down at another man's door like a foundling, and expect him to take care of it; and don't you see, if you are always sitting on your box waiting for a fare, they will say, 'If we don't take him, some one else will, and he does not look for any Sunday.' Of course they don't go to the bottom of it, or they would see if they never came for a cab, it would be no use your standing there; but people don't always like to go to the bottom of things; it may not be convenient to do it; but if you Sunday drivers would all strike for a day of rest, the thing would be done."

"And what would all the good people do if they could not get to their favorite preachers?" said Larry.

"'Tis not for me to lay down plans for other people," said Jerry, "but if they can't walk so far, they can go to what is nearer; and if it should rain they can put on their mackintoshes as they do on a weekday. If a thing is right, it *can* be done, and if it is wrong it *can be done without*; and a good man will find a way. And that is as true for us cabmen as it is for the churchgoers."

37

The Golden Rule

Two or three weeks after this, as we came into the yard rather late in the evening, Polly came running across the road with the lantern (she always brought it to him if it was not very wet).

"It has all come right, Jerry. Mrs. Briggs sent her servant this afternoon to ask you to take her out to-morrow at eleven o'clock. I said, 'Yes, I thought so, but we supposed she employed some one else now.'"

"'Well,' said he, 'the real fact is, master was put out because Mr. Barker refused to come on Sundays, and he has been trying other cabs, but there's something wrong with them all; some drive too fast, and some too slow, and the mistress says there is not one of them so nice and clean as yours, and nothing will suit her but Mr. Barker's cab again.'"

Polly was almost out of breath, and Jerry broke out into a merry laugh.

"All come right some day or night; you were right, my dear; you generally are. Run in and get the supper, and I'll have Jack's harness off and make him snug and happy in no time."

After this Mrs. Briggs wanted Jerry's cab quite as often as before; never, however, on a Sunday; but there came a day when we had Sunday work, and this was how it happened. We had all come home on the Saturday night very tired, and very glad to think that the next day would be all rest, but so it was not to be.

On Sunday morning Jerry was cleaning me in the yard, when Polly stepped up to him, looking very full of something.

"What is it?" said Jerry.

"Well, my dear," she said, "poor Dinah Brown has just had a letter brought to say that her mother is dangerously ill, and that she must go directly if she wishes to see her alive. The place is more than ten miles away from here, out in the country, and she says if she takes the train she should still have four miles to walk; and so weak as she is, and the baby only four weeks old, of course that would be impossible; and she wants to know if you would take her in your cab, and she promises to pay you faithfully, as she can get the money."

"Tut, tut, we'll see about that. It was not the money I was thinking about, but of losing our Sunday; the horses are tired, and I am tired too—that's where it pinches."

"It pinches all round, for that matter," said Polly,

"for it's only half Sunday without you, but you know we should do to other people as we should like they should do to us; and I know very well what I should like if my mother was dying; and Jerry, dear, I am sure it won't break the Sabbath; for if pulling a poor beast or donkey out of a pit would not spoil it, I am quite sure taking poor Dinah would not do it."

"Why, Polly, you are as good as the minister, and so, as I've had my Sunday morning sermon early to-day, you may go and tell Dinah that I'll be ready for her as the clock strikes ten; but stop—just step round to butcher Braydon's with my compliments, and ask him if he would lend me his light trap; I know he never uses it on the Sunday, and it would make a wonderful difference to the horse."

Away she went, and soon returned, saying that he could have the trap and welcome.

"All right," said he; "now put me up a bit of bread and cheese, and I'll be back in the afternoon as soon as I can."

"And I'll have the meat pie ready for an early tea instead of for dinner," said Polly; and away she went, while he made his preparations to the tune of "Polly's the woman and no mistake," of which tune he was very fond.

I was selected for the journey, and at ten o'clock

we started, in a light, high-wheeled gig, which ran so easily that after the four-wheeled cab it seemed like nothing.

It was a fine May day, and as soon as we were out of the town, the sweet air, the smell of the fresh grass, and the soft country roads were as pleasant as they used to be in the old times, and I soon began to feel quite fresh.

Dinah's family lived in a small farmhouse, up a green lane, close by a meadow with some fine shady trees; there were two cows feeding in it. A young man asked Jerry to bring his trap into the meadow, and he would tie me up in the cowshed; he wished he had a better stable to offer.

"If your cows would not be offended," said Jerry, "there is nothing my horse would like so well as to have an hour or two in your beautiful meadow; he's quiet, and it would be a rare treat for him."

"Do, and welcome," said the young man. "The best we have is at your service for your kindness to my sister; we shall be having some dinner in an hour, and I hope you'll come in, though with mother so ill we are all out of sorts in the house."

Jerry thanked him kindly, but said as he had some dinner with him, there was nothing he should like so well as walking about in the meadow.

When my harness was taken off, I did not know what I should do first—whether to eat the grass, or roll over on my back, or lie down and rest, or have a gallop across the meadow out of sheer spirits at being free; and I did all by turns. Jerry seemed to be quite as happy as I was; he sat down by a bank under a shady tree and listened to the birds, then he sang himself, and read out of the little brown book he is so fond of, then wandered round the meadow and down by a little brook, where he picked the flowers and the hawthorn, and tied them up with long sprays of ivy; then he gave me a good feed of the oats which he had brought with him; but the time seemed all too short—I had not been in a field since I left poor Ginger at Earlshall.

We came home gently, and Jerry's first words were, as we came into the yard, "Well, Polly, I have not lost my Sunday after all, for the birds were singing hymns in every bush, and I joined in the service; and as for Jack, he was like a young colt."

When he handed Dolly the flowers, she jumped about for joy.

38

Dolly and a Real Gentleman

THE WINTER CAME in early, with a great deal of cold and wet. There was snow, or sleet, or rain, almost every day for weeks, changing only for keen driving winds, or sharp frosts. The horses all felt it very much. When it is a dry cold, a couple of good thick rugs will keep the warmth in us; but when it is soaking rain, they soon get wet through and are no good. Some of the drivers had a waterproof cover to throw over, which was a fine thing; but some of the men were so poor that they could not protect either themselves or their horses, and many of them suffered very much that winter. When we horses had worked half the day we went to our dry stables, and could rest, while they had to sit on their boxes, sometimes staying out as late as one or two o'clock in the morning, if they had a party to wait for.

When the streets were slippery with frost or snow, that was the worst of all for us horses. One mile of such traveling, with a weight to draw and no firm footing, would take more out of us than four on a good road; every nerve and muscle of our bodies is on the strain to keep our balance; and, added to this, the fear of falling is more exhausting than anything else. If the roads are very bad indeed, our shoes are roughed, but that makes us feel nervous at first.

When the weather was very bad, many of the men would go and sit in the tavern close by, and get some one to watch for them; but they often lost a fare in that way, and could not, as Jerry said, be there without spending money. He never went to the Rising Sun; there was a coffee shop near, where he now and then went—or he bought of an old man who came to our rank with tins of hot coffee and pies. It was his opinion that spirits and beer made a man colder afterward, and that dry clothes, good food, cheerfulness, and a comfortable wife at home, were the best things to keep a cabman warm. Polly always supplied him with something to eat when he could not get home, and sometimes he would see little Dolly peeping from the corner of the street, to make sure if "father" was on the stand. If she saw him she would run off at full speed and soon come back with something in a tin or basket—some hot soup or pudding Polly had ready. It was wonderful how such a little thing could get safely across the street, often thronged with horses and carriages; but she was a brave little maid, and felt it quite an honor to bring "father's first course," as he used to call it. She was a general favorite on the stand, and there was not a man who would not have seen her safely across the street, if Jerry had not been able to do it.

One cold windy day, Dolly had brought Jerry a basin of something hot, and was standing by him while he ate it. He had scarcely begun when a gentleman, walking toward us very fast, held up his umbrella. Jerry touched his hat in return, gave the basin to Dolly, and was taking off my cloth, when the gentleman, hastening up, cried out, "No, no, finish your soup, my friend; I have not much time to spare, but I can wait till you have done, and set your little girl safe on the pavement." So saying, he seated himself in the cab. Jerry thanked him kindly, and came back to Dolly.

"There, Dolly, that's a gentleman; that's a real gentleman, Dolly. He has got time and thought for the comfort of a poor cabman and a little girl."

Jerry finished his soup, set the child across, and then took his orders to drive to Clapham Rise. Several times after that the same gentleman took our cab. I think he was very fond of dogs and horses, for whenever we took him to his own door, two or three dogs would come bounding out to meet him. Sometimes he came round and patted me, saying in his quiet, pleasant way, "This horse has got a good master, and he deserves it." It was a very rare thing for any one to notice the horse that had been working for him. I have known ladies to do it now and then, and this gentleman, and one or two others have given me a pat and a kind word; but ninety-nine out of a hundred would as soon think of patting the steam engine that drew the train.

The gentleman was not young, and there was a forward stoop in his shoulders as if he was always going at something. His lips were thin and close shut, though they had a very pleasant smile; his eye was keen, and there was something in his jaw and the motion of his head that made one think he was very determined in anything he set about. His voice was pleasant and kind; any horse would trust that voice, though it was just as decided as everything else about him.

One day he and another gentleman took our cab; they stopped at a shop in R—— Street, and while his friend went in, he stood at the door. A little ahead of us on the other side of the street, a cart with two very fine horses was standing before some wine vaults; the carter was not with them, and I cannot tell how long they had been standing, but they seemed to think they had waited long enough, and began to move off.

Before they had gone many paces, the carter came running out and caught them. He seemed furious at their having moved, and with whip and rein punished them brutally, even beating them about the head. Our gentleman saw it all, and stepping quickly across the street, said in a decided voice:

"If you don't stop that directly, I'll have you arrested for leaving your horses, and for brutal conduct."

The man, who had clearly been drinking, poured forth some abusive language, but he left off knocking the horses about, and taking the reins, got into his cart; meantime our friend had quietly taken a notebook from his pocket, and looking at the name and address painted on the cart, he wrote something down.

"What do you want with that?" growled the carter, as he cracked his whip and was moving on. A nod and a grim smile was the only answer he got.

On returning to the cab, our friend was joined by his companion, who said laughingly, "I should have thought, Wright, you had enough business of your own to look after, without troubling yourself about other people's horses and servants."

Our friend stood still for a moment, and throwing his head a little back, "Do you know why this world is as bad as it is?"

"No," said the other.

"Then I'll tell you. It is because people think *only* about their own business, and won't trouble themselves to stand up for the oppressed, nor bring the wrongdoer to light. I never see a wicked thing like this without doing what I can, and many a master has thanked me for letting him know how his horses have been used."

"I wish there were more gentlemen like you, sir," said Jerry, "for they are wanted badly enough in this city."

After this we continued our journey, and as they got out of the cab, our friend was saying, "My doctrine is this, that if we see cruelty or wrong that we have the power to stop, and do nothing, we make ourselves sharers in the guilt."

39
Seedy Sam

I SHOULD SAY that for a cab horse I was very well off indeed; my driver was my owner, and it was his interest to treat me well, and not overwork me, even had he not been so good a man as he was; but there were a great many horses which belonged to the large cab owners, who let them out to their drivers for so much money a day. As the horses did not belong to these men, the only thing they thought of was how to get their money out of them: first, to pay the master, and then to provide for their own living; and a dreadful time some of these horses had of it. Of course, I understood but little, but it was often talked over on the stand, and the Governor, who was a kind-hearted man and fond of horses, would sometimes speak up if one came in very much jaded or ill-used.

One day a shabby, miserable-looking driver, who went by the name of "Seedy Sam," brought in his horse looking dreadfully beat, and the Governor said:

"You and your horse look more fit for the police station than for this rank."

The man flung his tattered rug over the horse,

turned full round upon the Governor, and said in a voice that sounded almost desperate:

"If the police have any business with the matter it ought to be with the masters who charge us so much, or with the fares that are fixed so low. If a man has to pay eighteen shillings a day for the use of a cab and two horses, as many of us have to do in the season, and must make that up before we earn a penny for ourselves—I say, 'tis more than hard work; nine shillings a day to get out of each horse before you begin to get your own living. You know that's true, and if the horses don't work we must starve, and I and my children have known what that is before now. I've six of 'em, and only one earns anything; I am on the stand fourteen or sixteen hours a day, and I haven't had a Sunday these ten or twelve weeks; you know, Skinner never gives a day if he can help it, and if I don't work hard, tell me who does! I want a warm coat and a mackintosh, but with so many to feed, how can a man get it? I had to pledge my clock a week ago to pay Skinner, and I shall never see it again."

Some of the other drivers stood round nodding their heads and saying he was right. The man went on:

"You that have your own horses and cabs, or drive for good masters, have a chance of getting on, and a chance of doing right; I haven't. We can't charge more than sixpence a mile after the first, within the four-mile radius. This very morning I had to go a clear six miles and only took three shillings. I could not get a return fare, and had to come all the way back; there's twelve miles for the horse and three shillings for me. After that I had a three-mile fare, and there were bags and boxes enough to have brought in a good many twopences if they had been put outside; but you know how people do; all that could be piled up inside on the front seat were put in, and three heavy boxes went on the top. That was sixpence, and the fare one and sixpence; then I got a return for a shilling. Now that makes eighteen miles for the horse and six shillings for me; there's three shillings still for that horse to earn, and nine shillings for the afternoon horse before I touch a penny.

Of course it is not always so bad as that, but you know it often is, and I say 'tis a mockery to tell a man that he must not overwork his horse, for when a beast is downright tired, there's nothing but the whip that will keep his legs agoing—you can't help yourself—you must put your wife and children before the horse; the masters must look to that, we can't. I don't ill-use my horse for the sake of it; none of you can say I do. There's wrong lays somewhere—never a day's rest—

never a quiet hour with the wife and children. I often feel like an old man, though I'm only forty-five. You know how quick some of the gentry are to suspect us of cheating and overcharging; why, they stand with their purses in their hands, counting it over to a penny and looking at us as if we were pickpockets. I wish some of 'em had got to sit on my box sixteen hours a day, and get a living out of it, and eighteen shillings beside, and that in all weathers; they would not be so uncommon particular never to give us a sixpence over, or to cram all the luggage inside. Of course, some of 'em tip us pretty handsome now and then, or else we could not live, but you can't *depend* upon that."

The men who stood round much approved this speech, and one of them said, "It is desperate hard, and if a man sometimes does what is wrong, it is no wonder; and if he gets a dram too much, who's to blow him up?"

Jerry had taken no part in this conversation, but I never saw his face look so sad before. The Governor had stood with both his hands in his pockets; now he took his handkerchief out of his hat, and wiped his forehead.

"You've beaten me, Sam," he said, "for it's all true, and I won't cast it up to you any more about the police; it was the look in that horse's eye that came over me. It is hard lines for man, and it is hard lines for beast, and who's to mend it I don't know; but anyway you might tell the poor beast that you were sorry to take it out of him in that way. Sometimes a kind word is all we can give 'em, poor brutes, and 'tis wonderful what they do understand."

A few mornings after this talk a new man came on the stand with Sam's cab.

"Halloo!" said one. "What's up with Seedy Sam?"

"He's ill in bed," said the man. "He was taken last night in the yard, and could scarcely crawl home. His wife sent a boy this morning to say his father was in a high fever and could not get out, so I'm here instead."

The next morning the same man came again.

"How is Sam?" inquired the Governor.

"He's gone," said the man.

"What, gone? You don't mean to say he's dead?"

"Just snuffed out," said the other. "He died at four o'clock this morning; all yesterday he was raving— raving about Skinner, and having no Sundays. 'I never had a Sunday's rest,' these were his last words."

No one spoke for a while, and then the Governor said, "I'll tell you what, mates, this is a warning for us."

40
Poor Ginger

ONE DAY, WHILE our cab and many others were waiting outside one of the parks, where music was playing, a shabby old cab drove up beside ours. The horse was an old worn-out chestnut, with an ill-kept coat, and bones that showed plainly through it. The knees knuckled over, and the forelegs were very unsteady. I had been eating some hay, and the wind rolled a little lock of it that way, and the poor creature put out her long thin neck and picked it up, and then turned and looked about for more. There was a hopeless look in the dull eye that I could not help noticing, and then, as I was thinking where I had seen that horse before, she looked full at me and said, "Black Beauty, is that you?"

It was Ginger! But how changed! The beautifully arched and glossy neck was now straight, and lank, and fallen in; the clean straight legs and delicate fetlocks were swelled; the joints were grown out of shape with hard work; the face, that was once so full of spirit and life, was now full of suffering, and I could tell by the heaving of her sides, and her frequent cough, how bad her breath was.

Our drivers were standing together a little way off, so I sidled up to her a step or two, that we might have a little quiet talk. It was a sad tale that she had to tell.

After a twelvemonth's run off at Earlshall, she was considered to be fit for work again, and was sold to a gentleman. For a little while she got on very well, but after a longer gallop than usual the old strain returned, and after being rested and doctored she was again sold. In this way she changed hands several times, but always getting lower down.

"And so at last," said she, "I was bought by a man who keeps a number of cabs and horses, and lets them out. You look well off, and I am glad of it, but I could not tell you what my life has been. When they found out my weakness, they said I was not worth what they gave for me, and that I must go into one of the low cabs, and just be used up; that is what they are doing, whipping and working with never one thought of what I suffer; they paid for me, and must get it out of me, they say. The man who hires me now pays a deal of money to the owner every day, and so he has to get it out of me too; and so it's all the week round and round, with never a Sunday rest."

I said, "You used to stand up for yourself if you were ill-used."

"Ah!" she said, "I did once, but it's no use; men are strongest, and if they are cruel and have no feeling, there is nothing that we can do, but just bear it, bear it on and on to the end. I wish the end was come, I wish I was dead. I have seen dead horses, and I am sure they do not suffer pain. I wish I may drop down dead at my work, and not be sent off to the knacker's."

I was very much troubled, and I put my nose up to hers, but I could say nothing to comfort her. I think she was pleased to see me, for she said, "You are the only friend I ever had."

Just then her driver came up, and with a tug at her mouth backed her out of the line and drove off, leaving me very sad indeed.

A short time after this a cart with a dead horse in it passed our cabstand. The head hung out of the cart tail, the lifeless tongue was slowly dropping with blood; and the sunken eyes! But I can't speak of them, the sight was too dreadful. It was a chestnut horse with a long, thin neck. I saw a white streak down the forehead. I believe it was Ginger; I hoped it was, for then her troubles would be over. Oh! If men were more merciful they would shoot us before we came to such misery.

41

The Butcher

I SAW A great deal of trouble among the horses in London, and much of it might have been prevented by a little common sense. We horses do not mind hard work if we are treated reasonably, and I am sure there are many driven by quite poor men who have a happier life than I had when I used to go in the Countess of W——'s carriage, with my silver-mounted harness and high feeding.

It often went to my heart to see how the little ponies were used, straining along with heavy loads, or staggering under heavy blows from some low, cruel boy. Once I saw a little gray pony with a thick mane and a pretty head, and so much like Merrylegs that if I had not been in harness I should have neighed to him. He was doing his best to pull a heavy cart, while a strong rough boy was cutting him under the belly with his whip, and chucking cruelly at his little mouth. Could it be Merrylegs? It was just like him; but then Mr. Blomefield was never to sell him, and I think he would not do it; but this might have been quite as good a little fellow, and had as happy a place when he was young.

I often noticed the great speed at which butchers' horses were made to go, though I did not know why it was so, till one day when we had to wait some time in St. John's Wood. There was a butcher's shop next door, and as we were standing a butcher's cart came dashing up at a great pace. The horse was hot and much exhausted; he hung his head down, while his heaving sides and trembling legs showed how hard he had been driven. The lad jumped out of the cart and was getting the basket, when the master came out of the shop much displeased. After looking at the horse, he turned angrily to the lad:

"How many times shall I tell you not to drive in this way? You ruined the last horse and broke his wind, and you are going to ruin this in the same way. If you were not my own son, I would dismiss you on the spot; it is a disgrace to have a horse brought to the shop in a condition like that; you are liable to be taken up by the police for such driving, and if you are, you need not look to me for bail, for I have spoken to you till I'm tired; you must look out for yourself."

During this speech the boy had stood by, sullen and dogged, but when his father ceased, he broke out angrily. It wasn't his fault, and he wouldn't take the blame; he was only going by orders all the time.

"You always say, 'Now be quick; now look sharp!' and when I go to the houses, one wants a leg of mutton for an early dinner, and I must be back with it in a quarter of an hour. Another cook has forgotten to order the beef; I must go and fetch it and be back in no time, or the mistress will scold; and the housekeeper says they have company coming unexpectedly and must have some chops sent up directly; and the lady at No. 4, in the Crescent, *never* orders her dinner till the meat comes in for lunch, and it's nothing but hurry, hurry, all the time. If the gentry would think of what they want, and order their meat the day before, there need not be this blow up!"

"I wish to goodness they would," said the butcher. "Twould save me a wonderful deal of harass, and I could suit my customers much better if I knew beforehand—but there—what's the use of talking—who ever thinks of a butcher's convenience, or a butcher's horse! Now then, take him in and look to him well: mind, he does not go out again today, and if anything else is wanted, you must carry it yourself in the basket." With that he went in, and the horse was led away.

But all boys are not cruel. I have seen some as fond of their pony or donkey as if it had been a favorite dog, and the little creatures have worked away as cheerfully and willingly for their young drivers as I work for Jerry.

It may be hard work sometimes, but a friend's hand and voice make it easy.

There was a young coster-boy who came up our street with greens and potatoes; he had an old pony, not very handsome, but the cheerfullest and pluckiest little thing I ever saw, and to see how fond those two were of each other was a treat. The pony followed his master like a dog, and when he got into his cart would trot off without a whip or a word, and rattle down the street as merrily as if he had come out of the Queen's stables. Jerry liked the boy, and called him "Prince Charlie," for he said he would make a king of drivers some day.

There was an old man, too, who used to come up our street with a little coal cart; he wore a coal-heaver's hat, and looked rough and black. He and his old horse used to plod together along the street, like two good partners who understood each other; the horse would stop of his own accord at the doors where they took coal off him; he used to keep one ear bent toward his master. The old man's cry could be heard up the street long before he came near. I never knew what he said, but the children called him "Old Ba-a-ar Hoo," for it sounded like that. Polly took her coal off him, and was very friendly, and Jerry said it was a comfort to think how happy an old horse *might* be in a poor place.

42

The Election

AS WE CAME into the yard one afternoon, Polly came out. "Jerry! I've had Mr. B—— here asking about your vote, and he wants to hire your cab for the election; he will call for an answer."

"Well, Polly, you may say that my cab will be otherwise engaged. I should not like to have it pasted over with their great bills, and as to making Jack and Captain race about to the public houses to bring up half-drunken voters, why, I think 'twould be an insult to the horses. No, I shan't do it."

"I suppose you'll vote for the gentleman? He said he was of your politics."

"So he is in some things, but I shall not vote for him, Polly; you know what his trade is?"

"Yes."

"Well, a man who gets rich by that trade may be all very well in some ways, but he is blind as to what workingmen want; I could not in my conscience send him up to make the laws. I dare say they'll be angry, but every man must do what he thinks to be the best for his country."

On the morning before the election, Jerry was putting me into the shafts, when Dolly came into the yard sobbing and crying, with her little blue frock and white pinafore spattered all over with mud.

"Why, Dolly, what is the matter?"

"Those naughty boys," she sobbed, "have thrown the dirt all over me, and called me a little raga— raga—"

"They called her a little blue ragamuffin, father," said Harry, who ran in looking very angry; "but I have given it to them; they won't insult my sister again. I have given them a thrashing they will remember; a set of cowardly, rascally, orange blackguards!"

Jerry kissed the child and said, "Run in to mother, my pet, and tell her I think you had better stay at home today and help her."

Then turning gravely to Harry:

"My boy, I hope you will always defend your sister, and give anybody who insults her a good thrashing—that is as it should be; but mind, I won't have any election blackguarding on my premises. There are as many blue blackguards as there are orange, and as many white as there are purple, or any other color, and I won't have any of my family mixed up with it. Even women and children are ready to quarrel for the sake of a color, and not one in ten of them knows what it is about."

"Why, father, I thought blue was for Liberty."

"My boy, Liberty does not come from colors, they only show party, and all the liberty you can get out of them is liberty to get drunk at other people's expense, liberty to ride to the poll in a dirty old cab, liberty to abuse anyone that does not wear your color, and to shout yourself hoarse at what you only half understand—that's your liberty!"

"Oh, father, you are laughing."

"No, Harry, I am serious, and I am ashamed to see how men go on who ought to know better. An election is a very serious thing; at least it ought to be, and every man ought to vote according to his conscience, and let his neighbor do the same."

43

A Friend in Need

AT LAST CAME the election day; there was no lack of work for Jerry and me. First came a stout puffy gentleman with a carpet bag; he wanted to go to the Bishopsgate Station; then we were called by a party who wished to be taken to the Regent's Park; and next we were wanted in a side street where a timid, anxious old lady was waiting to be taken to the bank: there we had to stop to take her back again, and just as we had set her down, a red-faced gentleman, with a handful of papers came running up out of breath, and before Jerry could get down, he had opened the door, popped himself in, and called out, "Bow Street Police Station, quick!" So off we went with him, and when after another turn or two we came back, there was no other cab on the stand. Jerry put on my nose-bag, for as he said, "We must eat when we can on such days as these; so munch away, Jack, and make the best of your time, old boy."

I found I had a good feed of crushed oats wetted

up with a little bran; this would be a treat any day, but was specially refreshing then. Jerry was so thoughtful and kind—what horse would not do his best for such a master? Then he took out one of Polly's meat pies, and standing near me, he began to eat it. The streets were very full, and the cabs with the candidates' colors on them were dashing about through the crowd as if life and limb were of no consequence; we saw two people knocked down that day, and one was a woman. The horses were having a bad time of it, poor things! But the voters inside thought nothing of that; many of them were half drunk, hurrahing out of the cab windows if their own party came by. It was the first election I had seen, and I don't want to be in another, though I have heard things are better now.

Jerry and I had not eaten many mouthfuls before a poor young woman, carrying a heavy child, came along the street. She was looking this way and that way, and seemed quite bewildered. Presently she made her way up to Jerry, and asked if he could tell her the way to St. Thomas's Hospital, and how far it was to get there. She had come from the country that morning, she said, in a market cart; she did not know about the election, and was quite a stranger in London. She had got an order for the hospital for her little boy. The child was crying with a feeble, pining cry.

"Poor little fellow!" she said. "He suffers a deal of pain; he is four years old and can't walk any more than a baby; but the doctor said if I could get him into the hospital, he might get well; pray, sir, how far is it? And which way is it?"

"Why, missis," said Jerry, "you can't get there walking through crowds like this! Why, it is three miles away, and that child is heavy."

"Yes, bless him, he is, but I am strong, thank God, and if I knew the way, I think I should get on somehow; please tell me the way."

"You can't do it," said Jerry, "you might be knocked down and the child be run over. Now, look here, just get into this cab, and I'll drive you safe to the hospital. Don't you see the rain is coming on?"

"No, sir, no, I can't do that, thank you, I have only just money enough to get back with. Please tell me the way."

"Look you here, missis," said Jerry, "I've got a wife and dear children at home, and I know a father's feelings; now get you into that cab, and I'll take you there for nothing. I'd be ashamed of myself to let a woman and a sick child run a risk like that."

"Heaven bless you!" said the woman, bursting into tears.

"There, there, cheer up, my dear, I'll soon take you there; come, let me put you inside."

As Jerry went to open the door two men, with colors in their hats and buttonholes, ran up, calling out, "Cab!"

"Engaged," cried Jerry; but one of the men, pushing past the woman, sprang into the cab, followed by the other. Jerry looked as stern as a policeman. "This cab is already engaged, gentlemen, by that lady."

"Lady!" said one of them; "Oh, she can wait; our business is very important, besides we were in first, it is our right, and we shall stay in."

A droll smile came over Jerry's face as he shut the door upon them. "All right, gentlemen, pray stay in as long as it suits you; I can wait while you rest yourselves." And turning his back upon them, he walked up to the young woman, who was standing near me. "They'll soon be gone," he said, laughing; "don't trouble yourself, my dear."

And they soon were gone, for when they understood Jerry's dodge, they got out, calling him all sorts of bad names and blustering about his number and getting a summons. After this little stoppage we were soon on our way to the hospital, going as much as possible through bystreets. Jerry rung the great bell, and helped the young woman out.

"Thank you a thousand times," she said. "I could never have got here alone."

"You're kindly welcome, and I hope the dear child will soon be better."

He watched her go in at the door, and gently he said to himself, "Inasmuch as ye have done it to one of the least of these." Then he patted my neck, which was always his way when anything pleased him.

The rain was now coming down fast, and just as we were leaving the hospital the door opened again, and the porter called out, "Cab!" We stopped, and a lady came down the steps. Jerry seemed to know her at once; she put back her veil and said, "Barker! Jeremiah Barker! Is it you? I am very glad to find you here; you are just the friend I want, for it is very difficult to get a cab in this part of London today."

"I shall be proud to serve you, ma'am; I am right glad I happened to be here. Where may I take you to, ma'am?"

"To the Paddington Station, and then if we are in good time, as I think we shall be, you shall tell me all about Mary and the children."

We got to the station in good time, and being under shelter the lady stood a good while talking to Jerry. I found she had been Polly's mistress, and after many inquiries about her, she said:

"How do you find the cab work suits you in winter? I know Mary was rather anxious about you last year."

"Yes, ma'am, she was; I had a bad cough that followed me up quite into the warm weather, and when I am kept out late, she does worry herself a good deal. You see, ma'am, it is all hours and all weathers, and that does try a man's constitution; but I am getting on pretty well, and I should feel quite lost if I had not horses to look after. I was brought up to it, and I am afraid I should not do so well at anything else."

"Well, Barker," she said, "it would be a great pity that you should seriously risk your health in this work, not only for your own, but for Mary's and the children's sake; there are many places where good drivers or good grooms are wanted, and if ever you think you ought to give up this cab work, let me know." Then, sending some kind messages to Mary, she put something into his hand, saying, "There is five shillings each for the two children; Mary will know how to spend it."

Jerry thanked her and seemed much pleased, and, turning out of the station, we at last reached home, and I, at least, was tired.

44
Old Captain and His Successor

CAPTAIN AND I were great friends. He was a noble old fellow, and he was very good company. I never thought that he would have to leave his home and go down the hill, but his turn came; and this was how it happened. I was not there, but I heard all about it.

He and Jerry had taken a party to the great railway station over London Bridge, and were coming back, somewhere between the bridge and the monument, when Jerry saw a brewer's empty dray coming along, drawn by two powerful horses. The drayman was lashing his horses with his heavy whip; the dray was light, and they started off at a furious rate; the man had no control over them, and the street was full of traffic. One young girl was knocked down and run over, and the next moment they dashed up against our cab; both the wheels were torn off, and the cab was thrown over. Captain was dragged down, the shafts splintered, and one of them ran into his side. Jerry, too, was thrown, but was only bruised; nobody could tell how he escaped; he always said 'twas a miracle. When poor Captain was got up, he was found to be very much cut and knocked about. Jerry led him home gently, and a sad sight it was to see the blood soaking into his white coat and dropping from his side and shoulder. The drayman was proved to be very drunk, and was fined, and the brewer had to pay damages to our master; but there was no one to pay damages to poor Captain.

The farrier and Jerry did the best they could to ease his pain and make him comfortable. The fly had to be mended, and for several days I did not go out, and Jerry earned nothing. The first time we went to the stand after the accident the Governor came up to hear how Captain was.

"He'll never get over it," said Jerry, "at least not for my work, so the farrier said this morning. He says he may do for carting, and that sort of work. It has put me out very much. Carting, indeed! I've seen what horses come to at that work round London. I only wish all the drunkards could be put in a lunatic asylum instead of being allowed to run foul of sober people. If they would break their *own* bones, and smash their *own* carts, and lame their *own* horses, that would be their own affair, and we might let them alone, but it seems to me that the innocent always suffer; and then they talk about compensation! You can't make compensation—there's all the trouble, and vexation, and loss of time, besides losing a good horse that's like an old friend—it's nonsense talking of compensation! If there's one devil that I should like to see in the bottomless pit more than another, it's the drink devil."

"I say, Jerry," said the Governor, "you are treading pretty hard on my toes, you know; I'm not so good as you are, more shame for me, I wish I was."

"Well," said Jerry, "why don't you cut with it, Governor? You are too good a man to be the slave of such a thing."

"I'm a great fool, Jerry; but I tried once for two days, and I thought I should have died; how did you do?"

"I had hard work at it for several weeks; you see, I never did get drunk, but I found that I was not my own master, and that when the craving came on, it was hard work to say 'no.' I saw that one of us must knock under—the drink devil or Jerry Barker—and I said that it should not be Jerry Barker, God helping me; but it was a struggle, and I wanted all the help I could get, for till I tried to break the habit, I did not know how strong it was. But then Polly took such pains that I should have good food, and when the craving came on, I used to get a cup of coffee, or some peppermint, or read a bit in my book, and that was a help to me: sometimes I had to say over and over to myself, 'Give up the drink or lose your soul? Give up the drink or break Polly's heart?' But thanks be to God, and my dear wife, my chains were broken, and now for ten years I have not tasted a drop, and never wish for it."

"I've a great mind to try it," said Grant, "for 'tis a poor thing not to be one's own master."

"Do, Governor, do, you'll never repent it, and what a help it would be to some of the poor fellows in our rank if they saw you do without it. I know there's two or three would like to keep out of that tavern if they could."

At first Captain seemed to do well, but he was a very old horse, and it was only his wonderful constitution, and Jerry's care, that had kept him up at the cab work so long; now he broke down very much. The farrier said he might mend up enough to sell for a few pounds, but Jerry said, no! A few pounds got by selling a good old servant into hard work and misery would canker all the rest of his money, and he thought the kindest thing he could do for the fine old fellow would be to put a sure bullet through his heart, and then he would never suffer more; for he did not know where to find a kind master for the rest of his days.

The day after this was decided, Harry took me

to the forge for some new shoes; when I returned, Captain was gone. I and the family all felt it very much.

Jerry had now to look out for another horse, and he soon heard of one through an acquaintance who was under-groom in a nobleman's stables. He was a valuable young horse, but he had run away, smashed into another carriage, flung his lordship out, and so cut and blemished himself that he was no longer fit for a gentleman's stables, and the coachman had orders to look round, and sell him as well as he could.

"I can do with high spirits," said Jerry, "if a horse is not vicious or hard-mouthed."

"There is not a bit of vice in him," said the man. "His mouth is very tender, and I think myself that was the cause of the accident; you see he had just been clipped, and the weather was bad, and he had not had exercise enough, and when he did go out he was as full of spring as a balloon. Our governor (the coachman, I mean) had him harnessed in as tight and strong as he could, with the martingale, and the bearing rein, a very sharp curb, and the reins put in at the bottom bar. It is my belief that it made the horse mad, being tender in the mouth and so full of spirit."

"Likely enough; I'll come and see him," said Jerry.

The next day Hotspur—that was his name—came home; he was a fine brown horse, without a white hair in him, as tall as Captain, with a very handsome head, and only five years old. I gave him a friendly greeting by way of good fellowship, but did not ask him any questions. The first night he was very restless. Instead of lying down, he kept jerking his halter rope up and down through the ring, and knocking the block about against the manger till I could not sleep. However, the next day, after five or six hours in the cab, he came in quiet and sensible. Jerry patted and talked to him a good deal, and very soon they understood each other, and Jerry said that with an easy bit, and plenty of work, he would be as gentle as a lamb; and that it was an ill wind that blew nobody good, for if his lordship had lost a hundred-guinea favorite, the cabman had gained a good horse with all his strength in him.

Hotspur thought it a great come down to be a cab horse, and was disgusted at standing in the rank, but he confessed to me at the end of the week that an easy mouth and a free head made up for a great deal, and after all, the work was not so degrading as having one's head and tail fastened to each other at the saddle. In fact, he settled in well, and Jerry liked him very much.

45

Jerry's New Year

CHRISTMAS AND THE New Year are very merry times for some people; but for cabmen and cabmen's horses it is no holiday, though it may be a harvest. There are so many parties, balls, and places of amusement open that the work is hard and often late. Sometimes driver and horse have to wait for hours in the rain or frost, shivering with the cold, while the merry people within are dancing away to the music. I wonder if the beautiful ladies ever think of the weary cabman waiting on his box, and his patient beast standing, till his legs get stiff with cold.

I had now most of the evening work, as I was well accustomed to standing, and Jerry was also more afraid of Hotspur taking cold. We had a great deal of late work in the Christmas week, and Jerry's cough was bad; but however late we were, Polly sat up for him, and came out with a lantern to meet him, looking anxious and troubled.

On the evening of the New Year, we had to take two gentlemen to a house in one of the West End Squares. We set them down at nine o'clock and were told to come again at eleven. "But," said one of them, "as it is a card party, you may have to wait a few minutes, but don't be late."

As the clock struck eleven we were at the door, for Jerry was always punctual. The clock chimed the quarters—one, two, three, and then struck twelve, but the door did not open.

The wind had been very changeable, with squalls of rain during the day, but now it came on sharp, driving sleet, which seemed to come all the way round; it was very cold, and there was no shelter. Jerry got off his box and came and pulled one of my cloths a little more over my neck; then he took a turn or two up and down, stamping his feet; then he began to beat his arms, but that set him off coughing; so he opened the cab door and sat at the bottom with his feet on the pavement, and was a little sheltered. Still the clock chimed the quarters, and no one came. At half-past twelve, he rang the bell and asked the servant if he would be wanted that night.

"Oh, yes, you'll be wanted safe enough," said the man; "you must not go, it will soon be over." And again Jerry sat down, but his voice was so hoarse I could hardly hear him.

At a quarter past one the door opened, and the two gentlemen came out; they got into the cab without a word, and told Jerry where to drive, that was nearly two miles. My legs were numb with cold, and I thought I should have stumbled. When the men got out, they never said they were sorry to have kept us waiting so long, but were angry at the charge; however, as Jerry never charged more than was his due, so he never took less, and they had to pay for the two hours and a quarter waiting; but it was hard-earned money to Jerry.

At last we got home; he could hardly speak, and his cough was dreadful. Polly asked no questions, but opened the door and held the lantern for him.

"Can't I do something?" she said.

"Yes, get Jack something warm, and then boil me some gruel."

This was said in a hoarse whisper; he could hardly get his breath, but he gave me a rubdown as usual, and even went up into the hayloft for an extra bundle of straw for my bed. Polly brought me a warm mash that made me comfortable, and then they locked the door.

It was late the next morning before any one came, and then it was only Harry. He cleaned us and fed us, and swept out the stalls, then he put the straw back again as if it was Sunday. He was very still, and neither whistled nor sang. At noon he came again and gave us our food and water; this time Dolly came with him; she was crying, and I could gather from what they said that Jerry was dangerously ill, and the doctor said it was a bad case. So two days passed, and there was great trouble indoors. We only saw Harry and sometimes Dolly. I think she came for company, for Polly was always with Jerry, and he had to be kept very quiet.

On the third day, while Harry was in the stable, a tap came at the door, and Governor Grant came in.

"I wouldn't go to the house, my boy," he said, "but I want to know how your father is."

"He is very bad," said Harry. "He can't be much worse; they call it 'bronchitis'; the doctor thinks it will turn one way or another tonight."

"That's bad, very bad," said Grant, shaking his head; "I know two men who died of that last week; it takes 'em off in no time; but while there's life there's hope, so you must keep up your spirits."

"Yes," said Harry quickly, "and the doctor said that father had a better chance than most men, because he didn't drink. He said yesterday the fever was so high that if father had been a drinking man it would have burned him up like a piece of paper; but I believe he thinks he will get over it; don't you think he will, Mr. Grant?"

The Governor looked puzzled.

"If there's any rule that good men should get over these things, I'm sure he will, my boy; he's the best man I know. I'll look in early tomorrow."

Early next morning he was there.

"Well?" said he.

"Father is better," said Harry. "Mother hopes he will get over it."

"Thank God!" said the Governor. "And now you must keep him warm, and keep his mind easy, and that brings me to the horses; you see, Jack will be all the better for the rest of a week or two in a warm stable, and you can easily take him a turn up and down the street to stretch his legs; but this young one, if he does not get work, he will soon be all up on end, as you may say, and will be rather too much for you; and when he does go out there'll be an accident."

"It is like that now," said Harry. "I have kept him short of corn, but he's so full of spirit I don't know what to do with him."

"Just so," said Grant. "Now look here, will you tell your mother that, if she is agreeable, I will come for him every day till something is arranged, and take him for a good spell of work, and whatever he earns, I'll bring your mother half of it, and that will help with the horses' feed. Your father is in a good club, I know, but that won't keep the horses, and they'll be eating their heads off all this time; I'll come at noon and hear what she says," and without waiting for Harry's thanks, he was gone.

At noon I think he went and saw Polly, for he and Harry came to the stable together, harnessed Hotspur, and took him out.

For a week or more he came for Hotspur, and when Harry thanked him or said anything about his kindness, he laughed it off, saying it was all good luck for him, for his horses were wanting a little rest which they would not otherwise have had.

Jerry grew better steadily, but the doctor said that he must never go back to the cab work again if he wished to be an old man. The children had many consultations together about what father and mother would do, and how they could help to earn money.

One afternoon, Hotspur was brought in very wet and dirty.

"The streets are nothing but slush," said the Governor; "it will give you a good warming, my boy, to get him clean and dry."

"All right, Governor," said Harry, "I shall not leave him till he is; you know I have been trained by my father."

"I wish all the boys had been trained like you," said the Governor.

While Harry was sponging off the mud from Hotspur's body and legs, Dolly came in, looking very full of something.

"Who lives at Fairstowe, Harry? Mother has got a letter from Fairstowe; she seemed so glad, and ran upstairs to father with it."

"Don't you know? Why, it is the name of Mrs. Fowler's place—mother's old mistress, you know—the lady that father met last summer, who sent you and me five shillings each."

"Oh! Mrs. Fowler. Of course, I know all about her. I wonder what she is writing to mother about."

"Mother wrote to her last week," said Harry; "you know she told father if ever he gave up the cab work, she would like to know. I wonder what she says; run in and see, Dolly."

Harry scrubbed away at Hotspur with a huish! huish! like any old hostler.

In a few minutes Dolly came dancing into the stable.

"Oh! Harry, there never was anything so beautiful; Mrs. Fowler says we are all to go and live near her. There is a cottage now empty that will just suit us, with a garden, and a henhouse, and apple trees, and everything! And her coachman is going away in the spring, and then she will want father in his place; and there are good families round where you can get a place in the garden, or the stable, or as a page boy; and there's a good school for me; and mother is laughing and crying by turns, and father does look so happy!"

"That's uncommon jolly," said Harry, "and just the right thing, I should say; it will suit father and mother both; but I don't intend to be a page boy with tight clothes and rows of buttons. I'll be a groom or a gardener."

It was quickly settled that as soon as Jerry was well enough they should remove to the country, and that the cab and horses should be sold as soon as possible.

This was heavy news for me, for I was not young now, and could not look for any improvement in my condition. Since I left Birtwick I had never been so happy as with my dear master, Jerry; but three years of cab work, even under the best conditions, will tell on one's strength, and I felt that I was not the horse that I had been.

Grant said at once that he would take Hotspur, and there were men on the stand who would have bought me; but Jerry said I should not go to cab work again with just anybody, and the Governor promised to find a place for me where I should be comfortable.

The day came for going away. Jerry had not been allowed to go out yet, and I never saw him after that New Year's Eve. Polly and the children came to bid me good-bye. "Poor old Jack! Dear old Jack! I wish we could take you with us," she said, and then, laying her hand on my mane, she put her face close to my neck and kissed me. Dolly was crying and kissed me too. Harry stroked me a great deal, but said nothing, only he seemed very sad, and so I was led away to my new place.

Part Four

46

Jakes and the Lady

I WAS SOLD to a corn dealer and baker, whom Jerry knew, and with him he thought I should have good food and fair work. In the first he was quite right, and if my master had always been on the premises, I do not think I should have been overloaded, but there was a foreman who was always hurrying and driving every one, and frequently when I had quite a full load, he would order something else to be taken on. My carter, whose name was Jakes, often said it was more than I ought to take, but the other always overruled him. "'Twas no use going twice when once would do, and he chose to get business forward."

Jakes, like the other carters, always had the bearing rein up, which prevented me from drawing easily, and by the time I had been there three or four months, I found the work telling very much on my strength.

One day I was loaded more than usual, and part of the road was a steep uphill. I used all my strength, but I could not get on, and was obliged continually to stop. This did not please my driver, and he laid his whip on badly. "Get on, you lazy fellow," he said, "or I'll make you."

Again I started the heavy load, and struggled on a few yards; again the whip came down, and again I struggled forward. The pain of that great cart whip was sharp, but my mind was hurt quite as much as my poor sides. To be punished and abused when I was doing my very best was so hard, it took the heart out of me. A third time he was flogging me cruelly, when a lady stepped quickly up to him, and said in a sweet, earnest voice:

"Oh, pray do not whip your good horse any more; I am sure he is doing all he can, and the road is very steep; I am sure he is doing his best."

"If doing his best won't get this load up, he must do something more than his best; that's all I know, ma'am," said Jakes.

"But is it not a very heavy load?" she said.

"Yes, yes, too heavy," he said, "but that's not my fault; the foreman came just as we were starting, and would have three hundredweight more put on to save him trouble, and I must get on with it as well as I can."

He was raising the whip again, when the lady said:

"Pray, stop; I think I can help you if you will let me."

The man laughed.

"You see," she said, "you do not give him a fair chance; he cannot use all his power with his head held back as it is with that bearing rein; if you would take it off, I am sure he would do better—*do* try it," she said persuasively. "I should be very glad if you would."

"Well, well," said Jakes, with a short laugh, "anything to please a lady, of course. How far would you wish it down, ma'am?"

"Quite down, give him his head altogether."

The rein was taken off, and in a moment I put my head down to my very knees. What a comfort it was! Then I tossed it up and down several times to get the aching stiffness out of my neck.

"Poor fellow! That is what you wanted," said she, patting and stroking me with her gentle hand; "and now if you will speak kindly to him and lead him on, I believe he will be able to do better."

Jakes took the rein. "Come on, Blackie." I put down my head, and threw my whole weight against the collar; I spared no strength; the load moved on, and I pulled it steadily up the hill, and then stopped to take breath.

The lady had walked along the footpath, and now came across into the road. She stroked and patted my neck, as I had not been patted for many a long day.

"You see he was quite willing when you gave him the chance; I am sure he is a fine-tempered creature, and I dare say has known better days. You won't put that rein on again, will you?" For he was just going to hitch it up on the old plan.

"Well, ma'am, I can't deny that having his head has helped him up the hill, and I'll remember it another time, and thank you, ma'am; but if he went without a bearing rein, I should be the laughing-stock of all the carters; it is the fashion, you see."

"Is it not better," she said, "to lead a good fashion than to follow a bad one? A great many gentlemen do not use bearing reins now; our carriage horses have not worn them for fifteen years, and work with much less fatigue than those who have them; besides," she added in a very serious voice, "we have no right to distress any of God's creatures without a very good reason; we call them dumb animals, and so they are, for they cannot tell us how they feel, but they do not suffer less because they have no words. But I must not detain you now; I thank you for trying my plan with your good horse, and I am sure you will find it far better than the whip. Good day." And with another soft pat on my neck she stepped lightly across the path, and I saw her no more.

"That was a real lady, I'll be bound for it," said Jakes to himself. "She spoke just as polite as if I was a gentleman, and I'll try her plan, uphill, at any rate." And I must do him the justice to say that he let my rein out several holes, and going uphill after that, he always gave me my head; but the heavy loads went on. Good feed and fair rest will keep up one's strength under full work, but no horse can stand against overloading; and I was getting so thoroughly pulled down from this cause that a younger horse was bought in my place. I may as well mention here what I suffered at this time from another cause. I had heard horses speak of it, but had never myself had experience of the evil; this was a badly-lighted stable; there was only one very small window at the end, and the consequence was that the stalls were almost dark.

Besides the depressing effect this had on my spirits, it very much weakened my sight, and when I was suddenly brought out of the darkness into the glare of daylight it was very painful to my eyes. Several times I stumbled over the threshold, and could scarcely see where I was going.

I believe, had I stayed there very long, I should have become purblind, and that would have been a great misfortune, for I have heard men say that a stone-blind horse was safer to drive than one which had imperfect sight, as it generally makes them very timid. However, I escaped without any permanent injury to my sight, and was sold to a large cab owner.

47
Hard Times

I SHALL NEVER forget my new master; he had black eyes and a hooked nose, his mouth was as full of teeth as a bulldog's, and his voice was as harsh as the grinding of cart wheels over graveled stones. His name was Nicholas Skinner, and I believe he was the man that poor Seedy Sam drove for.

I have heard men say that seeing is believing; but I should say that *feeling* is believing; for much as I had seen before, I never knew till now the utter misery of a cab horse's life.

Skinner had a low set of cabs and a low set of drivers; he was hard on the men, and the men were hard on the horses. In this place we had no Sunday rest, and it was in the heat of summer.

Sometimes on a Sunday morning, a party of fast men would hire the cab for the day; four of them inside and another with the driver, and I had to take them ten or fifteen miles out into the country, and back again; never would any of them get down to walk up a hill, let it be ever so steep, or the day ever so hot—unless, indeed, when the driver was afraid I should not manage it, and sometimes I was so fevered and worn that I could hardly touch my food. How I used to long for the nice bran mash with niter in it that Jerry used to give us on Saturday nights in hot weather, that used to cool us down and make us so comfortable. Then we had two nights and a whole day for unbroken rest, and on Monday morning we were as fresh as young horses again; but here there was no rest, and my driver was just as hard as his master. He had a cruel whip with something so sharp at the end that it sometimes drew blood, and he would even whip me under the belly, and flip the lash out at my head. Indignities like these took the heart out of me terribly, but still I did my best and never hung back; for, as poor Ginger said, it was no use; men are the strongest.

My life was now so utterly wretched that I wished I might, like Ginger, drop down dead at my work, and be out of my misery and one day my wish very nearly came to pass.

I went on the stand at eight in the morning, and had done a good share of work, when we had to take a fare to the railway. A long train was just expected in, so my driver pulled up at the back of some of the outside cabs to take the chance of a return fare. It was a very heavy train, and as all the cabs were soon engaged, ours was called for. There was a party of four; a noisy, blustering man with a lady, a little boy, and a young girl, and a great deal of luggage. The lady and the boy got into the cab, and while the man ordered about the luggage, the young girl came and looked at me.

"Papa," she said, "I am sure this poor horse cannot take us and all our luggage so far, he is so very weak and worn out. Do look at him."

"Oh, he's all right, miss," said my driver, "he's strong enough."

The porter, who was pulling about some heavy boxes, suggested to the gentleman, as there was so much luggage, whether he would not take a second cab.

"Can your horse do it, or can't he?" said the blustering man.

"Oh, he can do it all right, sir; send up the boxes, porter; he could take more than that." And he helped to haul up a box so heavy that I could feel the springs go down.

"Papa, papa, do take a second cab," said the young girl in a beseeching tone. "I am sure we are wrong, I am sure it is very cruel."

"Nonsense, Grace, get in at once, and don't make all this fuss; a pretty thing it would be if a man of business had to examine every cab horse before he hired it—the man knows his own business of course. There, get in and hold your tongue!"

My gentle friend had to obey; and box after box was dragged up and lodged on the top of the cab, or settled by the side of the driver. At last all was ready, and with his usual jerk at the rein, and slash of the whip, he drove out of the station.

The load was very heavy, and I had had neither food nor rest since morning; but I did my best, as I always had done, in spite of cruelty and injustice.

I got along fairly till we came to Ludgate Hill; but there the heavy load and my own exhaustion were too much. I was struggling to keep on, goaded by constant chucks of the rein and use of the whip, when, in a single moment—I cannot tell how—my feet slipped from under me, and I fell heavily to the ground on my side; the suddenness and the force with which I fell seemed to beat all the breath out of my body. I lay perfectly still; indeed, I had no power to move, and I thought now I was going to die. I heard a sort of confusion round me, loud, angry voices, and the getting down of the luggage, but it was all like a dream. I thought I heard that sweet, pitiful voice saying, "Oh, that poor horse! It is all our fault." Someone came and loosened the throat strap of my bridle, and undid the traces which kept the collar so tight upon me. Someone said, "He's dead, he'll never get up again." Then I could hear a policeman giving orders, but I did not even open my eyes; I could only draw a gasping breath now and then. Some cold water was thrown over my head, and some cordial was poured into my mouth, and something was covered over me. I cannot tell how long I lay there, but I found my life coming back, and a kind-voiced man was patting me and encouraging me to rise. After some more cordial had been given me, and after one or two attempts, I staggered to my feet, and was gently led to some stables which were close by. Here I was put into a well-littered stall, and some warm gruel was brought to me, which I drank thankfully.

In the evening I was sufficiently recovered to be led back to Skinner's stables, where I think they did the best for me they could. In the morning Skinner came with a farrier to look at me. He examined me very closely and said:

"This is a case of overwork more than disease, and if you could give him a run-off for six months he would be able to work again; but now there is not an ounce of strength left in him."

"Then he must just go to the dogs," said Skinner. "I have no meadows to nurse sick horses in—he might get well or he might not; that sort of thing don't suit my business. My plan is to work 'em as long as they'll go, and then sell 'em for what they'll fetch, at the knacker's or elsewhere."

"If he was broken-winded," said the farrier, "you had better have him killed out of hand, but he is not; there is a sale of horses coming off in about ten days; if you rest him and feed him up, he may pick up, and you may get more than his skin is worth, at any rate."

Upon this advice Skinner, rather unwillingly I think, gave orders that I should be well fed and cared for, and the stable man, happily for me, carried out the orders with a much better will than his master had in giving them. Ten days of perfect rest, plenty of good oats, hay, bran mashes, with boiled linseed mixed in them, did more to get up my condition than anything else could have done; those linseed mashes were delicious, and I began to think, after all, it might be better to live than go to the dogs. When the twelfth day after the accident came, I was taken to the sale, a few miles out of London. I felt that any change from my present place must be an improvement, so I held up my head, and hoped for the best.

48

Farmer Thoroughgood and His Grandson Willie

AT THIS SALE, of course, I found myself in company with the old broken-down horses—some lame, some broken-winded, some old, and some that I am sure it would have been merciful to shoot.

The buyers and sellers too, many of them, looked not much better off than the poor beasts they were bargaining about. There were poor old men, trying to get a horse or a pony for a few pounds, that might drag about some little wood or coal cart. There were poor men trying to sell a worn-out beast for two or three pounds, rather than have the greater loss of killing him. Some of them looked as if poverty and hard times had hardened them all over; but there were others that I would have willingly used the last of my strength in serving; poor and shabby, but kind and human, with voices that I could trust. There was one tottering old man who took a great fancy to me, and I to him, but I was not strong enough—it was an anxious time! Coming from the better part of the fair,

I noticed a man who looked like a gentleman farmer, with a young boy by his side; he had a broad back and round shoulders, a kind, ruddy face, and he wore a broad-brimmed hat. When he came up to me and my companions he stood still and gave a pitiful look round upon us. I saw his eye rest on me; I had still a good mane and tail, which did something for my appearance. I pricked my ears and looked at him.

"There's a horse, Willie, that has known better days."

"Poor old fellow!" said the boy. "Do you think, grandpapa, he was ever a carriage horse?"

"Oh, yes, my boy," said the farmer, coming closer, "he might have been anything when he was young; look at his nostrils and his ears, the shape of his neck and shoulder; there's a deal of breeding about that horse." He put out his hand and gave me a kind pat on the neck. I put out my nose in answer to his kindness; the boy stroked my face.

"Poor old fellow! See, grandpapa, how well he understands kindness. Could not you buy him and make him young again, as you did with Ladybird?"

"My dear boy, I can't make all old horses young; besides, Ladybird was not so very old, as she was run down and badly used."

"Well, grandpapa, I don't believe that this one is

old; look at his mane and tail. I wish you would look into his mouth, and then you could tell; though he is so very thin, his eyes are not sunk like some old horses."

The old gentleman laughed. "Bless the boy! He is as horsey as his old grandfather."

"But do look at his mouth, grandpapa, and ask the price; I am sure he would grow young in our meadows."

The man who had brought me for sale now put in his word.

"The young gentleman's a real knowing one, sir. Now the fact is, this 'ere hoss is just pulled down with overwork in the cabs; he's not an old one, and I heerd as how the vetenary should say, that a six months' run-off would set him right up, being as how his wind was not broken. I've had the tending of him these ten days past, and a gratefuller, pleasanter animal I never met with, and 'twould be worth a gentleman's while to give a five-pound note for him, and let him have a chance. I'll be bound he'd be worth twenty pounds next spring."

The old gentleman laughed, and the little boy looked up eagerly.

"Oh, grandpapa, did you not say the colt sold for five pounds more than you expected? You would not be poorer if you did buy this one."

The farmer slowly felt my legs, which were much swelled and strained; then he looked at my mouth. "Thirteen or fourteen, I should say; just trot him out, will you?"

I arched my poor thin neck, raised my tail a little, and threw out my legs as well as I could, for they were very stiff.

"What is the lowest you will take for him?" said the farmer as I came back.

"Five pounds, sir; that was the lowest price my master set."

"'Tis a speculation," said the old gentleman, shaking his head, but at the same time slowly drawing out his purse, "quite a speculation! Have you any more business here?" he said, counting the sovereigns into his hand.

"No, sir, I can take him for you to the inn, if you please."

"Do so, I am now going there."

They walked forward, and I was led behind. The boy could hardly control his delight, and the old gentleman seemed to enjoy his pleasure. I had a good feed at the inn, and was then gently ridden home by a servant of my new master's and turned into a large meadow with a shed in one corner of it.

Mr. Thoroughgood, for that was the name of my benefactor, gave orders that I should have hay and oats every night and morning, and the run of the meadow during the day, and, "You, Willie," said he, "must take the oversight of him; I give him in charge to you."

The boy was proud of his charge, and undertook it in all seriousness. There was not a day when he did not pay me a visit; sometimes picking me out from among the other horses, and giving me a bit of carrot, or something good, or sometimes standing by me while I ate my oats. He always came with kind words and caresses, and of course I grew very fond of him. He called me Old Crony, as I used to come to him in the field and follow him about. Sometimes he brought his grandfather, who always looked closely at my legs.

"This is our point, Willie," he would say; "but he is improving so steadily that I think we shall see a change for the better in the spring."

The perfect rest, the good food, the soft turf, and gentle exercise, soon began to tell on my condition and my spirits. I had a good constitution from my mother, and I was never strained when I was young, so that I had a better chance than many horses who have been worked before they came to their full strength. During the winter my legs improved so much that I began to feel quite young again. The spring came round, and one day in March Mr. Thoroughgood determined that he would try me in the phaeton. I was well pleased, and he and Willie drove me a few miles. My legs were not stiff now, and I did the work with perfect ease.

"He's growing young, Willie; we must give him a little gentle work now, and by midsummer he will be as good as Ladybird. He has a beautiful mouth and good paces; they can't be better."

"Oh, grandpapa, how glad I am you bought him!"

"So am I, my boy, but he has to thank you more than me; we must now be looking out for a quiet, genteel place for him, where he will be valued."

49

My Last Home

ONE DAY DURING this summer the groom cleaned and dressed me with such extraordinary care that I thought some new change must be at hand; he trimmed my fetlocks and legs, passed the tarbrush over my hoofs, and even parted my forelock. I think the harness had an extra polish. Willie seemed half anxious, half merry, as he got into the chaise with his grandfather.

"If the ladies take to him," said the old gentleman, "they'll be suited and he'll be suited. We can but try."

At the distance of a mile or two from the village we came to a pretty, low house, with a lawn and shrubbery at the front, and a drive up to the door. Willie rang the bell, and asked if Miss Blomefield or Miss Ellen was at home. Yes, they were. So, while Willie stayed with me, Mr. Thoroughgood went into the house. In about ten minutes he returned, followed by three ladies; one tall, pale lady, wrapped in a white shawl, leaned on a younger lady, with dark eyes and a merry face; the other, a very stately-looking person, was Miss Blomefield. They all came and looked at me and asked questions. The younger lady—that was Miss Ellen—took to me very much; she said she was sure she should like me, I had such a good face. The tall, pale lady said that she should always be nervous in riding behind a horse that had once been down, as I might come down again, and if I did, she should never get over the fright.

"You see, ladies," said Mr. Thoroughgood, "many first-rate horses have had their knees broken through the carelessness of their drivers, without any fault of their own, and from what I see of this horse I should say that is his case; but of course I do not wish to influence you. If you incline, you can have him on trial, and then your coachman will see what he thinks of him."

"You have always been such a good adviser to us about our horses," said the stately lady, "that your recommendation would go a long way with me, and if my sister Lavinia sees no objection, we will accept your offer of a trial, with thanks."

It was then arranged that I should be sent for the next day.

In the morning a smart-looking young man came for me. At first he looked pleased, but when he saw my knees, he said in a disappointed voice:

"I didn't think, sir, you would have recommended my ladies a blemished horse like that."

"Handsome is that handsome does," said my master; "you are only taking him on trial, and I am sure you will do fairly by him, young man, and if he is not as safe as any horse you ever drove, send him back."

I was led home, placed in a comfortable stable, fed, and left to myself. The next day, when my groom was cleaning my face, he said:

"That is just like the star that Black Beauty had; he is much the same height, too. I wonder where he is now."

A little further on he came to the place in my neck where I was bled, and where a little knot was left in the skin. He almost started, and began to look me over carefully, talking to himself.

"White star in the forehead, one white foot on the off side, this little knot just in that place"— then looking at the middle of my back—"and as I am alive, there is that little patch of white hair that John used to call 'Beauty's three penny bit.' It *must* be Black Beauty! Why, Beauty! Beauty! Do you know me? Little Joe Green, that almost killed you?" And he began patting and patting me as if he was quite overjoyed.

I could not say that I remembered him, for now he was a fine-grown young fellow, with black whiskers and a man's voice, but I was sure he knew me, and that he was Joe Green, and I was very glad. I put my nose up to him, and tried to say that we were friends. I never saw a man so pleased.

"Give you a fair trial! I should think so indeed! I wonder who the rascal was that broke your knees, my old Beauty! You must have been badly served out somewhere; well, well, it won't be my fault if you haven't good times of it now. I wish John Manly was here to see you."

In the afternoon I was put into a low park chair and brought to the door. Miss Ellen was going to try me, and Green went with her. I soon found that she was a good driver, and she seemed pleased with my paces. I heard Joe telling her about me, and that he was sure I was Squire Gordon's old Black Beauty.

When we returned the other sisters came out to hear how I had behaved myself. She told them what she had just heard, and said:

"I shall certainly write to Mrs. Gordon, and tell her that her favorite horse has come to us. How pleased she will be!"

After this I was driven every day for a week or

so, and as I appeared to be quite safe, Miss Lavinia at last ventured out in the small close carriage. After this it was quite decided to keep me and call me by my old name of "Black Beauty."

I have now lived in this happy place a whole year. Joe is the best and kindest of grooms. My work is easy and pleasant, and I feel my strength and spirits all coming back again. Mr. Thoroughgood said to Joe the other day:

"In your place he will last till he is twenty years old—perhaps more."

Willie always speaks to me when he can, and treats me as his special friend. My ladies have promised that I shall never be sold, and so I have nothing to fear; and here my story ends. My troubles are all over, and I am at home; and often before I am quite awake, I fancy I am still in the orchard at Birtwick, standing with my old friends under the apple trees.

$\mathcal{M}$Y CALM SURPRISED ME. I had just come from my mother's funeral. How could I be doing this? John Gale came to the barn door. I gave him the two buckets, took the saddle and halter, and followed him to the wagon, wondering: What happened to Belle's harness? Did anyone take it off her, or was it not worth saving?

The colt stood at the gate, leaning so hard that the top bar made a cracking sound. He barely noticed me putting on the halter; all his attention was for the other horses. When I let down the bars, he jumped over them, almost pulling me off my feet.

"Whoa!" I couldn't stop him. He circled me, his head turned toward the horses. I meant no more to him than a post. "Whoa!" I cried. My voice came high and shrill. He would know—everyone would know—that I was afraid. ☞

Awards for

UNBROKEN

Publishers Weekly Best Book

Parents' Choice Gold Award

Notable Children's Trade Books in Social Studies
(NCSS / CBC)

Unbroken

ᖇ JESSIE HAAS ᖆ

A Greenwillow Book
HarperTrophy®
An Imprint of HarperCollins*Publishers*

AUTHOR'S NOTE

This story was inspired by the real-life story of Helen Watts Chase, who was orphaned under different circumstances in 1889. Like Harry, Helen had lived with an indulgent mother and was left to the care of an aunt with different ideas about raising children. Her story is included in *Roxana's Children: The Biography of a Nineteenth-Century Vermont Family*, by Lynn A. Bonfield and Mary C. Morrison, published in 1995 by the University of Massachusetts Press.

Harry is not Helen but came into existence because of her.

Harper Trophy® is a registered trademark of HarperCollins Publishers Inc.

Unbroken

Copyright © 1999 by Jessie Haas

All rights reserved. No part of this book may be used or reproduced in any manner whatsoever without written permission except in the case of brief quotations embodied in critical articles and reviews. Printed in the United States of America. For information address HarperCollins Children's Books, a division of HarperCollins Publishers, 1350 Avenue of the Americas, New York, NY 10019.

Library of Congress Cataloging-in-Publication Data

Haas, Jessie.

Unbroken / by Jessie Haas.

p.   cm.

"Greenwillow Books."

Summary: Following her mother's death in the early 1900s, thirteen-year-old Harry lives on Aunt Sarah's farm, where an accident with her spirited colt leaves her a changed young woman.

ISBN 0-688-16260-6 — ISBN 0-380-73313-7 (pbk.)

[1. Death—Fiction. 2. Grief—Fiction. 3. Orphans—Fiction. 4. Aunts—Fiction. 5. Mothers and daughters—Fiction. 6. Horses—Fiction.] I. Title.

PZ7.H1129 Wc   1999   98-10485

[Fic]—dc21   CIP

                                                                                 AC

First Harper Trophy edition, 2001

❖

Visit us on the World Wide Web!

www.harperchildrens.com

For Michael

One

OUR PENCILS SCRATCHED STEADILY. Every head was bowed, but we watched Miss Spencer and Reverend Astley from under our hands or hair.

He spoke close to her ear, and the welcoming smile went stiff on her face, then vanished as she glanced our way. Behind me Luke drew a faint hissing breath. Trouble for someone.

I wondered for whom, watched my hand scrolling out an elegant line of script across the page, so regular and well formed that I barely recognized it for my own, glanced out the high window, through which the sun streamed—

"Harriet Gibson."

My pencil clattered on the floor. Miss Spencer's face, full of compassion, was turned toward me. My heart squeezed.

"Bring your things, dear," she said.

Luke's breath hissed again, and I felt her fingers

touch my back. With numb hands I scrambled my books and papers into a pile and rose with them in my arms. Billy Booth gave me the pencil, with a sympathetic grimace. Then I was up the aisle, being ushered out of the room by Reverend Astley, and the thick oak door shut behind us.

"I won't keep you in suspense," he said, turning to face me the moment we were alone. "Your mother has been injured in an accident, and you must come home at once."

He took the books. His hand on my upper arm hurried me along the corridor as the clock struck the half hour. Nine-thirty in the morning—

"Is she—"

"Her condition is serious, but the doctor is hopeful." He opened the door for me. At the bottom of the stairs his buggy waited. He handed me up, climbed in himself, and turned the roan horse.

"What—what's wrong with her? What happened?"

Reverend Astley seemed to hesitate for a moment. "I don't know the details," he said finally. "An automobile was involved, and the horse took fright. Your mother was on her way back from bringing you to school, I understand."

A lump began to grow in my throat. We were late this morning. I'd jumped down over the wheel and run up the Academy steps without glancing back. Just "Bye!" over my shoulder, and the sound of Belle's hooves as Mother turned her.

Oh, please let her be all right. Please.

Barrett village blurred past, and we were out on the road, climbing between fields and pastures toward West Barrett.

Please.

"Don't look," the reverend said suddenly. "Close your eyes!"

Too late. There ahead of us was the buggy, shattered like a shot crow: broken shafts, broken axle, splintered top. It looked too fragile ever to have carried the two of us.

Farther along the sun gleamed on a motionless sorrel mound. Belle. I saw her white foot curled up toward her belly, as if ready for one last kick. The roan horse pricked his ears, and his steady trot faltered, but Reverend Astley touched him with the whip, and he clopped on.

A moment later we rounded the corner and saw West Barrett, small and high above us, just a straggling line of gray houses clinging to the hillside. Our house, smallest and grayest, leaned slightly toward the sawmill next door, as if it had gone deaf and were straining to hear what the saw was saying.

The bright moving spot behind the house was the colt, trotting back and forth. His neighs reached us even down here. Two years old, but he cried for Belle every time she left him. The sunlight suddenly glittered more brightly as my eyes filled with tears. Every morning and afternoon the hollow rang like this, and once or twice a week Mother said, "Thank goodness for that mill! At least we're not causing the only racket!"

The smell of sweat came back from the roan, and the fresh, wild scent of pine sawdust came, too, sinking down from the mill. Smoke rose from our chimney. Dr. Vesper's buggy stood in the yard. We pulled in beside it, and I leaped over the turning wheel and fell on my knees in the dirt. "Harriet!" Reverend Astley cried sharply, but I was already running up the steps.

The kitchen and sitting room were empty. I rushed through, toward the back bedroom and the sound of voices. Dr. Vesper's broad black waistcoat blocked the doorway. "Please," I said. He stepped to one side, and I stopped.

She didn't look like herself. She was as pale as the pillowcase, with a big red bruise on her forehead. Her eyes were closed, the lids bluish, and the room was very quiet.

I stepped softly toward the bed, looking at the quilt. Yes, it rose and fell. Yes, she was breathing.

After a moment she whispered, "Hello, Harry." Her eyes struggled to open. Her mouth formed a tiny curve, like a smile. "I made a mistake."

Her hands were under the quilt. I dropped to my knees beside the bed and touched her shoulder. "Oh, Mummy!"

The sound of tears was in my voice, and I heard a *tsk* from the other side of the bed. I looked up. Our neighbor Mrs. Brand sat there, in a flour-dusted apron. She shook her head. "Don't worry her."

At that Mother's eyes opened, smoothly and swiftly. She stared at the ceiling for a moment, unfocused.

Then slowly her eyes turned toward me. Only her eyes. All the rest of her was still. But a faint color touched her cheeks for a second. "You don't worry me," she said clearly, and under the quilt I saw her hand move.

Mrs. Brand looked up at Dr. Vesper. Then she reached across Mother and gently drew the quilt aside.

Mother's trembling fingers stretched up. I took them in my hand, and at their touch a chill struck inward at my stomach. She shouldn't be this cold!

Her eyes closed again. Through the window came the scream of the mill saw, the scream of the colt. "Poor Belle," Mother whispered. Then she seemed to be done talking. I didn't know if she was conscious anymore.

Behind me in the sitting room Dr. Vesper said, "No, I can't move her, not down this godforsaken hill!"

"I don't think this hill is quite God-forsaken," Reverend Astley said in a prim voice. On the other side of the bed Althea Brand stiffened and frowned.

"Oh, Judas, look at the time!" Dr. Vesper said. "I was sent for up-country!" He came in and leaned over me. His thick, wrinkled hand was beside mine, feeling Mother's pulse. Her eyelids didn't flicker.

"You'll stay, Althea, won't you?" he asked.

Mrs. Brand looked hard at him, as if trying to understand something. Then she nodded. "Yes, but I'm worried about my house. Harriet, run down quick and see if I left the kettle on. And look through and find that cat, won't you, and put her out?"

"But—" I was holding Mother's hand.

"Go on, Harry," Dr. Vesper said, giving my shoulder a squeeze. "You're young and quick. It'll just take a minute."

I couldn't say no. He was almost one of the family. But Reverend Astley could have offered! He could have let me stay. I brushed past him without excusing myself and hurried down the front steps, startling the horses.

Mrs. Brand's house was three doors down. I ran, past the windows with the white gauze curtains, past the faces. Into Mrs. Brand's house, the only other house in West Barrett with which I was familiar. We had lived here for eleven years, since I was two, and we smiled and spoke to everyone. But we were never invited past the kitchen. Althea Brand had set her back up against the other four ladies of the village and so made a point of not disapproving of us.

Of course the kettle was not on the burner, and the cat wasn't in the house either. I had scrambled through half the rooms and almost upset a lamp when I noticed her down in the little back garden, hunting. I banged out the door again and ran up the hill, feeling the drag of its steepness. Past our small field. The colt pushed against the gate, calling to me. I hurried past him and up the steps. If I got back quickly, I might hear what they were saying.

But as I came in, Dr. Vesper was laying Mother's hand back on her stomach and drawing the quilt up to her chin. "I will," he said, in a serious, reassuring voice. Turning, he drew me out to the sitting room.

"Now, Harry, I've got to go. Althea knows what to

do, and I'll be back just as quick as God'll let me."

"Is she—" I couldn't finish the question. No one had told me anything. Mother and I were all each other had, and no one would tell me anything, not even Dr. Vesper, who looked hard at me for a moment, as if considering it, but who just said, "Do what Althea tells you, and help her all you can. You're a good girl, Harry. Be brave!" He chucked me under the chin and hurried out the door.

"I must leave also," Reverend Astley said, taking my hand. "I'll pray for your mother's recovery."

My hand was stiff and unresponsive in his. Could he feel how much I disliked him? "Yes," I managed to say. "Thank you."

Then the sitting room was empty, the two buggies rattled away, and I was left with Mother and Althea Brand, the screaming mill saw, and the screaming colt.

Two

"WHY DON'T YOU GO CHANGE your clothes?" Mrs. Brand said when I came back into the room.

Mother's face was set like a mask. After a moment I saw her swallow.

"Water? Mummy, do you want a drink?"

No, her lips said soundlessly. I looked across the bed at Althea Brand. She sat straight in the hard chair, watching Mother's face with bright, steady eyes. She would do everything. It was all right to leave for a minute.

My schoolbooks were piled on the sitting-room table. Beside them was a pair of deerskin gloves that I didn't recognize—nothing special, just medium-nice gloves spattered with dark drops of something. The sun streamed across Mother's sewing machine. The dress she'd been hoping to finish by afternoon and to deliver when she picked me up from school lay as she had left it.

The clock ticked. A dying ember hissed in the kitchen stove. Slowly, making as little sound as possible, I climbed the narrow stairs to my bedroom.

It was the largest room in the house, at floor level, but the walls sloped sharply inward and ended in a strip of ceiling two feet wide. Light came in the gable ends, and the middle was shadowed. I walked over to look out the south window.

I was above the swallows here. I could look down on their backs. The land fell away sharply behind the houses, fifteen feet down to a narrow shelf of flat land, and then down again to the river. "If you ever get to the big city," Mother said to me once, "you won't feel like a rube. You've already lived in a skyscraper!"

I turned from the window and sat to unlace my boots. My fingers were shaking. I crushed them together in my lap and folded my body over them.

Don't cry. Don't. Crying makes it real. I clenched my teeth and threw my head back. "Don't let it know you're afraid," Mother always said of growling dogs and high-strung horses. I hugged myself hard, straining every muscle to a feeling of strength. But when I bent to the bootlaces again, my fingers still shook.

I slipped out of my school skirt and blouse and into the new calico dress Mother had just made me. We liked brighter calico than the West Barrett ladies. It was one more thing against us.

I started down the stairs, and halfway my feet just stopped. Pebbly silver wallpaper with green flecks, light above in the bedroom and light below in the kitchen, and I was suspended between, like a moth in a spider's web. I didn't know how I felt or how I was supposed to feel. Hope, or fierce prayer, or despair: if I chose one, I was settling things, and I didn't know how things really stood. Mother would have told me with one swift glance, but Mother's eyes were closed.

When they don't tell you, it's usually bad.

I found I was hugging myself again, leaning stiffly forward. Stop. Down one step, down the next, and into the kitchen, which smelled of warm tomato plants. The kitchen, with its geraniums and seedlings in the windows, its bright mats and the green china teapot, was Mother. The whole house was Mother, and it seemed to embrace me. I drew an easier breath and walked through the sitting room to her bedside.

There we sat through the morning. Mother's face looked troubled sometimes. A frown came between her brows and gradually smoothed away. But she never opened her eyes, and she never spoke.

The mill saw stopped. Noon. In the greater silence I could hear my stomach growl. Mrs. Brand must be hungry, too. "Would you like bread and jam? And tea?"

She nodded, and I went away to fix lunch. I was hungry, but when I took the first bite of bread, spread with blackberry jam we made last fall, I couldn't seem to chew it. I forced it down in a dry lump that hurt my throat and followed it with a swallow of too-hot tea. Althea Brand ate her slice of bread and drank her tea, never turning her gaze from Mother's face.

The saw started up. The sound seemed to waken

the colt's despair. He screamed again and again. There was no sign that his cries disturbed Mother. Her eyelids didn't flicker. But over the next two hours Althea Brand began to jerk in her chair at every neigh.

"Can you shut him up somehow?"

I couldn't. He wanted Belle, who lay dead beside the road. Would someone bury her, or would she be dragged away to rot in the back corner of a field? Pretty Belle. Without even closing my eyes I could see the exact outline of the white snip on her nose, how at its edges the white seemed to overlap the chestnut of her face like a smear of paint.

Mother drew a deep, long breath. We looked. A long pause followed, and then another breath came.

Althea Brand's eyes seemed to grow and darken. Her mouth got smaller. She stared intently into Mother's face. Then she reached across the bed and twitched the quilt back. "Take her hand!"

She pushed back the quilt on her own side, took Mother's other hand, and leaned forward so their faces were close. "Ellen!" she said sharply. "Ellen! You hold on now! You think of this child!"

Mother's hand was freezing, and the cold seemed to spread up my arm into my chest and throat. I couldn't speak.

Mrs. Brand leaned closer. "Ellen, don't you give in! What will become of Harriet if you give in like this?"

The slow, deep breaths went on, with terrible pauses between. Mrs. Brand began to chafe the back of Mother's hand, so hard it made a rasping sound.

"*Harriet!* Say something! Call her back!"

I opened my mouth, but only a whimper came out. "Muh!"

Mother's eyes opened, in the swift way she had whenever I was threatened. She was *there*. Her eyes glowed in her white mask of a face, and she turned and smiled at me tenderly. I felt tears on my cheeks.

Then she bit her lip and shook her head slightly, still smiling. "I can't." Just a whisper. "You'll be fine, Harry. I know."

"Mummy."

Very near the house and as loudly as he could, the colt neighed, as if trying to slam his voice into Belle and force her back to him.

"Be careful," Mother whispered. "And—" She paused, smiled and grimaced, as if at some small, amusing impediment, and shook her head again. "Andy will tell you— Yes, I'm coming!" She seemed to answer the colt. "Just a minute. Harry—" Her hand tightened slightly on mine. "Love . . . yes," she whispered. "Yes."

She smiled past me; her breath sighed out; the clock in the sitting room ticked, ticked. A longer pause, but the next breath would come. There! Trembling. Wasn't it?

Althea Brand's hand reached to Mother's face, tenderly touched her eyelids, and smoothed them shut. The breath was hers. She was crying.

I looked across at her, and she shook her head at me. "Harriet. Harriet."

My face seemed to be smiling. I didn't know what to do about it.

"You'll want to be alone with her." Mrs. Brand went past the end of the bed, fumbling in her sleeve for her handkerchief. I heard her in the kitchen, blowing her nose.

Mother lay smiling on the pillow, a little color in her cheeks. She looked as she had this morning. I would just bend over and whisper in her ear, and she'd wake up.

I bent, and something seemed to catch me, as if a sharp, hot stake had been driven through my body. Don't do that. Don't. Stay here, hold her hand, see her smile in the sunlight, while the sweet scent of mock orange hangs in the air.

I remember that Dr. Vesper came back at some point and led me from the room, made me drink some blackberry cordial.

I remember I was cold. Very cold. Not even Mother's thick wool shawl could warm me.

I remember them talking. They said Althea Brand would take me to her house. But when she wanted to, I shook my head. I couldn't really see anything. I didn't look at her. I shook my head, and they didn't make me.

"—lay her out in?" They wanted me to choose a dress. Her pretty green print. That was her favorite dress. Did I tell them that? The colt screamed and screamed, and Dr. Vesper said, "Somebody should shoot that son of a bitch!"

I could see him for a moment. He stood at the sitting-room window. He was crying. "No," I said.

"No," he said. "Oh, damn it all, Harry."

I didn't cry until I went upstairs, and I was alone, and I would always be alone. I used to feel a strong line from Mother's heart to mine whenever I saw her, and love moved along it like a telegraph signal. Now the line was cut.

I cried quietly until I couldn't be quiet anymore, and then I cried out loud. Mrs. Brand came up and rubbed my back for a while and went away again.

Dark came. I would never sleep again. My eyes were open, and the dark pressed against them.

> *She was driving out of our dooryard. I could see the whitewashed rocks and the pansies. She was driving Belle.*
>
> *I stood up. "But you're dead!"*
>
> *Belle stopped, and Mother reached down to me. I took her hand, and she squeezed mine. We looked into each other's faces. The sun shone around us, and I could feel the line, I could feel the love. Some of Mother's side hair was loose, and the sun caught the tendrils.*
>
> *Belle stamped. Mother smiled, drew her hand away, and shook the reins over Belle's back. I turned and watched them go down the hill. My heart was light and free and happy.*

My eyes opened against the dark. Happy. I didn't think I would ever feel happy again.

They *are* dead.

But they're all right. She was letting me know. She was telling me. It was clearer than a dream, and realer than a dream, because I knew all the time that they were dead. I *said* they were dead. It wasn't just a wish because if I'd had my wish, she wouldn't have driven away.

I wanted to get up and tell someone. They came. They're all right.

Outside in the dark all was quiet. No neighing. Maybe the colt had seen them, too.

Three

$\mathcal{I}$ AWOKE IN SUNSHINE. Swallows dived past the window, and the mill saw was singing.

I sat up under the sloped ceiling, with a heavy head and aching eyes. A stripe of cold ran down my back. My arms and legs had a cringing feel to them, as if they wanted to curl up tight.

But my heart felt clear and as open as the window. I could see her so precisely, in her bright calico dress just like the one I wore now. I could feel the press of her hand. It was real, not a dream. She had come back to tell me she was all right.

The shawl was still wound around me. I unwrapped it and walked to the window. Far below, the colt grazed intently, as if making up for lost time—snatch snatch snatch. The sunlight made a streak over his round back, sliding as he moved. Below him the willow branches stirred, the little river sparkled and splashed.

Mother loved this view. She must be out there

somewhere, folded invisibly into the air.

I turned, spreading my arms as if to catch something. Nothing stopped them, though, and the sunlight dazzled my eyes. I was desperately thirsty. A cup of tea . . .

When I came down to the kitchen, Dr. Vesper sat at the table. For a second my mind seemed to disconnect. Was she better? Was she only sick now, not dead?

He looked up wearily. "Morning, Harry. Tea?" The pot stood on the table. There was the smell of biscuits on the air and a plate with crumbs and jam in front of him.

I sat down. He poured out tea for me, then got up to take the biscuits out of the warming oven. He was making a guest of me in my own home. Around the happy freedom in my heart something seemed to tighten.

"Althy went home for a minute," Dr. Vesper said. His voice seemed deeper than usual, rasping and slow. It was made that way by sorrow. I wanted to tell him, "I saw Mother last night."

But he went on. "I need to tell you some things, Harry, and I have to be quick. Somebody needs me."

I sipped the tea. Too strong. We like it light, so the perfume comes through, and not the bitterness. This tea seemed to bite the back of my mouth.

"I'm the executor of your mother's estate," Dr. Vesper said. "You need to know how things are left, Harry."

How things are left? I could think only of the

closed door beyond the sitting room, the dimness and stillness that seemed to spread from there.

"You're to go to your aunt Sarah," he said.

"*What?*" Aunt Sarah hated us. She was my father's sister, and I'd seen her only a few times in my life.

"It's what your mother wanted. She said it to me, and she set it down in her will. 'Sarah's ways aren't my ways,' she said to me, 'but she'll be good to Walter's child.'"

"*When?* When did she say that? She didn't say it to *me!*" How could she not have said it to me? How could she have wasted precious moments of breath on *them*— Mrs. Brand, Dr. Vesper—while I was sent away?

Dr. Vesper looked straight at me. His eyes were bloodshot and red around the rims. "There's no reason not to tell you now," he said. "Your mother never expected to live to see you grown."

Around my head the air seemed to hum. "Why?"

"She had a bad heart, Harry. She didn't have much time left." He stopped abruptly and looked down.

"But why—" I couldn't even whisper. My throat squeezed shut.

"Your mother was . . ." His voice went down too deep. He paused and took a breath. "She said to me, 'Harry and I are going to be happy while we can. When we have to be sad, we'll be darned good and sad, but right now we'll be happy.' But she made her plans, too, and you're to go to Sarah."

"I can't stay here?"

He didn't hear it as a question. "That's all right," he

said in a reassuring voice. "The house will have to be sold anyway. I'll take care of that, and pay the debts, and anything left I'll put in the bank for you."

Sold? Our house? But she was *here*. This was where I saw her, driving past our white rocks. *Here*.

"Can you write Sarah a note, Harry?" Dr. Vesper was asking. "I'll stop by the farm this morning and tell her everything, but a little something from you might help things along."

I stood up numbly and walked to Mother's desk in the sitting room. With my back to the bedroom door, I took out the paper, opened the ink bottle, and wrote:

> *May 27, 1910*
> *West Barrett, Vermont*
>
> *Dear Aunt Sarah,*
> *Mother died about four o'clock yesterday afternoon. She left me to you.*
> *Dr. Vesper will bring this letter and explain.*
> *Your—*

Your what? The pen stopped, making a blot. Your . . .

> *Your affectionate Niece,*
> *Harriet Gibson*

Dr. Vesper came in behind me. I folded the note and gave it to him.

"Harry," he said, stopped, and cleared his throat. "Harry, just so you know, I'm named in the will if

🎗 19 🎗

something happens. Sarah isn't the only one you have. I'm named, too."

Then the kitchen door opened. Mrs. Brand was back, and Dr. Vesper, with a harried glance at the clock, departed.

"Do you want to sit with her?" Mrs. Brand asked.

Sit with her? Oh. Go in and sit beside her body. "No." I closed my eyes. "No. I . . . have to go back upstairs."

"Did you eat anything? Have some tea."

I shook my head and went past her. My heart felt swollen and heavy, and my head was heavy, and my throat had closed tight.

In my room I stood still. The sunlight reached toward me across the bare floor. Through the screen I could hear the swallows chortle to one another.

A bad heart?

Sold?

The air seemed thick, impossible to push through.

Debts? What debts did we have?

We. I always said "we." *We* always said "we," but part of her was *I*, and grown up, and keeping secrets. Debts, and a bad heart.

But she sent me to the Academy. How did she pay for that?

She drove me there and back every day.

She didn't have much time left.

My thick, heavy feet moved me toward the window. The bright grass. The sparkling river. The willows tossing and the swallows diving for flies . . .

It will have to be sold.

Mother and I made our own little world. What I wished and what I thought, my talents and my grades at school, mattered more to her than anything.

Without her I was no one. I must do what her words on a piece of paper told me. I must do whatever any adult told me. I couldn't even stay here, in the world we had made together. The house was her, the house was us, and it would have to be sold.

My hands seemed to rise by themselves, independent of my arms or will. My wrists felt numb and tingled, but above them, disconnected, my hands were strong. My fingers spread wide and pushed slowly into the screen, each fingertip making a separate indentation. With a *pop* and a *scritch* the thin, rusted wires began to separate and then to break.

I looked down on the bottle blue backs of the swallows. Down, down, on the bright green grass. Down, to the bottom of my skyscraper.

Folded invisibly into the air.

The saw blade paused for breath, and in the little silence I heard hoofbeats. My fingers jumped back, and broken wire stabbed them.

Up from the river the colt came galloping. His head was high, his nostrils wide, his ears flat back. He swept in a wide loop around the pasture, then stopped at the very edge where the land dropped down to the river and gazed out over the tops of the willows.

Playing. All by himself.

His head turned. He looked toward the pasture gate, thinking of his mother. He was just her color, bright chestnut. Beautiful. "Keeping a horse just to drive that girl to school is bad enough," the West Barrett ladies used to say, "but a useless colt into the bargain?" When I overheard that, I told Mother, and we laughed.

"Harry and I are going to be happy. . . ."

Tears were running down my face. "I just wanted to *ask* you," I said, into the glittering, empty air.

No answer came. She wasn't ever going to answer my questions again, and I was stuck here. I had been going to jump, and now I wouldn't, because of the bright running colt, and my fingers were stuck in the screen. The broken wires stabbed into them like porcupine quills.

A tearing sob burst out of me, another, another. The colt stared up at the high window, and shied, and ran. And up the stairs two at a time came Althea Brand. She burst into the room and cried, "Oh, good Lord in heaven!"

I looked over my shoulder to see her standing back a little, one hand up to her mouth.

"I'm *stuck!*"

She looked behind her and then came forward slowly, as if I were dangerous. I felt my hot face streaming with tears, my hot, throbbing fingers, but inside, a cold little shock. This is too much. This is more than she can do.

The tears stopped coming, all by themselves. I

sniffed hard and saw her wince.

"I'm sorry. Could—could you wipe my face?"

She came closer, fishing in her sleeve, then drew out a dampish handkerchief and mopped my eyes and nose. When that was done, she looked at my hands, and her normal expression of practical competence began to reappear. "Will the sewing shears cut that screen, do you think?"

"I think so."

"Then—" She started to turn, then stopped and looked hard at me. I looked back at her, knowing I must not be a reassuring sight. But I felt a hardness inside that was like her hardness, stiffening me all up the center.

"I will not jump out the window," I said.

She nodded once, as if that settled that, and went away.

I pushed my fingers forward to keep the screen from stabbing deeper. I watched the colt graze, listened to Althea's quick steps downstairs, feeling straight and quiet, suspended between one state and another.

You will have to be careful.

The thought presented itself that way, as if someone else were speaking. I belonged to no one. I must not ask too much and drive my friends away.

Althea snipped the screen away from my fingers and picked out the rusty, embedded fragments. "Come downstairs," she said, looking at the ten splayed rips in the screen as if the destruction pained her. I looked back at them as I followed her, ten spots of brightness,

23

where the sky and willow branches showed through clearly.

She sat me at the kitchen table, pumped a basin of cold water, and made me soak my fingers. "You stay put!" she said, darted down the road to her own house, and came back with an old pair of cotton gloves and a tin of ointment. She dried my fingers on a clean towel and began spreading the yellow, strong-smelling stuff over the cuts. On her left hand her two gold rings clicked together. The wide ring on her middle finger was grooved by the other, narrower one, which had rubbed against it for years.

"The wide one was her husband's ring," Mother told me once. "She's worn it since he died."

He died. Everyone must have died on Althea Brand, because she was alone, and she'd been alone as long as I had known her. Once, or twice, or many times she must have felt the way I did now.

I looked up at her face. It was paler than yesterday, holding something back. Maybe she was trying not to remember this feeling, or maybe it was always with her. Did it ever go away? Did you ever feel better? If you did feel better, maybe you hated yourself for that.

But I saw Mother. Last night I saw her.

Althea's yellowish old ear was near my face. Barely above a whisper I said, "I dreamed about her last night."

Althea looked up. Tears brimmed in her eyes, but a brilliant, wavering smile lit her face. "*Did* you? Then she's all right!"

I couldn't speak. I could only look.

"They come back to comfort us. That's what I believe."

"I woke up. I was so happy—" I clamped down to keep from crying.

"But you weren't fooled, were you? You *knew* she was gone. But she's all right. We can't understand it, but they *are* all right!"

Althea's face made me cry, she looked so happy, so reassured. As my tears started, she reached forward and gathered me into a hug, the first time ever. "You'll be all right, too, Harriet. I *promise!*"

I still couldn't eat. I made tea, our way, and sipped that.

"You've got to get something down you," Althea said. "I'll beg some milk from Julia Gould and make you a cornstarch pudding."

I shook my head. "She won't—"

"Oh, yes, she will!" Althea said. "She's dying for the news. She won't get it from me, but she won't care to miss the chance."

"*I* don't even know. What happened?"

Althea's eyes dimmed. "I don't rightly know, Harriet. A Model T came down this road, and I'd no more than watched it out of sight when back it came, and the reverend driving lickety-split behind it. Before I could get over here, the Model T man was off again after the doctor. Don't even know who he was."

"He left his gloves. On the sitting-room table."

"Andy Vesper will know," Althea said. "Now, this may take a few minutes. Will you be all right by yourself?"

She looked at me kindly. She thought I should go sit with Mother.

"I'll go check on the colt," I said.

The sun was high and warm on my head as I walked down the road, past the white rocks, through the heavy stream of scent from the mock orange bush. Those creamy four-cornered blossoms were Mother's favorite flower.

The colt came to the barway when he saw me there. He sniffed my pockets and hands. The lanolin smell beneath the gloves made him flip his lip in the air.

Then he sighed, looking off over my shoulder with a troubled expression. His muzzle pressed heavily into my palm. I could feel the teeth behind the velvet. His ears pricked toward the road, drooped back, and again twitched forward. His hope made tears run out of my eyes. More tears. I was so tired of crying.

I rested my forehead on his neck, feeling his animal warmth and the heat of the sun on his coat. He was all I had left.

My head came up so suddenly that the colt shied. *Did* I have him? Or was he among the possessions Dr. Vesper expected to sell?

I looked up at the house. It was full of our things—books, dishes, dresses and boots, and uncounted odds and ends. Was any of it mine?

I looked the colt over. He was in an awkward phase,

front and back halves growing at different rates. But he would be a good Morgan. The men who kept trying to buy him proved that.

"A horse is not an extravagance," Mother always said. "Without that mare I doubt you'd get an education."

Two horses *were* an extravagance, but we couldn't bear to part with him, and we were two people. "Someday we'll go our separate ways," Mother said, "or you can train him and sell him to pay for your college."

Now he was untrained. He couldn't take me anywhere, and he wouldn't bring in much money.

And if he wouldn't bring in much money, perhaps I would be allowed to keep him.

With stinging fingers, I broke off a branch of mock orange and carried it into the house. Althea Brand turned from the stove and made as if to move her pudding off the burner.

"No. I'll go in by myself."

The sitting room was quiet. Sunlight streamed in the window, and the sewing machine, silhouetted against it, looked like an animal grazing on the folds of fabric. Who would finish that dress? Was that one of our debts? *My* debts now.

I stood with my hand on the back of her chair. Here she sat every day, between my going to school and my returning. The pine-scented breeze coming through the screen was the air she used to breathe, while she bent over the fabric and pulled it through the machine, while her feet steadily rocked the treadle.

When I was little, I played beneath the machine or just sat there, tracing the iron lacework of legs and treadle with my fingers. Once a week I dusted the carved oak flowers and ribbons on the drawers. The sewing machine was our grandest piece of furniture and our most essential. Mother went to it late at night sometimes, saying, "I'm going to print us some money, Harry!" Sometimes I would go to sleep to the rock and thump of the treadle and that cough she got when she worked too hard.

If she had died of that cough, I would want to break up the sewing machine with an ax. I would want to kill myself, for my blindness and childishness.

But she didn't. I'll keep the sewing machine, I decided. She made our living with it. I should be able to make a living, too.

With that thought uppermost, I pushed open the bedroom door.

The hush stopped me. I could almost feel it on my face. Mother lay with her hands folded across the front of her green dress. Her face on the pillow looked like a wax carving, and not a good likeness either. The distant, reserved expression was all wrong.

I was surprised at how cool I felt. This wasn't Mother. This was what she'd left behind.

Her hands were like herself, though. There was the burn she got cooking last winter. Her wedding ring hung loosely on her finger. That hand was the one she'd reached to me last night. I remembered feeling the ring.

I stretched my eyes wide against the smarting tears.

Maybe she would come again tonight. If she didn't, that must be the last touch I remembered. I slid the branch between her hands, keeping it flexed so my fingers didn't even brush her dress. Then I laid my head beside hers on the pillow.

"Good night, Mother," I heard myself whisper. I went out to the kitchen before I could think about that.

Althea Brand stood at the stove, stirring briskly, while tears ran down her face. I didn't want to cry anymore. I stood back, hugging myself, and she didn't know I was there.

But when her tears began to drip and hiss on the stove top, it made me laugh. Then I couldn't help crying. We hugged each other, and that was still so strange it brought us around quickly. We spooned down warm cornstarch pudding and drank tea and waited for the doctor.

He came late in the afternoon, looking exhausted and in a hurry, sat down at the kitchen table, and handed me a folded piece of paper. "I'll leave you two to talk," Althea Brand said, slipping out the door.

I read.

Dear Harriet,
Of course you will have a home with us for as long as you need one. We will be down to the funeral. Please have your things ready as we must get back to milk.
I am very sorry.

Sincerely,
Sarah Hall

Dr. Vesper was looking skeptically at the cup of black tea Althea Brand had left him. Without raising his eyes, he asked, "What kind of letter did she send you, Harry?"

I gave it to him. He glanced over it, and his eyebrows jumped. "Well," he said, "guess that's all right then."

What in the letter had surprised him? What had Aunt Sarah said when he gave her the news? I didn't dare ask. I couldn't afford to hear anything that might make me hate her.

Instead I said, "I have to ask you some things."

At that moment he noticed my gloved hands. I looked down at them. The ointment had soaked through in dark, greasy patches.

He doesn't tell *me* everything, I thought, and folded my hands in my lap.

"What do you want to know, Harry?"

"Will you tell me what happened?"

He looked down again at his tea. "The horse bolted, and the buggy smashed, and . . . Sam came down from the mill and shot the mare. She had a broken leg."

"Mother said—she told me she'd made a mistake."

"I believe she did. It was John Gale in the car, big farmer from upriver. He said she tried to keep the mare on the road instead of turning off. He was coming down that hill standing on all three pedals, and he said to me, 'I could see her get her dander up, and she took hold of those reins,' and of course the jeestly thing backfired. If she'd just turned off . . . there was an open gate right there, she could have. . . ." His voice had been deepening, and now it squeezed off.

"He left his gloves," I said.

"John Gale? He's a good man, Harry. You'll see him tomorrow, I expect." He paused and cleared his throat. "The reverend been next or nigh you?"

"Not yet."

"He will be." Dr. Vesper took a wincing sip of tea. "Be civil, Harry."

My heart swelled, and my eyes prickled. It was so moving to be understood. I had to wait a moment before I could ask, "What did you mean, that you're named in her will?"

"I'm your mother's executor, and I'm partway your guardian. I'll be looking out for you."

"But—" My heart beat harder, but I made myself ask. "But I can't stay with you?"

He hesitated, glancing at me under his heavy brows. My stomach sank. Careful, I thought. Careful. Don't ask too much.

"You could for all of me, Harry," he said, "and the Old Lady agrees." The Old Lady was Mrs. Vesper. "But you do have family, and . . . there's lots of reasons to go to them. Your mother thought so. That's what she wrote in her will, and it's what she asked me to do on—yesterday."

"Oh. Then . . . what are the debts? Who do we owe money to? You can tell me," I said as he seemed to retreat. "I'm not a baby."

"That's right, Harry. I'll give you that." He thought

a moment. "I don't know the money amounts, but I believe it's the store in Barrett you owe, mostly, that and the Academy. And I should think the sale of the house would cover that. You'll come out free and clear and with a little bit left over."

"And when you sell the house—"

Dr. Vesper raised his head and looked straight across the table at me. "Yes?"

"What can I keep?"

He didn't answer right away. I could hear the hush. Did he think I was heartless, asking about *things* the day after my mother's death? *Was* I heartless?

"Harry," he said at last, "you've been thinking. What do you want to keep?"

"The sewing machine," I said. "The colt."

His eyes widened. He sat staring at me for a moment, and then he started to smile, sadly and wearily, but with a true sparkle in his eye. "Poor Sarah!" he said. "At most she'll expect you to bring a couple of carpetbags. I can't wait to see her face when you turn up with a big old sewing machine and an unbroken colt!"

Althea came back, and Reverend Astley arrived. How was I expecting to get my effects up to Sarah's farm, and did I really want the colt? And a sewing machine? A dress for the funeral, the time for the funeral, when the coffin was arriving, and how I would get down to Barrett. "And really, child, what *are* you going to do with that animal?"

The voices went on. My throat hurt, and my head ached. I felt as if I were thinning out somehow, getting ready to disappear.

Suddenly Dr. Vesper snapped his fingers. "Hey! John Gale was asking was there anything he could do for you. He'll bring your things up to Sarah's, and the colt, too, I should think."

That seemed to settle things. Soon the two men went away, and Althea and I were left alone. I was so tired I could hardly see her; she was just a blur across the kitchen table.

"We'll have some more tea," she said to me, "and then we'd better start packing."

Four

"Walter Gibson, 1873–1899. Ellen Gibson, 1877–"

Their names on the headstone steadied me. I stared at them, straining my eyes wide. I was alone now. Completely alone. She didn't come last night. Time was passing and carrying me away from her.

Many people had come to the graveside service. I couldn't look at them. Reverend Astley's words came through from time to time, though I tried not to listen.

"He maketh me to lie down in green pastures . . ."

I didn't want to cry. She was all right. She'd come back once to tell me. But though I clenched my teeth and squeezed my eyes shut, tears poured down my face. I had to strain my muscles tight to keep from sobbing aloud.

Someone nudged my arm. A handkerchief was offered. I wiped my face and blew my nose. An aura of lye soap clung to the handkerchief, which belonged to

Aunt Sarah. I held it to my nose, sniffing, and the sharp scent revived me.

"*Thou preparest a table before me in the presence of mine enemies. . .*"

I looked at the people now; it seemed to dry my eyes.

Aunt Sarah, beside me, was as solid as a sofa set upright, covered in straining black broadcloth. Her face was just as I remembered, heavy jawed, with big, rather staring eyes. She looked sober, but not tearful.

"*Surely goodness and mercy . . .*"

Next to her Uncle Clayton seemed small and loose in his clothes. Aunt Sarah had been born fourteen years before my father. Clayton was old enough to be my grandfather.

"*. . . house of the Lord forever.*"

Across from me Dr. Vesper stared into the grave with tears running down his face. I looked quickly at Mrs. Vesper—the Old Lady—who had one arm linked through his and her face hidden in a handkerchief. Althea Brand looked grim, and the four ladies behind her looked grimmer: the four ladies of West Barrett, who had come down the hill together, courtesy of a rented wagon from the sawmill.

Some of the millmen were there, too. I saw Frank Watts, who had taken Mother walking a few times, and Earl Cooney, who once got drunk and serenaded my window in error. There were quite a few of Mother's customers, wearing dresses she had made. Miss Spencer hadn't come. She'd be in class now, teaching Latin. But

Luke was there. Shaken with crying, she stood very close to her mother. While I watched, Mrs. Mitchell put an arm around her. I looked away.

Now here was a man I didn't know, clean shaven, squeezing his hatbrim in his hands and looking soberly at the ground. That would be John Gale, who had driven the Model T. And next to him—

My stomach jumped. Did I know this man? I seemed to remember him—he seemed to look exactly like himself—but who was he? He was thin and bent, and he must have had stomach trouble because he kept one arm pressed across his front—

No, he didn't *have* an arm, not a whole arm. His sleeve was pinned up, and what I'd thought was his forearm was just a large crease in his coat. He had a thin white beard, stained yellow around the mouth, and pale eyes that didn't stay fixed like everyone else's. Instead he looked around the cemetery, with a pleased expression that made me look, too, at the green grass and flowering mock orange and spiraea. There was nothing unseemly in his attitude. When he glanced at the coffin, he seemed almost grateful, as if for an invitation to some pleasant occasion.

It *is* pleasant, I thought. The sky was blue, the sun warm, and it warmed the grass until it gave off its green smell. I hadn't been able to forgive that this morning.

But Mother was all right. I remembered now how she'd reached her hand down from the buggy with a reassuring smile, while Belle stamped and snorted.

This day was always going to come. She had a bad

heart, and she knew she wouldn't live to see me grown—and she was all right. The man with the stained beard seemed to know that. The free way he held up his head and glanced around at the day, and respectfully at the coffin, told me that. Who was he? In spite of his thin, rusty, impoverished look, he was the most interesting person there.

Unexpectedly it was over. I'd missed the words I dreaded most: the earth, ashes, dust. People were coming toward me now. I held myself straight and clenched my fingers around Aunt Sarah's wet handkerchief.

First to approach was John Gale. He was pale, his skin furrowed like snow that's been rained on. His sad eyes met mine directly as he took my hand between his two warm ones.

"Miss Gibson? I'm as sorry as I can be," he said.

I couldn't answer. All I could do was nod.

"The doctor says I'm to transport your things—"

Aunt Sarah stirred. "That won't be necessary. Her uncle and I will bring her things up with us in the buggy."

John Gale gave my hand a strong squeeze and released it, turning to face Aunt Sarah. "Ma'am, I'm John Gale, and I caused the accident that took her mother's life. I'd like to help."

Aunt Sarah seemed to swell on a long, indrawn breath. Two spots of color burned on her cheeks, and her eyes flashed. "I thank you," she said firmly, "but no help is needed."

John Gale pressed his lips together and glanced at

me. He seemed full of courage still but unsure what to say next.

I couldn't help him. On her other side Uncle Clayton seemed to shrivel inside his clothes, and I wanted to shrivel, too. How could Dr. Vesper have let me keep the colt and the sewing machine? Didn't he know that was too much?

I looked for him but felt him first, a big, warm hand on my shoulder. "Hello, Sarah," he said. Then the other hand was on my other shoulder, and he was like a wall at my back. "You'll have a more comfortable ride up—has John been telling you? He'll bring Harry's things."

Aunt Sarah's whole face was red now, and her eyes were as hard as marbles. She looked from one man to another, and I was glad to be short and beneath her gaze. "I just don't see the need," she said.

"Well now, Sarah, Harry's bringing her whole inheritance with her." His hands gave me a squeeze, so small it must have been invisible. "It don't amount to much, but it's what she's got: three big carpetbags, as I understand, and a Singer sewing machine, and a two-year-old colt."

Aunt Sarah's chin worked visibly, and her eyes fixed on mine. I felt my knees start to weaken. I straightened them and hoped they would lock.

"Blame me if you like, Sarah," Dr. Vesper said, and her eyes lifted swiftly. She *did* like. "But Harry's made some good choices. Good Morgan that'll get her some-where someday, good sewing machine that her mother made a living with—"

Aunt Sarah sniffed. The sniff was directed at Mother, and I wanted to strike, right in the middle of the broadcloth waist. But Dr. Vesper's hands were heavy on my shoulders, and from Aunt Sarah's shadow Uncle Clayton said timidly, "Put the hoss in the pasture with the rest of the stock. No trouble, really."

Aunt Sarah looked down at me. I stared back at her, my cheeks and eyes burning. Her face changed in some way that I didn't understand. She turned to John Gale.

"Mr. Gale, it appears your help will be most welcome. You may follow us up to West Barrett."

She turned to go. I was expected to follow, but I couldn't move. I was shaking all over, ready to fall.

"Andrew!" I was hugged deep into a lilac-scented bosom. The Old Lady. "You can't allow this!"

"It's what Ellen wanted. They owe it to her to try, Sarah and Harry both."

"It's too much!" Mrs. Vesper said, wrapping her arms tighter around me and dropping tears onto my head.

I cried, too—shook all over with it, helpless. Oh, *Mother.* Did I really? Did I *owe* it to her to live with this horrible woman who despised us both?

Aunt Sarah would be climbing into the buggy. She'd be watching me with her marble blue eyes.

I drew back from Mrs. Vesper and used the lye-scented handkerchief. Dimly I heard her say, "No, Andy, I *won't* hush! Harriet, you've got a home with us if you need one. You remember that!"

Then Dr. Vesper drew my arm through his and led me toward the buggy. The four ladies of West Barrett were clustered at the wheel. Luke stood almost in our path. To my swimming eyes she appeared to waver like a reflection on the water. "Harry?"

No more hugs. Please. No more crying.

She hung back for a moment. Then she darted forward and gripped my hand hard. She was sobbing, but she managed to ask, "Will you come back to school?"

"I don't know."

She squeezed my hand again. Then she was gone, and Dr. Vesper was helping me up into the buggy, where I squashed in beside Aunt Sarah.

Uncle Clayton turned the white horse, and it jogged heavily up the street. Aunt Sarah was a hot bulk beside me. On the other side the strut of the buggy top dug into my shoulder. The breeze dried my face. I closed my eyes.

I could tell when we reached the edge of town by the roughness of the road, the shade, the tilt backward as the horse began to climb. Every day I'd made this ride, beside Mother, behind Belle. . . .

I kept my eyes closed as long as I could, wanting not to see the place where the grass was crushed beside the road from Belle's body being dragged away, the fragment of buggy hood that no one had picked up.

But my eyes opened too early. I turned to look at the people beside me. Aunt Sarah gazed straight ahead, lips pressed tightly together. Uncle Clayton just drove, looking around him curiously. I saw by his face when we passed the spot. His head turned until his eyes met mine. He jumped and looked straight ahead again. "Clayton is harmless," Mother always said. I closed my eyes again and listened for the sound of John Gale's team and wagon behind us.

When I walked into the house, my footsteps sounded hollow. The house was not much emptier—three carpetbags beside the door, the sewing machine folded down into its table—but it sounded empty.

I was alone for the moment. Outside Aunt Sarah directed John Gale and Uncle Clayton, horses tramped, and wagon wheels rumbled. Inside, it was still. Already it felt like someone else's house.

I climbed the stairs. On the bare mattress lay my calico work dress. A rectangle of sunlight reached along the floor. After a moment's hesitation I crossed to the skyscraper window. At sight of the long drop my stomach seemed to fall through my body. I braced my hand on the window frame. My fingers throbbed inside my black gloves.

Would I ever again be high enough to look down on a swallow's back?

The willows shifted above the bright water. The little river made its rushing sound, the saw sang, and right in front of my nose a mosquito climbed through one of the holes in the screen.

"Come on in," I whispered.

"Harriet?" Aunt Sarah called from the bottom of the stairs. "Harriet, where are you?"

I will hate my name, I thought. She'll make me hate my own name.

I went to the stairs and looked down to meet her eyes. Instantly I felt myself stiffen, the way a dog stiffens and bristles at a strange dog's challenge. "I'll *be* right *down.*"

Aunt Sarah's form seemed to broaden and fill the stairwell. Her eyes took on a glassy hardness. Without a word she turned away.

I sat on the bare bed, shaking. I don't fight. Though Lucretia and I call ourselves Luke and Harry, though we ride horses and climb trees, we aren't rough girls. I like people who like me, and before this I paid no attention to anyone who didn't.

But already I had made Aunt Sarah angry.

"Well, she started it," I whispered to the still room. "She started it."

I changed my dress. When I came downstairs, the carpetbags were no longer beside the door. John Gale and Uncle Clayton were carrying out the sewing machine, and Aunt Sarah stood in the kitchen, looking around and tapping her foot.

I looked where she was looking, at the tomato seedlings in the window, the pots and pans on their hooks, the teapot and the cups. Last night, packing, Althea and I had not known what I could take. If we removed anything but Mother's and my personal things, was it stealing from the creditors? And how much room would Aunt Sarah have? Would she be offended if I brought too much?

Now she seemed to blame me for leaving too much behind.

There was a knock at the door. Althea Brand stood just outside. She had ridden up behind us in John Gale's wagon, and she looked dusty and small.

"Come in," I said as she hesitated in the doorway.

"I just wanted to tell you good-bye, Harriet, and—"

"I want to give you a present," I said, interrupting. It had just come to me how good she'd been. She didn't have to take care of me. She wasn't even a relative. But she was Mother's friend, and she'd done what a friend should, just out of love.

"Here!" I said, snatching the green teapot from its shelf. Father gave the pot to Mother. It came from Boston, and before that, from China.

"Mother would want you to have it," I said.

Althea's eyes filled with tears. She sat down suddenly at the table. "Thank you, Harriet. I'll think of you both—" Her voice choked off.

Aunt Sarah let out an audible breath. "What about these tomato plants?"

"I don't know." I would have given them to Althea, but hers were already started.

"Bring them along," Aunt Sarah said. Uncle Clayton came to the door. "Clayton, those tomatoes!"

He clumped across the kitchen. Aunt Sarah went out.

I've forgotten something! I thought. Without knowing why, I hurried through the sitting room and opened the door. Mother's bed was bare now, too, and the thick hush was gone from the room. It looked empty and shabby.

I didn't even think, just pulled open the top bureau

drawer. There atop the stockings was the shiny leather wallet. "Your father's pocketbook," it was always called, and she never would make or buy anything prettier to carry her money in.

I pushed it into my pocket and walked out.

When I went to the barn for the colt's halter, I saw other things I'd been forgetting: brushes, bridles, liniment, and buckets. Uncle Clayton would have all those things, but these were mine, and there was my saddle on its peg. I began packing the gear into the buckets. It was dark and cool inside the barn. Behind me I could sense the warm sun and Aunt Sarah's hurry.

My calm surprised me. I had just come from my mother's funeral. How could I be doing this? John Gale came to the barn door. I gave him the two buckets, took the saddle and halter, and followed him to the wagon, wondering: What happened to Belle's harness? Did anyone take it off her, or was it not worth saving?

The colt stood at the gate, leaning so hard that the top bar made a cracking sound. He barely noticed me putting on the halter; all his attention was for the other horses. When I let down the bars, he jumped over them, almost pulling me off my feet.

"Whoa!" I couldn't stop him. He circled me, his head turned toward the horses. I meant no more to him than a post. "Whoa!" I cried. My voice came high and shrill. He would know—everyone would know—that I was afraid.

"Hang on!" Uncle Clayton said, somewhere on the edge of things. "By jing, he's a wild un! Keep hold—"

"Easy, boy." Big brown hands appeared above mine on the rope. "Easy." John Gale.

I didn't want to let go, but there was no room for me, and no need. Gale gave a couple of rough jerks on the halter, and the colt seemed to notice that someone had hold of him. His bright eyes remained fixed on the other horses, but he pranced beside John Gale without pulling. There was nothing left for me to do but follow them up the hill. My legs felt loose, and my throat hurt. The colt had always been so easy to handle. His wildness now felt like betrayal.

John Gale tied the colt's rope to a stout ring at the back of the wagon. The colt pushed against the tailgate, straining toward the broad rumps of the team. "Someone ought to ride with me," Gale said, looking doubtfully at me. "In case he gives me trouble."

"Clayton," Aunt Sarah said.

Then I must ride with Aunt Sarah. I walked quickly to the buggy, determined not to stop, not to look at the house.

I saw it anyway, gray and fragile as a wasp's nest, the worn clapboards gleaming in the sunshine. The geraniums looked out the kitchen window, and Althea Brand stood in the doorway, small and shabby like the house, clutching the teapot to her stomach. I waved and felt tears starting.

No. I pressed my hand hard against my mouth and climbed into the buggy beside Aunt Sarah. She turned the horse, and we started up the long hill.

Four

MOTHER AND I SPENT OUR LIVES in West Barrett and downhill. Only in August did we go up, to comb abandoned pastures for blackberries.

But we had come from uphill. The house I traveled to now was the one in which my father had been born and raised. Close to it was the little place he'd lived in with Mother and where I was born.

We climbed slowly through the pastureland, past farms and cornfields. The road was rutted from the recent mud season, dry enough for easy travel but not yet dusty. A couple of miles up, birches were beginning to take over some of the pastures. Their white trunks and lacy leaves made the grass look rich and green. We passed a cellar hole. The house had collapsed into it, and columbines grew over the silver clapboards.

"Whoa!" Aunt Sarah said suddenly. She pointed.

"What?"

"There!" she said, pointing harder. Down across a pasture a red-brown animal wandered through a birch grove.

"A—a *deer?*" I'd never seen a deer.

"We see them once in a while now," Aunt Sarah said. "She'll be in your uncle's bean field next!" She drove on.

We came out into the open now, and an empty green hillside stretched above us. I could see stone walls, and after a minute I saw a house.

It was yellow-gray, the color of goldenrod gone to seed, a two-story Cape with a big front door and a long ell. Beside it stood a gray barn fronted by a muddy yard. Cattle grazed on the slope below.

We crawled up the edge of this pasture until we came to a lane, and then along the lane to the farmyard. The horse stopped of his own accord at the barn door, and Aunt Sarah got out. Numbly I followed.

John Gale's wagon stopped behind us. The colt bobbed his head up, bumping against the tether. His eyes blazed. He'd never been outside West Barrett. The shelf of pasture and the riverbank had been his world.

Hugging myself, I walked back to him. He paid no attention, just twisted and turned and blew hot breath out of huge, reddened nostrils. Could I approach him? I seemed to see myself from above, and I didn't think so: thin and small and thirteen years old. A girl. An orphan.

As I hesitated, Uncle Clayton let himself down from the wagon seat and came back. He untied the rope, and the colt wheeled around him, coat flashing in the sun. His hooves cut the packed dirt.

Out in the pasture a horse whinnied. The colt flung his head high. He listened desperately for a moment. Then his eye seemed to soften with gladness, and he sent a ringing neigh out across the hillside.

He thinks it's Belle. My tears released again.

Through a blur I saw Uncle Clayton stumble toward the barway in the colt's wake. He slipped back the rails, let the colt through, and unclipped the rope.

The colt thundered down the hill in a violent blur of speed, neighing crazily. A blaze-faced work team trotted to meet him. He nearly crashed into them, and all three stood nose to nose. The colt sniffed first one, then the other. Then he raised his head and looked uphill.

Aunt Sarah had led the white horse to the barway. No horse could look less like Belle, but the colt screamed and raced back. The white horse ignored him, buckled his knees, and rolled.

The colt pranced around the rolling animal. His tail stuck straight up and streamed over his back. He still hoped . . . somehow he still hoped that one of these horses was Belle. I hugged myself.

"Hey!" said John Gale, on the wagon seat behind me. "Look!" He pointed toward the top of the barn. I followed his hand and saw a weather vane, a trotting Morgan, with high head and flowing tail.

"Oh." I looked downhill at the colt again. The weather vane Morgan was mature, deep-bodied, and my colt was young and weedy, but the look was there.

"Yes." John Gale drew a breath and let it out slowly, gazing around him. "Decent land," he said, "for hill land."

To me it looked shabby, as if there were more work here than two people could do.

I got two of my carpetbags out of the buggy and, weighed down with them, followed Aunt Sarah into the kitchen. It smelled of vinegar. The table was covered with oilcloth, and a yellow flystrip hung down, several dead flies sticking to it. But every surface shone. It was clean, with that peculiar smell cider vinegar makes when you wash up with it.

Aunt Sarah crossed the kitchen and opened a door onto a set of stairs. They were closed in and dark, turning a corner three-fourths of the way up and continuing a little more steeply. Any light from above was blotted out by Aunt Sarah's bulk.

My breath came shallowly, not seeming to get past my throat. I pressed my palm to the center of my chest and followed.

We came out into the light, in a narrow, steep-shouldered room not much different in shape from my room at home. Everything seemed gray: plaster walls, iron bedstead made up with a gray wool blanket, limp gauze curtains at the window. The vinegar smell was strong here.

It's like a hired man's room! I thought.

Aunt Sarah put the bags on the bed and turned to me, with the nearest thing to a smile I'd seen on her face. "This was your father's room," she said. "I thought you'd like to have it."

A hot feeling flooded my chest. I couldn't speak. I crossed the bare floor, listening to the sound of my bootheels, and looked out the window. The barnyard was below. A red hen scratched in the dung.

"Thank you," I made myself say. My voice came hard and raspy.

There was no answer. I turned. Aunt Sarah just stood there, not gimleting me with her eyes, as I'd expected, but looking at the room.

All at once she noticed me staring. "It'll look prettier when you've put your things around," she said, and turned toward the stairs.

My things. I sat on the bed beside my carpetbags. I hadn't brought my rug. I hadn't brought the little jug we filled with wildflowers all summer. I'd left all the pictures on the walls. What did I have in these bags except clothing? I didn't want to open them. My hands felt too weak to work the buckles.

Downstairs I heard shuffling feet. Uncle Clayton and John Gale must be walking the sewing machine in. A thump. Now their steps sounded lighter, heading out the door. I went down to say good-bye.

John Gale stood at his horses' heads, looking uncomfortable again. I tried to think what Mother would do, and then I walked over and held out my hand.

"Thank you."

He stood holding my hand, looking down at it. His

hand was hard and rough, with dirt ground in so deeply that scrubbing couldn't take it out, though otherwise he seemed like a clean man.

He heaved a sigh, as if trying to push a weight off his chest. "Miss Gibson . . . Miss—" He shook his head. "I'm as sorry as I can be." He gave my hand a squeeze and then climbed up into his wagon and turned it.

I stood watching it rattle down the lane. He turned down the rutted road to the valley and his own concerns. He would pass our house in West Barrett and the flattened place in the grass, go down the broad street by the Academy.

Aunt Sarah said, "Clayton, what time is it? I don't know whether I'm afoot or horseback!"

Uncle Clayton began fishing his watch out of his pocket. It seemed to hang on a very long chain. "Ha' past four," he said when he'd flipped the watch open and blinked at its face for a few moments.

"Then you've got time to fix that pigpen gate before you milk."

"Guess so."

"Go change your clothes, and I'll fix something to eat." She seemed to push us before her into the kitchen. Uncle Clayton disappeared into another part of the house. Aunt Sarah tied on an apron and began slicing bread.

"Shall I help you?"

She raised her head as if surprised and looked at me for a moment with the knife poised over the loaf. "No.

Thank you. Take a look around, why don't you? See where you're at."

My fingers twisted together, making all the little, inflamed stab wounds sting and throb. Look around. Was that what you were supposed to do on the afternoon of your mother's funeral?

I looked into the next room. It should have been the dining room, but Aunt Sarah had arranged it as a sitting room, with rocking chairs, a knitting basket, and a sewing machine in one corner. Not Mother's machine. I didn't see that anywhere.

A door at the back of the room opened, and out came Uncle Clayton, in overalls. Without the jacket I could see how his shoulders sloped. They didn't make a broad shelf, like Dr. Vesper's or John Gale's. They just fell away like the shoulders of a milk bottle.

He seemed embarrassed to see me and gestured vaguely at the room. "Yup, this here's the sittin' room . . . have to get an extra chair in here, I guess."

He opened another door. I glimpsed a hall, bright with sunlight. The knees of a stairway intruded on the left. Beyond was another large room, piled nearly to the ceiling with furniture. I saw beds, tables, couches, a forest of chairs, and, just inside the door, Mother's sewing machine.

The hallway was cold. Cold air flowed down the stairwell and brought with it a smell of vinegar and soda. From deep in the thicket of furniture came a scrabbling sound, like tiny claws on bare wood.

Uncle Clayton waded into the furniture. Dust

streamed up through the sunbeams as he put aside a set of hatboxes and three kitchen chairs. He came to grips with a straight-backed rocker and tried to lift it out. It caught on something, and his shoulders worked as he heaved at it.

"Clayton! You'll break it! Wait a minute!"

Uncle Clayton stepped back obediently. Aunt Sarah shoved something, tilted something else, and lifted the rocker straight up in one firm hand.

"There! If you'd use your head for something besides a hatrack— Now take it from me, will you?"

Uncle Clayton started forward guiltily and took the chair. As I stepped out of his way, I gained a new angle on the room. There was a fireplace. Gray and sepia faces frowned down from the walls: two men in uniforms from the time of the Civil War, a severe, heavy-jawed woman with practically no hair.

Aunt Sarah pushed Mother's sewing machine an inch or two deeper into the room and closed the door. "Come and eat," she said, as if none of this required explanation.

Was it like this when my father was a little boy? I'll have to ask Mother, I thought, and then remembered.

Six

THE MIRROR IN MY FATHER'S ROOM was murky and speckled. The girl who passed in front of it was the girl I'd glimpsed approaching the colt, the orphan. Her hair was done in two tight braids. Her face was a pale blur, with large dark eyes and a small mouth.

What kept catching my eye, and surprising me, was her dress, a leafy print with bright red berries. Didn't the orphan have anything more suitable?

Even away from the mirror I watched that girl. She sat silently at the table. She didn't ask for anything, took only what was passed. She couldn't seem to mark time properly. Did several days pass, or just one long day? In bed she lay with her eyes wide open. The lump in her chest was too hard for crying.

One morning the girl's aunt asked her to collect eggs. She tried to listen as she was told where to look. But out in the barnyard she remembered nothing. She stood among the crooning, scratching hens with her basket hanging at her side.

A hen strolled from behind the manure pile, clucking loudly. The orphan retraced this path, and in a sheltered spot by the side of the barn she found an egg. She picked it up and turned around.

A rooster's head, with gray, closed lids and gaping beak, lay on the manure pile.

I dropped the egg.

"Harriet! For crying out loud, give me the basket! Now follow me. I'll *show* you where to look."

Nooks and crannies all over the farm—that was where to look, because the hens roamed everywhere. Aunt Sarah even climbed into the haymow. She stooped and peered under the buggy. "Crawl in there for me, Harriet, will you?"

I crawled in. The egg felt warm. I would have liked to cradle it for a while, cup my hands gently around it. But this egg must go in Aunt Sarah's basket.

"That's all, unless they have a nest I don't know about."

I forced myself to speak. "Thank you for showing me."

She was counting her eggs, head bent and chin compressed into two large pillows. "That's all right." Her voice seemed forced, too. "Time to start dinner," she said after a minute. "We always have a big dinner on Sunday."

Sunday dinner. It was Sunday. I watched Aunt Sarah go away, puzzled at her stiffness. It was as if she were shy and on her best behavior. But this was her home. Why would she put on company manners?

Nearby, hens mused over things they found in the dirt. Roosters crowed. The horses and cattle grazed far down the field, the colt glowing among them like a new copper penny. He didn't answer my whistle.

I wandered to the sunny front of the barn and sat on the chopping block. A gray rooster approached. I've met some mean roosters. I pulled my feet back, wondering what this one intended.

He tilted his head and looked at me. Then he noticed a tiny feather on the packed dirt. He viewed it through one eye and then the other and began to chortle. *Ohhh, my, looklooklooklooklooklook!* He pecked the feather, ejected it with a headshake that set his dewlaps wobbling, then pecked it again.

I felt a deep breath lift my ribs. The sun warmed my face and shimmered on the rooster's feathers. *Ohhh, looklooklook!*

I raised my head, and saw for the first time that I was looking down on mountains. Or ridges, anyway, row on row of them, like ocean waves. They receded into the distance, each one a paler, more transparent blue. In the valleys morning mist still lingered, rising like whipped cream out of a bowl.

A high place. I thought of my skyscraper bedroom, where I had looked down on the backs of swallows. I looked quickly away, at the mustard-colored house and drab barn and the hill rising behind it, fringed with birches.

It was silent here. No mill saw, no river, no road for anyone to pass on. Somewhere along this ridge were the little house we lived in when I was too small to remember and the school where Mother was teaching when she and Father met. But were there any people, anywhere?

"Oh, Mother," I whispered. "Why did you send me here?" I felt proud of how I'd done at home. I'd grieved, without entirely forgetting the feelings of other people. I'd been wholehearted, brave, responsible.

Here I felt myself shrinking down. The orphan with her two braids, hunched on a stump. She really should be wearing brown.

Ohhh, look, the rooster remarked. As I watched him peck the feather, I saw in my mind the severed head on the manure pile, with its fringe of bruised and blackened feathers. . . .

The chicken roasting in the kitchen.

The chopping block!

I rose, to a *chuck-chuck-chuck* from the gray rooster, and felt the back of my dress. It was damp, and my hand came away stained with blood.

"Oh, no!" I almost sat down again and let everything close over me like dark wool. But as I bent, I saw the red berries on my skirt. "Don't they just make you *happy*, Harry?" Mother said when we chose the calico. "Let's have dresses just alike, so we can look at each other and be cheerful!"

Mother *chose* to be happy. I never understood that before.

"Ow!" The rooster was pecking my leg. I drew back to kick him, then realized what he was doing. He was pecking the berries.

"They're cloth," I said, drawing back. "They're not real."

He tilted his head to look at me through the other eye, as if much struck. Then he turned back to the ground and the tiny golden feather.

"Watch out for that, too," I said. "That's probably a bad omen."

In the kitchen the roast chicken smell was heavy. Aunt Sarah stood in her pantry, stirring. In the sitting room Uncle Clayton sat collapsed to one side, snoring gently.

At home I would know what to do. Here I wasn't sure what was allowed. "Aunt Sarah?"

She turned her head.

"I've got . . . blood." I held out the wet part of my skirt. "Should I—"

"Good heavens!" She dusted her hands on her apron and came out. "Is it your first time? Are you prepared?"

"Am I *prepared?*" I stared at her large red face. "Prepared for—*oh!*" She thought I'd been taken unawares by my monthly period. "I sat on the chopping block," I said.

Her face flushed even redder. "Well, goodness gracious, go to the sink and pump cold water on it! Surely you know how to do that!"

"That's exactly what I was *going* to do!" I said. "I

wanted to make sure you didn't mind!"

Her eyes brightened with anger. I felt how large she was, and my back stiffened. After a moment she folded her lips, swelling with a long, slow breath. "This is your home. You do what you need to."

An especially loud snore sounded in the other room, and a startled "What?"

"Nothing," Aunt Sarah said, turning back to the pantry. "Go on with your reading."

I rinsed the blood out of my skirt and stood with my back to the cookstove to dry it, looking around the clean, ugly kitchen. I felt shaken by the brush with Aunt Sarah. Was this going to be my life, quarreling with her over every little thing?

No, my life would be different. I would have a career, like Luke's sister, Vicky, who worked for a publisher. That was why schooling was so important.

Instantly Barrett Academy formed in my mind, complete with chalk dust; Miss Spencer's voice fading to a background drone when the algebra got too hard; the smell of horehound cough drops; Luke; and the little society the Academy made, with its teachers, the students from hill farms who boarded at Webb House, town kids who walked or drove in each morning. . . .

I felt the blood drain out of my head. I stared out the window at the transparent waves of ridges.

"Aunt Sarah!"

"Now what?"

"Aunt Sarah, how—how will I get to school?"

There was a pause. She came to the pantry doorway.

"School? You've finished school, haven't you? I understood you were through eighth grade."

"I'm at the Academy now, but how am I going to get there? Mother used to drive me—"

Two red spots burned on Aunt Sarah's cheeks. "You don't imagine *we're* going to drive you, do you? It's seven miles each way!"

"But what am I going to *do*?"

"*Do*? There's nothing *to* do! You'll stay right here and take up the life the Lord's given you!"

"I'll drive myself! I can drive—"

"Your uncle needs all three horses right here!"

I became aware of Uncle Clayton in the sitting-room doorway. He was shaking his head at me in some kind of warning. I looked back at Aunt Sarah. "Then I'll board there, I can stay at Webb—"

"And how would you pay for that? If you've got any money coming to you, girl, I've yet to hear of it! All I've heard about is debts!"

"But—" I didn't have words to go on with. Our lives had revolved around my schooling. Mother always made it the most important thing, and to Aunt Sarah it was nothing.

"I'm sorry," she said after a minute. Her voice had that forced-out sound again, or maybe it was forced *in*, holding things back. "It seems hard, but you have to face facts."

On the flypaper over the table a fly whined and whirred its wings in vain. I stared into Aunt Sarah's marble eyes. "Well, this is a fact," I said. My voice shook. "Mother wanted me to go to school."

Smack! Aunt Sarah hit the table with her open palm. "If your mother is an example of what education does for a woman, I'd like to see the schools close right down!"

My mouth hung open. The chicken sizzled in the oven. After a moment I asked, "What?" My voice came in a whisper. "What?"

Aunt Sarah pressed her lips together, as if trying to prevent more angry words from escaping. "Never mind."

"No! You tell me what you meant by that!"

Aunt Sarah's eyes widened, "I'll tell you what I mean! Your mother was an immoral woman! She got herself in trouble like any common trash, and she ruined my brother's life!"

"Sairy—" Uncle Clayton said, but my voice trampled his.

"What are you talking about?" My voice came full throated now, from the deepest part of my lungs. In one detached corner of my mind I was amazed. I'd never spoken this way to a grown-up, hardly ever to anyone. Aunt Sarah's arm twitched back as if she wanted to slap me. I stepped closer. *"What?"*

"If you're so smart," she said between her teeth, "then when is your birthday? When were your parents married? It doesn't take algebra to figure out that sum!"

I could only stare. After a minute I said, "I don't know when they were married."

"It was too darned late, I can tell you that!"

I understood what she was saying. She was saying that Mother was pregnant when she and Father married. I looked her square in the eye. "My mother was a wonderful person," I said. "The only mistake she ever made was sending me to you!"

At that she did slap me, right across the face. I hardly felt it. It was only a sound.

"Go to your room!"

I turned without speaking and rapidly climbed the stairs. I went straight to the mirror and looked at myself.

The orphan was gone. This girl had brilliant, glittering eyes and one cheek redder than the other. She looked so full of power that she might burst into flames at any moment.

I looked at her. I touched the reddened cheek.

"I will not stay here."

Seven

I found a pencil and a tablet of the ugly paper we used for algebra.

> *Dr. Vesper* [I wrote],
> *I will not stay here and listen to my mother being insulted. May I come and live with you? I will work hard and do everything I can not to be a burden.*
> *Please come see me as soon as you can.*
>
> > *Your grateful friend,*
> > *Harriet Gibson*

I folded it and addressed the outside. Now I began to hear the sounds downstairs: the ongoing angry rumble of Aunt Sarah's voice, an occasional protest from Uncle Clayton.

I went down. Aunt Sarah rounded at the sound of my step. "I thought I told you to go upstairs!"

I looked past her. "Uncle Clayton, I need this letter to go to Dr. Vesper. When do you go down for your mail?"

He looked away from me, only to recoil from Aunt Sarah's expression. "Wednesdays!"

Three more days. I looked out the window. Clouds lay in combed rows across the eastern sky, mirroring the rows of ridgetops. Below the pasture I saw the slender brown line of the road.

"Never mind." I walked out the front door.

The air felt cool. A rim of blue sky showed in the east, but from the west bigger, darker clouds were pushing in. I headed straight across the yard. Hens scattered. Only the gray rooster hesitated, eyeing the red berries on my dress. *Ohh, look.*

I plunged past him, along the rutted lane. Wind clapped the maple leaves. Down in the pasture the colt flung his head high and watched me. He hadn't given up hope that any moving creature might be his mother.

"I'll be back for you," I said to him. Everything was clear in my mind. I would walk down to West Barrett and stay the night with Althea Brand. In the morning I'd see Dr. Vesper and the lawyer, and I would figure out what to do next. I'd work as a hired girl rather than come back here. I'd live in a *barn*—

Something rumbled. I turned. Behind the row of maples loomed an enormous crinkled cloud. The rumble came again.

One thing I'd been well taught was to seek shelter at the first sign of a thunderstorm. I hesitated. I wasn't out of sight of the house yet.

But it was no part of my plan to be hit by lightning. I turned and walked toward the barn, ignoring the face at the kitchen window. The first fat raindrops were spearing into the dirt as I reached the haymow door.

Hens ran into the barn after me as the rain began to sheet down. I sat among them. The gray rooster strolled close. I picked up a handful of the chaff that lay all around me, dusty and golden, and held it out to him.

He drew back and pecked shrewdly at the chaff on the floor. What's so special about yours? he seemed to be asking. He scratched a long trough with one foot and inspected the results.

I looked past him, out the big door. The rain beat down. The stinging nettles bent and dripped. *Crack!* of lightning, thunder like a freight train on an iron bridge.

Against this background I saw myself arriving hot and sweaty at Althea Brand's. I saw myself on Dr. Vesper's doorstep, demanding shelter. I saw the looks on their faces.

No, not that way. Send the letter and wait.

A shower of chaff buried my foot. The rooster had drawn his line there, and now he pecked importantly, pretending to pay no attention to me. I tipped my hand to show him my chaff, and he drew back in alarm. I thought of Aunt Sarah's hand twitching back to hit me and how I had stepped forward to meet the blow. That side of my face hurt. I had never been slapped before.

I'd never been that angry.

"I don't believe it," I said. "It isn't true!" Everything Mother did was open, joyful, courageous. I couldn't imagine her getting married because she had to.

So why was Aunt Sarah lying? Why exactly did she hate Mother?

Mother was young, I thought, and full of charm, and educated. She was different, and people are like chickens.

Tears prickled my eyes. I could hear her saying, "People are like chickens, Harry. They'll always peck the one that's different."

My throat felt full and tight. Through my tears I watched the hens, so pretty with their wide, plump bodies and their tiny, tiny heads. We were both different, especially here where Aunt Sarah ruled. While Mother was alive, she protected me, but now I was getting pecked, too.

So why did she send me here?

Across the yard rain streamed out the eaves' spout and splashed into a barrel at the corner of the house. Smoke flattened black under the rain, puffed down, and tried to rise again. My father lived right here, as a boy. But I didn't remember my father. Being where he grew up couldn't make me happy.

Was it just that Mother thought Aunt Sarah *should* take care of me? That didn't sound like Mother. If there was one thing I knew, it was that Mother loved me more than anything in the world. She must have thought this was best for me.

"But *why?*" I tipped my head back and spoke up

toward the blackness. "Mother, why?"

Suddenly I felt something touch my hand. I looked down. The rooster was just drawing back as if he thought himself very clever, with a large piece of chaff in his beak. He crooned, *Ohh, mymymymy. Ohh, my*—

"You're funny," I told him. My voice was achy and rasping, but I could feel myself almost smile. I looked down at the letter in my hand, and I heard Dr. Vesper saying, "It's what Ellen wanted. They owe it to her to try."

I hadn't really tried at all yet. I'd just barely woken up, had just started to see where I was and who was here with me. In a way it felt worse than the gray zone where the orphan lived. It *hurt*. My throat ached with sorrow. But I was awake now, and I would try. One thing I knew, though: Mother wouldn't want me to stay here if it meant giving up my education.

Exams must be soon, I thought. Next week? Could I go down and take them? Could I afford the Academy? And how could I get there? Could I possibly train the colt by next fall and ride him down?

Dr. Vesper could answer some of those questions. Only I could answer the last one. I always meant to train him, I thought. I'll just have to get started.

Eight

THE RAIN STOPPED. The sun came out through the last long, fat drops and shone on the puddles as I crossed the yard.

They were eating. A place was set for me. I sat down, and Aunt Sarah served me without speaking. To my surprise I was hungry, and I didn't mind eating that rooster, though I'd seen his head on the manure pile and though he was cooked dry. Mother was a better cook than Aunt Sarah—not that we often aspired to a chicken. Popcorn and milk was our Sunday dinner.

I looked up and caught Uncle Clayton glancing from Aunt Sarah to me. He started when he met my eyes, and reached for another biscuit.

When the meal was finished, I helped Aunt Sarah clear away and wash dishes. It was while I was drying the platter that she finally spoke. "We'll have to learn to get along better." She was scrubbing the bottom of the roasting pan, with her big chin pillowed and her mouth tight.

We? I thought. Who started it? But it was the nearest she could come to an apology. I could understand that. I hate apologies, too. "Yes," I said finally, "we will."

That began a week of dancing: two steps forward, two back. No, I don't want your help with washing; then a brooding, emotion-filled silence the next day, until I understood that I *was* supposed to help iron.

Spend more time outdoors.

Where were you?

Where I was all Tuesday afternoon was trying to catch the colt. He'd always been friendly before, sometimes too friendly, dogging our heels when we caught Belle or repaired the fence. But the freedom of the big pasture had gone to his head, or else a week or so of neglect had caused him to forget me. He let me get close, but not close enough, until I lost my temper and threw the rope at him. Then he kicked up his heels and galloped away.

Wednesday Uncle Clayton went for the mail. He took two letters from me, one to the Academy, asking about examinations, and one to Dr. Vesper, asking him to explain the exact state of my finances. Aunt Sarah looked sharply when I handed the letters over but asked no questions.

I helped her bake. Heat rolled off the big stove, but she kept me well away from it. Not with any expression of tenderness; she just set me to work at the far table and watched sharply as I rolled out piecrust.

"You have a nice light hand," she commented. I heard the note of surprise and understood it for yet another insult to Mother. I pressed my lips together and didn't answer.

After a minute she said, "It's a nice day out. Go get some fresh air."

The kitchen was hot and dark, and sun shone outside the windows, but Aunt Sarah's voice made me want to stay right there at the table just to spite her.

Instead I went down into the pasture with a rope and a measure of oats. The colt flung up his head and watched me, but the work team only tipped their ears and kept on grazing. I went halfway down the hill and rattled the oats.

All across the field heads lifted. Ears pointed at me: cow ears and horse ears. I hadn't expected them all to notice, but the colt was looking, too. I shook the oats again, softly.

A cow stepped toward me. Like the slow start of an avalanche, others stepped, glanced at one another, sped up, until they all were trotting, shaking their big fringed ears, bucking, cantering. Now the horses came at a gallop.

I fled toward the gate, but two speckled heifers blocked the way. Hooves thundered behind me. I froze and ducked my head. When nothing hit me, I turned, and the team reached their big noses to the oats. The colt veered past them and started a swirl of cows milling around me.

"Bess! Chick! Go on!" I heard a popping sound.

Cows galumphed away to either side, and the horses backed up, flattening their ears. Then Aunt Sarah was beside me, large and hot, with a buggy whip in her hand.

"*Thank* you!" I said.

But Aunt Sarah looked into the measure. "Why on earth are you feeding good oats to these animals? There's plenty of grass!"

"I was trying to catch the colt—" I stopped myself. I hated the weak, excusing sound of my voice, as if I didn't have a perfect right to do what I was doing.

"Oh, so now he can't be caught?"

"I'll catch him," I said as we made for the gate.

"Well, don't waste good oats. They're too hard to come by." Aunt Sarah drew the bars back. How had she gotten in? I wondered. Did she slip between the rails or climb?

"Try apples next time," she suggested after a moment. "Might be a little more private!"

I looked at her quickly. That was almost a joke. "Thank you. Where are the apples?"

"In a bin down cellar. I'll show you." She paused. "What do you call that animal?"

We are having a conversation! I thought. "We—he doesn't really have a name." We could never decide on one. We were always reading a new novel with a new hero and trying that name. He was Laurie once, from *Little Women* "I call him Kid," I said, just to keep things going.

"I see."

The gray rooster jerked a shrewd glance upward as we approached. I offered him oats on the palm of my hand.

71

Ohhh, looklooklook. He came close, and I saw how beautiful his eye was, the green center surrounded by hot orange. He snatched an oat. I felt his wattle touch my fingers, and high above, Aunt Sarah cleared her throat.

"I hope you know better than to make a pet of a farm animal."

I ignored her, shaking the oats farther down my fingers. Above my head I heard a massive indrawn breath, and then she swept on ahead of me, toward the house.

She gave me some wizened russet apples, and I spent the afternoon by the brook. In the lacy shade of the birches I waited until the horses came to rest and drink. Then I ate an apple loudly.

The colt couldn't bear it long. He came and begged with an eloquent nose. I made him wait for the core, and I didn't even try to touch his halter. Instead I walked away, eating another apple. He followed and nudged, and at last I gave it to him.

I put my hand on the halter then, and scratched his ears, but made no attempt to hold him. The next day, when I went down with apples in my pockets, he came right to me.

I didn't know what to do with him once I had him. Once I'd had a plan. I had a book by Dennis Magner, the great horse tamer, and I was going to follow his directions, and the colt was going to be perfectly trained. People were going to marvel at how well a young girl had done. Now I led the colt around in a few circles, let him loose, and went for a walk.

The lane meandered past the barn to the crest of the hill. An old road ran along there, so rarely used that it was mostly grassed over. I followed it, passing another abandoned cellar hole, and after a while came upon a small brick building with a hole in the roof and a padlock on the door.

I peeked in one cobwebbed window. Rows of empty desks faced a blackboard. This must be the school Mother taught in. Here she first met my father.

I sat on the front step. They must have sat here together, after the children had gone home. There were only three children then, on all this broad hillside. It was an easy school to teach, Mother used to say, and in the afternoons Father came.

I looked off at the blue hills. She would like to know I was here. Maybe she did know. I could almost feel her shoulder nudging mine, and I stayed as long as the feeling lasted. The hills were dusky purple when I walked back along the ridge.

"Where in heaven's name have you been?" Aunt Sarah shattered my peace the minute I walked in. I could smell supper, but nothing was on the table.

"I went for a walk."

"And how was I to know that?"

Of course there was no answer. I should have told her. I faced down her angry eyes.

I would have told Mother because Mother loved me. Mother would worry. Aunt Sarah only wanted to be the boss.

Nine

THE NIGHTS WERE WORSE than the days. Aunt Sarah and Uncle Clayton went to bed at nine, and I was meant to go, too. When they'd closed their bedroom door, the house was silent. It was too quiet to turn in bed, too quiet to cry. Night after night I lay still and narrow, like a wrinkle in the blanket. I could hear how big that house was. I could sense its rooms crowded with ghostly furniture. Sometimes I was cold, sometimes I broke into a sweat, because it was real. It was true. Mother was dead.

Every time I got in bed I prayed that she'd come back in another dream, and dreams did come, but they were never like that first one. That one was *her*, and the dreams I had now were only me, trying to rearrange things in my mind.

Thank goodness for Aunt Sarah, I sometimes thought. All day long I braced against her. That was eighteen hours out of every twenty-four when I felt strong and wary and a little mean, and that was better than feeling crushed. How would I hold out, I wondered, when I was with someone who loved me? Uneasily I watched the road for my first visitor.

No one came.

Luke was at school, I reminded myself, and Althea Brand had no way to come, and Dr. Vesper was busy.

But on Saturday there was no school. Luke would be missing me. All morning, as I collected eggs, and led the colt in the pasture, and helped Aunt Sarah get dinner, and ate dinner, I was really down in Barrett watching Luke. She woke up—and as the day wore on, I woke her later and later in my mind—and negotiated to use Tulip, their phlegmatic horse. Maybe Mrs. Mitchell needed Tulip first. Maybe Vicky had come home, and there were family doings. But surely by lunchtime, or right after lunch, Luke was saddling and riding up the road. With her I turned my face away at the place where the grass was crushed, and with her tears sprang to my eyes as I went by our little gray house. Then up the silent hill, arriving just about two o'clock.

Tulip was a slow horse. Say three o'clock, or half past.

At four o'clock I was waiting hunched on the chopping block, my arms pressed tight against the hot, crawling sensation in my stomach. By five o'clock I knew: out of sight, out of mind. My friends might care while I was there in front of them, but they didn't care enough to come this far. Here I was, and here I'd rot, as far as anyone in Barrett was concerned.

In the barn milk hissed into Uncle Clayton's pails. My rooster pecked near my feet, the only creature in the world that willingly sought my company.

Two by two Uncle Clayton carried the milk pails to the house. When he came to let the cows out, Aunt Sarah came, too. "We need a bird for Sunday dinner," she said, and reached down and grabbed the gray rooster by the legs. He gave a squawk and hung blinking from her hand.

I stood up. "That's *my* rooster!"

Aunt Sarah barely glanced at me. "You can't get attached to farm animals. They aren't pets." She handed the upside-down rooster to Uncle Clayton and started to turn away. I felt the lump in my chest swell and crack.

"You have a dozen roosters! Kill one of the others!"

Aunt Sarah paused, stiffening. "Harriet," she said, "these are my chickens. I'll manage them as I see fit."

Something seemed to burst inside me. I stamped my foot. "You don't want me to have anything! You want me to *die!*"

She turned very slowly. Her face was blotched white and red, and she seemed gigantic, like an oceangoing ship. If I'd had any sense, I would have been frightened, but I stood my ground, thrusting my jaw at her. She said, in a voice so soft I could hardly hear it, "Clayton, kill that bird!"

"No!" I said. "Give him to me!"

Uncle Clayton's jaw sagged. He looked from me to

Aunt Sarah. The rooster's wings opened in a faint, dazed way.

"Harriet Gibson!" Aunt Sarah said. "You may not have been raised to respect adults, but you're about to learn!"

"I was raised *fine!*" I screamed the last word, so loud it slapped up a little echo off the side of the barn. "I was raised to respect *good* people! But you don't want me to have *anything!*"

"You've got that colt out there eating his head off! You've got a room of your own! Some children might be grateful, but your mother—"

"You leave my mother out of this!"

"Oh, yes, leave her out! She took my brother away from this farm; she disgraced herself and spoiled his life—"

"That is *not* true! You're lying!"

"Oh, look in your Bible, child! Read the dates!" She turned away from me contemptuously. "Clayton!"

I pushed past her and snatched the rooster out of his unresisting hand. The bird's legs were warm. I tipped him gently upright and settled him under my arm. "I'll be back for my things when I've found a place to live." My voice shook, but it sounded clear and brave. I turned and started down the lane.

I didn't see anything. I didn't hear. My body shook, and in my mind I yelled at Aunt Sarah. I did the whole fight again, only better. "If my mother had been a *bank robber*, she'd still be a better person than you are!" I screamed inside.

It felt glorious.

I stumbled. *Uhh-ohhhh,* the rooster murmured. I felt him shudder in my arms. His head bobbed with every step I took, jerking side to side as he tried to focus. I looked into his green and orange eye. She would have chopped his head off.

"I will never go back," I said. "This time nothing's going to stop me."

The long, low afternoon sun slanted through the trees. I turned down the main road, skirting the lower edge of the big pasture. I would find a place to live, I would send for Mother's sewing machine, and I'd earn a living for myself. She'd taught me to sew a seam; with thought, with practice, I could learn to design as she had, to make the little adjustments that turned an ordinary dress into something far more flattering.

Or I'd go out as a hired girl.

Oh, yes, I can see that! some part of me said, in a voice like Aunt Sarah's. A runaway orphan, as near illegitimate as makes no difference—

"That's a lie!"

Ohh, murmured the rooster. His chest vibrated on my arm. *Ohh, look!* He cocked his head, listening, and now I, too, heard hoofbeats, coming from downhill.

A buggy emerged from the shade of the birches, pulled by a horse I didn't know. We drew nearer each other. In the shadow of the hooded buggy a face began to take shape: an unbleached shirtfront—no, a long yellow-white beard.

The one-armed man.

The horse reached me and stopped of its own accord, puffing. It had deep hollows over its eyes and looked too fuzzy for this time of year, as if it hadn't shed out properly. It turned its head toward the rooster but didn't seem to have enough strength or curiosity to sniff.

I kept walking. As I passed the front wheel, a voice issued out of the dark buggy. "Well, hello there! You'll be Harry Gibson."

I stopped in my tracks. No one had called me Harry in a long time. I stared into the old man's clear, pale eyes and felt a sudden shock, the kind you feel when you miss the bottom stair. I knew him. Didn't I? But who was he?

"Where you goin' with Sarah's rooster?"

The top of my head prickled. "How do you know whose rooster it is?"

Movement beneath the beard seemed to indicate a smile. "Ain't many roosters on this ridge. Where you takin' him?"

Mother taught me not to talk with strange men. I glanced behind me. I could get over the stone wall quickly, if I needed to.

"Don't remember me, do you? It's Truman Hall, your uncle Clayton's brother."

Truman! I remembered the name. I remembered that Uncle Truman had been good to Mother and Father, and suddenly I remembered him, sitting at our kitchen table once or twice when I was very small.

"You came to the funeral."

He nodded. "I'da done better to come while she was alive, but it ain't easy with a horse this old. Jerry's done well to get me down to the birches today." Beneath and behind the seat, I noticed now, were bundles of dry twigs, tied together with strips of rag. "Kindling," Truman said. "I don't split it as easy as some folks." He shrugged his left shoulder, and the shortened arm moved within the sleeve.

"Where do you live?"

"Live in your house," he said. "House where you were born."

"Really? Where is it?"

He pointed uphill with his chin. I saw only the road and the empty green slope. "I was born there, too," he said. "So was your Uncle Clayton. I sold the place to your dad when they got married, bought it back from your mother when he died. You prob'ly don't remember it."

"No. I only remember West Barrett."

"Headin' back there?" Truman asked. "I see you're takin' along your supper!"

I glanced down at the rooster, lying warm and docile on my arm. "No, he—he's friendly. He likes me. She was going to kill him for Sunday dinner!" To my horror tears overflowed my eyes. "She has a dozen roosters, but just because I like this one—" I stopped myself.

Truman shook his head. "Sarah, Sarah, Sarah," he said, in a warm, musing voice. "Always did make bad worse. Little bit that way yourself, ain't you, Harry?"

"No! I never fight with people! It's *her!*"

A huge grin cracked Truman's face. He cocked his head and looked at me with an expression of pure delight. "Y'know, when I see Sarah pickin' you up at the funeral, I says to myself, Trume, I says, Sarah don't know it, but she's got a bobcat by the tail. Ohh, my!"

Ohh, my, the rooster echoed, shifting. I felt his wings try to flap, and I wrapped my arm closer around him.

"Mr. Hall, I need to be going," I said as politely as I could.

He leaned forward. One elbow rested on his knee. The other arm didn't include an elbow. "Now, youngster, listen. Are you dead set on runnin' away?"

"I'm not running away. I'm just leaving."

"Because if you ain't," he said, "it'd give me a lot of pleasure to have you in the neighborhood. Now, tell you what, c'mon up home with me. Bring your bird, and I'll shelter him for you. Then you and me and him can visit back and forth, and we'll study up how to civilize Sarah."

I hesitated. The sun was nearing the ridgetop, and the road below was deeply shadowed. It was a long way down to West Barrett, and the bird was shifting in my arms.

But would I really get into a buggy with a strange man? Would I really go back to Aunt Sarah a second time, after running away?

"Course, if you come with me, you've got to walk," Truman said. "Jerry'd catch his never-get-over if he had to haul us both."

He chirruped, and stiffly the old horse put himself in motion. I turned with the turning wheel and watched the buggy leaving. The hillside seemed wide and still and empty.

I took three long steps and caught up.

Ten

MY ARM WAS CRAMPING. I shifted the rooster. He opened his beak, and a screech came out that sounded like *help, help, help!*

Truman dropped the reins on the dash, set his foot on them, and took off his straw hat. He handed it to me. "Put that over his head. He'll feel better if he can't see too much."

The hat was worn and greasy, but the rooster stilled beneath it. I walked beside the wheel, and Truman leaned forward on his one elbow, gazing at the green hillside. He didn't speak. We neared the farm lane and very slowly passed it. I listened for the sound of other hoofbeats. Would Aunt Sarah really let me run away? Wouldn't she come after me?

"If Jerry was younger," Truman said suddenly, "I'd drive up and tell Sarah not to worry. But when a horse hits thirty, he's only got so many steps left in him."

"I *want* her to worry," I said. "It serves her right!"

He grinned again, as if something about me delighted him beyond measure.

We continued up the road about half a mile farther. A grassy lane branched off to the left. Jerry turned in there and stopped with a sigh, dropping his head to graze. Truman climbed down awkwardly and stood patting the old horse, looking across the blue folds of the hills.

I looked, too. We're so high, I thought. It made me feel calm and at home, as if I were looking out my own bedroom window.

"All right, Jerry." Truman pulled up the old horse's head, and we walked on either side of him. The lane seemed untracked and abandoned, but ahead I saw the sagging wall of a shed.

In a moment the whole house came into view: a low gray Cape, crumbling back into the hillside. The shed was swaybacked, and lichen grew on the roof slates, making them look thick and soft. Lilacs crowded tight to the house, and they were blossoming, though the lilacs at home had already faded. A shiver traveled up my spine. I don't remember this, I thought. I'm sure I don't remember.

Truman led Jerry into the shed, which was open on both sides. I watched with an unsettled feeling in my stomach as he unhitched and unharnessed. The lone hand seemed independently alive, like an animal.

He slung the harness onto the wall pegs and slipped the bridle off Jerry's head. Jerry shuddered his skin and ambled out the other side of the shed, down the green slope. I looked out after him. There was no fence in sight, only hens bobbing in the grass, looking like fat old ladies with their hands clasped behind their backs.

"Won't he run away?"

"Jerry ain't ambitious," Truman said. He looked around blankly, scratching in his beard. Then he fetched down a dusty bushel basket from a rafter peg. "Here, stick your bird under this. I'll put him with the hens after dark."

I put the rooster on the ground, and Truman lowered the basket as I took my hands away. A soft, weary *ohhh* and then silence.

I stepped back. Truman said, "Now, Harry. Thirsty?" I nodded.

"Set down on the step, and I'll fetch you a cup of water." He disappeared through a door in the shed, and I went outside.

The front step was a brown piece of sandstone, weathered and soft looking. I sat, curling my legs under me. A low purple-flowered plant with scalloped leaves grew all around the stone. Bees buzzed and stirred the blossoms.

That's gill-go-by-the-ground, I said to myself.

How did I know that? My gaze dropped to the edge of the stone, where a large chip was missing—

The back of my neck prickled. In my mind's eye I saw a baby's finger, pink and pointed, tracing the chip. *My* finger.

The door opened behind me. Cold, dog-smelling air flowed out. A dog came, too, a cow-dog, who flattened her ears at me in a friendly way. Behind her came Truman, with two tin cups in his hand. I took one, and he lowered himself onto the rock beside me. The dog squeezed in between.

"Well now, this is neighborly!"

I drank half my water in two big gulps. It was cold and sweet. "I remember this rock," I said after a minute. "I remember sitting out here."

"I remember you here," Truman said.

The rock was warm, and warmth spread into me. The place seemed to put its arm around me. I cradled the tin cup and looked over the rim, at the crooked, spindling bean poles, green grass and green trees, hills turning from blue to purple.

The dog sighed and nudged at my hands. I put an arm around her, brushing the rough cloth of Truman's coat with my elbow.

"What's her name?"

"Name? Seems to me I named her Nell. Call her Tippy nowadays." The dog flattened her ears at both names. "What you call that horse of yours?"

"He doesn't have a name yet. I call him Kid." I listened to the quietness of the hillside. It was the same hill Aunt Sarah lived on, but here I felt as if I belonged.

"What happened to your arm?" I asked.

The lines around his eyes deepened. "You asked me that the last time I talked to you."

"I don't remember."

"You wa'n't but four or five." Truman glanced down at where his left elbow should have been. "I took a bullet, and they cut it off."

"In the *war*?"

"Well, it ain't *the* war anymore. The War Between the States."

I'd seen the old veterans march in the Decoration Day parade; not very many of them anymore. I'd never seen Truman there. "Did it—did it hurt *terribly*?" It seemed like a stupid question, but I had to ask.

His eyes twinkled. "I can't remember," he said. "Three days later I couldn't remember. Seemed to hurt the other fellers, though, so I suppose it hurt me, too. God arranges so you forget some things, which I guess is a mercy."

I stared. I couldn't begin to imagine having your arm cut off. The worst thing that had ever happened to me was a skinned knee. No. The worst thing that ever happened to me was Mother.

"When did you stop missing it?"

"Miss it yet," he said. "First thing in the mornin', when I reach for my boots. After that—oh, I'm old now anyway. Wouldn't be able to do much even if I had two hands."

"But—" That wasn't really the answer to my question.

After a moment he seemed to understand. "When a thing like that happens, you don't feel it so sharp at first. You're kind of stunned. Then later, oh, Mother of God, it hurt! And you begin to sense how nothing's going to be the same. In a while, though, by the fall after it happened, I decided I was glad to be alive. And then little by little you get better."

I felt Tippy warm against my side, and Truman warm against the arm I had around her. Something inside me relaxed. Just to be understood, to have someone answer an unspoken question . . .

"I wish I could stay here."

Truman nodded slowly. "Come back," he said after a minute. "I'm just about always here."

"I thought someone would come visit me." I heard the hurt in my voice and would rather have hidden it, but the words tumbled out suddenly. "I wrote to Dr. Vesper, and I wrote to the Academy. There'll be exams soon. I thought Luke might—" A big hot air bubble rose in my throat and stifled me.

"Barrett Academy," Truman mused. "Still teach Latin, do they?"

"Yes."

"'*Amo, amas, amat,*'" he quoted. "'I love, you love,'"— and with a glance at Tippy—"'she loves.' That's about all I remember—no, wait! '*Gallia est omnis divisa in partes tres—*'"

"'—*quarum unam incolunt Belgae!*'"

"Yup, the good old Belgae. That's somethin', isn't it? After all that time there's still a place called Belgium on the map."

"I have to take my exams," I said. "I have to be ready for next year."

"You figure on goin' then?"

I didn't see the hills anymore. I saw Dr. Vesper at the

table, and Aunt Sarah standing up like a Roman column, and that long, steep road. "I don't know how," I said. "It's so far, and . . . I don't know how I'll afford it."

Truman's eyes scanned the landscape, with the look of calm delight that was particularly his. "You got time," he suggested.

"No!" I stood up abruptly, and Tippy stood up, too, waving her tail. "Nobody has time, not to be sure of. Look at Mother!"

He nodded slowly, conceding the point.

"And anyway, time—I've been there weeks already and—oh, *why* did she send me there?" Tears poured down my face. "She *hates* us! Aunt Sarah *hates* us! She says horrible things, and—*why?*" I collapsed on the stone again with my face on my knees.

Tippy whined and pawed me. Then she was pushed away, and Truman's arm wrapped around my shoulders.

He let me cry. When I got quiet, he said, "You want to ask yourself, Harry: where else could she send you? Her folks are gone, and Sarah's all that's left of Walter's folks. She had a right to ask Sarah, and she knew Sarah'd do her duty."

"Aunt Sarah hates us," I said in a thready voice, and sniffled massively.

Truman's arm came away. "Walk out back of the house, Harry, and get a handkerchief off the clothesline."

I obeyed. I was startled to see that it was nearly dusk. The bushes were dense shadows, and the last hen walked hastily into the coop.

I found the clothesline. Hanging on it were a pair

of overalls, some long underwear, and three blue bandannas, worn so thin I could see my hand right through them. I unpinned one, mopped my itching face, and blew my nose.

"Harry, come give me a hand with this rooster," Truman called from the back door of the shed. I heard him chuckle. "Give me a hand! Think that's funny?"

"Uh—"

"Your ma and Walter always laughed. Sarah just gets mad." His hand curved over the rim of the bushel. When the basket lifted, I closed my hands around the warm, drowsy rooster. I put him in the coop, and Truman closed the door, held it shut with one knee, and turned the peg.

"There! Now, Harry, I know you want Sarah to suffer, but I got to send you back."

I didn't answer. The peepers began their shrill piping somewhere near. It was night.

"I'd go with you," Truman said, "but I can't ask Jerry to make another trip. Tell you what—you take Tippy and keep her overnight. Then, why, I'll have to come fetch her, won't I? Tell Sarah she'll have company to Sunday dinner."

He got a rope from the dark shed and fastened it to Tippy's collar. "Go along now," he said. "I'll see you tomorrow."

I started down the grassy lane. After a minute I heard a shout behind me. I turned, and Truman called, "S'pose we'll have chicken?"

Eleven

BEYOND THE STONE WALLS the world was dark. Tippy and I got ourselves between the ruts, and the road rolled us downhill. I would have passed the farm lane, but Tippy hesitated there and whined.

"Thank you, Tippy." Suddenly I was so tired I could hardly keep walking.

After a few minutes I heard hoofbeats and buggy wheels behind me. Tippy and I stepped to one side and waited. A pale blur, a heavy, sloppy trot—that was Whitey, Uncle Clayton's buggy horse, passing. Ahead a window glowed yellow. I walked toward it as Whitey stopped, the kitchen door opened, and a tall black column filled the rectangle of light.

"Did you find her?"

"She didn't go there. Nobody saw her."

I trudged past the buggy, past the horse. I wanted to walk straight inside and sit, but Aunt Sarah blocked the way. She wore a peculiar expression. I could barely see it, let alone interpret.

"Why, here she is, Sairy!"

"Yes, Clayton, I can see that." Aunt Sarah turned, and I followed her inside. I smelled potatoes and salt pork gravy, and instantly I was famished. I sat at the table. Aunt Sarah brought the pan from the stove. My eyes wouldn't open normally. I squinted up at her.

"Did you leave my rooster up to Truman's?" she asked. How did she know that? I wondered, and then saw Tippy exploring near the stove for crumbs.

"Yes. He said, expect company for dinner to-morrow."

Silence answered me. I managed to widen my eyes and see her, but I couldn't tell anything of what she might be thinking.

Tippy slept on my legs, and for the first time here I slept all night long. I woke to the sound of the dog's toenails on the stairs, feeling . . . not good, not happy, but expecting something, ready to start the day.

After chores Aunt Sarah started cooking dinner, and I went out to catch the colt. He came for his apple, sighed when I caught him, but allowed himself to be led through the gate. I put the bars back up and turned him toward the barn.

In my mind I already had him tied and was putting on the saddle. In his mind the colt was right here, and a strange little two-legged animal was coming toward him. His eyes bulged. He sank back on quivering haunches.

"Oh, for goodness' sake! It's a *hen!*"

But hens didn't roam free in West Barrett, and the colt had never seen one. His forefeet plunged right, left, and he started to back. I hung on, shouting, "Whoa! Whoa!" Two more hens arrived and scratched vigorously at the fresh black hoofmarks. The colt backed against the bars.

"Come *on!*" I pulled on the rope, but he only pressed backward. The gate began to creak. He'd break it! "Come *on!*" I yelled. "Come *on!* Come *on!*"

"Easy," someone said behind me. Uncle Clayton was there, gently shooing the hens away. The colt eased off the gate, and his head came down a little.

"Never seen a hen before?"

"I—I guess not." And he had panicked, the way Belle panicked when John Gale's Model T Ford came down West Barrett hill.

The hens began to return, flowing around Uncle Clayton's legs like brook water. The colt's head came down another inch. "He's a smart feller," Uncle Clayton said. "Once he sees what they are, he'll be all right."

He turned back toward the house, leaving me alone with colt and hens and a quivering feeling that spread from my stomach out through my arms and legs. I knew what that feeling was. I was afraid.

I'd seen the broken buggy and Belle beside it, but I hadn't thought much about the moment when the automobile was coming and Mother decided to make Belle face it. The plunging hooves, Belle's sunlit back, the moment when it was too late, when the buggy was tipping and Belle wouldn't stop.

The colt sighed and dropped his head into my shoulder. His bones pressed against mine. I cupped one hand behind his ear, feeling his heat and the quick, leaping pulse. How many other terrifying sights lay between here and the Academy steps?

Just then I heard a squeak and a rattle, and Truman's old buggy appeared at the bend in the lane. Tippy trotted toward it, waving her tail.

The colt's chin drew into a tight, quivering cone. His ears swiveled, showing the swing of his reactions. At last he tried to bolt. I stood firm, and he trotted in a circle around me.

Truman stopped the buggy. "Harry!" he called. "Tell him, 'Trot!'"

"Trot!" I gasped, expecting somehow that this would stop the colt.

Nothing changed, but Truman said, "Now tell him, 'Good boy!'"

"Why?"

"He done what you told him, didn't he?"

"Good *boy!*" I said, and started laughing. "Trot, darn you! Trot! Good boy!"

Another circle and the colt stopped, staring at Jerry. At a nod from Truman I said, "Whoa! Good boy!," feeling like a fool. The colt continued to stare at Jerry while I maneuvered him through the gate. Released, he came to press against the rails and gaze as I turned back to Truman.

"Is that how *you* train horses? Tell them to do what they're already doing?"

"I don't train horses, but that's part of it. If you can't make 'em do what you want, make 'em think you want what they're doin'."

"I trained him to lead," I said, "and to pick up his feet. But I've never trained a horse to ride."

"No? And you more'n a dozen years old! Get up, Jerry." We headed slowly toward the barn, the colt following along the fence line as long as he could. "How old is that critter?"

"Two."

"That's young. He'll get over a lot of foolishness on his own if you give him a year." Truman climbed down at the barn door and tousled Tippy's ears.

"I don't have a year. I need to ride him by the end of summer."

Truman looked up. In the shadow of the barn his eyes were green and glassy, like the net floats Luke brought from the seashore. "Doesn't pay to hurry a horse."

I set my lips firmly and didn't answer.

When we'd unhitched Jerry and put him in a stall, we went to the house together. Truman stopped just inside the kitchen door, closed his eyes, and inhaled deeply. "Salt pork gravy! By jing, that smells good!"

Uncle Clayton stood in the sitting-room doorway. He made a small, startled jerk and looked quickly at Aunt Sarah. She was stirring something on the stove, surrounded by billows of steam. I couldn't see that she even glanced up.

Truman sat down at the table and began playing with a fork. Once again I noticed that there was only one hand; it was a moment when a man would naturally have used two. "I never saw a rooster as tame as that," he remarked, raising his voice slightly. "Just a little leery when I opened the door this mornin', but I had him takin' grain out of my hand in ten minutes. Lot of roosters'd just as soon scratch your eyes out—"

Aunt Sarah put a plate of biscuits on the table with a good deal of emphasis. She looked at him for a moment, pressing her lips together. "Truman, if you're looking for an apology, just ask for one!"

Uncle Clayton and I glanced at each other uncomfortably.

"You don't owe *me* an apology," Truman said. "And the bird's still alive, so if he and Harry are satisfied—"

Her face was alarmingly still. Was this his idea of civilizing her? It seemed more like a challenge. She stared at him without speaking for long seconds. Then she said, "Truman Hall, what have you done to that shirt?"

Truman glanced down at himself. Just below the edge of his beard was a neat three-cornered tear. "By golly—"

"Go take it off and put on one of Clayton's! I'll mend that just as soon as I get a minute."

Truman nodded meekly. "Thank you, Sarah. Don't know how I come to do that." The two men disappeared into the back bedroom.

Aunt Sarah turned back to the stove. "I don't need

that old fool to tell me when I've done wrong," she said after a minute, stiffly.

I didn't know how to respond. I felt my face get red.

"We do need to eat these critters," she said. "You won't go making pets out of all of them?"

"Oh, no," I said. "No."

She turned from the stove with the platter of salt pork. I took it from her and placed it on the table. Both of us were warm and red faced and glad to have Truman and Uncle Clayton return. Truman draped his torn shirt over the back of a chair. I touched it as I passed. The fabric was worn nearly as transparent as the blue bandanna I'd borrowed last night.

"I'll mend this," I said. It seemed only right; I had a feeling the shirt had been torn on my account.

Uncle Clayton bowed his head in a brief, silent grace, and I looked at his hair, lank and gray streaked with brown. Then we ate, and after the first awkward moments there was real conversation. True, it was all about farm work, just as the weekday exchanges had been. But Truman hadn't visited in a while, and the way the grass was coming along, the thin place where the beans weren't growing, the new pigpen gate, all had to be explained in expansive enough terms that I could understand them, too. Everything was work here. Everything was food and firewood and racing the summer to get both put away in time. It was a life Mother had turned her back on, by moving down the hill to West Barrett, by staking my future on an Academy education. But it was new to me, and the distraction, any distraction, was welcome.

After dinner we washed up, and I mended Truman's shirt in a neat, nearly invisible darn, as Mother had taught me. While he was changing again, Uncle Clayton harnessed Jerry and brought him to the front door. Aunt Sarah came out of the house with a covered pie carrier.

Truman climbed into the buggy and snapped his fingers to Tippy. She leaped up, looking sturdy and balanced after his awkwardness. Aunt Sarah put the carrier on the floor. "Now don't let that dog eat this!"

Tippy had indeed sniffed the plate, but all at once she stiffened and looked past us, down the lane. After a moment a buggy appeared. "As good as livin' on Main Street," Truman said, settling back against the cushion with a pleased, expectant look.

I recognized the horse now, and after a moment I could see Dr. Vesper's face.

"Well, they're all out waitin' for a man!" he cried, and pulled up close to Jerry. "Trume, you're looking almost human! Sarah, Clayton. Hey there, Harry!"

In this yard, among them all, he seemed young and boisterous, like a classmate of mine rather than my doctor and guardian. He didn't look exactly as I'd remembered him. *It hasn't been that long!* I thought.

"I'm here to take you down to Barrett, Harry."

"Really?"

For a second he looked surprised. "Why, yes. You're to stay with the Mitchells while you take your exams."

I had hoped he was taking me away for real and

always. It took me a moment to gather my thoughts. "I'll get my things."

Only then did I notice Aunt Sarah's silence. She stood very still beside Truman's buggy, her face rigidly composed.

Was I supposed to ask if I could go? My cheeks burned. To heck with that! I thought, forming the words deliberately in my mind, and I went upstairs to pack a carpetbag.

When I got into the buggy, I was at eye level with Aunt Sarah. She wore her marble look.

"I'll have her back sometime midweek," Dr. Vesper said.

"All right," said Aunt Sarah, as if it made little difference to her.

I looked over at Truman and Tippy. He had his arm around the dog. No, on that side Truman didn't have an arm.

"You go first, Andy," he said. "We don't care if we never get there."

Twelve

THE MITCHELLS LIVED on Barrett Main Street in a big brick house that once was white. As the paint wore away, the brick color showed through, a soft terracotta.

The house was as familiar to me as my own. Luke and I have been best friends since Mother first began to sew for Ida Mitchell. We were three years old, and we can't remember a time when we didn't know each other.

Still, I opened the front door a little timidly. Luke hadn't been waiting in the yard. Dr. Vesper drove off with a cheerful "Good luck!" and I was alone again.

"Hello?" I said, into the fern-filled front hallway.

Upstairs something banged, and Luke looked over the banister. Her dark braids hung past her face. "Harry! Hang on!"

She cascaded down the stairs, and I saw the exact spot, halfway down, where she remembered that things were different. She flushed and came more slowly. Is she afraid? I wondered. She looked afraid.

"Harry," she said, and stopped. She still had her mother and the big brick house, and she didn't know what to say to me. I felt sorry for her, a little.

"Hi," I said. "Were you studying?"

She nodded. "Algebra."

"I haven't even looked at it. Can we drill?"

Luke looked—what? Disappointed? "Sure," she said after a minute, leading the way upstairs.

Algebra, Latin, and history got us through the afternoon. Supper was harder. Beautiful Ida Mitchell, in the skirt and shirtwaist Mother had made her, dark hair swept up the way Mother used to wear hers, made me want to cry. I had to brace, make my words curt and few. She kept looking at me, and I could see her love and concern. I stared at my plate. I never had this problem with Aunt Sarah.

After supper we studied until Mrs. Mitchell made us go to bed. Then we laid out the corduroy-covered floor cushions I've been using since I first slept here, at age seven. I cried that first night, I remember. I was homesick, and even a hug from Mrs. Mitchell didn't help.

Now I lay in the dark with my eyes open. My heart hurt. I dug my fingers into the blanket. I always thought heartache was a figure of speech. I never realized it was literal.

"Huh!"

A hushed, gasping sound from Luke's bed. I listened. Her breath trembled. There was a tiny sniff and then another "huh!"

"Luke?"

Her breath stopped entirely for a second. Then came a big sniff, and she asked, "What?" in a steady, muffled voice.

"Are you crying?"

"No," she said, and gave another hiccuping sob.

I sat up. "What's the matter?"

"Nu-nothing."

"Oh."

I started to lie back down when Luke suddenly burst out, "Are you still my friend, Harry?" I leaned, frozen, on one elbow. "Because—you haven't said *anything* to me! I've cried every night, I feel so bad for you, and—and you just want to do algebra!"

She sat up among her tumbled white sheets. The moon was bright enough to show the dark flow of hair down her back. Tears glittered on her cheeks.

"Luke . . ." It's too much if *I* have to comfort *her*, I thought. It's too much.

"I'm sorry," Luke whispered. "I meant—I wasn't going to—" She threw herself facedown on the pillow. Her whole body shook with crying, and before I thought, I was on the bed putting my arms around her.

As soon as I touched her, I started to cry, too. I knew how bad she felt for me, and I knew that I felt so much worse than she could guess, and that she was full of relief not to be in my shoes and was ashamed. It was all one pain, and we cried into the same pillow with our arms around each other.

When we finally stopped, we both needed handkerchiefs—two each in fact because Luke uses dainty linen squares. They made me think of Truman's bandanna. With a hiccup I said, "My uncle—"

"Wait," Luke said. She went to her door and listened a moment. "Be right back."

It was several minutes before she returned and closed the door behind her. Something clinked when she sat down on the bed. In the moonlight I made out a tray, glasses, and a decanter.

"Mother's cherry cordial," she said. I heard the sound of pouring, and then she pushed a glass into my hands. "It's very res-restorative."

I sipped. The cordial was sweet in my mouth and hot all the way down to my stomach, and only after I'd swallowed did I taste the cherries. "It's good."

"Is it?" Luke took a swallow and choked. "Well! Kill or cure!" We sat shoulder to shoulder, leaning against the wall with our legs stretched across the bed, and I told her nearly everything, beginning with the house and ending with the colt.

"I have to train him. It's the only way I can keep coming to school—if I can even afford it. But he's afraid of *hens*, Luke!"

"What if you meet an automobile?" Luke whispered.

Then I'll see Mother sooner than I expected! I

thought. Taking a moment to steady myself, I said it out loud. Luke laughed, and sniffed, and sloshed more cordial into our glasses.

The tray, glasses, and cordial were gone when we awoke. We went apprehensively to breakfast, but Mrs. Mitchell only said, "Another time, girls, get up and make cocoa."

We went out onto the sunny street. We were both nervous about exams, but beyond that I dreaded walking through the Academy door. The last place I was happy was in Miss Spencer's classroom, in the moments before Reverend Astley walked in.

But we met Billy halfway there, and then some others. After the first moments, when each person flushed and looked down and my insides burned, they were glad to see me, full of questions that skirted around Mother and centered on my new life and future. There were exams to worry about, tips to exchange, and all the while Luke stood shoulder to shoulder with me. We'd shared all that could be shared. I felt strengthened.

The two days passed quickly. When Latin and algebra stared me in the face, I had to forget everything else. The rest of the time Luke and I were together. We walked by the river. We climbed trees. We cleaned an unused stall in the Mitchells' stable and mended the fence of the second paddock, so the colt would have somewhere to stay while I was at school.

We were surrounded by other projects that had started with a bang: a board across the crotch of a maple that was going to be our tree house, a wavering line of stones and rough earth that was our rock garden. I could see the paddock staying empty, the boards falling down again.

But if the colt never got here, then I wouldn't, and when would I see Luke? I pounded nails fiercely and tried to believe we weren't just playing.

After the last exam we walked to the graveyard. I wasn't prepared for the rectangle of bare earth, the threads of sprouting grass. It had not been very long, not as long as it felt. No one had carved the final date after Mother's name. Whose job was it to hire that done? I wondered. Beneath my father's name—*"Walter Gibson, 1873–1899"*—hers looked unfinished, as if no one cared.

I felt a hot rush of tears coming and looked quickly away. The nearest row of gravestones caught my eye. They were all Gibsons, like me: *"Melinda, wife of David Gibson, 1843–1873. David Gibson, 1842–1876. Edward, 1867–1890. Lettice, 1870–1892. Violet Anne, 1871–1895."*

"Who are they?" Luke asked.

I shook my head. "David and Melinda—they might be my grandparents."

Luke counted on her fingers. "They all died young. Lettice was only twenty-two."

"I don't know anything about them," I said.

Luke glanced at me curiously but didn't say anything.

It had always been a given that I had no family but

Mother, orphaned in a fever epidemic, and Aunt Sarah, who hated us. The family was here apparently. The dates, the names, the stones began to weigh on my heart like gray storm clouds. "Let's go!"

When dusk fell that evening, we were in a tree again. We could see Mrs. Mitchell, a white blur in the front yard, weeding her flowers. The window of Mr. Mitchell's study glowed yellow. We listened to the birds and frogs and the sound of an approaching buggy.

It stopped at the front gate. Mrs. Mitchell went to the fence.

"Hello, Ida," Dr. Vesper said. He sounded tired. "'Fraid I can't get Harry up the hill tomorrow. Spent all day delivering a baby——"

Did he deliver *me*? I wondered. He'd know if I came too early. I imagined asking him. I couldn't imagine asking him.

"Doesn't matter," Mrs. Mitchell was saying. "She's perfectly welcome to stay here."

Dr. Vesper hesitated. "Thing is, I don't want to get her in Dutch with Sarah."

"I see. Then I'll drive her up. We can take a picnic."

"I appreciate——whoa!" The hungry horse had made a move toward home. "She talk to you any, Ida? She was kind of mum with me on the way down."

"She's talked with Lu," Mrs. Mitchell said. "I've tried not to interfere. Nothing but time can heal Harriet, but Lu's been good for her. They'll remember this time together all their lives, I think."

Dr. Vesper made a grumbling sound. "That doesn't tell me what's going on up there." He leaned out of the buggy, pitched his voice low, and for a few moments the words didn't reach us. Then he sat up. "Tell her I'll be up soon and we'll have a business session. And will you stop by Althea Brand's on your way up? Thanks."

He drove up the street. Luke and I slipped quietly down the tree and through the back door, ready to be told the news.

It seemed a pleasant plan: a drive behind Tulip, a roadside picnic. It was only after we'd blown out the lamp and stopped talking that I began to see it happen: Luke and her mother meeting a car, the horse running down that steep hill.

That won't happen. Tulip's very calm.

But the buggy kept tipping over. Both of them were killed. Luke was killed. Her mother was killed. Always I was the one left alive.

It was my turn to stifle ragged breath and try to keep from sniffing.

In a few minutes Luke said, "Harry?"

"What if you meet a car?" I sobbed. "What if your mother dies, too?"

Luke started crying instantly. "I know, I know. I keep thinking that—"

We were crying too hard to stop ourselves. Luke got out of bed and took my hand. We went downstairs into the parlor, where Mrs. Mitchell was just rising, alarmed.

She put her arms around us and drew us down on

the sofa. "Oh, babies," she said. "Oh, babies."

"What's the matter?" I hadn't even noticed Mr. Mitchell in his chair.

When we could make ourselves understood, when we'd been given handkerchiefs and had blown our noses and only sobbed from reflex, we all sat on the sofa together. Luke's father hugged her, and Mrs. Mitchell kept her arms around me. Patiently they explained how Tulip had been taught not to fear automobiles. They had a Model T of their own and had spent hours on the job.

"I was just as afraid as you girls are," Mrs. Mitchell said, "but Tulip is well trained now, and he's the calmest animal God ever put breath in."

"But you can't guarantee," I said.

"No," Mr. Mitchell said. "Nothing's guaranteed. But we've done everything we could."

We went to the kitchen, all four of us, and made cocoa. Then Mrs. Mitchell settled us back in bed, as if we were indeed babies. Tomorrow I'd be back on the hill, a grown-up among grown-ups.

I wished I could always stay here.

Thirteen

BEFORE MR. MITCHELL went to his office, he took us out to the pasture. Tulip crunched oats, and Mr. Mitchell drove the Ford in circles around him. Tulip tossed his head, looking annoyed.

"You'll have to train your colt this way," Luke said, turning to me with wide, serious eyes. "Bring him down here, and Papa will help."

But how would I get him down, I wondered, when I couldn't lead him past a scratching hen? It was going to take so much work. I felt a stir of impatience to get home and get started.

We reached West Barrett just as the mill stopped for lunch. I saw Luke's mother struggle not to look at our house. Tears glittered on her lower lids.

Althea popped out the door as soon as we stopped. "Harriet!" She squeezed my hands gently, with a quick look at my fingers. It took me a moment to remember how I'd stabbed them on the screen.

The kettle whistled on the stove, and the green teapot stood ready on the table. Althea poured boiling water over the tea leaves. Then she said, "Ladies, I need to show Harriet something. Will you excuse us a moment?" She led me upstairs and opened the door of her spare bedroom.

Althea's spare room had been very spare: one old bedstead, one thin rug, one washstand. Now the bed was crowded with books, rolls of fabric, framed prints. Here were the pitcher we put wildflowers in and, next to that, our rotary eggbeater.

"Two o'clock every single morning," Althea said, "I sit straight up and think, 'But we never took *that*! She'll need such and so.' And along toward daybreak I walk up and get it. I told Andy Vesper, we didn't have time to think before, any of us, but I just couldn't square it with my conscience if I didn't rescue the things Harriet ought to have."

I touched the pitcher. Just a few weeks ago Mother had filled it with lilacs. "Thank you," I whispered.

"I thought it'd be just you and Andy," Althea said, "and more room in the buggy. But you take what you want right now, and the rest'll be here."

I looked at her, dried up like a raisin in her patched old dress. I wanted to say something, but I didn't know the words. I felt . . . *proud* of her, but a girl can't say she's proud of an old woman. I reached for her hand again and felt her hard old fingers squeeze mine.

After tea I made my choices. Luke came up with

me, looking sober. She would be thinking of the brick house on Main Street, with its rugs and ferns, its furniture and knickknacks. A house seemed permanent, but here was our house turned into a forlorn pile of objects. That could happen to anyone.

I took my rug, my quilt, a small pile of books, and the flower pitcher. Later we passed a rosebush blooming beside the road. I filled the pitcher with white roses, nourishing them with lemonade from our jug.

Tulip was a slow horse, and Mrs. Mitchell didn't hurry him. We stopped in one of the blackberry pastures and lingered over our picnic. Still, we got closer and closer, my stomach got tighter and tighter, and then we arrived.

I heard the clink of hoes on stone and found them in the potato patch. Aunt Sarah came toiling up the hill, like a potato herself in brown gingham. I looked at Mrs. Mitchell, light, slender, and graceful in dotted Swiss. She looked like Mother. There would be trouble.

She shook Aunt Sarah's hand. "Mrs. Hall, I'm Ida Mitchell. Harriet's mother was my dear friend. And this is my daughter, Lucretia, who is Harriet's dear friend."

Aunt Sarah stiffened, and I knew why. Behind her words Mrs. Mitchell was saying, clear as paint: This girl is not alone in the world. I take an interest in her.

Aunt Sarah didn't speak. Mrs. Mitchell went on. "My husband and I wanted you to know that we'll help when Harriet decides how to manage school. The horse can stay with us during the day, and Harriet herself can stay anytime she needs to."

"The horse isn't trained," Aunt Sarah said.

"He will be. Also, we spend two weeks at the seashore in August, and we'd like Harriet to join us this year."

Luke and I looked at each other. We'd heard nothing of this.

Aunt Sarah seemed to swell on one of her long breaths.

"Go help Harriet bring in her things, Lu," Mrs. Mitchell said. Color was beginning to glow on her cheekbones. I strained to hear as Luke and I collected my belongings and went inside.

I could make out nothing until I'd reached my room. Luke stopped at the top of the stairs, but I rushed to the window. They were right below me, and their voices came clearly.

"I'm to have the care and feeding of this child, but apparently I have no say in what happens to her!"

"Of course you have a say in what happens to her. But at her age and in her situation she must have a great deal to say for herself, especially about her education."

"I know what education did for her mother!" Aunt Sarah said.

I turned quickly from the window. Luke mustn't hear this. "What do you think?" I asked in as carrying a voice as I could manage. As I'd hoped, Aunt Sarah's voice sliced off.

"Oh, Harry, it's *awful!*" Luke looked around with tears in her eyes.

I shook out the rug beside the bed. "There! This

helps, and the quilt." I folded it over the back of the chair. "And the roses, of course." I put them on the windowsill, and glanced down. Aunt Sarah and Mrs. Mitchell had stepped apart from each other.

Mrs. Mitchell called, "Lu! I'm ready to go!"

Luke said, "We've got to get you out of here!"

When the rattle of the buggy wheels had died away, the place seemed still and empty. The afternoon was hot. Aunt Sarah had gone back to hoeing, and I was alone in the kitchen.

My footsteps were loud as I crossed to the pantry. I lifted the lid of the spring box and took out the dripping pitcher of buttermilk. I drank down a glass of it, rinsed the glass, dried it, and put it away. There! I'd left no trace. Nothing in this kitchen showed that I had ever been here. No task awaited my finishing, no book was left open on its face, no spot of color or life appeared; just drab cleanness and the smell of vinegar.

Vinegar Hill! I thought suddenly. That's the name for this place! It cheered me immediately, as if I'd struck a secret blow for myself. My unfinished task awaited me down in the pasture. I changed my clothes, went down, and caught him.

After Tulip the colt seemed extravagantly beautiful. His nostrils flared wide and thin like bone china teacups. His red-gold coat, with the veins close to the surface, seemed to promise a hot, sensitive nature. Mother and I had loved to look at him. He'd be just like Belle in a few years, we thought.

"Right now I'd be happy if you were a little more like Tulip," I told him. He snorted at hens. He shied violently at the currant bushes, which I could understand, because they had been veiled in white netting. But being terrified of an apple crate and the hay rake made no sense at all. I couldn't make myself say "whoa," and praise him when he balked and bugged his eyes, not when, from the potato patch, Aunt Sarah could see it all.

"Stop it!" I said sternly, and jerked the rope. Truman's way wasn't the only way to train horses.

During supper Aunt Sarah sat ominously silent, glancing toward me from time to time and pressing her lips tightly together. She must have been brooding all afternoon, and now she was trying to keep from saying something.

I felt hollow. I've never managed not to speak unwise words when they're on the tip of my tongue. I may know better, and for a while I may be able to congratulate myself on restraint, but the words always burst forth anyway, as if holding back only gave them a bigger head of steam. I think it's that way for everyone.

Suddenly Aunt Sarah said, "Does this dear friend of your mother's have any notion of work on a farm?"

I put down my fork and sat looking at her. I wasn't going to waste my powder defending Ida Mitchell, but in fact, she knew all about farm work. I remember her saying to Mother, "From the day I weeded my first acre of potatoes I've wanted to marry a man who lived in town." She was laughing at herself because Mr. Mitchell had been a farmhand when they met. "Love is blind!" she said.

Mother didn't laugh. "No, Ida," she'd said. "Love sees truly. Anything we do for any other reason is apt to be a mistake."

"How does she know we can spare you in August?" Aunt Sarah was asking.

"Don't know why we *couldn't*," Uncle Clayton said. Aunt Sarah and I both looked at him. He looked down at his plate, but he said, "We never do need anybody besides us and Trume."

"We have extra mouths to feed!"

"I'll be very happy to do my share of the work," I said. "I didn't ask to be taken to the seashore!"

"And I didn't ask for—" She clamped her mouth shut.

I sat stiff in my chair. Next she'd say that thing about Mother, and I would have to fight.

"Can you churn?"

I almost didn't understand the question. It took me a moment to answer. "I never have."

"I'd like you to take that over for me," she said.

"All right." I had no idea what I'd agreed to, only a surging determination to do it well and thoroughly.

Aunt Sarah's hackle was slowly going down. "A half day's work is plenty. I've never believed in working youngsters too hard."

What youngsters? I wondered. She'd had no children

that I'd ever heard of. How could she set herself up as an authority? But I only said, "Fine."

Uncle Clayton glanced from one to the other of us and seemed to think that the storm had blown over. He got up and went to look out the window. "Well, guess I'll cut hay tomorrow."

Aunt Sarah frowned. "That looks like mackerel sky to me."

I hated to agree with her, but it looked like mackerel sky to me, too—thin clouds laid across the blue like a fillet of fish with the flesh just pulling apart.

Uncle Clayton shook his head. "'Twon't amount to anything," he said, and yawned. "Time for bed."

Down on Main Street Luke and I would be climbing into a tree about now, the evening just beginning. Here at Vinegar Hill we washed dishes and headed to our bedrooms as the clock struck nine. It wasn't even dark out.

I put on my nightgown and drew the rocking chair near the window, where I could look out on the barn roof and the weather vane horse striding across the dim early stars. At home nine o'clock found the sewing machine still humming. I'd be setting a hem for Mother or maybe reading aloud. No question about her character would ever have crossed my mind.

Not that I thought Mother was perfect. When you live with people, you see them scratch and hear them sniffle. You know if they swear sometimes, on running a needle into their thumbs, and then scold if you do the same. You know if they're stubborn, and if they

🖙 116 🖘

listen to gossip, and if attention to detail might make their accounts true up.

I knew these things about Mother, but I never knew her to do anything big and wrong. Have a baby too early. Not tell that baby things she needed to know. Aunt Sarah hadn't said it again, but somehow, by not saying it, by not making me fight her, she'd caused the doubt to bite inward.

Was it true?

It couldn't be—but how could I *prove* that? "When is your birthday?" Aunt Sarah's voice nagged. "When were your parents married?"

My birthday was February 14. That much I knew. Mother and Father's wedding date was another matter. She had neither celebrated nor mourned their anniversary, just as we never visited his grave or came back here. Everything was forward with Mother, but there must be some record. A marriage certificate, perhaps. Althea and I hadn't thought to look for papers like that when we did our late-night packing. Would Dr. Vesper look before the house was sold? Or were those things already in the care of a lawyer?

All at once I remembered the wallet. I'd put it in the bureau drawer without even looking inside. It hadn't seemed to belong to me.

I carried the candle over and looked inside the wallet. A few coins weighted the bottom. There was a folded scrap of newspaper that, flattened out, proved to be a corset advertisement. Inside it was a crumbling red clover blossom. That was all.

I put the wallet back in the drawer and picked up my candle. The light wavered across the mirror and touched the wall behind.

That's not a wall, I realized. That's a door!

How had I never seen it before? True, everything was gray in this room, and true, the door was mostly concealed by the mirror. The mirror was what usually caught my eye, because of its odd surface. But not see a door? A short little door like this, with one corner lopped off by the angle of the rafters? I've been walking around half blind, I thought.

I mapped the house in my mind. My bedroom was in the ell. Here the house was a story and a half high. The rest of the house was a full two stories, and this door must lead to those upstairs rooms.

I felt behind the bureau. No latch. I brought the candle near the wall and angled it till I could see that yes, there was a thumb latch. The bureau was in the way and I couldn't reach it.

I set the candle on the floor and crawled up onto the bureau. My own white bulk came at me in the mirror. I squeezed one leg behind the frame, groped till I found the latch, and pressed my toe into its cold, smooth groove.

The latch squeaked open. Gently I nudged the door. It swung about six inches and stopped. All I could see was darkness. I squirmed farther over, my thigh pressed hard against the mirror frame, and it creaked.

The darkness seemed to jump. I stilled my breath,

listening to the silent house. No one spoke, but I could imagine Aunt Sarah lying wide eyed, waiting for the sound to repeat. I sat a long while, the mirror frame digging into my thigh.

At last I reached my foot into the dark room, found the edge of the door, and drew it toward me. When it was close enough, I shut it with my hand. I couldn't latch it. I'd have to leave it slightly ajar, and sometime tomorrow, when Aunt Sarah was outside, I'd run up here and close it.

First, though, I'd look inside.

Fourteen

$\mathcal{I}$N THE MORNING I learned about churning. One sat on the back porch in a rocking chair and pushed the churn, a barrel on rockers, with one's foot. One looked at the currant bushes or the maples on the hill or provided oneself with a book. A basket and half-finished gray vest showed that Aunt Sarah knitted as she sat here. There would be time to complete any number of vests.

Maybe I should learn to knit. I needed something to keep me from thinking, but whenever I tried to read, the people, even my favorite characters in my favorite books, seemed like paper dolls. Nothing was powerful enough to turn my mind from Mother.

Away on the hillside I heard the mowing machine clatter. Aunt Sarah stepped around the kitchen; bowls clinked; the oven door slammed. Then she came out to the back porch, tying on her straw hat. "Call me when it comes together. I'll be in the garden."

I waited long enough for her to get there. Then I dashed upstairs, pulled the bureau six inches out from the wall, and peeked around the edge of the open door.

The room beyond was empty. Absolutely empty.

A closet door stood open, and the closet was empty, too, except for the bed slats leaning in one corner. No curtains, no rugs, no cobwebs, hardly any dust. Across the room was another closed door.

I stared at the wide boards crossed by sunlight, at the creamy, violet-sprigged wallpaper. I had thought these rooms would be full of furniture. Why else would the front room be given up to storage except that the upstairs rooms were full?

This room was empty but not abandoned. It had been cleaned recently and smelled of vinegar and soda. What lay beyond the closed door, so flat and bland and white? I wanted to go open it, but it seemed a long way across the room, and Aunt Sarah might come back to the house. I didn't want her to find the churn deserted. I closed the door behind the bureau but left the bureau where it was, pulled away from the wall just far enough that I could slip behind it.

Back downstairs I rocked, and rocked, and thought of Mother, and cried. Still the butter wasn't done. I rocked some more, rocked with all my might and determination, until at last the yellow grains of butter floated in the milk and it was time to call Aunt Sarah.

Even as Uncle Clayton drove back from mowing, clouds began to gather, and by late afternoon it was raining. Aunt Sarah looked dark, but Uncle Clayton seemed perfectly placid.

"First cut of hay always gets rained on," he said. "I cut that weedy spot a-purpose."

"Seems to me after forty years a man could cut hay without it getting rained on!"

Behind his magazine Uncle Clayton murmured, "You should have stopped me, dear." Then he glanced at me and looked startled. He wasn't used to having his little flings of spirit witnessed.

When the long, wet day ended and we went to bed, it was actually dark. I waited, while the rain roared off the eaves, until Aunt Sarah would surely be asleep. Then I slid behind the bureau, sheltering the candle flame with my palm, and opened the door.

Darkness doesn't scare me, but this empty room seemed too large. Shadows lay thick in the corners. There was nothing to see here. I went straight across and opened the door on the other side.

I was looking out into a hallway. Another closed door stood opposite. I moved toward it and stopped with a gasp, sensing a black chasm to my right. I turned the candle so I could see.

Stairs. Just stairs.

I opened the next door: another room, also clean, also empty. It contained two closets, one piled with wool blankets, the other bare.

The hallway made a three-sided rectangle around the stairwell. At the other end was a third door. I already knew what I would find there, an empty room.

Why would anyone do that? Why take every stick of furniture out of these unused rooms and pile it in the front parlor? That room must have been very pleasant once, with the sunny windows and the fireplace.

Of course the fewer rooms you used in a house, the less work, but then, why was it so clean up here?

The rain continued the next day, steady and gentle. I didn't churn. Churning was every third day, depending on the milk supply. Instead I swept and dusted and washed the kitchen down with vinegar. After dinner I walked over to Truman's.

My oilskin could have been longer. It kept the upper reaches dry, but water rolled down and collected in the hem of my skirt, which also gathered moisture from the grass in the lane. The fabric slapped chill against my legs.

In Truman's yard the violets bloomed, each flower beaded with raindrops. As I walked past the sagging shed and the scent of crushed gillflower rose, the feeling of belonging came over me again. It was like the line that used to run between Mother and me, diffuse now, as if the love had become a cloud I walked into. Only here. Was she here? I paused and looked around. There was nothing to see but the violets and the trees, nothing to hear but the rain, nothing to feel but cold and wet, but—but something. Something was here that belonged to me.

I knocked. Tippy barked sharply, and after a moment the door opened. "Why, Harry!" Truman slipped his suspenders up over a sleeveless undershirt. The stump of his arm was in full view. I couldn't help staring. It looked so neat, sliced off square like a piece of meat at the butcher's. Shiny-looking skin stretched across the end.

"C'mon in!" He reached for his threadbare jacket, thrown across the back of the chair. When he'd shrugged into it, he looked ordinary again, as ordinary as a man could look with a flowing yellow beard and only one arm.

"Pull a chair up to the stove and get dry," he said. "I'll make tea."

I took off my oilskin and sat down, spreading my skirt and looking around the room. At first glance it seemed unbelievably cluttered. There was a cot in one corner and a woodbox in another, a table, two chairs, pots and pans, a sack of onions, a coat on the floor covered with dog hair. There were books on every surface and books through the open door in the next room.

But despite the clutter, the room was really simple. I never saw Truman look for anything. His hand just reached, and what he needed was right there. The canister. The teapot. The potholder—

Mother, I thought suddenly. It was as if I'd caught sight of . . . not her but something that belonged to her. What was it? Not the pans. Not—

"The curtains!"

"What about 'em?" A cloud of steam masked Truman's face as he poured hot water into the teapot.

"Those were here!" I said. "Weren't they? Didn't Mother make those?" They were white, with a strip of bright calico sewn across the bottom. Wasn't there a dress of that fabric?

"Yup, those were hers." Truman looked around. "Not much else. The cookstove. We figured it didn't make sense, her haulin' this stove downhill and me buyin' one and haulin' it up. So we come to terms."

That was after my father died, when Mother must have felt just the way I did now. How did she bear it? I wondered. I never knew how much grief hurt, so I never knew to ask her.

"How—how *was* she? After he died?"

Truman considered me, his fingers twisting a small section of beard into a spike. "I don't s'pose she put you down for three days," he said at last. "And you were a pretty hefty package about then, big two-year-old girl. But she held on to you, and that kept back the worst of it, I guess."

I knew what the worst of it felt like. It hurt, really hurt, in your body. Would it help having someone to hold?

Truman poured tea into the two tin cups. I wrapped my hands around mine and put it down in a hurry. Hot!

"So, Harry," Truman said, "come to visit your bird?"

I'd actually forgotten my gray rooster, dearest thing in life to me when I was carrying him down the road. "No, I'm here to tell you that haying's started." That was the errand I'd been charged with when I'd said where I was going.

Truman looked out at the dripping eaves. "Clayton's cut the weed field. What'd Sarah say?"

" 'After forty years I'd think a man could cut hay with*out* it getting rained on!' "

"You do it well," Truman said gravely. He reached into the skillet beside him and started to break off a chunk of biscuit. Then he paused. "By golly, if Sarah was here, she'd give me a piece of her mind! Excuse me."

"I was wondering how you cut bread."

"Same way I do a lot of things. I don't." He finished breaking the biscuit and handed it to me. "I generally dump the jam on a plate and dip into it. That suit you?"

"Why don't I spread it for us?" I said, spotting a knife on the table. Everything was clean. How did he wash his dishes? I wondered.

He settled back in his chair, stretching his long legs, and watched me spread the jam. "You're like your mother," he said after a minute.

"I am? How?"

He shrugged. "Manners, I guess. Kind manners."

"Am I like my father, too?"

"Oh, you're a Gibson, all right! You've got the chin!"

I put my hand up to hide it. "You mean, like *Aunt Sarah*?"

He smiled, the slow narrowing and arching of his eyes that reminded me of the years he'd spent outdoors, marching and fighting. "Just like," he said. "You look just like she did at the same age."

"You knew her then?"

"Oh, yes! Known Sarah since before she was born. The Gibsons—the old folks—wa'n't too very much older than me." He took a cautious sip of tea, eyes focused on something far away. "The old folks! Seems funny to call 'em that. They never did get old."

"My grandparents?" He nodded. "What happened to them?"

"What happened?" He looked down, and the bushy shelves of his brows hid his eyes from me. "They died, Harry. Awful lot of consumption on this hill, back when it was full of farms. I guess maybe that's died, too. Hope it has."

I tried to remember the dates on the gravestones, to make a story out of what he was telling me, but the numbers wouldn't come back. "How old were the children—I mean, my aunts and uncles? When their parents died?"

"Sarah, she was about fourteen when she was left to mother the rest of 'em. Your father was a baby."

My age almost. Only one year older. That girl who became Aunt Sarah must have felt the same way I did, the same way Mother did when my father died. She must have held on to baby Walter the way Mother held on to me, the way I would hold on to somebody, if there were anyone to hold.

Then why wasn't she nicer? Why didn't she show a little kindness?

Truman sighed aloud, like a word, and rubbed his big hand down his face. "We was proud of her. She raised all four of 'em, even after she buried her dad. I remember when that house was full of young folks. They'd have dancin' in the kitchen most Saturday nights. . . . I was quite a bit older, but that didn't stop me courtin'. But Sarah had those kids to raise, and Clayt had two arms."

He'd wanted to *marry* Aunt Sarah?

He sat with his chin on his chest for a minute and then took a big swig of tea. That was how the beard got stained, I noticed. "And then they started dyin'," he said. "Get into their twenties, they'd get that cough. Sarah fought it, every time. She was bound and determined, but you can't beat it. Hard times. Hard times. I don't know how she stood it. This arm of mine is kid stuff compared to that."

The empty rooms were their rooms. Of course. "What about my father?"

"He was sick already when he met your mother, though Sarah wouldn't see it. He knew what he had coming to him, and he told your mother, but he couldn't scare her off." Truman gazed past the stove. After a while his chest heaved, as if to push off sorrow. "All over now. They're together."

And I'm alone.

Truman said, "But you've heard this all a hundred times."

I'd never heard it once. Oh, I knew Aunt Sarah had raised Father, and I knew what he'd died of. But

Mother didn't tell her life as a story. I knew the events, but not the details, not the flow of one thing into another. The fever epidemic, the orphanage, school and love and widowhood—I knew they'd all happened, but Mother didn't look back, so I didn't either. I felt ashamed of my ignorance.

We sat silent. Outside, the drips slowed, and a breeze stirred the wet leaves. Of course Aunt Sarah hated Mother, I thought. She took away baby Walter. Mother might have shared, but Aunt Sarah never would have. It was all or nothing with her.

"So why is the house like that?" I asked. "Why are those rooms empty, and why is everything crowded into the front parlor?"

"Had some good times in that parlor," Truman said musingly. "But y'see, Harry, Sarah had to go on living there after all that happened. She had to manage some way." He glanced down at himself. "It's like this arm. Wa'n't hurt all that bad, but if they hadn't cut it off, 'twould have gone black, and the black would have spread into me, and I wouldn't be here."

"Oh." I was trying to see how Truman's arm and the house at Vinegar Hill went together. Cleaning out those rooms, where maybe they'd died, filling with furniture the room where they'd had good times together—was that like cutting off an arm with gangrene? What if I'd had to live in the house where Mother and I lived and where she died? What would I have done with her bedroom? Maybe rearranging the house was the closest Aunt Sarah could come to moving.

Truman gazed at the front of the stove as if it were a window. "Nothin's come out the way we thought it would. Here we thought that farm wouldn't be big enough to support 'em all, and maybe one of 'em'd want this place, and who else could they buy a little land from . . . and now the ridge is empty, and Clayt cuttin' back a little every year. He ain't a spring chicken, Clayt, for all he was the baby of the family."

"That's why Aunt Sarah hated Mother," I said. "She took my father away from the farm."

Truman shook his head, not disagreeing, just shaking his head at life. "That's about a tenth of it, Harry. Your mother was—well, you know what she was, and Sarah—Sarah ought to have had more scope. Ought to have gone to the Academy, and I s'pose Dave would have sent her if Melinda'd lived. She has great abilities, Sarah does, and we've all benefited from 'em, but it's been a narrow life, no denying that."

"I . . . see."

"Well, you don't see, Harry, but in time you will. You make sure you get your schoolin'. Sarah doesn't know what she missed—well, she does and she doesn't. But she played the hand she was dealt, like you're doin' now."

The hand I played was the Academy, the colt, my strength, and my sorrow: Mother's love within me. All this new knowledge was like another card I'd drawn from the deck. It changed everything, but for the moment I couldn't see how. "I should go," I said after a few minutes.

"Tell Clayton I'll be over."

The rain had given way to heavy mist. I walked slowly along the road, listening to drips and loud birdsong. Bright pink worms stretched and contracted themselves between the ruts. I saw a robin snatch one and fly away.

So Aunt Sarah was an orphan. Like Mother. Like Father. I come from a long line of orphans.

Everyone's an orphan, if they live long enough. But not everyone is orphaned young.

But Mother was happy. I knew now that she was happy on purpose, with sorrow in the past and sorrow sure to come, in debt, with a bad heart. *I* made her happy. She always made sure I knew that.

Before me, Father. Before Father, her school, her friends.

What's going to make you happy, Harry? I could be an orphan like Mother or an orphan like Aunt Sarah.

"But that's not fair!" I said out loud. Aunt Sarah must have been splendid. She raised them all, and Truman wanted to marry her—and then they died.

Just for a moment I felt bitterly ashamed. All I had done was hate her. When I said, "You want me to die," when she turned to me, blotched and still, she must have felt as if she'd been stabbed in the heart. "I'm sorry," I whispered.

She did try to kill my rooster. She did say those terrible things.

Still, pain could twist people. I'd felt it inside

myself, mean and sour. Mother must have known that about Aunt Sarah, but she also knew that Aunt Sarah had raised my father, made a good man of him. Sending me here, she sent me back to good as well as bad.

I reached the pasture gate and paused, looking across the hills. Somewhere down there West Barrett nestled among the trees, with the sawmill humming at its heart and no view at all. I would have missed this place. But in all those years, Mother came up again only as far as the blackberry pastures.

I heard a step and felt the colt's warm breath on my cheek. "Hello, Kid." I rubbed his hot, wet neck, and he pressed against my hand, tossing his head and grimacing.

Here was *my* baby. He'd been left to me as I'd been left to Mother, and baby Walter—my father—had been left to Aunt Sarah. I crawled between the bars, struggling against my wet skirt and oilskins, and put my arms around his neck.

He tried to rub his body along me. He must itch from the rain. "Hold still!" I moved along with him, hugging the muscular neck as it tossed, but then his shoulder pushed, my heel caught in a rut, and I sat down hard.

Legs; big, smooth joints; surprised, innocent face. Sweet breath clouded around me.

"Yeah, how *did* I get down here?" I clambered back; through the gate and leaned there, scraping mud off the back of my skirt with a flat stick. "No, I won't scratch you anymore!"

The colt heaved a sigh, gazing across the hillside. Lid

and lashes folded close over his eye, like calyx over bud. His breath and his warm, wet smell made an atmosphere around us. I breathed it, remembering his birth, remembering Belle's deep, soft-voiced whinny to him, remembering Mother's delight in the new little creature, and how everything about him had pointed us toward the future, when I was grown, when I was in school.

I hope I *can* train you, I thought. Everything had changed, but the future, the colt giving me independence, could still come true. If I could make it.

When I walked into the kitchen, Aunt Sarah said, "What did you do, sit down and make mud pies?"

"I—" I bit back a sharp answer. She brought the tin bathtub in from the back room and began to draw steaming water from the tank beside the stove.

"Get out of your wet things and into that tub. Your uncle's gone to town with the butter, so have a good long soak and get warm all the way through."

She turned back to her rolling pin. I peeled off my clothes, folded myself under the water, and gazed around the kitchen. Its very size made it ugly, and the snuff-colored wainscoting and the vinegar smell.

But scent it with mulling cider, fill it with young people, color Truman's beard brown, straighten Uncle Clayton's shoulders, and set them dancing . . .

"Who made the music?"

She turned her head. "What?"

"Tru—Uncle Truman said you had dances. Who made the music?"

She turned back to her piecrust. *Squeak, squeak* went the rolling pin. "I did."

I stared. As if she could feel my eyes, she said, "I had my father's fiddle. He taught me to play."

"But then you could never dance!" Not that I could imagine her dancing, but Truman had been courting her, and Uncle Clayton, too. Did that happen while she had a fiddle tucked under her chin?

"I wasn't much for dancing."

No, I could see that. Aunt Sarah played the tune, and everyone else danced to it.

Fifteen

THE NEXT MORNING the sun came out, and in the afternoon Uncle Clayton cut hay.

Big white clouds sprang up by the following noon. I watched them while I churned. At dinner Uncle Clayton glanced at the clouds only when Aunt Sarah's back was turned. His eyebrows worked like the brows of a worried dog. I didn't think, I'll tell Mother. I'd gotten over doing that. But without the words to choose for her, it seemed as if I missed half of what I was seeing. My mind felt like Truman's hand: mateless, distorted.

I could write her a letter, I thought, and that seemed so close to crazy that I went right out to catch the colt.

There was no reason for him to want to close his mouth around a piece of metal, no way for me to explain why he should. Reaching for a nose grown high as a giraffe's, prying open clenched teeth, listening to the grating of a snaffle being gnawed, I kept myself in the here and now.

As I turned the colt loose, Truman arrived. Uncle Clayton caught Whitey and hitched him to the rake. Aunt Sarah stepped out of the house, tying on her hat. Her sleeves were rolled up, showing her muscled arms. She climbed onto the rake and drove away up the hill. Uncle Clayton hitched the team to the wagon, and Truman, having put Jerry in a stall, brought two hay forks from the barn.

"Can't I help, too?"

Uncle Clayton glanced up the hill, where the rake had begun to clack. He opened his mouth, and it stayed open.

"Grab another fork," Truman said.

We rode out on the bumpy wagon to where Aunt Sarah had begun raking the hay into rows. There Uncle Clayton showed me how to roll each row into a tumble. He made the fork look intelligent, turning this way and that as if it could feel the hay and never wasting a motion. His tumbles were smooth and lifted neatly onto the wagon. Mine looked like crow's nests, and hay cascaded onto the ground when I lifted one.

Aunt Sarah drove the rake past and pulled up just above me. I struggled without looking up, waiting for her to send me back to the house and more empty hours.

"It's like kneading bread," she said. "*Fold* it."

"Oh." It didn't make sense, but nothing I was trying made sense either. I tried folding, and most of my small, shaggy tumble made it onto the wagon.

Truman had stayed up there. By wrapping his wrist around the handle, and bracing the handle against his shoulder, he could use a pitchfork. As we put the hay up, he placed it where he wanted it, trod on it a few times, and turned for the next forkful, eventually building a load as flat and firm as a mattress.

The sun beat on our backs, and then abruptly the world went dark and cool. We looked at the sky and worked faster. The rake clacked ahead, behind, above us, as Aunt Sarah circled the hillside.

Sweat stung my eyes. My hands were starting to blister. But I noticed suddenly that my chest didn't hurt. Quickly I turned my thoughts away, to the smooth ash handle of the fork, to the black snake that whipped away across the stubble. But I couldn't help noticing that just for this moment I wasn't actually unhappy.

Aunt Sarah finished raking. She wrapped the reins so Whitey would stand and came down the hill toward us. "Shall I get up there with you, Truman? It's getting pretty high." It was getting too high for me to reach, actually, and I was hoping we'd stop soon.

"Send Harry up," Truman said.

I was expected to climb up the smooth, round side of the load, but how? What would I hold on to?

"Here." Uncle Clayton drove his pitchfork into the side of the load, so the handle stood out straight. He made a stirrup with his hand. I stepped into it and then onto the fork handle, and then Truman's hand caught mine and pulled me up.

The horses' backs were small and far away. Aunt Sarah looked like a dumpy little doll. Truman handed me his fork. "Reach down," he said, "and take the hay they fork up to you. Don't go too close to the edge now."

What was too close? I wondered. The load felt firm beneath me, but the hay was slippery. I inched to the edge, clashed my tines with Aunt Sarah's, dragged her forkful of hay to the center of the load.

"Put it on this corner," Truman said. "If we build it even, we can still get quite a bit on."

Another forkful of hay nosed toward the edge of the load. I crept toward it. Don't be such a coward! I told myself.

Suddenly I felt a hand grip the waistband of my dress. "Go on," Truman said. "I got you."

He held my dress, and I reached down again and again, learning to feel safe at the edge of the load, learning what was too far. After a while Truman let go.

"Full load," Uncle Clayton said finally, and drove the wagon down the hill. I lay on the fragrant, scratchy hay and watched the sky. Beside me Truman leaned on his elbow, chewing on a straw.

Uncle Clayton drove into the barn and helped us off the load. I watched as he reached for a thin rope hanging against the wall. He pulled it, and down from the rafters with majestic slowness swung a huge iron jaw. It hung from a heavier rope that ran through a pulley at the peak of the rafters and down again to another pulley beside the barn door. There Aunt Sarah payed it through her hands, making herself a counterweight. If she didn't do that, I realized, the jaw would fall, and crush Uncle Clayton.

When it settled on top of the load, he spread it wide. It had a tooth on each corner, like a saber-toothed tiger. Uncle Clayton sank the teeth deep into the load, stepping on each one to push it deeper.

Meanwhile Truman brought Whitey to the barn door and hooked the heavy rope into his harness. Aunt Sarah got a fork and climbed over the half wall into the haymow.

She saw me standing by the team's heads, with no idea what was going on, and hesitated. "Are you tired?"

"No." I was, but I'd never say so.

"You could help me in here. Bring a fork."

I stood with her against the back wall. Truman led Whitey away from the barn, tightening the rope. It groaned through the pulleys, and a third of the load lifted slowly toward the ceiling, swaying and dripping hay. Its sweet green fragrance filled the air.

Then the jaw clicked onto its track, and the hay rushed above us toward the end of the barn like a ship under full sail. "Whoa!" called Uncle Clayton. He yanked the thin rope. *Whumpf,* the hay dropped into the mow. Aunt Sarah stuck her fork into the edge of the pile and glanced at me. "Do what I do," she said. I copied her, and together we pulled the hay in one mass back to the wall.

The whole process repeated twice. Then Uncle Clayton forked the remnants off the wagon and glanced at the sky. Patches of blue showed between the clouds now, and they were white, not gray. "Drink of water," he said, and crossed the yard to the house. Aunt Sarah caught up and passed him, to forestall some disaster like his drinking from the wrong pitcher.

"How you like hayin', Harry?" Truman asked, passing his gossamer-thin bandanna over his brow.

"I love it!"

Two weeks after dropping me off, Luke wrote:

Dear Harry,
Have you ridden him yet? I hope it's going well. Was your aunt mad after we left? Mama was so mad she swore! Don't let her crush your spirit, Harry. That's what Mama says she wants. Remember, we are here.
Papa says give your colt time to see for himself that things won't hurt him. He says a horse never forgets what he figures out for himself, but things you pound into his head go right out the other side. I can't wait till August, can you? Hazel says Billy misses you and carved your name in one of their trees, but I saw him holding hands with Mildred Dean, so I don't know. I think he likes all *girls.*
Write back.

Love,
Luke

Write back? How could I explain that everything was different from the way it had seemed? The empty hill was populated with people dead and gone. They bloomed slowly to the surface of my awareness, the way yeast springs to life in the proofing bowl. No one had spoken their names in years: Edward. Lettice. Violet Anne. No one spoke of them now, except Truman once in a while, but I knew about them. They lived inside me.

We hayed and hayed and hayed, and time slid by. I fell into bed exhausted and woke up aching. In the morning there was churning or housework. Just after noon I worked the colt. Then came haying and the hot sun, the smooth-handled pitchforks, stop and start of the team, clink of harness, Tippy's white tail waving as she hunted mice in the weeds—sweat, chaff, headache, and the sorrow emptying out of my body. In the hay-field I felt like a figure in a landscape painting, not like a person. It helped.

Aunt Sarah watched me closely. "Don't run with a fork!" she snapped when I did that. She made sure I wore a hat. She passed second helpings of dinner before I asked. Even so, the waists of my dresses began to hang slack.

And how was the colt? What would I have written to Luke if I'd managed to answer her letter? I had rid-den him—sat on him anyway—but no one saw it. He was standing beside the fence, surrounded by cows, and I just slid on. He didn't do anything, only curved his neck around to sniff my foot, and then ambled along the fence line, reaching under it to snatch bits of grass. When he turned downhill to chase a cow, I slid off.

Not much else was as easy as that. Every day he walked sleepy eyed to the gate, but as soon as he stepped over the bottom rail, his head came up, his neck stiffened, he began to bobble and step on me and look for things to shy at. Every day. The only sign of progress was that he now ignored hens.

Bridle him: the giraffe game. Saddle him: always easy. Then I would lead him behind the barn where the hay was just cut and circle him on the long rope, teaching him my language. Walk. Trot. Whoa. No. No. No.

One afternoon I led the colt to meet Truman. It was a cooler day than usual, with a light breeze stirring the leaves. The colt walked on tiptoes, flaring his nostrils. A bright patch of sunlight on the ground stopped him in his tracks. A rustle in the bushes set him trotting around me like a carousel horse. I gave him a sharp smack on the neck. "Cut it out!"

At the corner I paused, intending to wait for Truman. I'd never seen a car here, but this was the main road, and with the colt in this mood I didn't dare chance it.

He snatched at grass. "No, stand!" I brought his head up, and he gazed off across the fields, focusing on something I couldn't see.

All at once he turned to look uphill. A bush blocked our view of the road. Is Truman coming? I wondered, when suddenly I heard *knock—knock—knock-knockknock*, a small, dense sound, very close.

That's his *heart!*

Something's going to happen! I stepped closer. "It's all right. It's Truman. It's Jerry." He ignored me, straining his ears forward, each breath deeper and quicker than the last.

Then he began to back. I went with him, close to the trampling hooves. He ducked left. I went that way, too, blocking him, moving with him. If he pulled against me in this deep a panic, he would certainly get away.

He backed, ducked right, then stopped and snorted, as loud as a locomotive's brakes. I felt a mist on my face. He bobbed his head high, low, high again, stood still, and I risked a glance over my shoulder.

At the end of the lane Truman had halted Jerry. "Hey there, young feller!" he sang out. "Hey there!"

The colt's head came down three inches. His ears swiveled forward and back, and sheepish creases appeared in his eyelids.

"There," I said. "There." I scratched his shoulder, where Belle used to scratch him as they stood under the willow tree. He scratched back. "Careful," I said. "No teeth!" When the hardness went out of his scratching, he was calm, and I led him to greet Jerry.

"I heard his heart, Truman! I *heard* it: *bump—bump—bump-bumpbump.*"

"Like a pa'tridge drummin'," Truman said. "That was good, the way you handled him."

"I didn't do anything."

"That's right. You didn't yell; you didn't haul on him, or hold him too tight, or make any one of a dozen other mistakes. You kept your head."

I *did*? "Not on purpose," I said.

Truman's beard and hatbrim seemed to close toward one another, his face retreating behind them. He was grinning under all that hair, as if I'd just said something clever and important. "Maybe next time you will," he said.

I felt myself blushing and turned to the colt. His neck was low, and he stared into space, as if reliving his moment of terror. He looked exhausted. I stroked his neck. We'd been through something big together.

"He trusts you more," Truman said.

I looked down. I never wondered whether he could trust me. I was always wondering whether I could trust him.

Sixteen

*L*ATER THAT SAME AFTERNOON, while we were in the hayfield, Dr. Vesper drove up. His lightweight buggy bobbed over the bumps. The horse stopped and perked his ears at our wagon, cheerful and idle as a man on vacation.

"Hey there, Harry! You look as lean as a wolf!"

"Hi!"

"Been an epidemic of health in Barrett, so here I am. Give you folks a hand?"

"Last load," Uncle Clayton said. "Sairy, we can get this. Why don't you two go on and have your talk?"

"Ride with me, Sarah," Dr. Vesper said. "Between us maybe we can hold this buggy down."

"I'll bring the forks," I said, and followed the buggy down the slope. I could hear my heartbeat, the way I'd heard the colt's this morning. Soon I'd know—what? Something I didn't know now. Something I didn't want to know. I looked uphill. The load of hay bulked against the sky, and the two old men looked thin, bent, and knobby. I wanted to stay with them.

In the kitchen Aunt Sarah poured three tall glasses of buttermilk, and we sat at the table. Her face was brick red and sweating evenly all over, like the glasses.

Dr. Vesper held a cigar box in front of him. He fidgeted the lid up and down, up and down.

"Well, the house is sold," he said abruptly. "Didn't fetch quite what I hoped for, but your debts are paid, Harry, and you've got seventy-eight dollars in the Barrett Savings Bank."

"Oh." I didn't seem to feel anything. Seventy-eight dollars. "Who bought it?"

"Mike Callahan, the mill foreman. He married Bridget Murphy, and they've got two little girls."

"Oh." How much did tuition at the Academy cost?

"So here's your bankbook." He opened the box and handed me the little leather book. "You need me or Sarah to sign for you if you want to withdraw any of it. And here's the bill of sale for the house, and your mother's deed, and some other papers she had. I come near throwin' this box out, but Althea said we should look in it first."

He pushed the box across the table, and my fingers closed around it. Seventy-eight dollars and a cigar box.

Dr. Vesper took a long swig of buttermilk and folded his lips in on themselves. "Harry." He hesitated. "Well, I'll just spit it out, and then I'll know how you take it, won't I? John Gale's paid your shot at the Academy—three years up front, cash on the barrel."

I saw him watching me, kind and sharp. I heard Aunt Sarah's breath draw in, swelling with some unknown emotion. I must have looked blank because he reached across, squeezed my hand, and gave it a little shake. "You're *set*, Harry! Tuition's all paid!"

"I—" My head felt perfectly empty.

He had the sense to go on talking. "John, he didn't want me to tell you it was him. Thought you might not take it. I said the Academy'll take it, like a trout takes a fly! And I said I'd better tell you. No knowing what you might imagine otherwise. But John feels awful bad. Sold his automobile, so I hear—"

"Isn't—isn't it an awful lot of money?"

"No more 'n he can afford. He's pretty well off, John Gale. Wanted to pay it all now to make sure 'twas done, he said. Didn't want to rely on his heirs if anything should happen to him."

He glanced at Aunt Sarah. Something he'd just said was not true, and he was checking if he'd put it over on her. She stared at the tabletop.

"So I'll tell him, Harry, that you'll let him do this? You aren't offended?"

I tried to pull myself together. "Tell him—tell him thank you. I'll . . . write him a letter."

"Good girl. I guess it's no more than right, though it wasn't his fault. What do you think, Sarah?" He darted the question at her like a cow-dog nipping at the heels of a bull. Don't, I thought.

She looked at him, and at me. I noticed the fine netting of lines all over her face. "I think Harriet had better start making progress with that horse," she said, and pushed back from the table. "Doctor, will you stay to supper?"

Dr. Vesper smiled to himself and stood up. "No, thank you, Sarah. The Old Lady thought I might like to eat one meal with my knees under my own table. I was to give you a kiss, Harry. Walk me out to the buggy?"

A safe distance from the house, he puffed his breath out through his teeth. "Phew! That went better than I expected."

"What? What did you say that wasn't true?"

He draped his arm along the buggy wheel and studied me a moment. "You won't forget how to smile up here, will you, Harry?"

My face heated. I looked down. What an awful thing to say!

"Hey!" he said gently. He reached out and squeezed my shoulder. "Are you doing all right?"

I nodded.

"It's a lonely place," he said, "when you're the only young person."

"I guess so."

"Now you're mad at me," he said, making a wry, sad face. "In answer to your question, it's all true except the part about the heirs. We decided, me and Ida Mitchell, that if 'twas all paid up front, Sarah couldn't say no. Didn't make any difference to John; he meant to pay it all anyway. Now that was clever of me, and I've known you all your life, Harry, so don't you think I could be forgiven?"

"*All* my life?" I asked. "Did you deliver me? Were you here when I was born?"

His eyebrows jumped. "No, you were in too big a hurry. Your aunt Sarah delivered you."

Aunt Sarah delivered me? The first person whose hands ever held me was *Aunt Sarah*?

"Harry!" Dr. Vesper sounded sharp. "Look at me, will you? Is it really all right? Because I have the power to make other arrangements."

The words had hardly any meaning. I felt the way I did when I had the measles, when the world went oily and things melted into one another. "Yes," I said, wanting only to make him go away.

The wagon had come down the hill, and just outside the barn door Aunt Sarah was speaking to Uncle Clayton. Her face was red; her eyes were big and hard. Truman stood a little back from them, and he looked troubled, though it was hard to tell with Truman. He looked surprised, too.

When I joined them, her silence slammed like a door, and we got to work. She kept looking at me, as if every time I put my fork into the hay I was doing something utterly and typically wrong. But I hardly felt the blow of these glances. There seemed to be a still cocoon of air around me.

We finished. She and I went inside and put supper on the table, while Uncle Clayton milked and Truman fed the pigs. We ate. No one said anything except "Pass the butter." "Pass the salt." We washed dishes, and

Truman lingered in the rocker beside the woodbox, while the sky darkened. I folded the dish towel. "Good-night."

Truman stirred. "Harry," he said. His voice seemed to command attention. "Feelin' all right? You look a little peaked."

"Just . . . tired." I took the cigar box from the shelf where it had lain all evening and climbed the stairs, undressed and washed, put on my nightgown, and sat in the rocking chair beside the window, with the cigar box on my lap. I looked off at the apricot-colored sky. The weather vane horse trotted past tinted clouds. My fingers curled around the box lid. I felt the torn paper seal.

The house was gone, and I had seventy-eight dollars in the bank. The number made me feel poorer than when I had nothing.

There's the tuition, I tried to remember. That's richness. But everything seemed limited, boxed off and finished. Seventy-eight dollars, and whatever important papers might be in this cigar box, and that seemed the end of Mother.

I heard steps on the stairs. Aunt Sarah's head appeared above the rail. "Are you all right?" she asked, without giving the slightest evidence of caring.

"Yes."

The round head balanced there like a stone. I could hear her breathe. I looked down at my brown fingers on the lid of the cigar box.

"Don't sit up late," she said finally. The footsteps went down the stairs.

I flipped up the lid. The soft, dim light from the window showed the bankbook and a thin stack of papers. I turned them over, one by one.

Bills from the Academy and Fuller's store, stamped "Paid in Full." A bill of sale from The Estate of Ellen Gibson to Mr. Michael Callahan, for "house and two acres in West Barrett village, just east of and adjacent to Newton's sawmill." Bill of sale for same from William Gregg to Ellen Gibson, dated eleven years earlier.

The next piece of paper I almost missed—a small browned clipping from a newspaper. It announced the death of Walter Gibson, "the most recent of his family to perish from consumption. He was predeceased by his parents, his brother, and two of his sisters. He leaves a sister, Sarah Hall, a wife, the former Ellen Tate, and a daughter, Harriet. Those who knew Walter before sickness restricted his activity remember a kind and merry-hearted youth who showed great promise."

Next came a piece of paper that I never looked at because when I lifted it, underneath was Mother, smiling straight at me and looking exactly like herself.

I picked up the photograph and held it nearer the window. It was mounted on stiff cardboard, an eighth of an inch thick, with "Barrett Photographic Studio" across the bottom in swirly letters. Mother wore a dress I recognized as her second best, and she looked happy and confident. By her side, so darkly dressed that I hadn't seen him at first, stood a tall, knobby young man. Their hands were down between their two bodies, almost hidden, and wrapped around each other, into each other, as close as they could possibly get. The man's eyes were a little staring, as if he unexpectedly found himself on the brink of exhaustion.

I turned the picture over. Her handwriting on the back was as fresh as the last note she'd written me. "Our wedding day, June 30, 1896."

I knew now why Aunt Sarah hated Mother. I knew why she would make up things that weren't true. But I counted on my fingers anyway. June to mid-February. Nine months. Nine . . .

No, I'd counted June, and June was over when they married. I had to begin with July.

Eight months then. Eight.

Babies take nine months. Every baby. Nine whole months.

So?

So what?

So it was true. Aunt Sarah had told me the truth. Mother had been pregnant when she married.

I turned the picture over, and she smiled at me again. For a moment I felt the line of love from heart to heart, and then my heart squeezed tight and cut it off.

I was in this picture. I was right there, under the bodice of the pretty dress. I looked out the window. The sky was darker. The trotting horse was black.

Does this *matter*?

I knew, roughly, how babies are made. "You'll hear a lot of nonsense from other children," Mother said, "and I want you to hear the truth from me." Then she explained, and she laughed when I made a face. "I know, Harry! It's part of grown-up love, and when you're grown and in love, you'll understand."

"When you're grown and in love." Not "when you're grown and married."

But they *did* marry. They loved each other. Look at those hands.

Three years after this he died. Did she hold his hand then, as I held hers? I remembered the feel of her hand at that moment. I remembered the feel of it in my dream. I remembered the press of her wedding ring.

I don't care about this, I thought. But I felt hollow down the center of my body, down my arms and legs. When you cut a pear in half and lift out the core with a knife—that's what I felt like. Our past was shameful, and I had never known it. My life had been built on sand.

Were we ever really happy? I reached for my pillow and sat hugging it. "Why don't we ever see Aunt Sarah?" I remember asking. "She doesn't like me," Mother had said. There was never a reason, and I never noticed that, because there *couldn't* be a reason for not liking Mother. Not a real reason.

I had been happy. I had been confident. I was the daughter of the prettiest, nicest, most loving woman in town. A few sour old ladies disliked us, but that was because we were young and loved the world and dared to show it.

All along those ladies had been right about Mother. She was good and loving.

She broke the rules. She never told me. Our life was a lie. In every scene, when I thought I knew what was going on, she knew something else.

Did she really like blackberrying?

Did she actually like reading "Evangeline" and "Hiawatha" with me?

Did she love our house? *Did* she love our life? Was there ever, really, any *us*?

I stood up, and the window glass was right in front of my face. Out there the night was soft and black. Below me they slept, Uncle Clayton, Aunt Sarah.

I didn't want to see Aunt Sarah again.

I would walk out of the house right now. I would disappear.

But already I was exhausted, and where would I go? I didn't want to see anyone, my friends even less than Aunt Sarah.

I put my hands up to the glass and remembered hurting my fingers in my skyscraper bedroom. *"If you ever get to the city, Harry, you won't feel like a rube."*

The city. A room in a real skyscraper, high and lonely. The people below me would be as small as ants, and I wouldn't know a single one of them.

I really could go. I could sell the colt for train fare. Saddle-broken, he'd bring enough money to live on for a while. . . .

I crawled into bed and closed my eyes. Behind my lids it wasn't black and soft. It was gray, like lake water on a cloudy day. Train him. Train fare. Train . . .

Just before morning I dreamed I was riding Mother's sewing machine to New York City: *clackety-clackety-clack.*

Seventeen

IT DOESN'T MATTER.

I woke up telling myself that, before I remembered what I was pushing away. I opened the cigar box and looked at their faces—hers so joyous, his weary, far-seeing. I looked at their hands.

They loved each other. It doesn't matter when I was born.

I believed it with all my conscious might, but underneath I felt the wound. It was like the time I ripped the lace on my best dress. Mother tucked the mangled part out of sight, and people were forever complimenting me on the dress, but I never felt the same about it afterward.

I couldn't seem to rock steadily that day. Churning took all morning, and in the afternoon I rested, as Aunt Sarah had wanted weeks ago.

Now she wouldn't have minded if I worked myself to death. I felt the weight of her glance when I sat down after dishes. Uncle Clayton and Truman looked curious when I stayed there, while they went off to the hayfield. Aunt Sarah bunched her mouth, as if she knew exactly what was going on.

When they were gone, I went upstairs to my hot bedroom. I looked at the smiling face of my mother, the exhausted face of my father.

You did what only married people are supposed to do. That's bad, not like killing people, but like—like keeping a dirty house. Like drinking too much. Like cheating.

Mother's face looked brave and happy. Father's looked . . .

What if she *had* trapped him? What if she'd said, "I'm going to have a baby. You have to marry me?"

What if she *did* ruin his life?

He didn't have much life left when he met her. But he could have spent it at peace with Aunt Sarah, who raised him from a baby. He could have spent it in the house where he was born.

I put them away in the cigar box.

That afternoon the haying on Vinegar Hill was finished. They came in streaming sweat. The day had heated up beyond anything we'd seen yet this summer.

"It's a weather breeder," Uncle Clayton said. "I'll wait for a change before I cut the homeplace." Truman went home, expecting the haying to come to him in a few days.

But the heat increased, smothering us. A dress left

on the floor formed wrinkles overnight, as sharp as if they'd been ironed into the fabric. Paper was limp. Milk soured quickly.

My attic bedroom was stifling, even after the thunderstorms that blew up each afternoon and cooled the air outside. Uncle Clayton waited for a big storm and wind to bring in fresh air. After each rain he listened, smelled, tasted the air, and shook his head.

Meanwhile we churned and washed and baked, weeded, shelled beans, canned vegetables. I presented myself for each task as it arose and was shown how to do it. We didn't talk, Aunt Sarah and I, but I knew what she was thinking. I'd overheard her tell Uncle Clayton. I know she meant me to hear; I'd never once overheard her say anything about me before, and I'm sure she said plenty.

"I'm to house this child, but nobody believes I'm fit to raise her! That folderol about John Gale's heirs! That was cooked up, so I'd have no say in what happened, and look at her now! Not a word to say to any of us. Thinks she's too good, I suppose, with all that money laid out for her!"

A murmur from Uncle Clayton.

"I raised four children! I don't think I made too bad a job of it! But the way Andy Vesper acts, you'd think I'd just gotten out of a home for the feebleminded!"

Murmur.

"Well, let her get herself down there then! Though I have yet to see an inch of progress with that horse that's eating us out of house and home—"

"That horse's too young," Uncle Clayton said. "And she is, too. Y'ought to put a stop to that, Sairy, before she breaks her neck."

"Oh, yes, and I can just see that Barrett crowd if I did! They'd probably have me in jail for cruelty!"

She was right. I was making little progress. The scenes repeated so often, they formed an eternal present. On the long rope, I tell the colt to walk. He keeps trotting. I yank the line.

Leading him, I say, "Whoa." He bobbles toward me and steps on my foot. I push him with my elbow.

Passing the new pigpen gate, he stops and snorts and backs up fast. I put my hand up to soothe him, and he bites me. I slap him.

I ought to have begun riding him. At home I would have, in the little pasture by the river. Here I didn't dare. The pigpen gate frightened him day after day, and what if I was on his back when that happened? What if we met a car, a rooster, a farm wagon, out on the road? Before that happened, I had to drill the commands into his head, so *whoa* meant "stop" every single time.

But it was hard to keep going. It was no fun for either of us, and why was I even doing it? He would fetch more money if he were trained, but did I believe I was going to sell him? Did I believe I'd run away to the city and vanish? Not really. I didn't believe anything anymore.

The second hot Thursday I was in the pasture when Truman drove up. The colt had been evading me, slipping away with sour ears whenever I got close. Now he brightened and trotted to greet Jerry. I followed.

"Hello, Harry!" Truman's beard looked limp and more tea stained than usual. Sweat trickled down his face and lost itself in the yellow-white fringe.

"Hello."

"Been expectin' you every day. I s'pose the weather's kept you home."

I nodded. My mouth felt tight and small. I snapped the rope into the colt's halter. He flicked his ears back angrily, and I felt an inner flick of anger in response.

"Been workin' him hard, Harry?"

"Not hard enough!" I pulled the colt's head away from Jerry and led him through the gate.

"Looks like you could both use a day off," Truman said when we caught up with him. "Why don't you come visit me? Haven't seen your bird in a spell."

"Maybe." Just what I need! I thought. One more person who thinks I can't train this—

Thunk! on the top of my head. Roman candles shot off behind my eyes. "Ouch! Oh!" *Clunk!* again, from behind. I saw the colt's head swinging.

"Darn you, cut it out!" I slapped his neck, as hard as I could. He flung up his head, mouth pinched tight.

"Harry!" Truman said. "He didn't do that a-purpose! He was bitin' a fly!"

"Well, it *hurt!*"

"The fly hurt him. Put him up for the day, Harry. You're in no mood to handle a horse."

"He has to learn!" Now my hand hurt, too. "I don't

care if a fly does bite him; he has to behave!"

Truman started to speak and stopped. He sat looking at me from under the shelf of his brows. "Well," he said after a minute, "guess I'll take my own advice and leave you be." He flicked the reins at Jerry's rump. Jerry walked faster, a bumpy gait that seemed stiff in some joints, too loose in others, and that left me ever so slightly behind.

I had to hurry now beside the colt, who urgently wanted to keep up with Jerry. Already I felt greasy with sweat and bad inside. I had been disrespectful to an old man who loved me. Mother would be ashamed.

I'm ashamed of you, too! I retorted in my mind.

Even as I brushed the colt, the deerflies bit, and the bright blood welled up. I couldn't blame him for jumping and squirming.

It was the craziness I blamed him for, the frantic stamping at the lightest touch on his legs, even a housefly or a grass stem. It was the foolishness that made him jump and look resentful when I smacked and killed a fly on his flank. "You'll just have to put up with it!" I said through clenched teeth. "Other horses manage."

I clipped the long rope into the halter and unsnapped his tie rope. The colt ducked his head into my shoulder.

Automatically my hand came up to rub the glossy bulb of his ear. I hadn't done that, or scratched his neck, or hugged him in a long time. All I'd done was boss him, smack him, yank on his halter.

Had I been too harsh? It wasn't his fault he was only two. Maybe Truman was right. I would just work the colt briefly, and as soon as he did one good thing, I'd praise him and put him away.

I led him up to the flat hayfield above the barn. I could see Uncle Clayton and the team, small at the far end of the bean rows. Aunt Sarah and Truman were in the garden, Aunt Sarah like a big stump in her brown dress, Truman thin and angular as a heron. They were talking, about me, I thought. I turned to the colt.

"Walk."

He didn't budge. I waggled the buggy whip; he flattened his ears and obeyed, circling me at the end of the rope.

"Good— No!" He'd ducked his head, shaking it angrily, and now he started to trot. I pulled on the rope. "You *walk!*" He kept trotting, the mincing jig Belle used to do when nervous, which had always given me a stitch in the side. I jerked the rope hard. "*No! Walk!*"

The colt stopped in his tracks.

"*Walk!*"

He lashed his tail, bit a fly just behind his elbow, and at last did walk. His mouth was pursed, and his eye narrow. "Good boy!" I said when he'd walked a complete circle. "Now trot!"

He shook his head heavily, on and on, trying to dislodge a fly. The deerflies favored the ears and didn't shake off easily.

"Trot!" I said again.

He stopped, rubbed his head against his foreleg,

snatched a bite of grass.

"Now darn you, *trot!*" I snapped the whip.

The colt let out a deep, angry squeal, plunged into a gallop, and lashed out with both hind feet, all at once. He began to race around me, his body slanted toward the center of the circle, his head carried high like a lance. The rope pulled hard against my hand. I dropped the whip—it seemed to cling to my fingers—and grabbed the rope in both hands.

"Whoa!"

But the colt saw the team down in the bean field. The circle became a straight line as he charged toward them, and my braced feet lifted off the ground.

For a moment I was flying. Then I hit the grass and was raked across it, across the bumps and stubble. The rope slid through my hands. I couldn't seem to let go, until the knot in the end of it slid past my face, banged like a hammer at the base of my hands, and they opened.

I saw a bruised leaf of clover and a bare quarter inch of ground amid the stubble. The earth drummed, and slowly I knew that for the colt's hoofbeats.

I didn't want to move. The yellowed field spun and sank slowly, one quarter turn, another . . .

Something prickled my cheek. I lifted my head a fraction. Nothing moved on the broad grass horizon, but I heard voices.

The sun was hot on my back. I started to push myself upright. The ground burned my palms, and I fell flat.

I drew my hands toward me across the grass, palms

up. I didn't dare look at them. I propped myself on my forearms, rolled over, and sat.

Far away the colt raced across the bean field. The long rope flew behind him. Dirt and bean plants erupted in the air.

Uncle Clayton strained his reins tight. His hatbrim tilted as he looked uphill.

"Harry! Harry, are you all right?"

How could I be hearing him? He was so far away.

Not him. I turned my head, slowly. It felt huge and light, as if it were made of cork.

Aunt Sarah, running, almost here. Her face was mottled, red and white. Truman struggled far behind her, the stub of his arm jerking and flapping like a broken wing.

"*Harriet!*" She fell on her knees beside me. Her breath came in great gasps. "Say something!"

She looked so strange. I turned my eyes away from her. The colt had made a spiral of broken, trampled bean plants. Now he pranced around the team. He'd tangle them in the rope. . . .

"Where are you hurt?" Her big, hot hands pressed my head. I winced as she found the places where the colt's jaw had whacked me. She passed one hand down my spine.

Truman collapsed on the grass beside us. He was pale, and his breath trembled, his hand trembled, as he gently reached for one of mine and turned it over.

It looked like raw meat.

Eighteen

MY STOMACH HEAVED. I ducked my head onto my knees, pressed my mouth against my skirt.

"Rope burn," Truman said.

I'd had a rope burn once. It was just a pink-glazed line across my arm. . . .

They were turning both hands over now. I heard Aunt Sarah's breath hiss through her teeth. After a moment Truman said, "Not as bad's it looks." Truman has seen people shot with cannons, I thought.

"Are you hurt anywhere else, Harriet? Look at me!"

I raised my big head. I felt dreamy somehow. I didn't want to speak. Aunt Sarah felt along my legs and arms. I stared off at the little, distant figures in the bean field.

"Well, Harry? You *satisfied?*"

I jerked all over. Truman's beard was sucked down into the hollows of his cheeks. His eyes sparked.

"Y'drove that horse and drove him till you finally made him hurt you! I just hope—"

"Truman!" Aunt Sarah said, in a voice that was large and deep and soft. "That'll do! When this girl needs a scolding, I'll tend to it!" Her voice was so different it didn't seem like hers. It was changed the way Belle's voice changed when the colt was born, as if her labor had changed the shape of all her organs. I felt Aunt Sarah's hands, firm under my elbows. "Can you stand up, Harriet?" My name was musical in her mouth.

"I . . . think so."

As soon as I stood, the blood sank and throbbed in my hands. I had to hold them up in front of me, and then I couldn't help seeing.

"Close your eyes," Aunt Sarah said. "Looking makes it worse."

No. I felt better, now that I could see the skin in little crumbs and tatters, the blood trickling. This was no horror. It was like a skinned knee, only more so. A lot more so.

"Can you walk?" Her hot arm felt good around me. We stepped slowly together over the uneven ground. My legs were strong enough but seemed loosely connected. I was glad to reach the shade of the barn and sit down on a crate.

Uncle Clayton drove up, half standing on the cultivator and leaning back on the reins. The team pranced and huffed, ears flat, nostrils red. The colt trotted beside them. His rope was garlanded with bean plants, and brought along a bruised green smell.

"Whoa!" Muscle and tendon stood out on Uncle Clayton's forearms. "Harry, ye all right?"

"She's hurt her hands, Clayton," Aunt Sarah said. She was, for some reason, untying her apron.

Truman went past her, toward the team and the colt.

"Don't . . ." I said.

Truman held his hand out. He looked both commanding and ridiculous, thin and old and one sided, still, straight, and calm.

The colt shuddered away from him, blew out a fluttering snort, and snatched at grass. But when Truman didn't move, his interest seemed to sharpen. He pricked his ears and pushed his muzzle toward the hand, sniffing.

Calmly Truman wrapped his fingers into the loose noseband of the halter. The hand looked huge against the colt's delicate profile, against the great porcelain nostrils and the tracery of veins in the face. The colt's eye rolled for an instant. Sinews stood out in Truman's wrist, and the colt seemed to wilt.

"Help me with the gate, Sarah?"

They hurried down the yard, the colt sidling to avoid the dragging rope. He looked small to me, weedy and undeveloped.

Uncle Clayton got off the cultivator. He looked different, too; I couldn't say how.

"I'm sorry . . . your beans."

He pushed the apology away. "Won't miss 'em. Want some water?"

I did. He reached inside the barn for the tin dipper and held it under the stream that flowed continually from the soapstone pipe into the water tub.

When he brought the water back, I almost reached for it. I would have sworn I caught myself in time, that I never even twitched, but it hurt anyway. My face heated with it. I felt sweat on my temples.

"Here." Uncle Clayton put one hand on the back of my head. With the other he held the dipper to my mouth. He tilted it gently and accurately as I drank.

I looked up at his face, closer to me than it had ever been. A spiderweb of lines surrounded his eyes: squint lines and smile lines. His mustache had a kindly sweep.

The colt began to neigh. Aunt Sarah appeared, half running and pulling Whitey behind her. He plodded, and all her hurry only stretched his neck.

"Clayton, harness this horse for me!"

I didn't like to have Uncle Clayton bossed like that. But he snapped to the task while she hurried toward the house, half running again, with an extra little skip every few steps as if she couldn't bear her own weight and slowness.

I let my head tilt back till it rested on the hot barn boards. The world had slowed down and come into unnaturally clear focus. I saw Truman coming. I saw how old he looked, how his gait was loosened.

He went into the barn, brought out the milking stool, and placed it beside my crate, arranging it with some care. Then he sat down.

"There! Floatin', Harry?"

I didn't even want to nod. "Mmm." Truman knew all about being hurt.

"You'll be all right."

Some quality in his voice made me wonder, and I found that by gently rolling my head to the side, I could see him.

He was smiling. Deep in his beard, hidden under the straw hat that had tipped down over his eyes, he undoubtedly smiled. I saw his thin chest rise and fall, the undershirt limp with heat. Short white hairs curled at the base of his throat. He looked . . . satisfied. Amused and satisfied.

We didn't speak. The sun pressed on our fronts, and the hot boards burned our backs. Uncle Clayton harnessed and hitched Whitey. The team ducked their heads into each other's necks and stamped at flies.

The kitchen door banged. Aunt Sarah came carrying a carpetbag and thrust it under the buggy seat. "Can you two manage here? Take care of the milk right away, Clayton, and you'll have to churn tomorrow. I don't know how long I'll be gone. Harriet, let me help you." She put her arm around me, and we went to the buggy.

I couldn't get in. Truman at least had one hand; I had none.

"I'll give you a boost," Uncle Clayton said. I was lifted from the waist, as I hadn't been lifted since I was a little girl. I bumped my elbow on a strut and fell awkwardly on the seat with my hands tucked up near my chin.

The buggy sank as Aunt Sarah climbed in. She clucked to Whitey, and he heaved himself into a trot.

I couldn't help gasping at the jolt. Aunt Sarah slowed him, and that was better, until we hit a rock. Then all the blood in my body hammered into my hands. I bit down on my lower lip. Aunt Sarah noticed even that and made Whitey walk. I held my hands up out of my lap; it seemed to keep the bumps from transmitting to them.

The main road was even rougher and did away with the floating sensation. I was right down inside my body, inside my hands and sweating brow. When I swallowed, my tongue made a sticky sound.

"Fool!" Aunt Sarah said. "Why didn't I bring some water?" She stared intently at Whitey's slow haunches. She could have picked me up and run with me faster than this.

We crawled down the fence line of the big pasture. I could see the house and barn, the bright copper spot that was the colt flashing back and forth, the little toy team and the toy old men. Watching, I forgot to hold in my gasp when we hit the next washboard on the road.

Aunt Sarah reached under the seat and pulled her carpetbag forward, without slowing the buggy. I watched her hand fumble with the catch. She felt inside and drew out a flow of white muslin: my nightgown and hers.

"Fold these—no, you can't." She looked ahead at the empty road, then dropped the reins on the dash and put her foot on them. She folded the nightgowns into a broad pillow and put it on my lap. "Rest your hands on this. It might feel better."

I made myself notice the softness of muslin on the backs of my hands, the very slight cushioning, the very slight improvement. I made myself hold my hands so blood would not spot the cloth.

We reached the tree line. Here I had first met Truman. *Ca-thlop ca-thlop,* went Whitey's big hooves. Lacy shadows slid over his back. The sight made me dizzy. I looked down. Here was my nightgown sleeve. Here was a bit of lace, a building up and crisscrossing of one single thread. Mother made that lace. With my eyes I followed every crisscross, up and down, up and down.

Out of the birches now, between the old pastures where the blackberries grew. *Ca-thlop ca-thlop . . .*

"How do you feel?"

My mind had gone broad and shallow, like water spilled on a table. "All right. All right."

Ca-thlop ca-thlop, past a farm, past the pasture where I had picnicked with Luke and her mother, past the rosebush, the white roses all turned brown with rain and heat. *Ca-thlop ca—*

PUT-put-put-put!

Whitey stopped, raised his head high, and higher. He looked like a statue carved in ivory.

Put-put-POP-put!

A car!

Whitey's sides heaved. His nostrils fluted out in

wide cones with each breath. Far ahead the Model T seemed to leap and skip over the ruts, heading straight toward us. I heard a little whimper come out of my mouth, and I hid my face in Aunt Sarah's shoulder.

For a moment she was there, a warm wall. Then she was gone. The buggy jounced, creaked, and she was at Whitey's head. She gripped the reins close to the bit and forced his face toward the side of the road. "Whoa! You whoa! Stand—now shhh! Shhh!" The knuckles shone white on her big red hands. "Shhh, now!"

Whitey's breath rattled like falling hail. His hooves minced up and down. His tail swished. If he got away, there was nothing I could do to save myself, not even hang on. I looked at the ground, just three feet away. Jump! Jump now!

"Can you wave him by?"

I didn't understand. It was the same voice she was using on Whitey, mixed in with orders and hissing. One of Whitey's ears curved rigidly toward her. The other swiveled back and forth. "Harriet, can you wave him by? I can't let go—shhh! Whitey! Shhh!"

The car. Wave the car by.

The right hand hurt less than the left, but it felt heavy, stiff, and curled. The air hurt it, moving hurt it, and the driver of the Ford took a long time to understand. Then he came cautiously, creeping along the very edge of the ditch. He wore goggles and a long white scarf. Between them little could be seen of his face. He seemed more like a bug than a human, but his mouth dropped open in human curiosity as he passed.

When the sounds died away, Aunt Sarah came back, keeping the reins tight and smooth. They never sagged once, even when she climbed into the buggy.

"Now walk, you old fool!" Whitey set off high headed, almost prancing. It was several yards before his body slackened and his head came down.

For the first time since the car had appeared, Aunt Sarah took her eyes off him and looked at me. She looked away again. "Did that scare you?"

I couldn't understand why she was even asking. It had panicked me, disintegrated me. I nodded, barely. She seemed to see it out the corner of her eye.

"If he saw more cars, he'd get over his foolishness."

I listened hard to the words. My hands hurt more than I'd ever known anything could hurt. Even shame didn't matter. Talk, I thought. Maybe that would help. "The Mitchells trained Tulip," I said. My tongue felt heavy, and the words came slowly. "They can lead him from their Model T."

"Can they?" She didn't like to hear that the Mitchells had done something clever. "That must be handy, though."

"But Tulip is the calmest horse in the world." I wished talking helped more. "Tulip could fall asleep on an active volcano, Mother used to say."

Aunt Sarah's breath made a little snort. "The opposite of your critter."

"Yes." I glanced at my hands, and every nerve in my stomach twanged. I closed my eyes.

We met no one else. The stone walls and blackberry pastures slipped by. After a time I smelled fresh pine sawdust, and the roofs of West Barrett came into view, few and small among the trees. Down, down we dipped, past the mill, past the little gray house—

My heart knocked. Our door stood open, and two small girls in grubby pinafores sat beside the step, stirring the dirt in the flower bed with spoons. Red checked curtains at the windows . . . It wasn't our house anymore. I hadn't realized it would change.

Aunt Sarah pulled up at Althea's gate. Before she had to shout, the door opened. "Morning!" Aunt Sarah called. "Has Andy Vesper been this way?"

Althea shook her head, coming slowly forward. She stared at my hands. "What on earth—"

"It's a rope burn," Aunt Sarah said, as if that were nothing much. "If you haven't seen him, we'll go on down. Do you need a drink, Harriet?"

I nodded. Without a word Althea went back into the house. The pump handle squeaked, and she came out with one of her white mugs, cracked and tea stained. Aunt Sarah said, "Would you mind standing at this horse's head while I help her drink?"

Althea went to hold Whitey. She looked small and distant. Aunt Sarah held the cup to my lips, and I drank. Water slopped up my nose.

"I'm sorry," Aunt Sarah said.

"No . . ."

Whitey snorted and shoved his head against Althea. She nearly fell.

"Whitey! Stop it!" Aunt Sarah said. "We'll be going."

Althea didn't step out of the way, didn't come to take the cup, for several seconds. "Stop back," she said when she did come. "I want to know how Harriet is."

"All right." Aunt Sarah let Whitey go.

The Old Lady was weeding her garden, out behind the Vespers' low Cape. She straightened, looked hard at our buggy, and headed at once for the house. "He's up the street. I'll telephone."

We were left alone in the hot, sunlit yard. How—

"Come in!" Mrs. Vesper shouted from the doorway, and disappeared again.

How would I get down? On elbows, on knees, with Aunt Sarah's hands around my waist. She tied Whitey to the ring in the barn wall and opened the door for me.

"Yes, it's Harry!" Mrs. Vesper shouted into the telephone mouthpiece. "What? I don't—" She turned to look at me. "Oh, my goodness! It's her hands, Andy! Get right down here!" She clashed the earpiece back on its hook. "Harry, sit down! What can I—oh!" She hurried into her pantry and came back with a sweating pitcher. "Lemonade!"

Aunt Sarah stood in the middle of the room, hands hanging at her sides. Mrs. Vesper almost knocked into her, rushing at her cupboard. "Oh! Sit down! Won't you sit down?"

Aunt Sarah sank onto a kitchen chair, obliterating it from sight. She stared past me, past the wall, past the glass of lemonade that was put in front of her. After one quick look at her, Mrs. Vesper helped me drink.

We waited. The kitchen was dim and still. I could almost hear my hands throb.

A buggy rattled past the window, and a moment later Dr. Vesper came through the door. He looked at my hands and whistled. "What happened?"

None of us answered.

"Sarah! Snap out of it! Are you hurt, too?"

Aunt Sarah stirred and slowly turned to look at him, as if coming from a long way off. "No."

"Then tell me what happened!"

"Harriet was . . . training that horse of hers." Her voice was soft, almost too low to hear. "He . . . ran and dragged her."

"Rope burn," Dr. Vesper said as if that solved everything. "Come on in my office, and I'll patch you up."

I stood, feeling as if my legs were made of glass, and went with him into the bright little room off the kitchen. Aunt Sarah followed as far as the doorway.

He leaned over my hands, so close I could feel his breath, and looked them over methodically, section by section. "Harry," he murmured, "you've got to learn to let go!"

Aunt Sarah almost said something. I heard her breath draw in and then sigh out harmlessly.

"Well, it's not so bad but what it could be worse. Let's see what we can do."

I didn't watch. There was something wet that stung so much sweat popped out on my forehead. Later there was a dressing, and in the middle of that, while I stared intently out the window at the house next door, he suddenly pulled down on the fingertips of my left hand.

"*Aaah!*" It was a real shriek. Suddenly Aunt Sarah was right there beside me.

"Sorry," Dr. Vesper said. "But if it heals flat, it won't heal short. You'll thank me next time you play the piano."

I couldn't make even the first twitch of a smile. He finished the dressing; only the tips of my thumb and fingers showed. Then he started the other one. He was going to do it again.

"I'm going to do it again. Ready? There, was that so bad?"

Someone's hand gripped my shoulder. "Andy, don't be an idiot!" Aunt Sarah said.

"Now if you can, Sarah, I wouldn't mind you two staying until tomorrow afternoon. I can get a pretty good idea of what's going to happen by then. You can stay right here in the spare bedroom. Maybe Harry'd like to go lay down awhile?"

I nodded. My head felt huge again: big cork head. I followed Mrs. Vesper upstairs, into a hot, dim little room with two beds. Sat down. Aunt Sarah took my shoes off, and I placed myself on the pillow, hands at my sides, palms up.

I thought I didn't sleep. I thought my hands hurt too much. But after I had opened and closed my eyes a few times, it was evening.

Nineteen

WE DINED ON COTTAGE CHEESE, lettuce, and cucumbers. Aunt Sarah fed me, and Dr. Vesper looked pleased with himself.

I still felt exhausted and not at all like talking. Aunt Sarah and I went up to bed early. She undressed me and put on my nightgown. I didn't mind that she saw me naked, though I turned my eyes away while she changed, in case she minded. Everything seemed strange and simple. My hands took up my whole mind and left no room for nonsense.

I slept awhile and awoke to the sound of Aunt Sarah breathing. Crickets throbbed. A horse and buggy passed.

Then downstairs something trilled loudly over and over. Feet on the stairs. Dr. Vesper said, "Yup. Yup. Oh, good golly, no! I'll be there just's quick as I can." *Bang-bang-bang* up the stairs, shuffle and mumble in the next room, *ca-rumble* down again, and a short time later the horse clopped away.

I lay sweating. My hands hurt more and more, hot, like bars of iron in the blacksmith's forge. I sat up.

"Harriet?" Aunt Sarah had never been asleep. Her voice was clear and alert.

"I'm all right. I'm . . . hot."

She got up, big and white in her nightgown, and went softly to the washstand. She poured water into the basin and gently sponged my face. The water was cool, but my face heated it quickly.

"I want to go outside." I could hear a breeze out there, ruffling the leaves. "Can I just go sit?"

She drew a long breath, the beginning of "no," but then she said, "I don't know why not." She went to our door. "Mrs. Vesper, we're going to sit outside awhile. Don't get up."

Mrs. Vesper came to her door, all her buoyant gray hair reduced to one braid down her back. "There's chairs on the side lawn. Harriet knows."

We crossed the wet grass. My nightgown trailed, getting heavier, but I couldn't hold it up. I made my way toward the faint white glow of the chairs and lowered myself cautiously onto a surface I couldn't see— wet, like the grass, cool.

My feet were cool, too, and the breeze felt cool on my face. Far to the west thunder grumbled. Lightning flashed pink in the clouds.

"Clayton'll be pleased," Aunt Sarah said.

After a moment I asked, "Why?"

"Storm at night means a change of weather. It'll be nice tomorrow." All I could see of her was the white blur of her nightgown. I should say something to keep the conversation going, but my mind felt empty. My hands lay in my lap like live coals.

Aunt Sarah sighed. "I haven't slept a night off that hill in over thirty years," she said.

Quite a while went by before I asked, "When did you?"

"When I was a youngster, we went to the fair." Her breath made the little snort that was laughter for her. "Well, I didn't sleep that night either! We all bedded down in the backs of the wagons, and when our baby wasn't crying, the next baby over was! I saw sunrise from the very start that morning!"

I asked into the soft darkness, "Who was the baby?"

She didn't answer right away. Lightning lit the bottom of the faraway clouds. "That would have been Walter," she said.

My father. Then she was my age that night, and her mother was going to die soon.

"I hope things are all right up home," she said.

"Will Tr—will Uncle Truman stay at—" I couldn't say Vinegar Hill! "Where will he sleep?"

"He likes to sleep under his own roof." Aunt Sarah sighed again. We both thought, I suppose, of the two houses on the ridge: the gray one crumbling back into the ground on the homeplace, the goldenrod-colored one at Vinegar Hill, with its furniture-crowded sitting room, its empty top floor.

"Which was your bedroom?" I asked. "When you were my age?"

Again the pause before the answer. "Oh, we were always tradin'. Later on, after I was married, things settled down . . . but we'd swap six or seven times in a year. And *fight*? My goodness! I remember lockin' Letty in the closet. She stayed in there two, three hours because Mother was working outdoors. Mother said to me, 'Sarah, suppose the house had caught fire?' And I said, 'Then I'd be rid of that little pest!' I got a lickin' for that."

She's talking like a regular person, I thought. Like Truman, like Uncle Clayton. It made me realize that she'd always spoken proper English before this, like Mother, or Ida Mitchell. Tell me more, I wanted to say. While she'd been speaking, I was on the hill, rumpusing through the upstairs rooms with those children. When she stopped, I was in my hands again.

"Does it hurt bad?" she asked.

"Not too bad."

The wind came up in a strong, cool gust. The tree branches lifted and sighed. The night was blacker for a moment and then lit white. Thunder.

"It's a ways off," Aunt Sarah said, "but it's comin'. We'll have to go in soon. Here." Her white form lengthened out. She came behind me, and I felt her hands on my shoulders, rubbing strongly.

"Ow!"

"Too hard?" She rubbed more gently. "Funny how

this helps, even when the hurt is someplace else. When Ed broke his leg, he always wanted his shoulders rubbed. His mind would go where my hands were, he said, and he'd forget the hurt."

My heart didn't hurt anymore. All I had room for was the pain in my hands. My shoulders winced under Aunt Sarah's fingers. I'd been dragged, too, and my muscles ached, but that was nothing.

Lightning traced a crooked trail across the sky. Before the thunder I asked, "How did Ed break his leg?"

"Toboggan. He had to make himself a jump, mainly because I said he shouldn't. Well, he didn't figure he had to obey his sister."

Her warm fingers kneaded, the lightning flashed, a few cold drops of rain hit us, and I wondered, What is happening? She'd never said their names before. They might never have existed. Now she couldn't stop talking about them, that young orphaned family, quarreling and laughing.

"We'd better go in," Aunt Sarah said abruptly.

We got up and hurried across the lawn, hearing the rain come down the street behind us. Drops hit my back like stones as we reached the door, soaking through the muslin nightgown. By the time we got inside, it was sheeting off the eaves, roaring all around us. The house seemed a small shell, like an overturned canoe.

"Good, you got in!" Mrs. Vesper came into the kitchen, wrapped tight in a dressing gown. She lit a lamp, opened the cupboard, and handed Aunt Sarah towels. "Suppose Andy got indoors before that hit?"

We had no way of knowing.

"Come in where it's comfortable," she said, leading the way into the sitting room. "No use pretending to sleep while this is going on." I sat on the sofa, and Aunt Sarah put a pillow in my lap for my hands to rest on. She dried my hair and shoulders. Then she sat beside me, Mrs. Vesper took the large chair opposite, and we listened to the rain. It drowned out even the thunder, but lightning lit the room two or three times a minute, and sometimes we heard its electric crack.

Eventually that passed on to the east, and the rain settled to a steady, silvery *sssh* outside the windows. We sat in the circle of the lamplight, surrounded by darkness, not speaking, not needing to . . .

"—way to greet a man!" The windows were gray with the dawn, and Dr. Vesper stood dripping in the doorway.

Twenty

HE LOOKED AT MY HANDS after breakfast and seemed satisfied. "I'll look again in the afternoon, and then you can go home." I was rebandaged and set down to rest.

Mrs. Vesper washed the dishes, and Aunt Sarah dried them. Then she stepped to the door. The sky was deep blue. Raindrops sparkled on the grass, and the puddles shimmered.

"Harriet, where do your friends live? The ones who brought you home?"

"Down the street, not far." I'd been thinking about Luke this morning, wondering if I could go see her, wondering if I wanted to. Yesterday morning I didn't want to see anyone, especially a friend. That feeling was gone. I could remember it, but it seemed as if it had been someone else, and that someone else hadn't answered Luke's letter.

"Let's go visiting," Aunt Sarah said abruptly. "You feel up to a walk?"

"Yes." I felt miserable, in fact, not just my hands but my whole body. I had blotchy bruises all down my front. My arms and shoulders and back and neck ached. But they ached no matter whether I sat or stood or lay down. The only thing that helped was distraction.

Aunt Sarah looked me up and down. "I can't help that dress," she said, "but I'll do your hair again. I made a poor job of that." She was different this morning, firmer, concealing more.

We paced slowly up the street. I thought I must look strange in my crumpled, grass-stained calico, with my arms crossed in front of me and my hands bound up in white mitts. Aunt Sarah was definitely out of place. Every woman we met wore a dark skirt and white shirtwaist and had her hair swept up in an abundant-looking knot. Aunt Sarah was unmistakably of the hill farms, dressed in dirt-concealing brown from top to toe, her thin hair scraped back. She was frowning.

Why did she want to see the Mitchells? It was the last place I would have expected her to go. I wasn't afraid she'd say something awful. I had more faith in her now. But by the light of day I couldn't ask her questions the way I might have last night.

In the gardens delphiniums and roses lay on their faces in the wet grass. Broken branches littered the street. The Academy bell tower stood white and crisp against the blue sky, and the Mitchells' house seemed softer, pinker, grander than usual.

"Here," I said as Aunt Sarah was about to pass.

Her lips tightened as she looked the house over. A flush came up in her face, and I felt her expand with a long breath. Then she pushed the gate open and walked up to the front door.

She knocked. They would never hear that. This house was so large, so protected by its front hall, that they only heard the bell. Aunt Sarah might not see the bell, and we could go away.

She knocked again, and then her large red hand went to the bell handle. She gave it a firm, scornful twist. I heard the buzz deep inside the house, and footsteps. The door opened.

"Put it—" Mrs. Mitchell said, and then she stopped with her mouth open.

She was swathed in an apron, splashed from dishwashing, and her hair was up in her early-morning knot, slightly askew. Her face grew pink as she looked at Aunt Sarah, and her hands went on drying themselves mechanically. At last she glanced down at me.

"Harriet Gibson, my goodness gracious! What on earth have you done?"

"The horse got away from her," Aunt Sarah said. "May we—"

"Oh, come in, come in! Lu!"

Luke appeared from the direction of the kitchen, drying a frying pan. She dropped it. "Harry!"

"How badly— When—" We were all crowded in the hall, and Mrs. Mitchell was pushing at her hair distractedly.

"Yesterday morning," Aunt Sarah said, sounding matter-of-fact. "The young horse pulled away, and she got a rope burn. And that's why we're here. It's plain she'll never get the animal trained before school starts, and I concluded I should come talk to you."

Luke and I looked at each other.

Mrs. Mitchell seemed to marshal her forces. "Yes, I—Lu, will you take Harriet upstairs? Mrs. Hall?" Aunt Sarah followed her into the sitting room.

We started upstairs. "Harry, are you all right?" Luke whispered.

I looked down over the banister, at the black and lonely frying pan on the polished floor. "I'm— It hurts a *lot*," I said as we reached the landing. "It hurts a *lot*."

We heard Aunt Sarah's voice in the sitting room. "Come on," Luke said, and pushed open the door of her sister's room. She crossed softly to the grate in the floor. I followed and looked straight down onto Mrs. Mitchell's untidy bun.

Luke knelt. I didn't dare. My hands' helplessness seemed to uncoordinate my whole body. I stood close and heard Mrs. Mitchell say, "We wouldn't dream of taking money. Harriet eats nothing."

"I've seen her put away a man-size supper," Aunt Sarah said dryly, "but that was after haying."

"Yes, but we—" Mrs. Mitchell paused and looked up.

She didn't speak, and her expression didn't change, but Luke sank back from the grate with a red face. "Come into my room," she said.

We sat on the edge of the bed, quiet for several minutes. "I never got a letter from you," Luke said finally. "Won't she let you write?"

"Of course she lets me. I just . . . didn't." Luke flushed. "I'm sorry. I felt . . . I can't explain. I . . . felt too bad."

Luke sat looking at me. At last she nodded, as if she understood. "You're here now," she said, putting her arm around me. "Tell me what happened."

"He . . . bolted." I didn't want to talk about it because I'd been abusing him, really. I made him bolt. "He dragged me, and then the rope slid through my hands, and he ran down into the bean field."

"Were they mad?"

"No. No, they were—" They were nice. All three of them. They all jumped to help me just as if I were their child.

As I was.

Why this should cause sorrow to swell in my throat I didn't know. Luke didn't ask any more questions. We sat side by side on the bed until her mother called us down.

Aunt Sarah looked—I don't know how she looked. I didn't know what to make of her expressions anymore. Mrs. Mitchell looked to her as if expecting her to speak, but she didn't.

"Harriet," Mrs. Mitchell said finally, "we've been discussing this coming school year. Would you like to stay here with us?"

Aunt Sarah stirred. That I understood. In her mind

it was all settled, and what was the use of asking me? I was a child and would do what I was told.

"I . . . thank you," I said. "I'd like that very much." My voice sounded small and prim. It would have drawn a frown from Mother. She'd have wanted a bigger, warm reaction.

"You're to bring us a dowry of butter and potatoes," Luke's mother said, with a nervous laugh. She hadn't even consulted her husband, and the interview with Aunt Sarah had rattled her. I should come to the rescue.

"But no beans," I said. "After what my horse did to that bean field, there won't be any to spare!"

That had been the right thing to say. They both smiled and relaxed a little. Inside me Mother approved. Oh, hello, Mother, I thought.

But where did I live now? Where did I belong? My heart ached, strangely, for Vinegar Hill and the two old men up there worrying.

Aunt Sarah had friends to visit, and I spent the day with Luke and her mother. They'd been about to embark on a lesson in puff pastry. The butter was on ice, and something extraordinary had been promised Mr. Mitchell when he came home to supper, so the project could not be put off.

I watched awhile. They were scratchy with each other, a little more so when I left the room and went to rest on the sofa. "I can't *do* it," Luke wailed once, and her mother's sigh carried all the way to the sitting room.

"Watch me one more time."

It was past noon by the time Luke came in with a tray of sandwiches and lemonade. "I *hate* puff pastry. I wish I'd never said I wanted to learn!"

"Did it come out all right?"

"Oh, *Mama* says it did! I think it looks awful!" She took a big bite of sandwich and then looked at me, pop-eyed, over bulging cheeks. Swallow. "Oh, Harry, you can't eat! I forgot!" She picked up a sandwich, dripping chicken salad, and pushed it at my lips.

"Wait. Slow down."

A bite for me, a bite for her, we worked through lunch. Sometimes Luke mixed up the sandwiches. When she gave me lemonade, it sloshed down my front, and we laughed. But inside I felt hollow.

Mrs. Mitchell had gone to see her husband at his office. We waited for her. We couldn't climb trees. We couldn't play cards. I didn't want to walk; standing made my hands hurt.

Finally we went out to the big hammock. Luke steadied it while I got myself balanced in the middle, and then she gently pushed me. That hammock was treacherous; it could buck you off like a wild horse if you weren't careful. Now Luke kept her hand on it at all times, and we didn't speak.

The gate latch clicked. The hammock shuddered as Luke looked up. Then she ran to meet her mother, and I lay absolutely still, feeling the hammock sway. If it tipped, I would either catch myself with my hands and hurt them, or not use them and hurt the rest of me. I hardly dared roll my eyes.

Slowly Luke and her mother came into view, arms around each other's waists, heads close together. Two dark heads, two sets of dark eyes, two smiles shaped the same.

"Oh, Harry, I forgot!" Luke rushed to me. The hammock trembled and lurched, and she firmed it again. "Papa says yes, of course, and he's very happy you're coming to stay!"

Mrs. Mitchell put a hand on Luke's shoulder. "We're all happy, Harriet. My only regret is that I misjudged your aunt so badly."

"Yes. I mean, me too." I couldn't look away from her hand on Luke's shoulder, the wedding ring glittering in the sun. Luke and her mother. You must be very careful, Harry, a voice inside me said. You must never come between them.

I smiled and said the right things, and thought, I want to go home.

Twenty-one

"THIS IS YOUR HOME now, Harriet," Mrs. Mitchell said, giving me a kiss at the door.

Mrs. Vesper said after the rebandaging, "You'll stop in for ginger cookies this winter just as if this was home?"

After Althea Brand had assured herself that I'd be all right and had reassessed Aunt Sarah, she told me, "Now, Harriet, this is your home, too. You come right in whenever you need to." She hugged me when we left and shook hands with Aunt Sarah.

We drove past the gray house. I turned my face away but heard the little girls' voices: "You be the driver!" "No, you! I want to be the horse!" I felt scalded all down my center.

But as we climbed above the sound of the sawmill, Whitey's head swung up and he stepped out eagerly. The sun was in our eyes, but by turning my head and squinting, I could see how fresh the grass looked, how everything sparkled.

Up the long hill between the fields, between blackberry pastures white with blossoms, through groves of birches. I didn't know the road well enough to be sure of each landmark. Three times we crested a rise and I expected to see the big pasture and the goldenrod-colored house.

But at last there it was. The air was so clear that every detail stood out, even the tiny weather vane horse silhouetted against the brilliant sky. Milking was over. The last cow lumbered through the gate and followed the rest downhill. A small, slope-shouldered figure put up the bars behind her, gazed down at the road, then turned and motioned. A second figure joined him.

"Look! There they are!" I almost pointed. One bandaged hand lifted involuntarily, and it hurt, but not as much as I'd expected.

"Now what kind of a mess do you suppose they've made of that kitchen?" Aunt Sarah asked.

As we turned into the lane, the colt saw us. He galloped up the hill, then trotted with us along the other side of the fence. His step was bouncy, and he carried his tail high. It flowed out behind him like the weather vane horse's tail.

"Not a notion in the world of the trouble he's caused," Aunt Sarah said. She almost sounded admiring.

I could hear the hens now. Tippy sat in the yard, wiggling all over and flattening her ears as we approached. Truman and Uncle Clayton seemed to hold back for a moment, as if they felt shy. But as Whitey stopped with a last *ca-thlop* and a heavy sigh, Uncle Clayton came to my side of the buggy and just stood looking at us. He seemed worn, almost transparent. His eyes shone, and I felt tears in mine.

"Harry. Sarah." His Adam's apple bobbed. "Didn't think you'd stay so long."

"Andy wanted to keep her overnight. Help her down now, Clayton."

I wiggled to the edge of the seat, and he scooped me out, one arm under my knees and one behind my back. For a second it felt like a hug. Then he set me on my feet.

Truman still hung back, his hand twisted into Tippy's collar. He looked shabby and tired. "Hush now!" he said when Tippy barked at me. "She can't pet you."

I felt shy with him. I'd have patted Tippy if I could, and brushed Truman's hand with mine, but that wasn't possible, and already Aunt Sarah was herding me into the house.

The familiar smell of vinegar greeted my nose. Aunt Sarah paused on the threshold, looking around critically. The kitchen looked clean enough to me, and ugly, and pleasantly familiar. But I wasn't home yet. "I'll be right down," I said, and climbed the dark, narrow stairs.

Behind me I heard Aunt Sarah step to the pantry to check on the milk, pause at her stove, and say, "Good gracious, Truman, don't you know how to clean up any better than this? Is there any more kindling? And get Clayton to pick me some green beans."

The last sunlight just slanted into my room. The cigar box was on the bureau.

I picked it up between my two sets of bandaged fingertips, carried it to the window, and sat down. It had been easy to flip the lid up before. Now it slipped away from the gauze once, twice. The third time I pressed harder, which hurt, but worked. Mother smiled up at me.

I felt myself flush, and tears prickled the backs of my eyes. "Hello," I said.

I reached into the box with my huge white hands. They pawed at the stiff cardboard, catching under one edge, dropping the other, then catching up the thinner papers beneath, and all the while burning hotter. At last I had the photograph pressed between my mitts, and I propped it in the window.

From there she seemed to lean toward me, as carefree and daring as a schoolgirl. The picture was miserably small and still, nothing but a pattern of gray tones on paper. I wanted Mother—real, warm, and bigger than me, hugging, laughing, answering questions. There was no getting around that.

Still, meeting her photograph eyes, I felt the love, though the line was tiny, thinned, and stretched, though I was going on in time and Mother wasn't. The warmth that had flooded me, the inner light that had come from my dream on the night she died, surrounded me again. "Hello, Mother," I whispered.

I looked at Father now. I wished I could remember him. I could see him only as a stranger, with a chin like mine and Aunt Sarah's, with exhausted eyes and that hand clinging to Mother's hand. I felt so sorry for him.

Where were the shame and hurt I'd been tangled in only yesterday morning? They were gone, skinned off with my palm prints. It's not supposed to work like that, I thought. You're supposed to think things through, come to conclusions. All I knew was that the bad feeling was gone, so far gone that I couldn't understand it anymore, and that I loved them. They were people, weakness and strength mixed together, and whatever they did, they did out of love. They'd loved each other, and they'd loved me, and somewhere in the unknowable universe maybe they still did.

"Harriet?" Aunt Sarah's voice at the bottom of the stairs. "Are you all right up there?"

I heard the step creak under her foot. "Be right down!" I said. I didn't want her to come up and see them now. But I left them on the windowsill, and I whispered, "See you later."

Truman had just brought in a basket of kindling, and Aunt Sarah was bent over the firebox. "This stove is stone cold! What did you two eat?" She didn't let him answer. "Harriet, are you tired? You can rest in the sitting room."

"I'll . . . go outside," I said. I was tired. My eyes prickled with it. But I'd had a lot of sitting today, a lot of being cared for, a lot of Aunt Sarah, though I felt guilty even thinking that.

Uncle Clayton was bent over in the garden. Whitey grazed near the pasture fence, the marks from the harness still wet on his body. The colt stood sniffing him, pricking his ears thoughtfully. He raised his head when he saw me.

I went to the fence. He hesitated for a moment, then came to me, sniffed my bandages, flared his nostrils at the smell of carbolic and ointment. He lifted his muzzle to my face. I felt the prickle of whiskers, the strong muscular lip against my cheek, the sweet, warm breath. I couldn't pat him, couldn't do anything but kiss the velvet skin at the corner of his mouth. "Hi, Kid," I said. "Hi. I'm sorry."

He sighed, sending the breath tickling into my ear and down the back of my neck. His eye was dark and soft, half closed, and he seemed very young.

Too young. I'd made the same mistake Mother made: pushed too hard. Thought I could control a horse by sheer strength of will, whereas it took something else: time, understanding, and probably other things I hadn't learned about yet.

"You're just a baby," I said. His lips opened against my cheek. He was about to experiment with a nip, and I stepped back.

"All smoothed over?" Truman was there behind me. He stepped up to the fence and rubbed his hand along the colt's neck.

"It was my fault," I said.

"Usually is. Any fight between a horse and a human, I blame the human every time."

"You told me—"

"I know I did." He leaned over the fence and scratched the colt's chest. The colt raised his nose high in the air, grimacing and working his upper lip. "Blame myself," Truman said in a lower, gruffer voice. "Ought to have stopped you when I seen the state of mind you were in. What was it, Harry? Some trouble with Sarah?"

He looked quite grim suddenly, and I didn't want him angry with Aunt Sarah for no reason. "No. I . . . found out. About my parents."

"Found out what about your parents?" He looked baffled, and my heart lurched. Had I made another mistake?

"You know . . . when I was born."

He shook his head slightly.

"Eight months," I said. "Not nine. I counted." He continued to stare at me, those clear greenish eyes huge in his bony head. Surely he knew how long babies take—didn't he? He was an old bachelor, but he must know that. "I don't care about it," I said. "I don't mind anymore. . . ."

All at once Truman seemed to understand. His eyes widened, he drew a deep breath, and then he laid his arm along the fence rail and bowed his head on it.

When he straightened, the skin above his beard was rough and red. "Now listen to me, Harry!" His voice was lower than I'd ever heard it, almost strangled sounding. "Your mother fell in the barn the day you were born. That's why you came a little early. She never told Walter because he felt bad enough already, her doin' his chores in her condition. And she darn sure never told Sarah, for the same reason!"

"How do you know?"

"I ain't a fool, and I made Andy Vesper tell me!"

It crossed my mind that Truman might be lying. He might be telling me what I wanted to hear. But no, I could so easily check with Dr. Vesper, and anyway, it sounded right. It sounded *exactly* like Mother.

But just because it sounded right didn't mean it was right. Mother was an adult, with more sides to her than I'd ever seen. She was young, and the man she loved was going to die soon. She could have been pregnant when they married. I felt stupid now for thinking it so easily, for not thinking of other explanations, but it could still have been true, and it didn't matter.

"It was Sarah set you on that track, wa'n't it?" Truman said. "Nothing else'd start a young girl countin' on her fingers like a darned old maid, about her own mother! Well, Sarah, I've let you go your length, but you get a piece of my mind before you're too many minutes older!" He swung away from the fence.

"No!"

He looked back at me. His eyes blazed, and for the first time I could envision Truman going into battle. But not now. Not against Aunt Sarah, whom he'd loved, one way and another, all her life.

"It's my fight," I said. "I'll handle it. Anyway, I already didn't care, even before you told me. I think—"

It was too complicated to say; my mind and heart were too full. "I don't care," I said again.

"*I* care!"

"Thank you," I said. "But I'll handle it."

Our eyes locked on each other for several more seconds. Then Truman turned away and kicked a pebble, hard. It hit the side of the barn and ricocheted off. "All right! Have it your way! By golly, Harry, you get stubborn from both sides of the family, don't you?"

"I suppose."

Truman ducked his head and laughed shortly. "Ordinarily I wouldn't recommend gettin' dragged by a horse. But it seems to have served you well."

"Served me right!"

"We all make mistakes," Truman said. He let out a sharp sigh that seemed to carry off the rest of his anger. "You know, if you'll let him, Clayton'll take your youngster in hand. He ain't what you'd call masterful, but Clayt can get a horse to see things his way. And I hear there's no hurry now."

"No."

He shook his head in a wondering way, leaned his elbows on the rail again, and gazed off at the pasture and the blue hills.

The colt nudged him and, getting no response, wandered downhill, snatching a bite of grass here and there. All at once he bucked and squealed and galloped menacingly at a cow.

"Well," Truman said, "long as you're all right, Harry."

"Truman!" Aunt Sarah called from the front step.

"Supper's about ready, and I want Harriet to rest!"

"Course, your troubles ain't over," Truman said as we turned toward the house. "You're closer'n two spoons right now, but she'll always know what's best, Sarah will. Unless you plan on cavin' in to her, sometimes you'll have to fight."

"I know."

"Next time it comes up," he said, "I think you ought to tell her."

"You mean . . . ?"

"What I just told you. And it'll come up again, make no mistake. Sarah never quits, and she never uses a popgun if she's got a cannon handy. When she throws that at you again, you ought to tell her the truth. Can't hurt Walter anymore, and I think you owe it to her, Harry. She ought to start thinkin' better of 'em. She ought to have that comfort."

It was like starting over as a baby, eating supper with no hands, except as a baby I probably didn't mind helplessness and things dribbling down my chin. Aunt Sarah was deft, and when needed, she chased the dribbles rapidly with a spoon, the way mothers do. It made me cross, though, and it would be this way for at least a week. Dr. Vesper insisted on absolute cleanliness, and he'd swaddled my hands so I couldn't be tempted to use them.

"I'll start hayin' the homeplace tomorrow," Uncle Clayton remarked over his tea. He glanced out the window at a tiny puff of cloud, golden with the last rays of sun. "Guess you won't be able to help us, Harry."

"Ride over and visit anyway," Truman said.

"Tomorrow I have to churn," I said. "I can still churn."

"Tomorrow you have to *rest*," Aunt Sarah said, wiping my chin with a damp cloth. I glanced at Truman and away, before the sparkle in his eyes could make me smile. I *would* churn. I'd sit in the rocker before she even poured the cream, and she'd say, "All right, a few minutes then," and I'd have my own way. I did know how to get around Aunt Sarah.

A wide yawn interrupted my thoughts. Without hands I couldn't hide it, and a moment later I yawned again. "Better say good-night," Aunt Sarah said. "I'll be up in a minute to help you change your clothes."

I climbed the stairs. There was time, before Aunt Sarah followed, to put Mother and Father's picture away. I was about to, but I paused, looking at them, and as I heard her step on the stairs, I decided to leave them where they were. No time like the present!

Aunt Sarah brought a candle and set it on the bedside table. It threw a soft glow directly onto the windowsill, touching the edge of the picture. She didn't glance that way. She was looking around the room. "It's awful hot up here!" It was true. The stale heat lingered in the corners of the room, like the remnants of a fever. "It must have been terrible during that hot weather. Why didn't you mention it, Harriet?"

She crossed the room and pushed the bureau aside with her hip. The murky mirror shuddered. She opened the door beyond, and after a moment cool air began to flow through my window, moving toward the next room.

Aunt Sarah paused in the doorway. "I'll move you over here tomorrow," she said. "That way you won't get the heat from the kitchen," She stood looking into that bare room for a moment. I leaned over and nudged the candle, so the warm glow lit Mother's face. Aunt Sarah turned and came toward me, the nightgown draped over her arm. I saw her see the picture.

She stood looking for a moment, and then she reached across the candle flame and picked up the picture. My heart beat harder: Mother and Aunt Sarah, face to face. She gazed and gazed, her eyes dark and wide.

"He *was* sick," she said finally, as if to herself. "I didn't realize . . . "

Then she seemed to remember that I was there. She looked down at me, huge in the twilit room, the photograph small in her hand. The candle lit the underside of it, lit the date in Mother's handwriting, lit the sudden glitter in Aunt Sarah's eyes.

"You'll want a frame for this," she said, "so you can have it on your table." Gently she propped the picture back in the window, a little farther over than I'd had it, so the candlelight fell only on Father's face, but never mind that for now.

"Stand up," she said, "and let me help you into your nightgown."

NATIONAL
VELVET

Enid Bagnold grew up "all over the world." Her father was a colonel of the Royal Engineers, whose work took him to many British colonies. When she was twelve, Enid was sent back to boarding school in England, then to finishing schools in France and Switzerland.

When World War I began, Miss Bagnold joined the VAD (Voluntary Aid Detachment) and worked first in a hospital, then later as an ambulance driver for the French Army. She was the first woman to drive an ambulance into war-torn Verdun.

Enid Bagnold lived in Rottingdean, Sussex, in the beautiful chalk down country where Velvet and her family lived. Like the Browns, the author and her four children—a girl and three boys—loved horses. When Enid's daughter Laurian was thirteen, she illustrated the first edition of *National Velvet*.

National Velvet, like so many books which young people love, was originally written for adults. It became a best-seller and was a selection of the Book-of-the-Month Club. Later it became a movie, starring Mickey Rooney and Elizabeth Taylor.

Enid Bagnold wrote many stories, articles, and plays, several of which have appeared in American magazines. Two of her plays, *The Chalk Garden* and *The Chinese Prime Minister*, were produced on Broadway. *The Chalk Garden* was also adapted for the movies.

NATIONAL VELVET

ENID BAGNOLD

AN AVON  CAMELOT BOOK

AVON BOOKS, INC.
1350 Avenue of the Americas
New York, New York 10019

Published by arrangement with William Morrow and Company, Inc.
Library of Congress Catalog Card Number: 99-94526
ISBN: 0-380-81056-5
www.avonbooks.com

First Avon Camelot Printing: December 1999

CAMELOT TRADEMARK REG U.S. PAT. OFF AND IN OTHER COUNTRIES, MARCA REGISTRADA,
HECHO EN U.S A

Printed in the U.S.A.

OPM   10   9   8   7   6   5   4

To Roderick and Laurian

~ ONE ~

Unearthly humps of land curved into the darkening sky like the backs of browsing pigs, like the rumps of elephants. At night when the stars rose over them they looked like a starlit herd of divine pigs. The villagers called them Hullocks.

The valleys were full of soft and windblown vegetation. The sea rolled at the foot of all as though God had brought his herd down to water.

The Hullocks were blackening as Velvet cantered down the chalk road to the village. She ran on her own slender legs, making horse-noises and chirrups and occasionally striking her thigh with a switch, holding at the same time something very small before her as she ran. The light on the chalk road was the last thing to gleam and die. The flints slipped and flashed under her feet. Her cotton dress and her cottony hair blew out, and her lips were parted for breath in a sweet metallic smile. She had the look of a sapling-Dante as she ran through the darkness downhill.

At the entrance to the village the sea was pounding

up the sewer with a spring gale behind it. She passed to the third cottage, stopped at the door, opened it, let a gush of light onto the pavement, closed it and carried her tender object inside.

Edwina, Malvolia and Meredith sat in their father's, Mr. Brown's, sitting room just before suppertime. It was dark outside and hot inside, and outside in the darkness the Hullocks went up in great hoops above the village. There was an oil stove in the corner of the sitting room and lesson books on the table. The ceiling was low and sagged. A lamp with a green glass shade lit the table. There was no electric light. Donald, the boy of four, was asleep upstairs.

Edwina, Malvolia and Meredith were all exactly alike, like golden greyhounds. Their golden hair was sleek, their fine faces like antelopes, their shoulders still and steady like Zulu women carrying water, and their bodies beneath the shoulders rippled when they moved. They were seventeen, sixteen, and fifteen. Velvet was fourteen. Velvet had short pale hair, large, protruding teeth, a sweet smile and a mouthful of metal.

Mr. Brown was swilling down the slaughterhouse, as Mi Taylor was away for the day. The sound of the hose swished at the wooden partition which separated the slaughterhouse from the sitting room.

"He went beautifully!" said Velvet, and laying down a tiny paper horse on the table she wrenched at the gold band that bound her teeth back and laid it beside the horse.

"Father'll be in in a minute," said Edwina warningly.

"It's going in again directly I hear a sound," said Velvet and sitting down she swept the band into her lap.

"Look at him," she said lovingly, taking up the paper horse. "I must unsaddle him and rub him down." The heads were bent on the lesson books again and Velvet took a tiny bridle of cotton threads from the horse. Then going to a shell-box on the sideboard she brought it to the table.

"It's just supper," said Mally. "You'll have to clear."

Velvet opened the box and took out a stable rubber two inches square, a portion of her handkerchief, hemmed round. Laying the little horse flat on the table she rubbed him with delicacy in circular motions, after having taken a paper saddle from his back.

The horse was a racer cut from the *Bystander.* He stood three inches high and had a raking neck and a keen, veined face. By dint of much rubbing the paper had given off a kind of coat, and now as Velvet rubbed there came a suède-like sheen on the horse's paper body. He was dark, most carefully cut out, and pasted upon cardboard. The bridle was made by the fingers of a fairy, noseband, chinstrap and all, in black cotton.

"He has a high action," said Velvet. "A lovely show canter, but a difficult trot. I didn't jump him today as he needs to settle down."

In the shell-box other horses lay.

"There's a marvelous picture of mares on the back of the *Times* today, but you can't cut a single one clear. They're all mixed up with the foals."

"I saw it," said Velvet. "I called at the Post Office. But it was no good."

"I called in too," said Mally. "They said in the Post Office that one of us looking at the *Times* was enough. We'd better take turns."

"Yes," said Velvet. "You can't think how lovely it was galloping up there. It was nearly dark. He never put a foot wrong. Somehow you can trust a horse like that."

"It's blood that counts," said Mally darkly.

"I haven't got the racing saddle cut right," went on Velvet. "I wish I could find a picture of one. I ride short when I ride this horse and with this saddle the knees come right off onto his shoulder."

"You need kneeflaps," said Edwina.

"I suppose there's not time," said Velvet, "to take the chestnut down for a stand in the pond? His hocks are still puffy."

"It's not you to lay tonight," said Mally. "You've got ten minutes. Don't let Father see. . . . Mind your band! It's fallen!"

Velvet dived under the table, picked it up, and examined it anxiously. Opening her mouth she worked it painfully in with both hands.

"S'bent a bit," she gasped. "It's a terrible band . . ."

"It's no good. Don't go on! Get on down to the pond."

Velvet packed the racer in the shell-box and carefully abstracted a smaller horse, a colored picture of a polo pony cut from the *Tatler*. Putting the box away she slipped through the door with the chestnut and was gone.

A door at the other end of the sitting room opened and Mrs. Brown came in. She stood and looked at the daughters for a moment—an enormous woman who had once swum the Channel. Now she had become muscle-bound.

Towering over the lamp she threw her shadow across the books and up the wall.

She said: "Lay supper." And went out.

"Meredith," said Edwina mechanically without looking up. Meredith got up and began to collect the books. When all the books were gone the two sisters sat tilting

4 ⬍

their chairs back so that Meredith could get the white cloth over the edge of the table past their knees. When this was done all their chairs came forward again. Kneeling by the Victorian sideboard Meredith pulled out plates, bread-knife, platter, sugar, knives and forks and salts and peppers.

The street door opened and Velvet stood on the mat. She had her shoes in her hand and her bare ankles were green with slime. Mrs. Brown who had come in glanced at her and took a duster from the sideboard. "Wipe them up," she said and threw the duster onto the mat. Velvet mopped her slimy ankles, whispering to Mally, pointing with her finger towards the door—"Stars like Christmas trees. Terrible stuff in the pond. Spawn. I stood five minutes."

"We ought to get some," said Mally. "I'll get a bottle after supper."

"Any spawn," said Mrs. Brown without looking up, "goes on a tin tray."

"Yes, mother."

"Larder," said Mrs. Brown.

Velvet put her shoes in the corner and the horse in the shell-box and disappeared. The others sat in silence till she came back with the tray.

Cold ham, jam, butter were placed on the table, and a dish of radishes.

Mr. Brown came in by the slaughterhouse door, rubber boots drawn to his thighs, his sleeves rolled up, his hands wet from the hose. He passed through the room on his way to wash for supper. Velvet and the three golden greyhounds sat on in brooding silence. A smell of liver and bacon stole in from the kitchen.

The two doors, that on the street and that on the kitchen, opened suddenly together. Out of the black hole of the street came Mi Taylor, brushed up for supper. Mrs. Brown came in from the kitchen carrying the liver and bacon.

The room filled with smells. Mr. Brown came in putting on his coat. Everyone sat down, Mi last of all, pulling up his chair gingerly.

"Well . . ." said Mr. Brown, and helped the liver round.

Meredith went out and fetched in the jugs of coffee and milk.

"Bin over to Worthing?" said Mr. Brown.

"I have," said Mi.

"Got that freezing-machine catalogue for me?"

"Shops shut again."

"Good gosh!" said Mr. Brown, exasperated. "Don't you ever learn the shut-shop day in Worthing? Whadyer do then?"

"Had three teeth out. Dentist was all there was open."

"Oh, Mi, where?" said Velvet.

Mi opened his jaw and pointed to a bloody wound.

"Oughter eat pap for it," said Mr. Brown. "It's pulpy."

"S'got to learn to harden," said Mi.

"Donald asleep?" said Mally.

"This hour gone," said Mrs. Brown.

They ate, sleek girls' heads bent under the lamp, Mr. Brown and Mrs. Brown square and full and steady, Mi silent and dexterous with his red hair boiling up in curls on his skull.

Jacob went grinning round the table from sister to sister.

"Nobody feeds him," ordered Mi under his breath.

His red hair boiled up on his skull fiercer than ever at Jacob's presumption.

The yard spaniels remained in the street on the doorstep through meals. They lay and leaned against the front door, grouped on the step, so that the door creaked and groaned under their pressed bodies. When the door was opened from the inside they fell in. When this happened Mi sent them out again with a roar.

Jacob had been allowed in all his life. His fox terrier body, growing stout in middle age, still vibrated to a look. His lips curled and he grinned at the blink of a human eyelash. His tail ached with wagging, and even his hips waggled as he moved. But under cover of these virtues he was watchful for his benefit, watchful for human weakness, affected, a ready liar, disobedient, boastful, a sucker-up, and had a lifelong battle with Mi. Mi adored him, but seldom said a kind word to him. Jacob adored Mi, and there was no one whom he would not sooner deceive. At meals Jacob wriggled and grinned from sister to sister, making a circle round Mi, whose leg was scooping for him.

Just outside the slaughterhouse was a black barking dog on the end of a string. This dog had a name but no character. It barked without ceasing day and night. Nobody heard it. The Browns slept and lived and ate beside its barking. The spaniels never opened their mouths. They pressed against doors and knee and furniture. They lived for love and never got it. They were herded indiscriminately together and none knew their characteristics but Mi. The sisters felt for them what they felt for the fowls in the fowlyard. Mi fed them.

But Jacob's weaknesses and affectations and dubious sincerities were thrust upon everyone's notice. When Velvet came in at the front door, and pressing back the leaning spaniels, closed it, Jacob would rise, wriggle his hips at her, bow and grin.

"How exquisite, how condescending, how flattering!" said he, bowing lower and lower, with his front legs slid out on the floor and his back legs stiff. But if asked to go for a walk not a step would he come outside unless he had business of his own with the ashbin, or wanted to taunt the chained and raging dog with the spine of a herring dragged in the dust.

The chained dog chiefly barked. But sometimes he stopped rending the unheeding air and lay silent. Then he would whirl out on his chain like a fury and fall flat, half choked. And Jacob would stand without flinching, banking on the strength of the chain, and think, "You poor one-thoughted fool . . ."

The Browns loved Jacob as they loved each other, deeply, from the back of the soul, with intolerance in daily life.

As the girls ate, a private dream floated in Velvet's mind. . . . It was a little horse, slender and perfect, rising divinely at a jump, forefeet tucked up neatly, intelligence and delight in its eager eye, and on its back, glued lightly and easily to the saddle . . . she, Velvet . . . Gymkhana Velvet. As she took the visionary jump in dream her living hand stole to her mouth. She pulled out the torturing band and hid it in her lap. Mi's eyes were on her in a flash, he who never missed anything.

"Be windy for the Fair Thursday," said Mrs. Brown.

"It's coming in wild from the southwest," said Mr. Brown.

"Always does when it comes in at all," said Mrs. Brown. "Three-day gale."

All the trees in the dark village outside attested this. They were blown like fans set on one side. The rooks shuffled and slept in them, waving up and down among the breaking twigs. The village street was white with rook-droppings.

"Put that in again, Velvet," commanded Mrs. Brown.

"She got it out again?" asked Mr. Brown, looking up sharply.

"It aches me an' aches when I eat," said Velvet.

"Ache or no, argue or no, that band cost me four pound ten and it's solid gold an' it goes in," said Mr. Brown. "I'm not going to have a child like a rabbit if I can help it. You girls have got your faces for your fortunes and none other. I've told you often enough."

The three golden greyhounds sat up straighter than ever and Velvet fumbled with her teeth.

"It's got hooked up."

"Unhook it, then," said Mr. Brown. He sat back, satisfied, commanding and comfortable, and pulled the radishes towards him. Then he passed the dish around.

"Take a radish, Velvet."

"Couldn't bite a *radish!*"

"Go without then," said Mr. Brown happily, and leaned back to light his pipe.

All the Browns tilted their chairs. Nobody ever told them it would hurt the carpet. They ate, ruminated, and tilted. Only Mrs. Brown sat solid and silent. She did not talk much, but managed the till down at the shop in the street. She knew all about courage and endurance, to the last ounce of strength, from the first swallow of overcome timidity. She valued and appraised each daughter, she knew what each daughter could do. She was glad too that her daughters were not boys because she could not understand the courage of men, but only the courage of women. Mr. Brown was with dignity the head of the family. But Mrs. Brown was the standard of the family. When Velvet had fallen off the pier at the age of six her mother went in thirty feet after her, sixteen stone, royal-blue afternoon dress. A straight dive, like the dive of an ageing mammoth. The reporter from the *West Worthing News* came to make a story of it and said to Edwina, "Your mother swam the Channel, didn't she?" Edwina nodded towards her mother. "Better ask *her*." "What's past's past, young man," said Mrs. Brown heavily and shut her mouth and her door.

Mi Taylor's father had trained Mrs. Brown for her swim, trained her when she had been a great girl of nineteen, neckless, clumsy, and incredibly enduring. Mi himself had been a flyweight boxer, killed his man, got exonerated and yet somehow disqualified, tramped the country, held horses, cleaned stables and drifted nearer and nearer to the racing world, till he knew all about it except the feel of a horse's back. Arriving somehow in the ebb of Lewes races he had been taken on by Mr. Brown for the slaughterhouse, for running errands, and lately even for negotiating for stock.

Mrs. Brown stared at him when he came with a look of strange pleasure in her hooded eyes. Mi Taylor, the son of Father Taylor! He knew all about her, Taylor did. The only one who ever did. He knew what she was made of. He'd had the last ounce out of her. He and the doctor at her five confinements, those men knew. Nobody else, ever. Mi was his son. Mi was welcome. He could stay. Henceforth he ate with the family and lodged in the extra loose-box. And Araminty Brown, embedded in fat, her keen, hooded eyes hardly lifting the rolls above them, cooked admirably, ran the accounts, watched the shop, looked after the till, spoke seldom, interfered hardly ever, sighed sometimes (because it would have taken a war on her home soil, the birth of a colony, or a great cataclysm to have dug from her what she was born for), moved about the house, brought up her four taut daughters under her heavy eye, and thought of death occasionally with a kind of sardonic shrug. Nobody could have said exactly whether she had a dull brain or no. Ed and Mally and Meredith behaved themselves at the wink of one of her heavy eyes. Velvet would have laid down her stringy life for her.

"Yer ma," said Mi, " 'sworth a bellyful. Pity she weighs what she does."

"Why?" said Mally.

"Binds her up," said Mi. And it was not constipation he was thinking of.

"Mi," said Mally to her mother, "thinks you ought to be riding in Lewes races."

Mrs. Brown made a noise in her nose.

"What?" said Mally.

"That's all right," said Mrs. Brown.

"You can never tell what Mother's thinking," said Mally to Velvet.

"She doesn't think where we do," said Velvet. "She thinks at the back."

In the sitting room at the close of supper Mrs. Brown stretched out an arm and turned the lamp lower.

"Box," said Mr. Brown, indicating the sideboard. Edwina rose and brought him his small cigar.

The shadows whirled.

"Monday," said Mrs. Brown.

"Driving night," said Velvet.

"What I was thinking," said Mrs. Brown. "Get on off!"

"First?" said Velvet.

"First," said Mrs. Brown.

Velvet hunched her shoulder blades and sniffed. Was driving worth it? She never could make up her mind. Out of bed it didn't seem so, but in bed it was worth while.

"Hush!" she said suddenly and held up her hand. "Cough . . ." she said, and went to the slaughter-house door.

"Gone to rub Miss Ada's chest," said Mi, grinning.

In the sitting room the books for homework came out again.

"Gotta see a boy," murmured Mi as he went out into the street.

Velvet lit the hurricane lamp standing in the corner of the empty slaughterhouse and passed through to the shed where the old pony lived.

Miss Ada was an old pink roan gone grey with age, her ears permanently back, a look of irritation about her creased nostrils, backbone sagging, horny growths on her legs.

"Hullo," said Velvet and opened the door. Miss Ada moved definitely round and turned her backside on Velvet.

Velvet put her hand on the quarters and the skin twitched irritably.

"You never do anything about being decent!" said Velvet. "Have you got a cough?"

Miss Ada bent her head suddenly and rubbed the itch off her right nostril onto her leg, and as she did it she flashed a robust, contemptuous look at Velvet. "Is there sugar?" said the look, "or no sugar? I want no subtle-ties, no sentimentalities. I don't care about your state of heart, your wretched conscience-prickings, your ambi-tious desires. Is there sugar or no sugar? State your reasons for coming to see me and leave me to brood."

Velvet produced a piece of sugar and the pony bent her head round with a look of insolence, as though she still suspected the sugar to be an imitation lump. She took it with her lips, but she pressed her old teeth for a minute on the child's palm, and at this trick, as old as Velvet's childhood, Velvet thrust her arms over the sagging backbone and buried her face among the knobbles of the spine. The pony munched her lump stolidly, flirting her head up and down as though she were fishing for extra grains high up among her teeth.

"If we had another pony," said Velvet, "nobody would love you less. But we can't go on like this, it's awful. The gymkhanas all coming and nothing to ride. And you hate all that. It puts you in your worst mood."

The door opened and Mally came in.

"Has she got a cough?"

"She hasn't coughed since I've been here," said Velvet.

"Get over, you awful old thing!" said Mally, "and let me pass."

"Don't, Mally . . ."

"The only way is to be as horrid to her as she is to us."

"I've left the lamp down there. Hang it up somewhere. I can't reach the hook."

Mally hung the lamp carefully out of way of the straw. The two sat up on the manger together. The pony, utterly disgusted, drew her ears back almost flat with her head, hung out her twitching underlip and faced round at an angle from them, her tail tucked sourly in.

"Look at her!" said Mally. "What a mount!"

Velvet took out her band and wrapped it in her handkerchief.

"Don't you leave it here," said Mally. "It won't

help us any. It was your band-fiddling that went wrong at supper.''

Mally got up onto the manger's rim, reached to a ledge of wood below the window and took down two sticks of dark gold paper.

"Crunchie?" said Velvet, her face lighting.

"I got them this morning."

"On tick still?"

"Yes. She was cross but I swore we'd pay by Saturday."

In the gold paper was a chocolate stick. Beneath the chocolate was a sort of honeycomb, crisp and friable, something between biscuit and burnt sugar. Fry's chocolate crunchie. Not one of the sisters ate any other kind of sweet that year. It was their year's choice. The year before it had been Carmel Crispies.

"We must pay her. She's a wispy woman. She's pappy."

"Aren't you queer about people. Always cutting 'em down to the bone."

"I don't like people," said Velvet, "except us and mother and Mi. I like only horses."

"Pity you weren't a boy."

"I should a bin a poor thin boy. With muscles just on one arm. From meat chopping."

"As it is," said Mally, "we're all going into tills. Into cages. To count out money."

"I'm not," said Velvet, examining her crunchie. "Do you like the end best or the middle?"

"I like the ones that don't seem cooked. Sticky in the middle."

"I wish I had a proper coat with checks," said Velvet.

"You? Why, Edwina's never had one."

14 ⚊

"Edwina isn't me. I'm not going to be a jersey-jumping child in a gymkhana any more."

"I don't know how we're going to do anything in the gymkhanas at all. Miss Ada's turning sourer and sourer on us. She'll end by refusing to go into the ring."

Miss Ada, seduced by the smell of the chocolate, turned slowly towards them, approaching by fractions.

"It's all right, Mally, I'll give her a bit of mine," said Velvet. "You bought 'em."

"It doesn't matter who bought 'em," said Mally. "We're all owing together. . . . She can have a crumb of mine too. Don't blow so, you idiot! She's sneezed her crumb off my hand!" Miss Ada stooped her head and began a vain search for one chocolate crumb in two inches of dingy straw.

The stable door opened and Mi put his head in.

"Meredith in here?"

"No . . . Whad' you want'er for?"

"*Canary Breeder's Annual's* come. Come on last post."

"Don' know where she is," said Malvolia. "She won't be fit to live with for weeks."

"Mi . . . Mi . . . Mi!" called a voice from the dark.

"In here. He's got your *Canary Breeder.*"

"Mother said so! Oh. . . . I'll come in. Give it to me!"

Meredith took the book from Mi. "You've taken off the wrapper," she said disappointedly; "I like to take it off myself," and leaned back against Miss Ada, unconscious of the pony's body.

" 'Nother time you can fetch your own *Annual,*" said Mi.

"Bet you don't remember next year," said Mally.

"Listen to this! Listen to this! It's what I always

thought!'' said Meredith. ''Listen to Mr. Lukie. He says (J. Lukie, Esquire, it's signed) he says, 'Cod liver oil should be given to mating birds. My own birds did magnificently on Poon's Finchmixture Codliver . . .' '' Miss Ada removed her support sharply and Meredith sat violently on the straw. ''Blast!'' she said, without looking round at the pony, opened the *Annual* and searched again for the page.

''Yes, but his birds were already mating,'' said Mally. ''You keep wanting to give them the cod liver oil to make them mate. It doesn't make them mate. Lukie doesn't say it does!''

''I don't see why . . .'' said Meredith, still hunting for the page. ''You've got to be lively to mate. Vital or something. Cod liver oil gives vitality. I read it . . . it's here . . . 'gives vitality to the mating bird.' ''

''Miss Ada'll step on your hand if you leave it there,'' said Velvet.

Meredith got slowly up, reading as she rose. ''It doesn't say whether it's the cock bird or the hen. Which do you think it is, Mi?''

''Cock before, hen after,'' said Mi.

''There you are!'' said Meredith. ''I *wish* Mother'd let me order it.''

''You got it all over the sofa last time.''

''But I've got a fountain pen filler now. I've trained the cock on drops of water. He's as good as gold. The hen makes a fuss. I could do her in the yard.''

''Bed,'' said Edwina from the darkness outside.

They filed out without a word, Meredith reading to the last by the flare of the hurricane lamp. The spring gale had gone. The spring sky was indefinite and still, with a star in it. There was a new moon.

''Are you coming, Velvet?''

16 ◄

"You can't leave Miss Ada with nothing when we've used her stable. I'll be a second." She opened the corn bin and Miss Ada dropped ten years off her looks. She plunged her nose on the two hands that cupped the corn and ducked her head to sniff out the droppings before they sank too far in the straw. Velvet, alone, saw the new moon. She bowed three times, glanced round to see that no one saw, then standing in the shadow of the stable door she put her hands like thin white arrows together and prayed to the moon—"Oh, God, give me horses, give me horses! Let me be the best rider in England!"

⇝ TWO ⇜

The next morning Meredith had to take some suet and a shin of beef over to Pendean. School was at nine. It was the last day of term. She rose at six. Mi called her on his way downstairs. He heated the coffee left over from last night and gave her three sardines between two pieces of bread. Then Meredith went out to saddle Miss Ada.

Miss Ada had a crupper to her saddle, partly because the hills were so steep and partly because she had no shoulders. Meredith forgot the crupper and left it dangling. She put the girths on twisted, put the *Canary Breeder* in the basket with the suet, and started off. Miss Ada tapped smartly up the village street on the tarmac. The flints on the church shone like looking-glass. Meredith trotted east into the rising sun. Her toes were warm and the sardines and the bread and coffee digested comfortingly. Over the Hullocks and down into the valleys, sun and shadow, cup and saucer, through the tarred gate, the wired gate, the broken gate, and finally into the Pendean valley and to the house. She gave in the beef and the suet, would have stopped to talk to Lucy the farm daughter (only Lucy had a temperature), started on the home journey, crupper still dangling, and Miss Ada restive now from the sore of the twisted girth.

"We'll go the Dead-Horse-Patch way," said Meredith suddenly, aloud; and then disliked the sound of the spoken words in the lonely landscape. One of Miss Ada's ears came forward. They were above the village now, though still two miles away. There were two ways down to the sea level. One by the two steep fields and the chalk road whence she had come up, the other by two more steep fields, two gates, a broken reaping machine, a cabbage field, to a haystack—and a place where a horse had once dropped dead.

For thirteen years Miss Ada had said that place was haunted. She had told Mr. Brown so plainly when Velvet was crawling. And he had never insisted with her, but let her come down the way she had planned for herself by the chalk road. Now to Meredith's mind came the desire to take Miss Ada the way she had never been taken by Edwina, Malvolia, Velvet or herself.

Even before the division of the ways the intention became communicated to the pony. A hardening took place, a clenching of spirit. A weight came into Miss Ada's head. She hung it provocatively upon her bit. Meredith sat uneasily and watchfully in her saddle.

Miss Ada's way was to the left. Meredith's was to the right. Miss Ada had two methods of getting her way. Either she didn't cede at all, or when Meredith pulled she ceded too fast and whipped round. This method she chose and the saddle slipped over on the too-slack girths. Meredith fell off. Miss Ada with a look of sudden youth flicked her heels, cantered to the wire fence, stooped her head and cropped. The basket with the *Canary Breeder* had fallen too and Meredith, getting up, picked up her *Annual,* glanced at Miss Ada and after a minute sat down in the sun to read. She was now faced with a walk home. Nobody ever caught Miss Ada once she was loose. She would go home her own way and at her own time.

Meredith read comfortably what Mr. Lukie had to say, then closed her book and trudged off.

"You'll look an idiot!" she said partingly to Miss Ada. "Coming home with your saddle all upside down." The whites of Miss Ada's eyes glinted as she cropped. Meredith went down towards the Dead-Horse-Patch. When she was out of sight Miss Ada moved off by the way she had intended to go.

Meredith ran down over a steep field that lay in shadow with its back to the rising sun, then up the opposite slope with the sun shining on her back. Over the rise she saw a rider in the distance nearing the haystack that stood at the edge of the cabbage field, the haystack where the legendary horse had laid down and died. The rider coming towards her, she could not see at first whether he was walking or trotting. . . . Then came a flick of movement and he was off. The horse as usual had shied at the Dead-Horse-Patch.

When Meredith reached him he was on his feet dusting himself down, a tripper-rider, a great lad with loose flannel trousers and bicycle clips. The horse, like Miss Ada, was cropping feverishly as though it had never seen grass before.

"You got Mr. Belton's Bumble Bee," said Meredith.

"What's the matter with him? Seen a ghost?" said the young man.

"Yes, he did," said Meredith.

"Eh? How? You had a fall too?" eyeing the green-grass stain on her hip.

Meredith looked round to see if Miss Ada was in sight.

"Bin sliding," she said.

"Can we catch the horse?" said the tripper.

"Maybe," said Meredith, "but I shouldn't think so. I got to be in time for school."

"Jumped his whole length sideways," said the tripper.

"They always do, here," said Meredith, edging gently towards the horse.

"Why here?"

"There's a ghost in the ground. A horse ghost. Steams up mornings and evenings. Specially early when there's a dew drying off." Her hand was within a foot of the reins, extended soothingly. The young man saw her intention and ran round the other side. The horse, startled, removed itself another length away.

"You mucked it," said Meredith. "I must get on."

Miss Ada got home first. Velvet was putting saltpeter on her girth-gall as she stood in the sunlight on the street by the front door. The saddle was pitched up on the railings. The front door was open and Mr. Brown, bareheaded, was enjoying his after breakfast pipe.

"My girl," he said when he saw Meredith, "yer fifteen, annt you?"

Meredith nodded and stood still before him.

"Seven years you've saddled that pony and put her bits of leather on her, and to this day you onny hang 'em round her like blind cords. She's got a sore'll take a week to heal."

Miss Ada looked at Meredith with smug reproach.

21

"If it was canaries . . ." muttered Velvet, dabbing with a rag.

Meredith glowered at Velvet as she passed her to go in for her school books.

Inside the sitting room Mi was telling Donald to get on with his porridge. It was cold porridge, turned out of a cup. There was a hole in the top and treacle was poured inside. Donald was laying a sap from the side into the center.

"You aren't eating what you cut out," said Mi, cleaning a rat trap with emery paper and the rust covering the cloth in showers.

"I am," said Donald. But he wasn't.

"Donald done yet?" called Mrs. Brown. "I'm washing the plates."

"He's fiddling," said Mi.

Mrs. Brown came to the door. "You get down and bring that porridge in here," she said as she rubbed a plate.

The sweetness of Donald's face remained unchanged. He watched the treacle run out down the sap. "I dooon't . . ." he drawled.

Mrs. Brown gave no second chances. It was her strength.

She took Donald in one great arm and the plate of porridge in the other and removed him. The sweetness of his face was still unchanged.

"He'll never eat that," said Meredith. "You're sitting on my atlas."

Mi pulled it out from beneath him. "He never eats anything he's fiddled with," said Mi, "because it's turned into something else in his mind. Hark to them hammering . . ."

"You'd never think, to look at the Green, that there'd

22 ━

be a Fair in twenty-four hours. Just a lot of old sticks and men hitting them in.''

"It'll be ready. You won't be though.''

"I'm just going. Last day. Holidays tomorrow.''

"All four hanging round the house all day. Life'll be a joke.''

"This bit a millet, Mi," said Meredith, dragging a length out of the sideboard drawer. "Stick it in for the male, Mi, *please.* . . .''

"Them birds . . ." Meredith blocked the light in the doorway and was gone.

"Blast and blast and blast . . ." said Mi softly. He had caught his finger in the rat trap.

"Blast," said Donald softly in the doorway. His silver hair hung in a lock over his forehead. His eyes were film-eyes and blue, with film-lashes. His platinum-blond, Hollywood head was set on a green jersey. His bottom was bare and his pants hung down unbuttoned.

"You've got off your pot!" said Mi threateningly. "Get on back." Donald disappeared again into the inner room, his behinds gleaming like the white polish of two peeled and hard-boiled eggs.

Edwina went in to Worthing for a piano lesson. Mally, Meredith and Velvet waded through a last day of grammar and map reading behind the walls of the village school. The children's voices droned behind the windows and the hammering on the Village Green increased. At break the children watched the hammers from the corner of the asphalt yard. The greasy pole was up, the cokernut shies were up, there was a frail porch with "Welcome" written on it.

Marks for the term were read out, and prizes given. Malvolia got *Hiawatha.*

At home it was steak and kidney pudding for dinner and Mr. Brown poured in the boiling water through a hole in the suet. Velvet kept her band in and swallowed whole. The kidneys went down like stones. Mr. Brown finished his *Meat Fancier* as he ate. Donald ate his meat well and said gently some six or seven times, "Is it castle puddings?" Nobody knew. His question was not insistent but soft. Sometimes he said it through his meat.

"Yer spitting, Donald," said Mi.

"I *said*," said Donald, dreamily. . . .

Mrs. Brown looked at him. "It is," she said.

"You never used to tell *us!*" said Velvet.

"Times," said Mrs. Brown, "I don't do what I always did."

Malvolia cleared the plates. Mrs. Brown fetched in a city of castle puddings and a jam pot full of heated jam. She served Donald, the baby, first. Two castle puddings and a dab of jam on the plate. He looked at his two puddings and began to examine them. He drooped his Hollywood head like a smiling angel.

"Fiddling again," said Mi ominously. "You wanted 'em too much."

"Yore putting it into his head," said Mally.

Edwina walked in and put down her music roll and her hat. She pulled a chair up.

"Your bit's there," said Mrs. Brown, "on the sideboard."

"Guvner an' me we wash," said Mi into his plate. "Funny how men wash for girls an' girls don' wash for men."

"Anybody knows boys are dirtier than girls," said Mally.

"Meybe. But grown men wash freer than women." Edwina sat down, ignoring criticism.

"Get on, get on," said Mrs. Brown to Donald.

"I am gettin' on," said Donald, and opened his mouth to show that it was full.

"Bin turning round and round," said Mi. "Give a swaller."

"Can't swaller," said Donald, " 'tisn't slidy."

"Isn't he lovely!" said Velvet, coming out of a dream quite suddenly and looking as though she had seen him for the first time. "Shall I teach you to ride, Donald?"

"You've put him off proper," said Mrs. Brown.

Donald opened his eyes and struggled with his mouth. Then he leant over his plate and spat out the revolving mass. "Yes," he said, when he was empty, "yes, when? Now?"

Mrs. Brown rose slowly, took her own empty plate away to the sideboard, moved calmly and without anger round to Donald.

"You'll finish alone," she said, and gathered him up. Donald and his plate sailed into the back kitchen.

"Well, really, Velvet," said Edwina.

"He doesn't care," said Velvet. "Wouldn't he be lovely in the under six?"

"On Miss Ada?" said Mally.

"She's too wide really."

"You want a little narrow thing like Lucy's Rowanberry."

"Lucy never can find anyone small enough to ride Rowanberry anyway."

"Could we start him, Father?" said Velvet.

"Eh?" said Mr. Brown, struggling to leave his page.

"Teach Donald. So's he could be ready for the under six?"

"Under what?" said Mr. Brown. "The under what?"

25

"Gymkhana," said Velvet. "The class for children under six. Six years."

"Ask your mother," said Mr. Brown, and returned to his page.

"Then that's that," said Velvet, rising happily. "Can I get down?"

There was no answer.

"F'whatayave received thank God," said Velvet to no one in particular, and disappeared into the kitchen.

"Did you give 'em that millet?" said Meredith suddenly.

"Forgot," said Mi.

"F'whatayave received thank God," said Meredith with a dark look at him, and shot from the room. Mr. Brown pushed back his chair.

"You girls said your grace?" he said, getting up.

"F'whatayave received thank God," said Edwina. And the meal was finished.

The candle in the scarlet-painted candlestick was burnt low and had a shroud. The bottle-candle was high and gave a good light.

Spring and evening sky showed between undrawn cotton curtains.

Mrs. Brown sat on a stout mahogany chair before her dressing table, and Velvet knelt behind her unhooking her dress from neck to waist at the back. The dress was dark blue rep, built firm. It was like unhooking a shrunk sofa-covering. Hook after hook Velvet traveled down till at last she reached far below the waist. Then Mrs. Brown stood up and the dark blue dress dropped to the floor, leaving her in a princess petticoat like a great cotton lily. The stings of this, untied at neck and waist by Velvet, disclosed her in bust-bodice, stays and dark-blue cloth knickers.

"The iodine's in the wall cupboard," said Mother.

Velvet went to the wall cupboard and extracted the iodine from an army of bottles and jars.

" 'N' the cotton wool," said Mother.

Velvet, behind her, undid the strings of the bust-bodice. Got down to bedrock, she knelt and examined the wound.

"Mus' take your stays off, Mother."

Mrs. Brown rose and drew breath. Working from the bottom up she unhooked the metal fencework within which she lived, and sat down again. "Star out," she said, staring through the window. The star was like a slip of silver tinfoil plumb between the hang of the curtains.

"M'm," said Velvet, and she glanced at the star over her mother's shoulder. "Metal's worked right through the top of the stays and cut you," said Velvet.

"Ought to get whalebone," said Mrs. Brown, sniffing at her own economy.

"Yes," said Velvet, "you ought. S'made a nasty place." She dabbed the iodine on the abrasion caused by the jutting shaft of the stays. "Hurt?"

"Stings," said Mrs. Brown. The star winked and stuttered.

"Stick on a band-aid piece," said Mrs. Brown.

"Thur's a tin'n the cupboard."

Velvet stuck the plaster onto the wide hard back.

Mrs. Brown glared at the star.

"Pray to God y'don't get fat, child," she said.

Velvet sat back on her heels aghast.

"You can't *be*," said Mrs. Brown, "what you don't *look*."

"You can, you can!" said Velvet. "You *are,*
Mother!"

"Maybe," said Mrs. Brown. . . . "But you gotter
dig. You gotter know. You gotter believe."

Velvet put her thin arms on her mother's shoulders
and kissed her on the enemy fat. She winced at a sign
of regret or weakness in the beloved mountain.

"There's nothing, *nothing* you can't do, Mother.
You've got us all beat. Mi thinks you're godalmighty.
N'we all do."

Mrs. Brown smiled in the glass. "Chut, child! Don't
mount up in a torment. M'not grumbling. M'out of condition, but it came on me. I'm only saying . . . you
poor, thin hairpin . . . KEEP thin! There's no song an'
dance . . ." Mrs. Brown was bolting herself back into
the fence. She stood upright.

"S'awful to grow up," said Velvet.

"Nope," said Mrs. Brown.

"Why isn't it?"

"Things come suitable to the time," said Mrs.
Brown.

The thin slip, the quivering twig looked back at her
mother.

"Lot o' nonsense," said Mrs. Brown, "talked about
growing up." She stepped into her princess petticoat
and drew it up. "Tie me," she said. The candle in
the red candlestick drowned itself in fat and went out.
"Childbirth," said the voice, gruff and soothing, talking
to the star and to the child (and the child knelt at the
strings of the petticoat), "an' being in love. An' death.
You can't know 'em till you come to 'em. No use guess-
ing and dreading. You kin call it pain. . . . But what's
pain? Depends on who you are an' how you take it. Tie

28 ⚊

that bottom string looser. Don't you dread nothing, Velvet.''

"But you're so mighty. Like a tree,'' said Velvet.

"Shivery to be your age. You don't know nothin'. Later on you get coated over.'' (Silence, and the hypnotic night.) "S'a good thing to be coated over. You don't change nothin' underneath.''

"All the same it's awful to grow up,'' said Velvet. "All this changing and changing, an' got to be ready for something. I don't ever want children. Only horses.''

"Who can tell?'' said Mrs. Brown.

"I've got Me,''- said Velvet, putting her thin hand across her breast. "I can't ever be anything else but Me.''

"You're all safe,'' said Mrs. Brown carelessly, stooping with grunts to pull up her dress. "You got both of us, you *an'* me. Say your prayers now an' get along.''

"Not yet, not yet.''

"Say your prayers, I say. Down on your knees an' say your prayers. You go plunging off this time o' night, don't you? Getting into your bed all of a daze an' a worry. Say your prayers, I say!''

Velvet went on her knees in the middle of the floor. Mrs. Brown sat down, the dress in wreaths around her, and took a knife to her nails.

"Ah . . . v'Farver . . . ch . . . art'n'eaven,'' mumbled the voice from the floor. The blue in the window had gone and the star had companions.

". . . power n'a GloryamEN. Mother . . .''

"Yes.''

"You're all right, aren't you?''

"M'as good as living forever. Get on off to bed. N'I'm not comin' to say good-night. Father is.''

Velvet kissed her. "Come an' say good-night . . .''

"No, I'm not. Hook me up before you go." Velvet nicked up the great line of steely hooks to the top.

"Now go." Velvet went.

"Child gets all alight at night," said Mrs. Brown to herself.

Velvet's head came back round the door.

"Good-night, Mother—where are you going?"

"Down the village."

"What for?"

"Will you GO!"

Mrs. Brown went down the village with the key of the empty shop in her pocket. She had accounts to finish. The Hullocks rose above her in hoops into the sky. The stars floated in the olive glaze of the weedy pond. The boys and girls were hushed, black and still, against the doorways. Edwina stood like a statue at the cobbler's doorway as her mother passed, but her mother knew her.

"Growing," muttered Mrs. Brown as she went on. "Poor lass has to hide it."

The beautiful boy beside Edwina breathed again. He was golden-haired, and trying for the police. He felt he had no real chance for Mr. Brown's Edwina, and he had no idea he was her first, her breath-taking first man.

"What'll Velvet . . . ?" murmured Mrs. Brown, looking a moment at the sky, and seeing Velvet's bony, fairy face. "What'll men say about my Velvet?"

The sound of hoofs striking on metaled road came out of the darkness, and down the street, all alone, galloped a horse. Bodies shot out of the doorways and shouts sprang from shadows. Something black and white and furious raced down the street. Mrs. Brown stopped and stepped off the pavement. With a striking of hoofs, sparks flying on the flints, a piebald horse, naked of leather, wild and alone, slid almost to his haunches and

30 —

stood stock-still, shaking and panting. He lowered his head.

"A suitor for Velvet!"

A suitor for Velvet. The horse glared at Mrs. Brown. It had strange eyes, a white wall eye and one of darkest blue. The light from the corner street lamp swam in its eyeballs. It trembled and glared; then at Mrs. Brown's slowly extended hand, shook its neck with a shudder, half reared and, turning, galloped off up the street towards the Hullocks.

"That perishin' piebald from Ede's," exclaimed a voice.

"That you, Mr. Croom?"

"Give me a turn," said Mr. Croom. "That's the third time this week that creature's got loose. Ede says he'll raffle him for the Fair. Wouldn't be a bad idea. Wonderful what you get for those raffles."

While Malvolia and Meredith were undressing, Velvet was driving her big toes with long pieces of tape. She lay on her back in bed, her knees bent, talking in a monotonous voice like a sleepwalker.

"Careful through the gate now. Mind now. Get on, Satin!" and she gave the side of her thigh a switch with a light twig she held in her hand. The long tapes ran through her fingers which she held on her stomach, and both her knees pranced up and down—a restive pair of well-matched chestnuts in the shooting wagonette. With another switch and a spring forward the knees rose slightly in the air, were drawn back firmly by the reins, reined in, and stood still before the porch of the old castle. . . .

The door opened and Mr. Brown surveyed the spectacle of his youngest daughter, bare to the waist, her nightgown fallen on her chest, the bedclothes peeled to the floor, her eyes bright and her toes chained to her hands by tapes. Mally was cleaning her teeth in her drawers. Meredith was covering the bird cages.

"Mother says it's time," he said, removing his pipe. "Ah . . . yer daft, Velvet."

"I'm only allowed on Mondays. I've two minutes more."

"Where'd you get it from, I want to know? D'you other girls go driving nights a week?"

"I used to," said Mally. "Now I'm bigger, Mother says I'll break the bed."

"Where's the baize off the cages gone to?"

"Velvet's used it under Miss Ada's saddle. That time she got a sore back."

"What's that you got on them?"

"It's Edwina's knickers she had for the party. They got burnt, drying."

"Shame burnin' your good knickers. Canaries wake early with that thin stuff. Thought I heard 'em yesterday morning. Where's Edwina?"

"Be up in a minute. Just gone down the street a second."

"There . . . I've finished!" said Velvet, fishing for the bedclothes from her bed. "The chestnuts hardly needed a rubdown. They were cool. I've left the roan cob for tonight. He can stay out to grass."

"Daft as a sparrow," said Mr. Brown at random. "I doubt if a girl ought to be what you are." Stooping, with his pipe in his mouth, he flung the bedclothes up on top of her, blew out the candle and made for the door.

"I'm not in bed!" said Mally.

"Then you ought to be," said Mr. Brown. "Say your prayers." And disappeared.

*　　*　　*

Velvet heard the cruelty and wild abandon of the iron feet and shuddered and sat up, excited. It was too late to move. The horse was gone. Gone into the sea? Was it a horse? The bed clung round her like protecting arms.

"Did you hear it?" (from the bed beside her).

In three beds three bodies were upright. Edwina's bed was empty. Then, after the pause, the iron feet plunged back again, and too late all three were at the window. The door opened and the curtains blew.

"Edwina!"

"Yes. Hush." Edwina was panting. She had flown up the street and up the stairs.

"Father put the light out?"

"Yes. What horse . . ."

"Did he say 'bout me not being here?"

"I daresay he thought you'd gone with Mother. What horse . . ."

"Piebald. Ede's piebald. Let me . . ."

"Didn't know Ede had a piebald. How d'you know what . . . ?"

"Be quiet. Get back. I'm getting into bed."

"Aren't you going to wash?"

"No."

"TEETH?" said Mally, impressed.

"NO."

"You bin with Teddy," said Mally with satisfaction, getting back to bed.

"You shut up," said Edwina. "Won't tell you about the horse."

"Thur's nothin' to tell. Piebald horse. Farmer Ede's. Teddy's told you that."

"Huh, an' near ran into Mother!" snarled Edwina, naked, pulling her dressing gown over the clothes tumbled on the chair.

"Mother? What's it done to Mother?" said Velvet sharply.

"Mother was in the street," said Edwina in a wasp's voice, pulling on her pajamas.

"Touched her? Knocked her?" said Velvet, flashing out of bed.

"Keep your hair on," said Edwina.

"Shut up!" sobbed Velvet and flew out of the door and down the stairs.

"Now you fixed yerself!" said Mally calmly. "Now they'll know you bin out with Teddy. You know well Mother's not hurt."

"Of course she isn't hurt. Should I be here!" hissed Edwina.

"Stringing Velvet off like a catapult! First, you go off with boys. Second, you upset Velvet. Third, you'll be found out. Fourth, Velvet'll be sick all night. *Sense,* haven't you?"

"Be . . . quiet . . ." said Edwina, in bed, in a dull strangled voice. "Meredith . . . Merry . . . Get her back . . ."

"What did the horse do to Mother, 'Dwina?"

"Sorta bowed to her. Slid to a full stop and hung its head and really sorta bowed to her. An' it reared and dashed back up the street home again. Get Velvet, Merry."

Father was sitting looking at nothing in the living room. He was just tipping his chair and swaying.

"Father!" said Velvet, scared, in the doorway, "is Mother all right?"

"Fine," said Father without moving. He turned his eyes slowly.

In the shadow behind the sideboard sat Mi mending Jacob's collar.

"There's bin a horse down the street . . ." said Velvet uncertainly.

"Gallopin'," assented Father round the stem of his pipe.

There was a pause.

"I dreamt it hit Mother," mumbled Velvet.

"You did?"

"Yes. But it *was* a horse. That wasn't the dream."

"I just come up the street," said Mi. "Yore ma's sitting with the blinds up, in the shop, totting up."

"I'll go back," said Velvet. "It was a dream." She turned and saw Meredith's face come round the doorway from the dark stairs.

"I had a dream, Meredith," she said. "I'm coming back."

Mi put the collar down and crossing to Velvet bent down and felt her ankles. "Cold as railings," he said. "I'll getchu a brick. Keep your stomach steady." He disappeared into the kitchen and Velvet turned back to the stairs. Suddenly, at the stairhead something caught her jumping heart. She was back in the room again at her father's side, by his tipping, swaying chair.

"You all right, too, Father?" she whispered. He put his arm round her and pulled her on his lap. "You get them teeth straight!" he said to her, and rocked her meditatively while his pipe smoked up through her cotton hair.

⚊ THREE ⚊

The back window on the yard was blocked with cactus pots. In front of the window stood the fern table with two big ferns in brass holders.

The street window had pots of blue and red and pied cineraria standing along its shelf, looking like a Union Jack. The eastern light of the morning burst through the cactus greenery on Mally laying the table with a darned and yellowing cloth. She clattered the crockery on from the sideboard, and the girls' voices called from the larder and kitchen.

"Mice bin at the bottom. . . . It's all run out!"

"Mice where?"

"Porridge packet. They've made a hole."

"Don't cut the rim off the toast, 'Dwina. I like 'em with the binding."

Mi looked in with a packet in his hand. "Whur's Velvet?"

"Vel V E T!"

"Coming down now."

"Mi's got your pumice."

"Mi?" said Velvet, coming through the attic-stair door. "Oh, thank you, Mi."

"Do it now," said Mi.

"Clean my band before breakfast!" said Velvet, outraged.

"Yer pa's sure to ask."

"I do it AFTER breakfast! What's the good a-doing it before!"

"Acids of the night," said Mi and disappeared.

"Acids of what?"

"Get on an' do it," said Mally.

"You'd think that band was jewelry!" said Velvet and went into the scullery.

"Cost more than your mother's engagement ring," said Mr. Brown, passing through to the slaughterhouse. "She grumbling again?"

"Gone to clean it," said Mally. "Kedgeree!"

Mother brought in the soup basin of kedgeree. Donald stumped near her skirts. Edwina and Velvet came in and, sitting down, began to eat.

"I bin sick in the night," said Donald.

"You haven't," said Mr. Brown. "Get on your chair."

"Why haven't I?" demanded Donald.

"Don't let him start whying!" said Mally.

"Why haven't I, I say?" demanded Donald. "Tell me why, I say?"

"Get onto your chair and don't let's hear any more about it," said Mrs. Brown.

"Why haven't I, I say?" Donald held on. "You changed my sheets. The new ones was cold."

"I changed your sheets for other reasons," said Mrs. Brown. "Now get on."

"The new ones was horrible," muttered Donald, subsiding. "Is it kedgeree?"

"Did you wash your neck, Velvet?"

"Yes, Mother."

"Before your frock or after your frock?"

"After."

"Then don't. Your frock's soaking. Where's Meredith?"

"Canary's loose."

Mr. Brown opened the door again and came in.

Donald brightened. "I was sick in the night, Daddy."

"Donald!"

"I was sick all over . . ."

Mrs. Brown removed Donald and the kedgeree to the kitchen.

"Lie. He wet his bed," said Mally.

"Oh," said Mr. Brown and helped himself to kedgeree. "I heard your mother moving about. Why don't she leave him wet. He won't hurt. He's no more than damp."

"Bad for his habits," said Mrs. Brown, returning. She sat down and drew the marmalade towards her.

"I've caught her!" Meredith came in glowing.

"Take your kedgeree into the kitchen and let Donald tell you how sick he's been," said Velvet.

"You'll do no such thing," said Mrs. Brown. "That child gets on one idea like a railway track. It's you and your stomach, Velvet, that puts him onto it."

"Can't help my stomach," said Velvet. " 'D'give anything in the world to change it."

"You'll grow out of it."

"Sixteen, you said."

"Sixteen, I said."

"Why sixteen?"

"You eat," said Mrs. Brown.

"Can I come back now?" Donald appeared in the doorway, holding his plate unsteadily in his fists.

"Yes, if you've finished."

"I've finished."

"All?"

"All except the bones. Jacob's eaten them."

"Oh . . ." Velvet flew up and left the room. "Mi!" she called into the yard from the kitchen. "Jacob's eaten fishbones!"

Donald lifted his plate to the sideboard and the spoon flew over his head to the floor.

"That child say he finished?" demanded Mr. Brown.

"I finished," said Donald.

"It's all on his plate still," said Mr. Brown, and went on reading his paper.

"Velvet!" called Mally. "It's a do, Velvet! Come back. Jacob hasn't got a bone."

Velvet appeared in the doorway.

"Donald," said Mrs. Brown, turning full on him, "have you told me a story?"

"It *was* a story," said Donald gravely.

"Do you know what a story is?"

"No," said Donald.

Mrs. Brown removed him to her bedroom.

"Piebald's gone down the street again," said Mi, putting his hair in at the door and disappearing. The four sisters rose and streamed from the room. Mr. Brown, glancing up once and half turning round, went on with his paper. Mrs. Brown returned.

"Donald sorry?" said Mr. Brown.

"He's thinking," said Mrs. Brown. "He isn't sure. Girls gone?"

"That piebald of Ede's got loose again," said Mr. Brown. There was peace and silence.

The tiny windowpane between the cineraria was filled with black and white and the piebald went back up the street at a hand gallop. After his metal feet the street rustled with running shoes.

"That animal'll knock down a pram one of these days," observed Mr. Brown. "Seems to make for the sea."

"Curious horse," said Mrs. Brown. "Climbs out in the night when the moon's up."

"Don't he jump?" said Mr. Brown.

"Jumps a house," said Mrs. Brown. "Sort of rodeo, so they say. . . . Yes, Donald? What is it?"

"I'm sorry," called Donald in muffled tones through the door.

Mrs. Brown opened the door.

"I'm sorry I was sick in the night," said Donald.

"Child'll make a lawyer," said Mr. Brown.

Meredith returned to the room.

"He went right through the poles they're hammering up for the Fair," she said. "Then down to the Post Office, an' slid about and up the Chalk Road back onto the Hullocks again. Mr. Ede was just going by 'n his cart. Cursed."

"He'll get into trouble if that horse hurts someone," said Father. "Mi done his breakfast?"

"Had it early. He's got given a glass tongue. Ate it in his room."

"Well, tell'm I want'm at twelve for six sheep." Mr. Brown passed away through the slaughterhouse door. Mi came in from the street.

"Six sheep at twelve, Father says."

"M'm. Piebald jumped a five bar gate with a wire on the top. Sailed over."

"Who says so?"

"Fellow."

"Is it broke?"

"The gate?"

"No. The piebald."

"Ede says it's as quiet as a lamb. Just can't bear to be shut up. Bit mad."

Mi blew his nose carefully, polished it, replaced his handkerchief and went for the yard door.

"You got a bit a time?" said Meredith.

"Get on an' do your canaries. Gotter sweep my room."

"Done my canaries. I'll come an' sweep yours."

Mi sniffed and went off. Meredith caught up a broom which stood beside the wall.

"You put that down," said Mi, who knew she had taken it without turning his head. "S'yer ma's own." The broom was meekly put back. Meredith followed him.

Mi's room was outside, next to Miss Ada. It was an old loose box that had fallen into disrepair. He took great pride in it and kept it spotless. Just within the door, which was propped open for freshness with a garden rake, was a large hole in the floor filled with rotting wood. The wood round the edges of the hole gave way like toast and Mi had marked a white ring round the hole and written in paint "Step further than this." He took his own broom and began to sweep.

"S'got no hairs on it," said Meredith, standing about and in the way.

No answer. Mi did not like criticism. He swept the dust of the room vigorously into a heap, then propelled it with his brush over a portion of the painted line and into the hole in the floor. Picking up an old milk bottle by the neck he rammed the dust horizontally under the floor boards.

"Now whadjer want?" he said.

"Hammer'n nails," said Meredith.

"Go out of the room then. Thurs no call fer you to see where I keep things."

Meredith went outside into the sunny yard and stood with her back to the wall on the far side of the door. Honorably she looked away and straight before her. Mi went to his bed and abstracted a hammer and tobacco box of nails from under his mattress.

"How big?" he called.

Meredith measured her thumb joint. "Inch an' a half."

"Whafor?"

"Hang my Roller cage."

"Find a joist then. It's rubble and such in between." Mi came to the doorway with the hammer and nails.

"D'you think . . . ?" began Meredith.

"No," said Mi shortly. "You get into yer own hot water fer puttin' yer own nails in the house. Yer pa's down the village."

"I know," said Meredith. "S'why I'm hurrying."

She disappeared with the hammer and nails, and Mi took down his shaving mirror and polished it with his handkerchief. He replaced a drawing pin or two on the corners of his series of "Grand National winners" pinned round the walls, and set the kettle onto his Primus stove that he might scald out his milk bottle.

Velvet and Mally appeared in the yard and hung about.

"Where's Merry?"

"Hammering," said Mi.

Silence fell and the kettle hummed. Mally and Velvet looked with envy from the yard into the loose-box bedroom.

"Wish I had a room of my own," said Velvet. "So I could hang up pictures."

Mi came to the door, and holding the milk bottle over the hole in the floor poured the scalding water into it.

"I've earned it," said Mi when the last drop was in.

"Why?"

"Full-grown," he said, and sucked the gap in his teeth. He looked at them, long and straight. They looked back.

"They're puttin' that piebald up to raffle," he said at last, and yawned deceptively.

"Raffle!" said Velvet. "Raffle!" A pause. Then— "Anybody might get it?"

"Anybody with a shilling."

"Cost on'y a shilling? You got a shilling, Mally?"

"Nothing at all."

"Nor I've got nothing . . ."

"Oh, a shilling's easy got."

"But we ought to have five. Donald ought to have a chance."

"You'll never get five!"

"That's whur yer wrong," said Mi. "I'll give you five. You kin pay me back in yer time. I got a tip from a perisher."

"Oh, Mi darling! What perisher?"

"Togged-up perisher that was swanky and windy and couldn't sit his horse in his best suit."

"What'd you do?"

"Fellow hired Belton's May Day and went out galloping. Top boots, spurs and checks, an' a bowler with a string on it.''

"Where were you?''

"Just walkin'.''

"Oh, Mi! You were sitting behind the haystack with the ghost!''

"Had to sit somewhere.''

"Tell us . . .''

"I saw May Day go out. Galloped out. Perisher'd never heard of walkin' or trottin'. Half the sky was dancin' up an' down under 'is bottom, so I legged up the other way an' come to the haystack.''

Pause.

". . . an' he galloped round,'' egged Velvet.

"I see him coming down towards the haystack, May Day blowy and sweaty an' the ghost waiting for them as jolly as a daisy.''

"Oh . . . Mi . . . YOU . . . SAW it.''

"IT? No, s'not my kind. It's a horse ghost. Perisher was red in the face an' lumbering along. Toes pointin' down and not even clutching with his calves. Not clutchin' with anything. Heaving like a sack. Stock all out of place under his ear, having a high old seven and sixpence worth. . . . Whoop . . . went May Day when the ghost made a pass at her. Sprung right across the road an' the perisher fell *on* the ghost, far's I c'd see. Serve it right, too. Real vicious horse that must've been that got killed there. To have a ghost like that. Why, you can't miss making a bit in that place. Every hiring fellow that comes down from London spins off at that haystack. You on'y got to sit behind it and pick up the bits.''

"They don't all tip you, though.''

"Most do. This one give me five. Here you are!''

Mi pulled two half crowns out of his pocket and handed them to Velvet in trust for them all.

"Thank you awfully, Mi. I'll give it you back. Swear." And she hooked both middle fingers over her index fingers and held them up.

"Witches' stuff!" said Mi contemptuously. "Keep yer word and don't crack yer fingers. And see this, Velvet, I'm a fool to do it. That piebald's as big a perisher's the fellow that tipped me the five. 'M going up to look at him this afternoon and likely I'll be sorry when I see his murdering white eye."

"Can we come too, can we come too?"

"You got yer muslins to iron."

"MUSLINS!" said Velvet, outraged.

"Yer ma's just wrung 'em out of the suds. I seen 'em. For the Fair."

"I'm not going to wear MUSLIN," said Velvet with a voice of iron.

"You'll wear what yer told," said Mi placidly. "I'll slip up after dinner. Nearer one. I got them sheep at twelve. Sounds I won't get any dinner. See Donald . . ."

Donald was beautifully dressed in a fresh striped blouse and grey pants the length of a coat cuff. The insides of both ankles were fastened up with sticking plaster and his silver hair had just left the prongs of a damp comb. The brown of his arms was a mixture of coffee and silk.

"Whur's the stinkin' ants?" said Donald.

"What's that?"

"A stinkin' ant jus' stung me."

"Where'd it sting you?"

"On my thumb," said Donald clearly, and held up his thumb.

There was no mark of any kind on the pink thumb.

"Say 'stinging,' " said Mally. "Ants don't sting. It was a wasp."

"Go on," said Mi. "Don't be s'old-fashioned. He'll say 'stinkin' ant' till he says 'stinging wasp' . . . and it'll all come natural."

Mally looked down her nose at Donald. "You're soft, Mi," she said. "You bin and killed something, Donald."

"It wanted to be dead," said Donald. "A very little ant."

"Throwing the blame on the ant!" said Mally. "I thought as much!"

Donald made a pass with his foot. "Thur's another one," he said. "They all want to be dead."

"Nice excuse!" said Velvet. "Stop it, Donald!"

"Every one of those ants," said Mally, taking a deep breath and blowing out her cheeks, "has got an aunt an' an uncle an' little brothers an' . . ."

"This one hadn't," said Donald, and ran away.

"S'awful to be so pretty," said Velvet, looking after him. "He's like an actress."

"Actress, my boot," said Mally. "He's a common murderer."

"Likes to see things stop," said Mi. "Anybody's the same. You better go iron them muslins. Sooner you get them ironed, sooner you see the piebald."

"Be in towels yet," said Velvet. "Mine was too short last summer. It'll look like a ham frill this."

"Got to get on," said Mi. "Frittering my morning away . . ." and disappeared.

"He won't go an' see that piebald without us?" said Velvet.

"What about the blasted muslins?" said Mally.

"Better go."

"Here's Meredith! What's the matter, Merry?"

"Went down the street," said Meredith. "Looking at the rooks' nests. Dropped a splodge. A rook dropped a splodge . . ." She was wiping her eye furiously with her dress. "Gummy," she said, "S'gummy stuff . . ."

"Get in under the tap," said Velvet. "It's lime. P'raps it's quicklime."

Meredith ran blindly into the scullery holding her eye. The lime ran off at the touch of water.

On the scullery ledge was a board with four objects on it like babies in long clothes, old bath towels, used for keeping the best washing evenly damp. Mally cautiously undid the first.

"It's them," she said, as though she had smelt a drain.

"What?" said Meredith.

"Muslin, ducky, for the Fair. Our muslins."

"Muslin!" said Meredith, stiff with offense.

"Muslin," said Mrs. Brown from behind with a soft and heavy certainty. "An' your white woolly pullovers on top. You'll be warm an' you'll be pretty. Get on upstairs and look over your stockings for holes."

"STOCKINGS! We're not going to wear STOCK-INGS!"

Mrs. Brown sat down on the scullery chair.

"We'll get it all over," she said. "I'll run through it. You'll wear your long black Christmas stockings, WITH supporters, fastened to them calico belts I bought you for the Christmas dance. You'll wear white petticoats that go with . . ."

"PETTICOATS!"

"Petticoats. That belongs to the dresses. (Or should.) You'll wear your muslins, an' your pullovers, an' your black lace shoes . . ."

"SHOES!"

"If you get a shock over everything, Velvet, you'll be ill an' you won't go at all. When you have muslins you have black shoes an' when you have black shoes you have stockings, or your heels rub . . ." (Edwina came through the street door.) ". . . an' you'll iron your muslins . . ."

"MUSLINS!" said Edwina in exactly the same tone as the others.

"We've been through all that," said Malvolia. "Black shoes, black stockings, petticoats, supporters, belts, pullovers . . . P'raps you'd like to sit down an' rest, 'Dwina? Go on, Mother. We're to iron our muslins when?"

"Father's at the bottom of this . . ." muttered Edwina.

Mrs. Brown reached for a long-clothes baby and unrolled it. "Damp yet," she said, trying it to her cheek. "Soaking. They'll stay damp till the evening in the shade. You can iron them after tea. Go on and look over the stockings."

Edwina, Malvolia, Meredith and Velvet passed through the little black door onto the stairs.

The canaries were singing and shouting in the breeding cages and the new wooden cage, recently put up by Meredith, hung insecurely and crooked from the nail she had borrowed.

"You got it up," said Velvet.

"It's all soft stuff in that wall," said Meredith.

"Nail's going to come out," said Mally—and they pulled out the drawers to look over the stockings.

Edwina held up her calico petticoat and measured it against her willowy figure. "Dressed up in muslin!" she muttered.

"But I thought you liked dressing up," said Mally. Edwina made no reply.

"Not dressed up enough is your trouble," said Mally.

"It's time I had . . ." murmured Edwina, preoccupied and searching in a drawer . . . "something . . . more . . ." and she found what she was looking for.

"I'll wear it over the muslin," she said, holding up a tennis skirt of white flannel. "It's a bit yellow. I've got a blue leather belt somewhere."

"You'll make us look like a lot of dressed-up babies," said Mally, half enviously. "And Mother won't let you."

"I'll slip it on last thing," said Edwina. "Mother doesn't really care. It's Father. The top'll look like quite a nice muslin shirt. I wish I could cut off the bottom."

"Well, that's your trouble," said Mally. "My goodness, I wouldn't dare."

"Where's it kept?" said Velvet.

"I had it in this bottom drawer," said Edwina. Velvet turned and stared at her. After a pause she cleared her mind. "I mean the piebald," she amended.

"Oh, I meant to tell you!" said Edwina. "They're going to raffle it to-morrow . . ."

"We know," said Mally. "Mi said so. And he's given us five shillings to have a ticket each. Even Donald."

"*Lent* us," said Velvet.

"I meant lent us. Where do we get the tickets?"

"They've got books at the Post Office. Books of tickets."

"Let's go down and choose early ones."

Edwina stuffed her skirt back in the drawer. The stockings lay in tight black balls on the bed.

"Come on, Meredith . . ."

"You go. I'll come in a minute."

Edwina, Mally and Velvet clattered down the stairs and left Meredith stooping beside a cage.

Velvet put her head back in at the door.

"Shall I get yours or will you get your own?"

Meredith answered without looking round. "The female's ill."

"Which is it?" said Velvet, coming nearer.

"Africa," said Meredith in a low voice.

Africa had been a male until she had been discovered to be a female. Now she lay in the palm of Meredith's hand, cloaking her eye with a little sagging hood.

"Is it the heat?" said Velvet, awed.

"I don't know," said Merry. "Get me the brandy. It's on the bottom shelf in the sideboard. In Father's flask."

While Velvet went for the brandy Meredith reached for her fountain-pen-filler, her left hand groping in a drawer, her eyes steady on the faint yellow bird.

"Draw the blind," she said to Velvet who had returned. Velvet drew the blind behind the roaring cages and all song dropped like a flag when the wind has failed. There was a sickroom silence and anxiety.

"How much?" asked Velvet.

"One drop."

But Africa died. She died in the palm of Merry's hand without a sound or a sigh or a movement. She seemed to miss a little breath and go smaller, and Velvet, startled, glanced round, as though a whiff of life had drifted out of Africa.

"I can't hold her now she's dead," said Merry, her teeth chattering. "Take her off my hand."

"Tip her off," said Velvet, wincing too.

"Go on. Take her! I'll scream."

Velvet took her and laid her with distaste on the bed-table by Merry's bed.

"Horrible," said Merry. "It's a corpse. Poor little Africa. She's gone away."

"I truthfully," said Velvet in a low voice, "thought I saw her go."

"How?"

"When she went small. Just something."

"What?"

"Air."

"That was her spirit," said Merry suddenly, looking at her intently. Velvet and Meredith stared at Africa.

"I should like her just not to be here," said Merry savagely. "I should like her to be all buried and finished."

"Perhaps Mi will."

"No, he won't. He'll say, 'Bury your own bird.' "

"Mother will," said Velvet.

"Will she?"

"Yes, come on. Leave it there." Velvet flipped up the blind again and all the canaries cantered straight into open song. "Go on down to the Post Office an' I'll be down in a second."

"Who's got the shilling?"

"Mally has," said Velvet. They'll be waiting for you. Don't get my ticket for me!"

"No—" Merry ran down the street.

"Mother," said Velvet, opening the scullery door. "Africa's died."

Mrs. Brown turned. "Merry know?"

"Yes, she died in her hand. Just now."

"Where's Merry?"

"Gone down to the Post Office. But she can't touch

Africa. She hates her dead. Could you bury her, do you think? She's on the table by Merry's bed.''

''I'll see to her,'' said Mrs. Brown. ''Bring her down.''

''I can't touch her either,'' said Velvet. ''She's . . .''

Mrs. Brown looked at her.

''You know when a thing's dead . . .'' said Velvet uselessly. Then after a pause she went slowly upstairs and brought down the dead bird in her hand. Mrs. Brown reached up to a shelf for a little cardboard box. She put Africa inside and shut the lid. Velvet raced down to the Post Office.

In the sultry midday, with the Hullocks steaming above them, a little group of parcel-posters and stamp-buyers was jesting over the book-tickets. Edwina and her sisters stood in the shadow, their eyes grave and full of choosing. They were weighing the flashing, unequal importance of numbers.

The blacksmith was having his joke.

''Stand up, gentlemen,'' he shouted, ''the horse is yours! Shilling a go for a mad piebald gelding. Or is it a stallion, Mr. Croom? Not clean gelded, eh? Thought as much. Mr. Ede done it on the cheap an' left a chip.''

''Not a bad thing to have a horse for a shilling,'' suggested Mr. Croom. ''You can always sell it for something.''

''Not so easy done,'' said the blacksmith. ''You got to feed it an' lodge it meanwhile.''

''Ede says it'll ride quiet,'' said Mr. Croom. ''He *says* it will. Anybody know?''

''I seen him ride it,'' aid a voice. ''Went along quiet an' dull. He had a basket on his arm too. An' he opened a gate and let the basket fall. Never turned a hair.''

''What's the matter with it that he wants to raffle it?''

"He can't tie it up an' he can't keep it in. Jumps any wall. Go sailing over the moon if you'd let it. Kink in its mind about being tied up or shut in. Ede's tired of catching it. Besides he's afraid it'll do a damage in the village. Bought it cheap in Lewes Market, but it's no good to him."

Some tickets were bought but there was no rush on them. Edwina walked out of the corner to the counter.

The raffle book was *one* to *two hundred,* got out in ink hurriedly by Mrs. Ede.

"He'll likely make his ten pound on him," said Mr. Croom. "That's more'n he paid for him at Lewes."

Solemnly the four girls lined against the counter and gazed at the book.

"I've thought of forty-seven," whispered Mally.

"But did you make yourself or did it come?"

"That's what I don't know."

"I've got ten . . . printed on my brain, large . . . in red letters," said Edwina.

Silence.

"It's like a visitation," persisted Edwina in a whisper.

Silence.

"But perhaps I'm meant to avoid it," she ended.

Each girl stretched her mind and tried to tremble to the finger of God.

"I'll have 119 please," said Velvet unexpectedly and firmly to the postmistress.

She paid her shilling, and the other three watched her, envious and dismayed.

"What did you . . ." began Mally.

"I don't want to talk about it," said Velvet, low, and walked out of the Post Office into the street.

The others followed her with tickets in their hands.

".We just took them anyhow," said Edwina, rather cross. "What's the good of thinking!"

"Have you got one for Donald?"

"Number One."

"Well, there we are anyway," said Mally. "Let's go an' pin them in the Bible. It's dinner time."

Meredith instantly thought of Africa. As they walked back towards the house Africa was like a yellow shade upon her mind. Where did she lie? Would she be visible again to the eye or was she packed up for ever? Mrs. Brown called to them from the door. "Wash your hands quick," she said, "it's hot dinner."

"I'll wash mine in the scullery," said Merry and fled through the sitting room.

Velvet whispered to the others, "Africa's dead."

Mrs. Brown turned off the scullery tap that Merry might hear what she said. "Your little bird's buried," she said. "Cage is all cleaned an' I've put the cock in there. The greeny cock. But he's got no food or water yet. Run up an' see to him."

Merry turned with streaming eyes and kissed her. "I'll rearrange them," she choked, and went upstairs to the bedroom.

They sat down to dinner without Mr. Brown or Mi, and Mrs. Brown brought in the joint. Merry joined them, a little flushed, but peaceful.

A squawking and bleating came muffled through the wall.

"That's the last," said mother. "Father'll be in soon."

"Row those sheep make," said Mally.

Edwina got up to get the red jelly from the sideboard.

"We've taken five tickets, shilling tickets, for a raffle

for the Fair tomorrow," said Velvet. "They're raffling that piebald."

"The piebald?" said Mrs. Brown. "Ede getting rid of it? Well, I'm not surprised."

"But what'll Father . . ."

"Time enough to worry when you get it," said Mrs. Brown. "Got that jelly, 'Dwina? It's there behind the pickles."

"Where's Donald?" said Velvet.

"Slep' on. But he ought to be woke now. You get him, Velvet."

Velvet got up and went out by the yard door. She pressed the spaniels back with her foot as they struggled and changed places, smelling the joint.

Jacob came wriggling and smiling round the wall. He was late in, having been down the village to the sea, watching the trippers unload from the buses.

The whole day's heat was shimmering in the yard. The splendor of the heat stood upright like a tank of water. Dust moved in it and midges poured up and down. Immediately she faced the yard Velvet went into a vision. The bones and stones and boxes and dogs of the yard dropped away below and she was mounted on a cliff beside the piebald, on the hip of a cliff overlooking the sea. The sea was pale and a ship swam up in a haze on the sky. The piebald stared like a lunatic at the cobbled wall which bound his field. Velvet choked as she stared with him, and saw the grasses wave at the foot of the cobbles. The wall gave way as they cleared it and sank together, the sea rushing up. A gull's wing zipped and she saw the indigo shadow, and with her knees she felt the ribs spring in arcs from the horse's spine. His boundless heart rushed into hers. The soles of her feet cramped against the impending waters.

"I've woke," called Donald from the shade where he lay on a mattress in Miss Ada's unused cart—its shafts propped on an upright barrel. Velvet crossed the yard and opened the little door at the back of the cart. "Get up," she said, but the child only stared half-awake at the sky. She took him by his bare legs and pulled. His shirt left his pants and began to turn up over his arms.

"Can't walk. Carry me," he said. His teeth chattered. "I'm shivery," he said, and bumped his heavy head onto her thin chest as she struggled with him.

"That's only sleep," she said. "It's dinnertime. You've slept too long."

Merry opened the sitting room door. "Are you coming?" she called.

"I've slept too long," moaned Donald at the door, in Velvet's arms.

"Get down an' walk," said Mrs. Brown.

"Slept *too* long," he wailed self-pityingly.

"A little tap water an' you'll feel better," said mother She took him and he wept a little and was carried away. He reappeared in a few minutes bright and silky. "I slept too long," he said in quite a different voice, engagingly, socially.

"Yes, we heard," said Mr. Brown who had come in. "Get up on your chair now. Here's your plate."

"The meat's sour," said Donald instantly, putting his nose to his meat.

"Poor lot those sheep," said Mr. Brown. "It's the drought. Bit ribby, weren't they, Mi."

"Dog bin racin' 'em," said Mi.

"It's sour," said Donald, giving his plate a push.

Mrs. Brown glanced over. "He's got capers put on his. Take them off, 'Dwina."

"It's you that's sour," said 'Dwina to him, getting

up and stooping beside him. "Oh . . . Mother, he's spat at me!"

"Spit came out," said Donald, a little anxiously.

"Fractious," said Mr. Brown. "Sit down, 'Dwina, and get on both. I heard Ede's going to raffle that piebald animal that got loose."

There was no response. Everyone, thinking hard, ate silently.

"You oughter take a ticket, Velvet," said Mr. Brown genially.

"We've all . . . we've all taken tickets," said Velvet softly, unable to believe her ears. Mr. Brown's face changed. He had meant to make a joke.

"He'll be meat if you get him," he said after a pause, and not genially at all.

Velvet's face flushed faintly.

"Cabbage is stringy," said Donald, and created a diversion.

"He's possessed," said Mr. Brown vexedly. The condition of the sheep had annoyed him.

Edwina and Mally cleared the plates and brought in gooseberry fool. Velvet fetched the milk pudding from the oven. They started with fresh life on the fresh food.

"Want you s'afternoon, Mi," said Mr. Brown. The girls grew tense, and waited, spoons still.

" 'Bout five," said Mr. Brown, and the breath of anxiety was let out again, and the spoons moved on.

The chairs were pushed in. "F'whatweave received . . . thank God!" they said as one voice and fled.

~FOUR~

The piebald cropped in just such a field, on just such a Hullock as Velvet had dreamed. There was the haze and the ship. Mi, Edwina, Malvolia, Meredith and Velvet stood in a row leaning against the cobbled wall. There was a long and watchful silence. The wild thyme smelt warm and looked pink. The sea lay below, not blue but dove-grey. The coping of the wall was hot and rough.

"Stands marvelous," said Mi at length.

Another long appreciative silence.

"See his bone . . ." said Mi.

Mi made a click with the gap in his teeth and turned to look at Velvet. "What's that number of yours?"

"119."

"Well, there!"

"What?"

"You ought to have a horse!"

The piebald looked up and saw them. Stared. Then cropped again.

"Seems quiet," said Edwina.

"Huh. No knowing. Think he's under fifteen hands?"

"Think he's more," said Velvet.

"See his white eye?"

They saw it. They saw everything. Their eyes, like birds' eyes, flickered over his startling patches of black and white. He was white in bold seas, and black in continents, marked in such a way that when he moved his white shoulders and his white quarters flashed, and his black body seemed to glide.

"Showy," said Mi.

Velvet climbed the wall into the field.

"He'll be off!" said Mally warningly.

Velvet went among the hot grasses toward him. She knew him. She had already ridden him in her dream. He cropped, head towards her, but watched her coming. She walked steadily and straight and began to talk in low tones. He raised his head and looked at her as firmly as she looked at him. She paused. He walked several paces towards her with confidence. No quirk or tremor or snort of doubt.

"See that!" said Mi, hanging against the wall.

They saw Velvet pat him and run her hand slowly down his neck onto his shoulder.

"She'll be that upset now," said Mi, "if she don't get him."

Velvet moved away. The animal followed her, flashing and jaunty. He had a white mane, a long white tail, pink hoofs, a sloping pastern, and he struck his feet out clean and hard as he walked.

"Isn't his neck thick?" said Edwina.

"Bit," said Mi. "Bin gelded late."

The piebald, whose desires were gone, had kept his pride. He walked after Velvet like a stocky prince. Thick-necked, muscular, short and proud. He left her a few paces from the wall, and stood looking, then turned and cropped quietly.

"Gotter be back," said Mi.

Velvet hung a moment longer by the wall, then all five in silence turned downhill. There was a wild snort behind them and the thunder of feet.

"He's off!" said Mi, turning sharp. "It's set him off!"

The piebald and his white tail raised and his head arched like a Persian drawing. He was galloping down the field towards the corner.

"Stop! Stand! He's never going over that!"

The ground had dropped away so sharply at the far corner that the original builder of the cobbled wall, to keep his coping straight, had heightened the wall itself. It was five feet two at the end of the field, with a fine downhill takeoff. The horse sailed over like a dappled flying boat. It was a double spring. As he was high in the air he saw also to his hind feet and drew them up sharply.

". . . AND to spare," said Mi quietly, nodding his head. "A horse like that'd win the National."

"You don't mean it, Mi!"

"Gets his hocks under. Got heart. Grand takeoff. Then when he's up in the air he gives a kind of second hitch an' his feet tuck up so he's on'y a body without legs. See him look before he took off? See his ears flitch forward and back again? You on'y got to sit on him."

"Oh, Mi, why don't you ride?"

". . . Got a nasty sort of look of Man-of-War too," pursued Mi, unheeding.

"Who was Man-of-War?"

"Man-eatin' stallion," said Mi.

60 ━

"But a black and white horse like that doesn't look like anything to do with a race."

"Ever hear of the Tetrarch?"

"No."

"Looked like a rocking horse. Sorta dappled. Mr. Persse his trainer was. One mornin' he was sittin' eatin' his egg an' a stable lad rushed in an' screamed out, 'That colored horse can beat anything!' an' rushed out again."

"And what did he win?"

"Didn't win anything so marvelous because they ran him as a two-year-old. But he sired twenty-seven thousand pounds!"

"How'd you know so much, Mi?"

"Used to read when I was up there," Mi jerked his finger north, away from the sea.

"Why did the stable boy rush in?"

" 'Cause he won, didn't he, in the gallops in the morning."

"The piebald Tetrarch?"

"He wasn't piebald. Not even grey. He was colored. Grey and roan and white. Mottled. They got him for a mascot. Just for a stable companion. And he brought them a fortune."

They walked down the slopes, wrapped in the eternal drama of the last being first.

"An' Mr. Persse," said Velvet, lifting her boy's face to the sky, "he rushed out?" She wanted to sit again over the breakfast table with Mr. Atty Persse. (The heavenly, escaping past—)

"He rushed out," said Mi, warming, "and he said: 'Where's that boy? I'll wring his neck!' "

"Why?"

"He had a feel the boy was right."

"Well, and . . ."

"When you gotta good thing you keep it dark, don't you! Not shout all down the passages and right through the kitchen an' go back runnin' an' grinnin' like a fathead to the stables."

"Mustn't anybody know when you think you're going to win a race?"

"Money passes," said Mi. "Fortunes. Thousands. Millions. It's like the City."

"Do they race a lot in the North?" asked Velvet.

A landscape glittered behind her voice. There were icicles in it and savage fields of ice, great storms boiling over a flat countryside striped with white rails—a chessboard underneath a storm. Horses were stretched forever at the gallop. Tiny men in silk were brave beyond bearing and sat on the horses like embryos with their knees in their mouths. The gorgeous names of horses were cried from mouth to mouth and circulated in a steam of fame. Lottery, The Hermit, the great mare Sceptre; the glorious ancestress Pocahontas, whose blood ran down like Time into her flying children; Easter Hero, the Lamb, that pony stallion.

"Race?" said Mi. "*All* the time." And Velvet knew she was right.

"If I won that piebald," said Velvet, "I might ride him in the Grand National myself."

"Girls can't ride in that," said Mi contemptuously.

"Girls!" said Velvet, stopping still beside him so that they all drew up. "Who's to know I'm a girl?" She cupped her face in her two hands so that her straight hair was taken from it.

" 'Tisn't your hair," said Mi, and his eyes fell on her chest. "Flat's a pancake," he said. "You'd pass. There's a changing room though."

"What'd you undress for?"

"Change your day things for your silks."

"But you needn't undress to your skin. You could keep the same vest."

"It *could* happen . . ." said Mi. "It never has. You got to get your horse first."

There was a silence as they walked.

"There he goes!" said Mi. The piebald was galloping below them, making as usual for the village. "Heavy galloper. Plunges as he goes."

"He's lovely," breathed Velvet, simply. They started to run. Below them they could see a sweeper at the entrance to the village wave his broom at the horse.

The piebald leaped round him and galloped on. He disappeared between the first houses on the street. Soon he was out again, driven away by men and boys whom they could see standing by the sea wall, and headed up the curve of the Hullocks again, still galloping, his white mane and tail flying.

"Carthorse and Arab in that animal," said Mi, pausing to look. The piebald tired on the steep hill and slowed to a trot, then stood still. He looked over his shoulder at the village below him.

"He's homesick," said Velvet suddenly. "He wants people. He hates it up there on that high field. Would he let me get near him?"

"Never while he's loose like that, an' after he's galloped," said Mi. "Not worth the trouble. What about those muslins?"

"Come along," said Edwina. "We've got to get them done. Don't keep staring at him, Velvet. He'll never belong to any of us, and if he did the Lord knows what Father'd say!"

After tea they did the muslins.

"Ironing's lovely," said Meredith. They had forgotten their antagonism to the frocks. The irons were hot and had polished shoes that slid over the steaming damp of the muslin surface. There were two irons and Meredith and Mally ironed while Velvet waited sitting by the cactus window. They used the supper table. The frail muslin hardened and blanched as the irons poked and slid, and Edwina made a racket in the room above looking for her blue leather belt. Father passed through the room in his rubber boots. He had been hosing.

"They want a steak. Over at Kingsworthy. Got to be there before breakfast," he said.

"Before breakfast!"

"That's what I said," said father. The door shut.

"What sort of a cook wants a steak before breakfast?" said Mally, shooting the nose of her iron in among the front pleats.

"Man-eating cook," said Edwina, standing in the doorway with her belt over her wrist. "Sucks 'em raw before she lights the stove."

"It's Mr. Cellini's, Kingsworthy," said Velvet. "He's got that chestnut we saw at the Show last year."

"Don't fiddle with the cactus," said Edwina. "The leaves break off."

Velvet folded her hands in her lap. "Sir Pericles," said Velvet. "He was called Sir Pericles, that chestnut. Won the novice's jumping."

"I'll go with the steak," said Meredith. "I'd love to. I'll go just as early as I awake, I'll creep out and get Miss Ada. Mother could leave the steak on the table overnight."

"Why couldn't we take it this evening?"

"Then they think it's today's meat."

"But it will be, anyway!"

"Yes, but they think it's fresher if it comes tomorrow."

"There!" Mally took her muslin dress and held it up by the puff sleeves.

It was stiff and fresh with ironing and almost stood by itself.

"It's like a paper bag," said Velvet. "Seems a pity to wear it. D'you want to start, Edwina, or shall I start mine?"

"I'm only wearing the top of mine. I've cut it off."

"Gosh! You *have?* You've been an' cut it?"

All the three heads were raised towards Edwina as she took this step into the future. They contemplated her for a second, then accepted her. Velvet got up and began to unroll her frock and lay it out.

"Ay . . . Merry. Look out! What's that . . . it's blood!"

Meredith shot one hand to her face. "It's my nose," she cried from under her hand.

"It's dropped on the muslin. Get me a rag!"

"Here's the ironing duster! Hold your head off the dresses! Lie down on the cold scullery floor. It's brick."

Donald appeared in the doorway from the street and watched Meredith as she ran into the scullery holding the duster to her face.

"She hurt herself?" he asked.

"Her nose is bleeding," said Velvet.

"I laugh when my nose bleeds," said Donald.

"Your nose hasn't ever bled," said Velvet briefly.

"I would laugh if it did," said Donald, and went.

"Merry marked her muslin?" said Mrs. Brown, coming in from the scullery.

"Great drop," said Mally.

"Put it under cold water," said Mrs. Brown. "Not a

touch of soap an' no hot. It sets it. It's Africa's made her nose bleed."

"I'll go with the steak tomorrow then," said Velvet. "There's the Fair an' all. She better keep still."

"What steak's that?"

"Father said Mr. Cellini wanted a steak before breakfast."

"Funny time," said Mrs. Brown.

"I'd like to go anyway," said Velvet. "I might see the chestnut."

That night, before the Fair, they went to bed early.

"Africa!" said Meredith, wildly and suddenly in the middle of the night. And slept again.

~ FIVE ~

Velvet's dreams were blowing about the bed. They were made of cloud but had the shapes of horses. Sometimes she dreamed of bits as women dream of jewelry. Snaffles and straights and pelhams and twisted pelhams were hanging, jointed and still in the shadows of a stable, and above them went up the straight, damp, oiled lines of leathers and cheek straps. The weight of a shining bit and the delicacy of the leathery above it was what she adored. Sometimes she walked down an endless cool alley in summer, by the side of the gutter in the old red brick floor. On her left and right were open stalls made of dark wood and the buttocks of the bay horses shone like mahogany all the way down. The horses turned their heads to look at her as she walked. They had black manes hanging like silk as the thick necks turned. These dreams blew and played round her bed in the night and the early hours of the morning.

She got up while the sisters were sleeping and all the room was full of book-muslin and canaries singing. "How they can sleep!" she said wonderingly when she became aware of the canaries singing so madly. All the sisters lay dreaming of horses. The room seemed full of the shapes of horses. There was almost a dream-smell of stables. As she dressed they were stirring, shifting and tossing in white heaps beneath their cotton bedspreads. The canaries screamed in a long yellow scream, and grew madder. Then Velvet left the room and softly shut the door and passed down into the silence of the cupboard-stairway.

In her striped cotton dress with a cardigan over it she picked up the parcel of steak that had been left on the kitchen table and drank the glass of milk with a playing card on the top of it that Mrs. Brown had left her overnight. Then she got a half packet of milk chocolate from the string drawer, and went out to saddle Miss Ada.

In the brilliance of a very early summer morning they went off together, Miss Ada's stomach rumbling with hunger. Velvet fed her from a bag of oats she had brought with her up on the top of the hill. There were spiders' webs stretched everywhere across the gorse bushes.

Coming down over the rolling grass above Kingsworthy, Velvet could see the feathery garden looking like tropics asleep down below. Old Mr. Cellini by a miracle grew palms and bananas and mimosa in his. Miss Ada went stabbing and sliding down the steep hillside, hating the descent, switching her tail with vexation.

Velvet tied Miss Ada to the fence, climbed it and crept through the spiny undergrowth into the foreign garden. There was not a sound. Not a gardener was about. The grass-like moss, spongy with dew so that each foot sank in and made a black print which filled with water. Then she looked up and saw that the old gentleman had been looking at her all the time.

He had on a squarish hat and never took his eyes off
her. He was standing by a tree. Velvet's feet went down
in the moss as she stood. His queer hat was wet, and
there was dew on the shoulders of his ancient black
frock coat which buttoned up to the neck; he looked
like someone who had been out all the night.

Raising one black-coated arm he rubbed his lips as
though they were stiff, and she could see how frail he
was, unsteady, wet.

"What have you come to do?" he said in a very
low voice.

"Sir?"

He moved a step forward and stumbled.

"Are you staying? Going up to the house?"

"The house."

"Stay here," he said in an urgent tone which broke.

Velvet dropped her own eyes to her parcel, for she
knew he was looking at her and how his eyeballs shone
round his eyes.

"How did you come?" (at last). She looked up. There
was something transparent about his trembling face.

"On our pony," she said. "I rode. She's tied to the
fence. There's some meat here for the cook, to leave at
the back door."

"Do you like ponies?" said the rusty voice.

"Oh . . . yes. We've only the one."

"Better see mine," said the old gentleman in a different tone.

He moved towards her, and as they walked he rested
one hand on her shoulder. They walked till they came
to the open lawns and passed below some fancy bushes.

He stopped. And Velvet stopped.

". . . if there was anything you wanted very much,"
he said, as though to himself.

Velvet said nothing. She did not think it was a question.

"I'm very much too old," said the old gentleman. "Too old. What did you say you'd brought?"

"Meat," said Velvet. "Rump."

"Meat," said the old gentleman. "I shan't want it. Let's see it."

Velvet pulled the dank parcel out of her bag.

"Throw it away," said the old gentleman, and threw it into a bush.

They walked on a few paces.

Something struck her on the hip as she walked. It was when his coat swung out. He looked down too, and unbuttoned his coat and slowly took it off. Without a word he hung it over his arm, and they walked on again, he in his black hat and black waistcoat and shirt-sleeves.

"Going to the stables," said he. "Why, are you fond of horses?"

There was something about him that made Velvet feel he was going to say good-by to her. She fancied he was going to be carried up to Heaven like Elisha.

"Horses," he said. "Did you say you had horses?"

"Only an old pony, sir."

"All my life I've had horses. Stables full of them. You like 'em?"

"I've seen your chestnut," said Velvet. "Sir Pericles. I seen him jump."

"I wish he was yours, then," said the old gentleman, suddenly and heartily. "You said you rode?"

"We've on'y got Miss Ada. The pony. She's old."

"Huh!"

"Not so much *old*," said Velvet hurriedly. "She's obstinate."

He stopped again.

"Would you tell me what you want most in the world? . . . Would you tell me that?"

He was looking at her.

"Horses," she said, "sir."

"To ride on? To own for yourself?"

He was still looking at her, as though he expected more.

"I tell myself stories about horses," she went on, desperately fishing at her shy desires. "Then I can dream about them. Now I dream about them every night. I want to be a famous rider, I should like to carry dispatches. I should like to get a first at Olympia; I should like to ride in a great race; I should like to have so many horses that I could walk down between the two rows of loose boxes and ride what I chose. I would have them all under fifteen hands. I like chestnuts best, but bays are lovely too, but I don't like blacks."

She ran out the words and caught her breath and stopped.

At the other end of the golden bushes the gardener's lad passed in the lit, green gap between two rhododendron clumps with a bodge on his arm. The old gentleman called to him. Then he walked onward across the grass and Velvet and the gardener's boy followed after. They neared a low building of old brick with a square cobbled yard outside it. The three passed in under the arched doorway.

"Five," said the old gentleman. "These are my little horses. I like little ones too." He opened the gate of the first loose box and a slender chestnut turned slowly towards him. It had a fine, artistic head, like horses which snort in ancient battles in Greece.

"Shake hands, Sir Pericles," said the old gentleman,

and the little chestnut bent its knee and lifted a slender foreleg a few inches from the ground.

"But I've no sugar," said the old gentleman. "You must do your tricks for love today."

He closed the gate of the loose box.

In the next box was a grey mare.

"She was a polo pony," he said. "Belonged to my son." He still wore his hat, black waistcoat, and shirt-sleeves. He looked at the gardener's boy. "I need not have bothered you," he said. "Of course the grooms are up." But the gardener's boy, not getting a direct order, followed them gently in the shadow of the stables.

The grey mare had the snowy grey coat of the brink of age. All the blue and dapple had gone out of her, and her eyes burnt black and kind in her white face. When she had sniffed the old gentleman she turned her back on him. She did not care for stable-talk.

In the next loose box was a small pony, slim and strong, like a miniature horse. He had a sour, suspicious pony face. There were two more loose boxes to come and after that a gap in the stables. Far down the corridor between the boxes Velvet could see where the big horses stood—hunters and carriage horses and cart horses.

The gardener's boy never stirred. The old gentleman seemed suddenly tired and still.

He moved and pulled a piece of paper from the pocket of his waistcoat. "Get me a chair," he said very loud. But before the boy could move a groom came running swiftly with a stable chair.

The old gentleman sat down and wrote. Then he looked up.

"What's your name?" he said and looked at Velvet.

"Velvet Brown," said Velvet.

"Velvet Brown," he said and tapped his pencil on his blue cheek. Then wrote it down. "Sign at the bottom, boy," he said to the gardener's boy, and the boy knelt down and wrote his name carefully. "Now you sign too," he said to the groom.

The old gentleman rose and Velvet followed him out into the sunlight of the yard. "Take that paper," he said to her, "and you stay there," and he walked from her with his coat on his arm.

He blew himself to smithereens just round the corner. Velvet never went to look. The grooms came running.

The warm of the brick in the yard was all she had to hold onto. She sat on it and listened to the calls and exclamations. "Gone up to Heaven, Elisha," she thought, and looked up into the sky. She would like to have seen him rising, sweet and sound and happy.

In the paper in her hand she read that all of his five horses belonged to her.

Taking the paper, avoiding the running and the calling of the household, she crept back through the garden to Miss Ada. When she got home she could not say what had happened, but cried and trembled and was put to bed and slept for hours under the golden screams of the canaries. At four o'clock Mally burst in and cried:

"They've drawn! They've drawn! We've got the piebald!"

"Whose ticket?" said Velvet faintly.

"Yours, oh, yours. Are you ill?"

"Mr. Cellini's dead," whispered Velvet. "Just round the corner!"

Mally stood transfixed to the floor. "They're bringing the piebald home," she said, staring. She could not be bothered by the death of Mr. Cellini.

Hearing a sound she ran to the window.

"It's here, it's down at the very door!" she called.

"Get Mother," said Velvet, who could not move because the room was swaying.

Velvet went to Mr. Cellini's funeral. As an heiress. She did not bury him in her heart till then. The nights before she had seen him only smashed, but living. Seen his face with its looks. Could a look be smashed? That night before the funeral, the horses in her dreams galloped downhill. By the head down, like rockets. But when she had been to his funeral and walked in her winter black tarpaulin mackintosh, among his relations, her eyes like sad lights in her head and her bony teeth, veiled in gold, like a war chief's trophy across her thin face, then she knew he was still and folded and she could turn to the horses.

Mr. Brown was quite agreeable to the horses. It was all in the local papers, and lovely pictures of the girls looking like three gazelles. And Velvet? Velvet looking like Dante when he was a little girl.

Mr. Brown saw it was good for trade. "You'll be wanting a field," he said.

"But they've been kept in," said Velvet.

"Keep them in you won't, my girl. And it's summer."

"But next winter?" said Velvet.

"Next winter'll take care of itself."

There were six horses now.

The strange piebald won at the Fair had been put that night by Mi into the Tablet Gully. In this narrow valley there was a tablet to a dead man, but the name had gone. The tablet said he died gathering moss in the snow, overwhelmed in a snowstorm and fallen down a mountain.

74

In all the ninety miles of the Hullocks there was no moss; there was no snow; no mountains to fall down, but only the curving breasts of hillsides. Still the legend of the nameless man remained intact, and here the pie-bald grazed, flashing like black and ivory in the dapple of the valley. He was six miles from the village and he had not yet attempted to break loose. He could not see a chimney or a roof from where he cropped, or hear any sound but the sheep who filled his valley. The food was new to him, richer than in the high burnt-up fields above the village, and his attention was caught, and his nostalgia for the time assuaged.

Now that the excitement in the village had blown out Mr. Brown began, and well he might, to fuss about expense.

"A man who leaves a butcher's daughter five horses might leave her some money to keep them with," he said.

"Why do you suppose he left them to you, Velvet?" asked Mally for the hundredth time.

Velvet looked at the table and said, "It was a joke he made with himself at the last minute."

"Just leave her," said Mrs. Brown calmly. "Don't keep on asking, Malvolia."

It was the green summer dawn of the day the horses were due to arrive. Velvet woke up and she could hear the birds' feet walking up and down on the roof.

"Swi—ipe!" said one canary in a very loud voice, and all the sisters woke.

At breakfast Velvet sat back in her chair, a little yellow.

"Chew your toast well," said Mrs. Brown, "and don't drink your milk. It'll lay loose."

"Is it eleven or half past that they're coming?" asked Edwina.

"Don't talk about it," said Mrs. Brown. "Leave the subject alone." Velvet faintly chewed.

At nine she had a strong drink of peppermint, and some whitish powder of her mother's choosing. Sitting close to the kitchen stove she slowly recovered. Every now and then the sisters looked in at the door at her anxiously.

"Shall I ever grow out of it, mother?" asked Velvet once.

"Yes," said Mrs. Brown, like a palmist, "when you're sixteen."

The room, crammed with furniture, was faintly green as the light struck through the cactus window. The cactus pots were arranged on glass shelves. They were well cared for, of different sorts, and six of them were in peculiar flower. The street door was shut, the yard door was open. On one side of the room the mahogany sideboard stretched from wall to wall, with its bottles of vinegar, old decanters, a set of green wineglasses, salts, peppers, A1 and Demon sauces, and in the middle the Sheffield dish cover, 30 inches long, that covered the joint on Sundays. The lamp, used at night in winter, stood on a table by itself. The dinner table, round, covered with a Paisley cloth, filled the center of the room. The window on the street was blocked with cineraria. Motes of blue from the flowers floated on the belly of the dish cover.

Velvet held the shell-box of paper horses in her hand, like something to which she was being disloyal.

All the girls had on striped cotton frocks too big for their thin bodies. Edwina and Malvolia had belted theirs in with leather belts bought in the village, but the dresses of Meredith and Velvet hung loose on them.

"Half the village outside in the street," said Mr. Brown complacently, coming in with his pipe out of the sunlight. "Seems to have got round."

"Not surprising," said Mrs. Brown, "with three reporters coming here."

"This family's cut out for the newspapers," said Mr. Brown, putting his arm on her vast shoulder. Mrs. Brown said nothing.

"Got your strong knickers on?" said Mrs. Brown presently.

"Yes," said Velvet.

"What's that for?" said Mr. Brown. "She's not going to ride this string of racers she's getting."

"They're hacks. Little hacks," said Velvet.

Mrs. Brown rose.

"See to Donald," she said. "He's frittering his time."

But at that moment, as they fidgeted, the door opened and Donald walked in, all buttoned up and shining and his brow as black as thunder.

"Who's buttoned you?" asked Mrs. Brown.

"Mi's buttoned me," said Donald savagely.

"Huh!" said Mrs. Brown.

They measured each other.

"You forgot me," said Donald.

Mrs. Brown said nothing. Donald strutted down the room and out into the yard.

"Seems upset," said Mr. Brown.

Mi came in.

"I'll thank you not to button him again," said Mrs. Brown.

"Any sign of the horses?" said Mr. Brown.

"Early yet," said Mi, "but the whole village is waiting on the Green."

"Most of 'em's outside," said Mr. Brown, motioning to the flower-window with his pipe. The flower-window was black with faces. "Ask Mr. Croom in."

Mi opened the door and spoke through the crack of it. Mr. Croom, the grocer, came in.

"Wonderful," said Mr. Croom, "Velvet gettin' them horses."

Mr. Brown got up and looked at his watch, which lay under a tumbler on the sideboard. "Getting on time," he said, and Velvet, sitting at the stove, felt suddenly light and warm.

"Whur's the little chap?" said Mr. Croom. "Donald?"

"I'm here," said Donald through the half-open yard door.

"I got silver an' gold for you," said Mr. Croom.

"More'n he deserves," said Mrs. Brown.

Donald came in brightly with his sweet smile.

"Silver an' gold," said Mr. Croom, holding out a net bag full of chocolate coins covered in silver and gold paper. "Foreign," he said, "Dutch stuff. But Donald won't care."

"Say thank you," said Mr. Brown.

"Thank you," said Donald, with his heart in his face. He took the bag and wandered away.

"Fine chap," said Mr. Croom.

"Cup of coffee, Mr. Croom?" said Mrs. Brown.

"If you're making any." Mr. Croom peered through the street window. "Quite a stir in the village."

"Yes," said Mr. Brown.

" 'Strordinary thing," said Mr. Croom. "Like a tale."

"Yes," said Mr. Brown again. "Took to Velvet, I suppose."

"Ever seen him before, Velvet?" said Mr. Croom.

"Yes," said Velvet faintly. "Once. At the Lingdown Horse Show."

"Better leave her," said Mrs. Brown. "Turns her stomach."

"Well, well . . ." said Mr. Croom regretfully. "Yes."

Mr. Cellini swam across the ceiling, frailer than memory, like a cobweb.

Mr. Brown rose again and looked at his watch on the sideboard. "Should be here," he said.

"Where's your gold and silver bag?" said Velvet suddenly to Donald.

"I put it away," said Donald.

"Don't you want it?" said Mr. Croom, hurt.

"No," said Donald. "I might want it some day."

"What you got there instead?"

"It's my spit bottle," said Donald, holding up a medicine bottle on a string.

He walked a little further into the room and dangled the bottle, showing a little viscous fluid in the bottom.

"That's my spit," he said.

"He's collecting his spit," said Velvet.

Donald applied his mouth at the top and with difficulty dribbled a little more spit into the neck.

"D'you let him do those sort o' things?" said Mr. Brown to Mrs. Brown.

"Take it outside," said Mrs. Brown. "Here's your coffee, Mr. Croom."

Edwina, Malvolia and Meredith burst the street door open with the crowd behind their shoulders. "Over the hill! You can see them!" Meredith panted, and all three disappeared.

Mrs. Brown picked up Donald, his spit bottle swinging. "Put your cardigan on," she said to Velvet. "Keep warm an' you'll be all right."

They all went out, the crowd following them, and turned up the chalk road.

"Where's Mi?" said Velvet suddenly.

"Got a half dozen sheep to fetch," said Mr. Brown. "Be here any minute."

"Poor Mi," said Velvet, and walked on, rapt with happiness.

Over the brow of the hill five horses moved down towards them.

"Ther's three grooms. My word, ther's three of them," said Mally, who had joined the procession. The grooms were walking the horses, two horses to a groom, then one alone at the back. As they reached the foot of the grass slope and stepped on to the flashing chalky road in the sun, the black crêpe could be seen on the arm of each walking groom. They were bowler-hatted, and round each bowler a band of crêpe was tied. The head groom, walking in front with the grey mare and Sir Pericles, had a rosy face and a fine black coat of good cloth. The others wore dark grey.

The horses were halted at the entrance to the village.

The head groom produced a slip of paper. "Miss Velvet Brown?" he asked. Mr. Brown stepped forward, Velvet close behind. Her thin face shone, smile alight, frock ballooned under cardigan, legs bare and scratched. "I'm Velvet," she said.

She walked up to Sir Pericles, transfigured, touched him gently on his neck, took the rein from the groom.

"We'll go down to the house," she said softly. "I'll lead this one home."

"Better let me," said the groom. Velvet stared at

him, shook her head, and walked on leading the shining horse.

"Daft today," said Mr. Brown to the groom.

"Mind she don't let him go then," said the groom.

The procession went on, Velvet first with her horse, Mr. Brown at her elbow, the horses and the village people following. "Keep the boys back! Don't let them frighten the horses!" said the old head groom.

"Keep back there," said Mr. Croom mildly, and the boys ran and skipped. Edwina and Malvolia and Meredith went ahead, turning to look over their shoulders.

"Better stop!" called Edwina.

The procession drew up and halted as it reached the street. Half a dozen sheep had arrived unexpectedly from a farm for the slaughterhouse, and Mi was striving to get the last three in. He ran about in his Sunday clothes, put on for the arrival of the horses. They could hear him cursing. The three sheep skipped, butted and ran. "Yer poor slob!" yelled Mi to the last one, bounding like a hare to keep it out of the main road. He turned it, and the last of the sheep went dingily behind the great wooden door. With the clatter of delicate feet on brick the horses moved on till they reached the sunny square before the cottage.

Donald was swinging his bottle before the door. He had not kept up with the procession.

"Keep that child in!" called Mr. Brown. But Donald swung his bottle gently, and Mrs. Brown did no more than lay a finger on his head.

The horses were drawn up facing the doorway and the second groom took over the bunch of leather reins. They ran like soft straps of silk over his fingers, narrow, polished, and flexible.

"Better take this into the house and read it over,"

suggested the head groom to Mr. Brown, handing him a typewritten sheet.

Mr. Brown glanced at it and called to Velvet. Together they went in at the door and sat down at the little fern table inside. Mr. Brown pushed the ferns gently to one side and laid out the sheet.

"One chestnut gelding. 14 hands. Seven years old, *Sir Pericles*. 1 snaffle bit, bridle, noseband and standing martingale. 1 Ambrose saddle, leathers and stirrups. 1 pair webbing girths."

And underneath this Velvet wrote "Velvet Brown."

"One grey polo pony. Mare. 15 hands. Nine years old. *Mrs. James*. 1 straight pelham, etc. . . . martingale . . . soft saddle and sewn girths."

And underneath Velvet wrote "Velvet Brown."

"1 child's pony, chestnut. 12.2 hands. Gelding. *George*. Snaffle bit and double bit. Soft saddle and sewn girths, etc."

And Velvet wrote "Velvet Brown."

"1 cob pony, for hacking or cart. 13.3 hands, dark bay gelding. *Fancy*. 1 double bit, etc. . . . old leather saddle, and harness for cart."

"Velvet Brown."

"1 Dartmoor filly, two years old, unbroken. 11 hands. Halter only. *Angelina*."

"Velvet Brown."

When Velvet had written her name for the fifth time, carefully, in ink, and with her breath held tight, her father touched her arm, and they both returned to the sunlight of the street. Mr. Brown gave the paper to the head groom.

"What are you doing with them straight away?" said the groom.

"Turning them into a field of mine," said Mr. Brown.

The groom hesitated. "Warm weather, but they've none on 'em been out at night yet. Won't hurt the little filly."

"They'll have to be out now," said Mr. Brown, with a slight rise of voice, as though he were being dictated to.

"Will they eat sugar?" said Mally.

"All except the grey mare," said the groom. "She likes apple."

Mally brought sugar out of her cotton pocket. Meredith went for an apple.

"Shall you be selling them, sir?" said the groom a little hesitatingly to Mr. Brown.

"They're mine!" said Velvet suddenly.

"We've not decided anything," said Mr. Brown. Velvet's soul became several sizes too large for her, her mouth opened, and she struggled with speech. Mrs. Brown's hand fell on her shoulder, and her soul sank back to its bed.

"I suppose you are fixed up with a man?" said the head groom tentatively. "I have a place myself, but . . ." He made a gesture towards the other two grooms.

"I'm a butcher," said Mr. Brown firmly. "My girl goes and gets herself five horses. Five! We've seven all told, with that piebald. If she has to have horses she must look after 'em. We've fields in plenty, and there's oats in the shed, and I've four girls all of an age to look after horses. Beyond that I won't go. I'll have no fancy stables here. I'm a plain man and a butcher, and we've got to live."

"Eh, yes," said the little old, rosy-headed groom. "Shall we unsaddle them and turn them into the field for you?"

"Saddles'll have to go in the slaughterhouse," said Mr. Brown. "Through with them sheep yet?" he said to Mi.

"Ain't begun," said Mi.

"Well then, you can put the saddles in the sun here on the wood rail, and lead 'em to the field in the bridles. Head collars they have on 'em. P'raps you'd better leave the bridles here."

The head groom went up to the girths of Sir Pericles, but Velvet's thin hand was on his arm. "I'm going to try them all first," she said.

Mr. Brown heard what she said, though he made no sign. He looked at Donald, then at his wife. She made no sign either.

"Fetch your gold sweets now!" said Mr. Brown heavily and with unreality to Donald, tweaking his chin, and retired from the whole scene towards the slaughterhouse.

"Let's go round to the field," said Velvet, with confidence, to the groom.

"Wait a bit," said Mrs. Brown. "You'll have a little something first. Edwina, there's that bottle of port. Bring it out. And glasses. Mr. Croom, you'll join too, a drop won't do anybody any harm."

Edwina and Mally brought out the fern table, a tin one, the sacred table that was never moved.

Velvet as the heroine, Edwina as the eldest, the head groom as the guest, and Mrs. Brown as the hostess sat down at the table and sipped a sip from the thick glasses of port. The village stood round at a respectful distance, and Mally and Meredith walked among the horses. Sir

Pericles dropped his neck and nuzzled by the head groom's pockets. The second grooms shared a glass between them. Then they all went up to the field to try the horses.

Velvet mounted Sir Pericles. She had ridden Miss Ada for eight years, hopped her over bits of brushwood and gorse bushes, and trotted her round at the local gymkhana. Once she had ridden a black pony belonging to the farmer at Pendean. She had a natural seat, and her bony hands gathered up the reins in a tender way. But she had never yet felt reins that had a trained mouth at the end of them, and, as she cantered up the slope of the sunny field with the brow of the hill and the height of the sky in front of her, Sir Pericles taught her in three minutes what she had not known existed. Her scraggy, childish fingers obtained results at a pressure. The living canter bent to right or left at her touch. He handed her the glory of command.

When she slid to the ground by the side of the head groom she was speechless, and leaned her forehead for a second on the horse's flank.

"You ride him a treat," said the groom. "You done a bit of riding."

"Never ridden anything but her old pony," said Mi, his hair rising in pride.

"The mare here's harder," said the groom. "Excitable, and kind of tough."

He shot Velvet's light body and cotton frock into this second saddle. Her sockless feet, leather-shod, nosed for the stirrups. The groom shortened the leathers till they would go no more, and then tied knots in them. Mrs. James, the mare, broke into a sweat at once. She flirted her ears wildly back and forwards, curved her grey neck, shook her bit, gave backward glances with her black eyes, like polished stones in her pale face.

"Mind! She don't start straight! She'll leap as she starts, and then she'll settle. She was Mr. Frank's polo pony an' she's not really nervous but she's keen."

There was scum on the mare's neck already, and the reins carved it off onto the leather as she shook her head. Mrs. Brown, holding Donald by the wall, watched quietly. Edwina, Mally and Merry sat on the gate.

"Hang on!" said the groom, and let go. Mrs. James, with a tremendous leap, started up the field. Her nostrils were distended, her ears pricked with alarm. She thought she carried a ghost. She could not feel anything on her back, yet her mouth was held. Velvet, whose hand had slipped down to the bridge of the saddle at the first leap, settled more steadily and lifted her hand to the reins. Mrs. James snorted as she cantered, like a single-cylindered car. She was not difficult to ride once the first start had been weathered. They rounded the field together; then Velvet got up on the pony George. George threw her as soon as her cotton frock touched his back.

"Get up again," said the head groom and held the pony tighter.

"Walk him, walk him," said the groom warningly. "Trot before you canter or he'll buck!"

George stuck his head out in an ugly line, and Velvet tried gently to haul him in. The whites of his eyes gleamed and his nose curled. He snatched at the bit when he felt her pressure and stretched his neck impatiently. Velvet's lips could not tighten, there was too much gold; but her eyes shone. She twirled the ends of the long reins and caught him hard, first on one shoulder, then on the other.

"She'll be off!" said Edwina.

"Not she!" said Mi. "It's what he's asking for."

George curved his neck and flirted archly with his bit, then trotted smartly back to the gate. Velvet dismounted and turned to Fancy, the cob.

Fancy was no faster than Miss Ada, and somewhat her build. He trotted round the field sedately.

"That's the lot," said the groom. "The filly's not broke."

"I must try George again," said Velvet.

"You bin on the lot," said Mrs. Brown. "Come home now."

"But Merry and Mally . . ."

"The horses'll get all of a do," said the head groom, "if they get too many on 'em. Better let them graze now, and tomorrow they'll be more themselves."

The horses were turned loose and the saddlery carried back to the slaughterhouse, where it was straddled over iron hook-brackets among the sheep's bodies.

The head groom stayed to midday dinner. The two others went down to the inn. It was Irish stew, with dumplings and onions. As the groom ate, he gave Velvet advice on how to catch the horses. His hat with the crêpe on it was laid on the sideboard.

"They haven't been out since last summer, and they're sure to be a bit wild at first. But you want to be up there, sitting on the wall, and just feeding them and coaxing them for a bit before you try to catch them. Mrs. James, she's wily. Sir Pericles'll do anything in the world you tell him. He knows a lot and what he knows is all pure goodness. Mrs. James is what you might call worldly wise. The pony's just pure cuss. He'll jump his own height if you can ever get him to believe in you. You can use a bit of stick on him. He's suspicious of kindness. But never touch Sir Pericles with anything. He'll break his heart and go sour. Fancy, she's no temperament. The little one, Angelina, wants playing with an' fondling, like you might fondle this dog here." Jacob grinned and bowed.

"Nice dog," added the groom. Jacob trembled with expectation. But the groom, pulling a piece of gristle out of his mouth, only laid it on the edge of his plate.

"You haven't asked about food, Velvet," said Edwina. But Velvet, who couldn't manage dumplings and onions, looked more ready to be carried to bed.

"Food now," said the groom. "But they're to be out to grass entirely? Well, well. . . . They'll just have to get accustomed to it. It's to be hoped they won't blow their bellies out the first day. But the grass is thin up there and that's a mercy. If they get colic you'll have to bring 'em in and sweat 'em and draught 'em. Whisky and rum together's the thing."

"Half and half?" said Mi abruptly.

The groom looked at him. "You'll be taking 'em on, I daresay?" he said hopefully.

"Mi won't waste his time," said Mr. Brown with authority. "The girls must learn what there is to learn."

"Leave it, leave it," said Mrs. Brown. "It'll settle itself."

"My band makes me retch," whispered Velvet to her mother.

"Grumble, grumble, grumble," said Mr. Brown, who had heard.

"Ho! I gotta huge, *huge* caterpillar in my greens!" said Donald, holding it up.

"It's dead!" said Mally. Velvet put her face in her hands.

Mrs. Brown rose and took a plate off the sideboard.

"Put it there, Donald," she said firmly, "and not another word about it."

"Let me see it," said Merry, leaning forward. Mr. Brown looked up, frowning. "There's manners about caterpillars," he said sharply. "Put them aside and *say nothing.*"

"It's done me!" said Velvet through her hands. "Can I go?"

"Yes, you can go," said her mother. Mr. Brown looked up again. "No good keeping her," said Mrs. Brown. "She'll vomit."

⬸ S I X ⬿

"Donald yelling on the Green!" called Mrs. Brown from the scullery.

Mi, with a bridle on his knees, in the living room, rose and looked through the flower-window.

"Mally's got him up in front of Mrs. James," he said. "S'e all right?"

"Can't see what's wrong with him. He's screaming awful."

"Mally," called Mrs. Brown, opening the front door. "Stop it. He's got a pin or something."

Mrs. James was cantering jerkily round and round the Green at what Mally believed to be a show canter. Donald, sitting on the edge of the saddle in front of Mally, had his arms over her arms and his bare legs were sinking beneath her knees, preventing her grip. He was scarlet in the face, his mouth was open, and he was screaming. His head jerked madly up and down as Mrs. James bounded. With difficulty Mally pulled up.

"Can't get off," called Mally (for Donald was half underneath her), then slid off in a heap with the child in her arms. Mrs. James sprang away in fear and trotted into the yard. Donald, sobbing, began at once to search in the grass.

"Whatever's the matter, Donald?" said Mrs. Brown from the doorway.

"Lost my sixpence. My chocolate sixpence," screamed Donald, hysterically turning over every tuft.

"Good gosh, is that all?" said Mally, rubbing her knee. She got up and went after Mrs. James.

"Lost his sixpence," said Mrs. Brown to Mi, closing the door and returning to the scullery.

"Ain't lost his nerve," said Mi, polishing the bit.

"Lot o' work we get out o' you, Mi!" said the butcher, coming in from the shed. "Place slimy with sheep stomach! Get on cleaning, do. Bits and leathers and irons and horses . . ." He disappeared again.

Mi grinned, put the bit on the sideboard and followed him. The little living room was dark and empty. Jacob parted the fringe of the sofa covering with his beaded nose and stole out, dragging his hindquarters after him with a yawn. He glanced round, grinned too, and leaped upon the sofa, turned round once or twice, scraped primevally with his foot and lay down.

Mi stuck his head back through the slaughter-shed door.

"Ha!" he said, and sprang for the sofa. Jacob was underneath again in a flash of white.

When the horses had been with the Browns a month, life readjusted itself and everything was easier than had been thought.

The horses had lost flesh a little in the dry, sea-blown field, and were very slightly out of condition. Mi knew it, but did not speak of it to Velvet. Velvet frowned and put her fingers into small hollows on the haunches, but said nothing. On the whole it was as well, for, corned-up as the horses had been when they arrived, the four girls would have had much more difficulty with them.

In the mornings they rode them in the field, and Mi, when he could sneak away, constructed jumps out of old packing cases, branches and bean poles, carrying up his precious hammer and nails. In the late afternoons they cantered over the Hullocks high up above the sea, preferably just before sunset. Mi watched them go off with a queer look in his eye, a look old Dan had worn when he saw Araminty Brown strike out from the brim of the land. There are men who like to make something out of women.

Velvet and Edwina usually rode Sir Pericles or Mrs. James. Mally liked her battles with George, and Mere-dith who never knew sufficiently what she was doing, was safest and happiest on Fancy.

"What shall we do when the summer's over?" said Velvet one evening to Edwina, as they rode along a chalk track on a ridge. "We can't keep Sir Pericles and Mrs. James out."

"It'll be murder," said Edwina.

"Mother'll do something with Father," said Velvet.

While they cantered in a stream Merry always formed the tail. She went with a loose rein and trusted God. Fancy plodded along and minded his path. Merry liked the air whistling round her forehead, and the shifting clouds reflected on the Hullocks. She watched for partridge and thought of her canaries. The arrival of the horses had not disturbed her at all. The partridges rose and went skimming away sideways and downhill like falling arrowheads. The rooks tossed about in the sky like a tipcart of black paper in a whirlwind. The larks hung invisible and the hawk hung visible. But Meredith, glancing at them, knowing them, was reminded only of Arabelle, of Mountain Jim, of Butter and Dreadnought Susan. She was not romantic about wild birds. She liked her power over her little yellow flight at home.

"When we bring out Donald, what'll we start him on?" began Velvet. (This was a favorite theme.) Donald was to ride, youngest, in the under-eight. He was to ride well, for the sake of their honor, but capital might also be made of his youth and his silver hair. He was to ride home up the village, carrying the silver cup he had won as best-boy-rider in the under-eight. But what on? That was the everlasting question.

"George is the narrowest."

"George would have him off in a second."

"Do you suppose . . ." began Meredith, but nobody listened to her. Mating was her mania. She was certainly going to talk about mating.

They walked their horses slowly down the chalk road leading to the village and reached the field.

"Who's got the key? Meredith, you had the key?"

Meredith fumbled under her cotton frock. Not one of them had riding breeches.

"It was in my knickers pocket," she said, turning her brown knickers almost inside out.

"You've lost it!" they all said instantly. Edwina got down and, undoing a bit of wire, took the gate off its hinges and opened it from the wrong side.

"I've got it!" said Mally suddenly, fishing in her knickers.

They rode up to a little lean-to allotment-shed with a padlock where they kept the saddlery and the rubbers. The horses were rubbed down and turned loose, and, wiring up the gate's hinge, the girls sauntered back along the road to the village.

"Let's see that schedule again," said Mally.

Velvet drew it out of her pocket. They came to a stop and sat on a flint bridge over a stream. The setting sun picked out the flints like pieces of glass.

" 'Novices jumping,' " said Velvet, pointing to an item many times underlined. The whole program was ready to drop to pieces.

"*Children's* Novice jumping," corrected Edwina.

"Well, of course! Sir Pericles couldn't do anything else. It'll be three foot."

"Three foot six, Mi says."

"Are you sure?"

"Well, you know what he is. He never likes to be wrong."

"Find out how he found out, anyway."

"George can jump three foot six."

"Easy, if he wants to," said Mally.

"About money," said Velvet. "We ought to look at it that way. There's more to be won in the jumping than in potatoes or bending. But there's most to be won in the hurdle races. Most of all. Pounds."

"But we . . . You wouldn't do that?"

"I don't know," said Velvet. "It isn't so awful. It's only low hurdles and a hustle."

"Don't you remember the way some of them crashed last year?"

"There's no need to crash like that," said Velvet. "It's the men who crash, not the women."

"Why is that?"

"I think they must be wilder," said Velvet.

"They win more too," said Mally.

"Sometimes women win," said Velvet in her clear voice, lifting her boy's face just a little.

"Would they let you?"

"Oh, yes, in gymkhanas. It's the size of the horse that counts. It doesn't matter who rides. It's 'Open.' It doesn't says 'Adults.' See in this one? First prize £3."

"We'll just have to borrow our entries, and pay them back out of prizes."

"But if we don't get any prizes?"

Nobody answered.

"Who can we borrow from?"

"We haven't paid Mi yet for the tickets for the raffle. And there's sixpence owing on Mar's Bars and twopence on Crunchies."

"Those are only shillings!" said Velvet impatiently.

"We are going to win pounds. We must just borrow again."

"Couldn't we sell something?"

"We ought to sell Miss Ada," said Meredith.

There was a silence like the silence of wasps before attack.

"I wasn't thinking!" said Meredith hurriedly.

"I should think not!" said Mally.

"But there's something in it," said Edwina. "We've got too many horses. If we sold the piebald we'd have money to pay for all the other horses."

"If anybody ever sells the piebald," said Velvet slowly, "I might as well die."

"Well, it's borrow or sell," said Edwina. "Come along. We've got to feed them still."

The sky green, the sun almost gone, they returned, buckets of oats mixed with chaff carried between them. They pulled branches of reeds and switched the horses off as they tried to steal each other's buckets. George ate with the whites gleaming in the corners of his eyes, and, as he finished, his ears went back. Then with a rush he stormed another bucket, and the evening rang with the clatter of iron shoes and zinc buckets over-turned. Mrs. James ate steadily and could lash out if interrupted. Sir Pericles was nervous and would rather not eat at all than be hurried. Fancy threw his bucket over, mixed his oats with earth. Angelina got the leavings. Unbroken, she was definitely out to grass and was only a crumb-picker, like a dog.

The stars came out as they watched the horses eat.

"Mrs. James, Mrs. James," said Velvet suddenly, with love. And the mare laid her ears back at such nonsense.

"Why do you love her?" asked Meredith.

"She is like Mother," said Velvet.

"Oh. . . . How?"

"She is," said Velvet. "Aren't they wild and lovely in this field at night! Look how their eyes shine! Look at Angelina's! Got kitten's eyes."

"Come . . . up, Mrs. James!" said Mally, tugging.

"What's a matter?"

Mally had the mare's off-fore in her hands. "Shoe gone. I thought so. Now there'll be shoeing bills. Had you thought of that?"

"That's upkeep. Father'll pay," said Edwina.

"Yes, but pay and pay, and there'll come an end. There's nothing coming in on these horses," said Mally.

"At Pendean . . . at Pendean . . ." said Velvet, stammering and desperate all at once.

"You won't make a fortune anyway. And you may break your neck. Mother won't let you do it."

"If I get the entry money, I'll enter. She won't know till I'm down at the starting post."

"Come along," said Edwina, holding the gate.

The horses who had finished hurried after them. They were shut out at the gate and hung their heads over into the dark.

"Cat in the ditch!" said Mally as they walked. They all saw the two fiery points among the dark weeds.

"Shush!" said Edwina, jumping suddenly to the brink of the ditch. The eyes winked and blew out.

"Cats' eyes shine like thieves' lamps," said Velvet. "What's for supper?"

"I just bin wondering," said Meredith.

"It's the two lobsters Father brought!" said Mally suddenly. "Mother said she'd do 'em hot . . . ." They ran, buckets clanking.

The spaniels, pressed against the door, yelped as Mally pushed them aside.

The living room smelt alive with hot lobster—a red, entrancing smell.

Edwina snatched a little parcel that had come by post from off the sideboard.

"What's that!" said Velvet and Mally instantly.

"Mine," said Edwina. She shot up the stairway to the bedroom.

All three streamed after her.

"I wish I had a room of my own!" panted Edwina, turning on them at bay from the dressing table, the parcel in her hand. "I shan't . . . I won't undo it."

"Hey!" called Mrs. Brown. "Father's come! Come on down. Never mind washing. It won't stand a minute."

In a few seconds they were all grouped round the table as keen as the dogs outside.

Mi appeared from nowhere.

The lobster was borne in on a vast dish, surrounded

by a bank of rice. It was chopped up, thickened with flour, buttered, and boiling hot.

"Where's that sherry?" said father, diving for the cupboard. "There was a drop."

"You'll cool it down," objected Mrs. Brown.

"Poof!" said father. "Where's the darn thing? Here it is . . ." He got the bottle and poured half a glass over the lobsters. "Turn it over then."

Mrs. Brown took up a spoon and turned the steaming lobster in the sherry. The helpings were ladled out, a lot of rice and a fair share of lobster. They ate.

"Poor Donald," said Velvet.

"Sleeping like an angel," said Mi.

"Empty angel," said Mally. "No lobster inside him."

"Stir him up if he had!" said Mi. "My word . . ."

At the thought of Donald stirred up with lobster to worse excesses they fell still again and continued to eat.

"No dog eats shellfish," said Mr. Brown sideways to Jacob, who was bowing at him.

"How d'you know?" asked Mally.

"Kind o' law," said Mr. Brown. "My father always said it to his dogs."

"Give him a bit an' see."

"Can't spare any," said Mr. Brown.

Jacob mooned under the table.

"Father, Mrs. James's lost a shoe," said Velvet.

The storm broke swiftly over the supper table.

"Oats an' shoes an' soon there'll be bits o' saddlery . . . nothing to show for it . . . nothing but pleasure and a lot o' girls being spoiled for school . . ." The storm blew in a wind of indignation and as it blew, Velvet was conscious of her father's case. It was a good one. There was no benefit to him in the horses. The lovely creatures ate, and were sterile. They labored not, and ate and ate, and lost their shoes. Velvet had no answers and no comfort to offer. And all her promises were child's promises and air until she could carry them out.

When supper was over and cleared, and Father was standing in the street with his pipe, she pulled out the gymkhana schedule from the dresser drawer, and bent her urgent face over the yellow paper.

Mechanically her hand went up to rock the gold binder and lay it in her lap.

"You *would* choose to-night!" said Edwina, giving her a shove with her elbow.

Velvet stared at her.

"Get your band in," said Edwina. "You always do it when he's angry."

Velvet stared at her still. A gust of loyalty to her father shook her heart. Edwina had a way of talking. . . . She eyed Edwina sideways. Edwina was rough, and she looked as fine as wire. Something about the beauty of the antelope face caught Velvet's attention. Suddenly she wondered if Edwina would save her if she were drowning. Then studied the schedule again.

"Seven two-and-sixes," she said finally.

"Make it eight. That's a pound," said Mally. "Wherever d'you suppose we're going to get that from?"

"Let's look again and see if there's anything we can leave out," said Meredith.

"No point in doing that," said Velvet. "It's just as difficult to borrow seventeen and six as a pound."

"Queer idea," said Mally.

"Why queer?"

"Thinking saving doesn't matter."

"We got nothing," said Velvet. "We got nothing, have we?"

"Nothing."

"Then we might as well ask for what we want as ask for less."

"Who you going to ask?"

"Don't know," said Velvet. "I'll have to see. Let's work it through once more."

There was a rustle by the door and she put her hand in.

"Let's go to Miss Ada."

They filed out across the yard, and stood and sat by Miss Ada's manger.

Miss Ada stood droopingly and sour. She had not seen much of them lately.

"Give her something to brighten her up," said Edwina. "She's looking a crime."

Velvet pulled up her frock.

"You've always got sugar in your knickers," said Mally. "How does mother let you have so much?"

"I buy it."

"*Buy* it?"

"I promised Mr. Croom I'd pay after the gymkhana." She fumbled. "Here's a bit."

Miss Ada took it in her exasperated manner, and turned her back on them.

" 'Children's Bending,' " read Velvet. "That's Mally. On George. 'Children's Potato Race.' Me on Mrs. James. 'Children (Novice) Jumping.' Me on Sir Pericles . . . and on the piebald."

"The piebald!" The three voices snapped in the stall like whip-cracks. "The piebald! But you've never ridden him."

100 ⸺

"I shall have ridden him by then. Remember how he jumped the wall?"

"Yes, but . . ."

"I shall have ridden him. I'm going over tomorrow afternoon."

"We'll all go. Tomorrow afternoon," said Meredith.

"I'll ride him quietly up and down the valley. We'll take Sir Pericles and change the saddles. His ought to fit the piebald. There's nothing wrong with the piebald, except that he hates being shut in square fields with walls. Or else he likes jumping walls. Where's the list?"

"There's the Threadneedle Race. That's me."

"Who'll thread your needle?"

"Mother."

"Then you'll have to tell her you're racing?"

"At the last minute. She'll do it. What is the fuss about racing? You've got to sit on and go round. It isn't even like a professional race, where they catch their legs in yours, if you're an amateur, an' throw you off."

"How d'you know?"

"I read about it in the Libra'y."

"Where'd you get the penny?"

"On tick again," said Velvet wearily. "There's an old book there on the National."

"What National?"

"The Grand National," said Velvet, with an undertone in her voice like a girl in love.

"The next's a Wheelbarrow Race," said Mally, reading.

"We can't all do everything," said Velvet, "because of the money. We must choose. Anyway, we've worked it out. We've eight half crowns."

"Where?"

"I mean that's what we're going to borrow."

"When's the closing day for the entries?"

"Friday," said Velvet. "I must get the pound by then."

"Bed yer ma says," said Mi, putting his head in at the door of the stable.

In the dark, when the light was out, Mally remembered. "What was that parcel, 'Dwina?" she asked.

Edwina, settled herself angrily further into the clothes. "Not a minute by myself. . . . *Never* by myself!" she whispered into her pillow, and the tears of growth and self-pity heated her eyes.

Very soon they were all asleep, and the dreams waved like palm leaves over the room.

~ SEVEN ~

The sun poured down on the beach. The Hullocks blazed, hot and grey with burnt grass in the late gymkhana summer. Horses were everywhere, creeping over the dun hills, silhouetted on the skyline like plumes, plunging down the skyline to the sea. Donald came in to midday dinner, shoeless, with painted toenails.

"What's he got on his feet?" said Mally, Velvet and Meredith all together, with gimlet eyes and sharp voices. Donald climbed onto his chair and placed his ten scarlet toes on the table.

" 'Dwina did me," he said. He looked pleased.

"Where's 'Dwina."

"Up in your bedroom."

Down came Edwina, blowing on her last finger. She held up her two hands, ten drops of deep crimson madder at the tips.

"The parcel!" she said tauntingly and with triumph. "Wet still. Don't touch!"

There was a silence.

"Have you got stuff to get it off?" asked Velvet in a cold voice.

"I'm not going to get it off."

"It won't wear off . . ."

"It'll stay like that for three weeks."

"Gymkhana's Friday week."

"Well?"

"D'you think you're going," said Velvet, "to ride Mrs. James with those red nails?"

"Why not?"

"Men have played polo on Mrs. James," said Velvet, choking, "an' you . . ."

"Coming!" called Mrs. Brown from the kitchen, with the dish.

"Look at the boy's feet! Who's dolled 'm up?" said Mr. Brown from the street door.

"I got PAINTED feet," said Donald with satisfaction. " 'Dwina done it."

Mr. Brown paused and looked at 'Dwina. He saw her nails and still he looked. She shuffled a little and took her seat at the table. Mrs. Brown came into the room with the dish of oxtail, glutinous, steaming, crusts of toast swimming.

Mr. Brown sat down and began to help the food. Mi slipped in and took his seat. Jacob caught the door on his shoulder and squeezed in, squirming, as it closed. Mally, Velvet, Merry, everyone was silent. When the food was all around Mr. Brown observed that Donald's toes were one thing. Then he paused. Velvet waited, almost in pity, for what was to fall upon 'Dwina.

But father was strange. He only said, "I'm not against yer fingers, Edwina. Looks kind of finished to me. Yer getting on, too. Time you worried about your appearance. Donald's toes is just silly."

"What's he done to his toes?" said Mrs. Brown, eating.

Donald arranged them again upon the tablecloth. His mother looked at them and went on with her dinner.

"Looks like my garnets," she remarked. "An' can you count 'em, Donald?"

So it was left to Velvet to undo Edwina. She clinched her spirit and knit it up again. When dinner was over she waited for Edwina in the bedroom where she knew she would come to look again at her bottle of nail polish.

From the height of the window, beyond the canary cages, the immortal Hullocks browsed, burnished and lit, at two in the afternoon. Bowed like silver barrels they were set in rows endwise to the sea. Like pigs, like sheep, like elephants, hay-blond with burnt grass. Velvet's mind stuttered like a small candle before the light and the height and the savage stillness of the middle afternoon. As she gazed her heart rolled slowly over, a wheel on which something is written. Edwina seemed to her small and distressed. The piebald horse, the light of her mind, walked slowly across her imagination. She leaned upon a cage. Merry opened the door and saw her.

"Looking at my canaries?" she asked, warmed to her marrow, like a mother whose baby is patted.

"No," said Velvet, turning round. Then seeing Meredith's face—"I was at first, and then I looked outside at the Hullocks. We're going over to the piebald as soon's Mally's washed up."

"What are you going to do about 'Dwina's nails?" said Meredith, and came towards the cages.

"Nothing," said Velvet. "She can have her nails if she likes."

"And ride Mrs. James?"

"If she likes to," said Velvet. "It's a disgrace to us but she can."

"I thought you minded so."

Velvet said nothing. Then she poked her finger in at Mountain Jim. "Will he sit on it?"

"On mine he will!" said Meredith eagerly, and opened the cage door. Mountain Jim bowed and fluttered his wing tips. Then descended to her finger and twisted his layered neck and cocked his easy head.

"You like them better then the horses, don't you?" said Velvet wonderingly.

"Nobody else wants them," said Meredith. "And they're small. They're like a doll's house."

"Why, there's a new one!"

"Mi bought it for me," said Merry in a small, touched voice, "because of Africa. This morning. That new mate got it for him."

"What mate?"

"The plumber's mate. The boy with the glass eye. The cat got it an' it's got no tail, but Mi says rub it with oil an' it'll grow. Hair oil he says. He's going to give me a teaspoonful of his."

"Does Mi use hair oil?"

"No, he doesn't use it, but he bought it."

"Merry," said Velvet, "nobody's thought what we're going to wear at the gymkhana."

"Our knickers."

"Yes," said Velvet, pondering. "Yes, our knickers. Every other child will have jodhpurs. I suppose they'll *let* us ride? In knickers?"

"Oh, I should think so," said Meredith, cleaning out the drinking pots with her finger. "Look at Butter bowing!"

Butter opened her wings and bowed from her perch.

"She can't make up her mind to go from perch to perch without doing that," said Meredith. "She laid another useless egg this morning. Just drops them about."

"Are you sure it's useless?"

"I put it in water an' it floated. It's sterile."

"Does Mi say—"

"That's what Mi says. Float 'em. No good if they float."

"Mi comin' with us to the piebald this afternoon?"

"It's such a long way to walk," said Merry. "If only he would ride."

"Nothin'll ever make him," said Velvet. "He won't even talk about it."

Donald came round the bedroom door with naked feet and painted toes. He carried a postcard in his hand. "You gotta postcard. From Aunt Em."

"For me?" said Velvet.

"Sfer Meredith."

Meredith took it. "She's at Brighton. Just her love . . ."

"Thurs a picture," said Donald. He looked at it. "What is it? It's a church."

"No, it's a palace," said Meredith, reading the printed inscription. "It's the Pavilion at Brighton. 'Where George the Fourth lived,' it says."

"Who's George a Fourth?" asked Donald.

"Was a king . . . lived in this palace."

"Whur's he now?"

"Oh, he's dead. Ages ago."

"Who died 'im?"

"Nobody died him. He just died."

"Well, whur's he now?"

"Well, dead, Donald. Like everybody. Everybody dies."

"Why?"

"Well, they do. You will an' I will an' old people do."

"Do what?"

"Die."

"Who died that king then? Who died him, I say?"

"Velvet," said Meredith, exasperated. "You tell him. I got to finish these canaries."

Velvet considered Donald with a mild expression. He was frowning. His lovely face was angry.

"Where's your spit bottle?" she asked.

"Ts'full," said Donald, his whole face lighting with radiance. "I'll get it, shall I?"

"Yes," said Velvet, "only hurry up."

"You didn't do much," said Merry.

"He didn't really want to know," said Velvet. "He just wanted to be angry. Bin smacked or something downstairs. He knows all about death. Look how he trod on those ants."

"Perhaps he didn't like a king being dead. A king's not like an ant. He's coming with his beastly bottle."

Donald fell on the top step and his bottle was smashed. It had been the work of weeks. The stairs ran with spit and blood and tickled with broken glass. The house was rent. Mr. Brown, Mrs. Brown, Mi and all the sisters picked him up.

Mally cut her knee kneeling on the glass. Edwina read to Donald, who had to have a stitch in the ball of his foot. Mrs. Brown kept Merry to help her with the washing.

In the end Velvet took Sir Pericles and rode alone to Tablet Gully.

In Tablet Gully the piebald cropped, moving from tuft to tuft in sun and shadow, and flashing as he moved. The bone of his shoulder, thrown up by his stooping neck, rippled under his sliding skin. His parti-colored mane hung forward over his neck, and his long tail tipped the ground.

He swung round with the sun. His teeth tore evenly as he worked. Now his quarters could be seen, slightly pearshaped and faulty, but strong. His hocks, too thick, but straight and clean, waded in the burnt grasses. He lifted a sloping pastern finished with a pink hoof, and bit a fly off his leg. The clouds reared overhead, the legendary gully with its dead man's tablet was heavy with steady sun and shielded from the wind.

Among the scabious flowers on the north slope sat Velvet, steady as a gorse bush, cross-legged, and watching the horse. She had tied Sir Pericles to a gate in the valley behind her.

Sitting like a Buddha, dreaming of the horse, riding the horse in dreams. A piece of cake and a Mar's Bar beside her in a paper bag, and the insects hummed and the mauve August flowers hardly moved. Just to look at him her heart beat violently with ambition. Her strong and inexperienced imagination saw no barriers. She was capable of apprehending death and of conceiving fame—in her own way, not for herself but for her horse. For a shilling she had won this wild creature that did not know its strength. In this valley, tucked away, she had got glory. What she meant to do made her heart beat afresh. She looked steadily at the piebald as though she pitied him. Eating his grass, prince, with his kingdom waiting for him! Her hand stole out and pulled the Mar's Bar from its bag, and she sucked its heavy stump, made from milk chocolate, toffee and nuts.

All the Hullocks were creeping with dowdy animals at livery. But here in Tablet Gully moved on its clever legs this living horse. Pulling gently at a blister on her heel she rode him in her mind. She would dazzle the world with this spot of luck, she and the creature together, breathing like one body, trying even to death, till their hearts burst. She would place her horse where he belonged, in history. She clasped the Mar's Bar like a prophet's child, with both hands.

"Leaders have been cut from coaches to do it . . ." she whispered as she rose. "Even horses out of carts. Why not him?"

A halter made of rope lay behind her and picking it up she walked gently down the valley holding it behind her frock. The piebald stared at her, interested. He loved humanity, and had it not been for the exceptional grass in Tablet Gully would have been off to the village long before this.

Frankly he watched her come, nostrils slightly distended and both calm eyes upon her, the blue eye and that white eye where the pied color streaked across his cheek. She paused beside him and slipped the halter over his head. He shook his neck to free it from flies and came with her willingly.

They reached Sir Pericles, who snorted at sight of them and danced his hindquarters, looking from side to side, catching his soft nose on the reins. How could his mistress walk so out of valleys leading horses? He was intrigued and excited, jealous, pleased to see her again. Velvet loosed and mounted him, and the piebald walked sedately at their sides, striking out his forefeet in his own peculiar gait.

They reached a field not far away, enclosed by a stone wall, and Velvet changed the saddle and bridle,

110 ━

tying Sir Pericles with the halter to the gate. She mounted the piebald, and walked and trotted him quietly in large circles. His mouth was a mixture of lead and rubber. He had no notion how to obey the bit but imagined that to turn his neck was all that was wanted. He would trot onwards with his neck turned to one side like a horse that has no face. Velvet had to rock him with her knees to get him out of his orbit, and even then it was no more than a bewildered stagger to one side. She set him into a canter. It was clumsy and gallant, and accomplished with snorts. He flung his powerful white head up into the air and nearly smashed his rider's precious band. Sir Pericles watched. The flashing piebald snorted excitedly round the field. Above him sat the noble child, thin as famine, bony as a Roman, aquiline nose and domed white forehead, tufted loonily with her cotton hair. Velvet, with her great teeth and her parted lips, her eye sockets and the pale eyes in them, looked like a child model for a head of Death, an eager, bold, young Death. She was thinking of something far outside the field. She was thinking of horses, great horses, as she sat her horse.

Turning in a flash in the middle of the field she drove him on with her knees. They went at the wall together. Over the grasses, over the tufts and mounds, both knitted in excitement, the horse sprang to the surge of her heart as her eyes gazed between his ears at the blue top of the flint wall. She bent slightly and held him firm and steady, her hands buried in the flying mane firm on the stout muscles of his neck. She urged him no more, there was no need, but sat him still. He was a natural jumper. She did not attempt to dictate to him. They cleared the wall together, wildly, ludicrously high, with savage effort and glory, and twice the power and the force that was needed. Velvet felt his hindquarters drop when they should have hitched. But there was so much space to spare that the piebald could afford it. Nevertheless it was an intemperate and outlandish jump.

She rode him back to his own valley and loosed him, then returned home alone on Sir Pericles, parading in dreams. As she approached the village she was outlined against the sunset, on the brow of a Hullock. Stirrups short, angled knee and leg etched on the side of the saddle; childish, skeleton hands waving with the ebb and flow of the horse's mouth on the reins; hands that seemed knotted and tied like a bunch of flowers with streamers going from them, swinging together, knuckle to knuckle, thumb to thumb, while she sat erect above them, her face held on the wand of her body. The straw hair floated and stared above the wide-open eyes.

Sir Pericles walked like Velvet sat. His soft mouth held the snaffle as a retriever carries a bird. Yet he arched his neck as though his bit were a bit of thorns, and his long, almond, Chinese eyes looked both backward and forward at once. He seemed to be watching from either end of the agate stuff that was his window, watching Velvet's leg, watching the horizon before him. The oxygen in the evening air intoxicated him. In the eye of little Sir Pericles something soft and immortal shone.

Velvet had laid down the piebald and her ambitions and was thinking comfortably of the coming gymkhana. In her mind she rose at white-painted gates and fences. Her knees crisped with her thoughts in the saddle and she leaned forward. Sir Pericles never altered his tossing walk. His head and tail, both like plumes, flirted, and he walked within her dream with a spot of gold upon his eyeball.

It was not the silver cup standing above the wind-blown tablecloth that Velvet saw—but the perfection of accomplishment, the silken cooperation between two actors, the horse and the human, the sense of the lifting of the horse-soul into the sphere of human obedience, human effort, and the offering to it of the taste of human applause. All this she had learned already from the trained mouth and the kneeling will of Sir Pericles.

And as the dim sense of this understanding sighed up and down her body it entered too into Sir Pericles' nerves, and through his nerves to his comprehension. Velvet lived her round of jumps, lips parted, the sunset shining on her golden mouth. She rose and fell at the triple bar, the water jump, the gate, the imitation wall. She heard the hands, palm on palm, threshing the noise of applause. Sir Pericles dreamed it too, a wild dream beyond his understanding, but to be recognized when the taste came again.

His hoofs came down sweetly on violets, grass and knitted thyme, clanking on a flint, breaking the crisp edge of a wheel rut. He took in everything, behind, before, and from the body astride him. Below, the chimneys were smoking up like poplars and a light was lit in the cobbler's shop.

They sidled together down the steep grassy banks towards the village.

"Velvet!" said Mally out of the darkness by the bottom gate.

"That you, Mally. Open the gate."

"Who's wired it up like this?" Mally wrenched at the twist of wire. She opened it and horse and child passed through. "The piebald's out again. Nobody knew you bin riding him but us. Came thunderin' down the street ten minutes ago."

"Where's he now? Father angry?"

"Went down to the sea as usual, an' slid about. Went crackin' up a side street. Father doesn't know. Better not let him. He's bin carrying on about the horses. It would be the limit if he found the piebald had started cracking down the street again."

"F'e broke a leg!" said Velvet in a voice of horror. "F'e did! Might. Easily."

"You can't go after him now. It's pitch. Thurs stars coming."

Sir Pericles gave a whinny. There came a sharp, near answer, and the piebald stalked out of the shadows, gleaming in the dusk.

"He's here!" Velvet's marveling whisper, as she slipped off Sir Pericles and held out her hand. The piebald came nearer, breathing hard.

"Mount, mount!" said Mally. "Get on again! He'll follow. He won't think you want to catch him."

"What'll we do with him?" said Velvet as she scrambled back.

"I'll go an' get a halter and we'll try an' put him. . . . Put him in Miss Ada's box tonight and put her in the toolhouse!"

The piebald followed, threshing his head, snorting the pleasant village smells, till they reached the yard of the cottage. He drooped his neck for the halter like a horse born in a kitchen. Soon Miss Ada stood among the spades and shovels.

"Poor old darling Ada," said Velvet, as she pushed the shovels to safety behind a wooden case. "Get half the bedding from the loose-box, Mally. The piebald won't miss it. He's never had any before. I'll get Ada some oats to make her happy."

"What'll Father say . . . about the piebald being in?"

"He won't know. I'll take him back early in the morning."

"Bet he neighs in the night. We'll shut both doors. He might try and jump the bottom one. Let's give him . . . What'll we give him?"

"Just hay," said Velvet. "He's not accustomed to oats."

"D'you know . . ." said Mally suddenly, pausing with an armful of hay.

"What?"

"He'll be worse than ever after this. He'll be coming back every night to get a night's lodging and a supper! You never saw . . ."

"What?"

"The way he came down the village street, slipping and sliding and snorting and his eyes shining."

"He's like a prince!" said Velvet.

"Eh?"

"Just a thing I thought," said Velvet. "I pretend he's a prince."

At supper everyone ate with memories behind them. Edwina had been kissed by Teddy for the first time. Her nails had shocked and enchanted him. Merry had oiled the canary's stump, and was worrying about what she should call him. She had got a list of gods' names and a birthday list of girls'. It was so hard to know the sex of canaries.

Mally and Velvet were thinking of what they had got in the stable, the prince who might kick up a row in the night. Donald was asleep now, stitches in his foot, blood and spit mingled in his dreams. He yelped from time to time in his sleep like a puppy.

"Whur's Jacob?" said Mr. Brown suddenly as he ate.

"After the bitches," said Mi, with resentment.

"Seem bad this August."

"Bitches? Terrible they are. Crown's got one an' Ede's got one. That Jacob he . . ." Words failed, and slightly redder than before Mi continued to eat.

As the door opened for the pudding's entry they heard the impatient hammer of a hoof on wood. Mr. Brown continued to munch his bread. Mi sat up and his eyes flickered upon Velvet's face.

"I'm not hungry any more. Can I get down, Mother?" said Velvet.

"Say your grace," said Mr. Brown.

"F whatayave receivedthankGod," said Velvet, pushing her chair in, and went out in the dark. At the corner of the yard and the road four apple trees were enclosed by a broken fence. They were laden with little sweet apples and the ground was littered with the wind-blowings. She gathered two handfuls and went to the stable with them.

Mi hung about the yard all the evening, whistling for Jacob and looking down the road. Once he opened the top portion of the loose-box and looked in, grinning.

"Gettin' on all right?" he enquired. Velvet was sitting on the manger.

"He's quiet while I'm here," said Velvet. "But I can't stay here all night. Where's Father?"

"Gone down to finish the bills," said Mi. "I thought he better."

Later in the evening Mally swinging on the gate by the apple trees saw Jacob coming up the empty road.

"Bitches good?" she asked him, flinging him a block of lichen off the gate post.

"Succulent," said Jacob, making a half circle round her.

"Go an' tell Mi about it!" said Mally.

Jacob went, bowing and grinning. Mi walloped him and gave him his supper.

Later in the night the house was quiet, the piebald quiet (for he had Velvet in her nightgown sitting on his manger), the moon rose steadily. At two o'clock the moon began to sink. Mi came to the stable door and looked over the top. He wore his sleeping clothes, several old sleeveless jerseys, and a pair of shorts.

"Get to bed now," he said. "I'll do a bit."

Velvet lowered off the manger. "Here's six quarters left," she said, pointed in the manger. "Give him a piece every time he seems restless."

"What is it?"

"Apples," said Velvet. "I bin feeding him bits all night."

"You'll make him loose," said Mi. "Where's the sacking pieces?"

"In the corner. An' ties. Ties off the hay bales."

At five the sea was running up with a gale behind it and pounding in the sewer. The day broke in flashes of light and the elms soughed in the wind. The piebald's tail and mane were flung about as Mi led him out into the yard, his hoofs bound up in sacking. Velvet met them in the road.

"How'd you wake?" asked Mi.

"An't bin asleep," said Velvet. "I just heard the wind. Isn't he good!"

"Perisher," said Mi.

"Oh, no," said Velvet. "Oh, no. Wait while I get a bridle."

She returned with a sniffle-bridle belonging to Sir Pericles, one which they had brought in to clean the night before.

"Gimme a leg up, Mi," and he jumped her onto the warm, round back.

"Key of the field's behind the manger. Come up an' help me get Sir Pericles. I got to ride back on him."

Mi walked beside her up the road to the field in the gale.

"Blowing awful up there," he said, looking to the Hullocks.

"Seaweed's smelling like drains," said Velvet, looking at the wild and shining east.

" 'Tis drains," said Mi, sniffing. "Lota nonsense they talk about seaweed. You had anything to eat?"

"No, I forgot."

Mi grunted with disfavor. "Fer a sickly girl you give yerself something to do!" he said.

"An't sickly. M'wiry," said Velvet. "Shove the gate wider. I'll stub my knee!"

Sir Pericles trotted down gladly, tail flying.

"Halter's under the stone in the corner," said Velvet.

Mi picked it up. Sir Pericles came willingly enough. The two horses hustled clumsily through the gate.

"Good-by," said Velvet and went off across the reedy ditch, riding the piebald and leading the chestnut.

"Why don't you ride the other?" shouted Mi, but his voice blew back into his mouth as he called into the gale coming off the sea.

He watched the horses go up the chalk road and break into a canter on the crest. His old mackintosh flapped on his bare legs and the wind tore at the roots of his red hair. "If she were a boy . . ." he said longingly to himself. With that light body and grand heart he would get her into a racing stable. He knew of many up North. He had friends here and there. She'd be a great jockey some day. Fancy wasting those hands and that spirit and that light weight on a girl. "No more'n a skeleton," he said. "An' never will be, likely. She'd ride like a piece of lightning. No more weight'n a piece of lightning.'' He thought of her mother . . . and of his old father. ''Velvet an' her. A feather an' a mountain. But both the same.''

Boom . . . went the sea on the cliffs. The savage blow came up the valley. Mi hated water. Brought up by the Channel trainer he had edged back inland as soon as he could. He couldn't stand the waves and the empty trough that sucked and soaked along the lip of the beaches. It turned his head, and he went up the village whenever he thought of the sea. ''How she ever!'' he thought, with his mind's eye fixed sharp on Mrs. Brown. Great, wallowing woman, half submerged, water pouring backwards and forwards over her shoulders, threshing across the water like a whale. A stormy dawn when she had landed. ''Bet old Dan was pleased,'' he thought. ''Wasn't many swimming the Channel those days.''

His mind went back to Velvet. He too, like her, was longing to place his dream in history. This child, Velvet, was good for something.

He turned back to his bed, shivering, Velvet in his thoughts.

And hungry, sick, delicate, blown so that she could hardly breathe, Velvet in the grip of horses and of the gale went on across the blunt and unprotected Hullocks. Great skies slipped out of the folds, unfurled, and stood a thousand miles above her. The sight battered against unseeing eyeballs, was drunk into the marrow of something older than her brain. Flags and pennons and beacons waved above the high land as she sat below, thinking in slow brown drops of thought, sure of her future, counting her plans, warm in expectation, glorious butcher's Velvet, eyes cast down upon the moving shoulders of mortal horses.

~EIGHT~

Mi raised thirty shillings for the gymkhana. He borrowed it from his girl for Velvet's sake. That is to say he treated love worse than he treated adventure.

"Your girl," said Velvet, frowning in thought. "Which girl? Didn't know you had a girl."

"Nor I had. Met her at the dance last night," said Mi. "Pleased as Punch, she was. Lent me the money too." So Mi behaved badly, and Velvet knew it. But neither she nor Mi cared when they set their minds firm.

On the day of the gymkhana, about mid-morning, it grew suddenly very hot and the rain came down in sheets. Inside the living room, polishing the bits, it was like the tropics. The girls' faces were wet. Rain came down outside on full leaves, making a rattle and a sopping sound. Everything dripped. The windows streamed. The glass was like glycerine.

"Oh, lord," said Mally, "oh, dear, oh, lord!"

"We've only two mackintoshes. Velvet's has stuck to the wall in the hot cupboard. Won't it rain itself out?"

"The grass'll be slippery. What about their shoes being roughed?"

"We've no money," said Velvet, "for roughing."

"If Mi had a file . . ." said Mally.

"A file's no good. You want nails in."

"I'm sweating," said Edwina. "Can't we have a window open?"

She opened the yard window and the rain came cracking in over the cactus.

"Hot's a pit in here!" said Mi, coming in from the yard and taking off his dripping coat. "The yard's swimming. Everything's floating."

"Will they put it off?"

"The gymkhana? No, it'll be over soon. It's a waterspout. There's a great light coming up the way the wind's coming from. Your ma going to serve the dinner early?"

"Yes, at twelve," said Edwina. "We better clear now. Put the bridles and things in the bedroom. Better Father doesn't see too much of it!"

"He knows, doesn't he?" said Meredith.

"Yes, he knows, but he doesn't want to think too much about it."

At dinner they had sardines instead of pudding. Mrs. Brown always served sardines for staying power. Dan had dropped them into her mouth from the boat as she crossed the Channel.

Donald considered his on his plate.

"I'll take your spines out, Donald," said Meredith.

"I eat my spines," said Donald.

"No, you don't, Donald. Not the big spine. The little bones but not the big one in the middle. Look how it comes out!"

"I eat my spines, I say," said Donald firmly with rising color, and held her knife-hand by the wrist.

"But look . . . they come out lovely!" said Merry, fishing with the fork. The spine of the slit sardine dangled in the air and was laid on the edge of the plate. Quick as lightning Donald popped it into his mouth with his fingers and looked at her dangerously.

"I crunch up my spines, I like them," he said.

"Leave him alone," said Mother.

"D'you eat your tails too?" said Merry vexedly.

"I eat my tails and my spines," said Donald, and the discussion was finished.

At one the rain stopped and the sun shone. The grass was smoldering with light. The gutters ran long after the rain had stopped.

"Keep up on the hog," said Velvet, as the horses moved along. "We don't want 'em splashed. Gutters are all boggy." They were well on the way to the gymkhana, held in the football field at Pendean.

"We look better in our mackintoshes!" called Mally. "I'm glad it rained."

"I'm steamy," said Edwina. "Merry, you can wear mine. You'll look better."

"I'm all right. I don't want it, thank you, Edwina."

But Edwina was struggling out of her mackintosh. "You'll look better. You're all untidy. . . . Put it on!"

"I don't want it!"

"You're a bully, 'Dwina," said Mally. "You jus' want to get rid of it an' not sweat."

They turned up a chalk road between a cutting and in a few minutes they could see below them the gathering of horse vans in the corner of Pendean field, the secretary's flagged tent, white-painted jumps dotting the course, and a stream of horses and ponies drawing along the road below.

The soaking land was spread below them, and the flat road of the valley shone like a steel knife. Getting off their horses they led them down the chalk path between blackberry bushes, and in ten minutes of slithering descent they were at the gates of the gymkhana field.

"Competitors' passes," murmured Edwina and showed their pasteboard tickets.

They picked out a free tree in the field and established themselves.

"Here's someone's program!" said Mally. "Squashed and lost. Sixpence saved!"

They crowded round to read it.

After endless waiting the band arrived. Then the local broadcaster rattled up, mounted on its ancient Ford, and settling into its position against the ropes, began to shout in bleak, mechanical tones . . . "Event Number One! Event Number One! Competitors in the Collecting Ring, please . . . PLEASE."

Instantly the field was galvanized. Children and ponies appeared from behind trees and hedges and tents. Mally mounted George and rode towards the ring.

In five minutes it was over and Mally was back again. George had had no idea of bending. Nor Mally either. They had broken three poles on the way up and were disqualified.

"We haven't practiced!" said Mally, trying to carry it off.

But Velvet, busy saddling Mrs. James, made no reply.

"Here's Jacob!" said Edwina suddenly. Jacob sprang lightly against Mrs. James's flank and grinned. "Mi must be here."

"Event Number Two!" shouted the Voice, and Vel-

vet mounted, and made for the Collecting Ring. Seeing
Pendean Lucy waiting at the gate for the first heat, she
thrust up beside her. The bar fell and Velvet, Lucy and
three others, two boys and a fat little girl, were let out
to the potato posts.

"You know what to do?" shouted the starter, his flag
under his arm. "Leave the posts on your right! Take
the furthest potato first! . . ."

Velvet tried to take it in but the trembling of Mrs.
James distracted her attention. Mrs. James had broken
already into a sweat of hysteria that had turned her grey
coat steel-blue.

They were lined up, the flag fell, and Mrs. James
made a start of such violence that Velvet could not pull
her up at the fifth post. Six strides were lost before they
could turn. Lucy was cantering down the posts with her
potato and Velvet heard the jingle of the bucket as the
potato fell neatly into it. The heat was over, and Mrs.
James, too big, too wild, too excited, too convinced that
she was once again playing polo, was left three potatoes
behind when the winner had drawn up beside the Starter.
Pendean Lucy won the first heat. . . .

"Five shillings gone . . ." muttered Velvet with hu-
miliation as she trotted slowly back to the tree. Mi was
there standing beside Sir Pericles.

"Five shillings gone, Mi," said Velvet aloud to him.

"It's a gamble," said Mi. "Keep yer head. Afternoon's young."

"Jumping . . ." said Mally. "It's the jumping now.
Which you jumping first?"

"Sir Pericles."

The blazing sun had dried up the burnt grass and the
afternoon shone like a diamond as Velvet sat on Sir
Pericles in the Collecting Ring. Mi wormed his way

between the crowds against the rope. Lucy came on her roan pony, but the pony refused at the Gate. Twice and thrice times, and she trotted back disqualified. A schoolboy in a school cap quartered in purple and white, rode out. His almost tailless pony jumped a clear round. Jacob wriggled with excitement between Mi's legs.

"Number Sixteen!" called the Broadcaster.

Sixteen was Lucy's elder sister, a fat girl in a bright blue shirt.

"Blasted girl!" said Mi under his breath, as the blue shirt cleared the first and second jumps. His heart was in his mouth, but he spat whistlingly and joyfully between his teeth as the pony landed astride the wall, and scrambled over in a panic, heaving the wall upon its side.

It seemed they would call every number in the world except Velvet's.

"Break her nerve, waiting!" grumbled Mi. He could see her cotton hair bobbing as she sat.

A small girl came, with pigtails. A little shriek burst from her throat each time her chestnut pony rose at a jump. The plaits flew up and down, the pony jumped like a bird. A clear round.

"Darn!" said Mi. "Two clear rounds."

"Number Fifteen!"

Out came Velvet from the black gap between the crowds. Sir Pericles arched his neck, strained on his martingale, and his long eyes shone. He flirted his feet in his delicious doll's canter and came tittupping down over the grass. Velvet in her cotton frock stood slightly in the stirrups, holding him short—then sat down and shortened her reins still more. Mi's stomach ran to soup.

"Got her stirrups in her armpits . . ." sighed Mi approvingly. "Little swell!"

There was nothing mean, nothing poor about Sir Pericles. He looked gay as he raced at the first jump.

"Too fast, too fast!" said Mi, praying with his soul.

The horse was over safely and had his eyes fastened on the next jump.

"Haul 'im in, haul 'im in!" begged Mi of the empty air. "He'll rocket along . . ." He saw Velvet's hands creep further up the reins, and her body straighten itself a little. The horse's pace decreased. It was the double jump, the In-and-Out. Sir Pericles went over it with his little hop—one landing and one take-off. Mi saw Velvet glance behind—but nothing fell. And the Gate. The Gate was twelve paces ahead.

He cleared the Gate with one of his best jumps, an arc in the air, with inches to spare.

"He'll do the wall," said Mi with relief.

He did the wall, but a lath fell at the stile. Half a fault. She was out of it then. Mi yawned with fatigue. He had held his breath. His lungs were dry. Jacob was gone from between his legs. He looked round, then turned again to the ropes to wait for the piebald.

There were no more clear rounds till the piebald came, and when it came a murmur went up from the villagers who stood in the crowd.

"Jumping *that* animal!" said a voice.

"Why, that's the one she won at the raffle!"

The piebald strode flashing into the sun. He paused, stood still, and gazed round him. Velvet's knees held him steadily, and she sat behind his raised neck without urging him on.

"I don't expect anything . . ." she whispered. "Do what you can. Keep steady. You're all right."

"You next," said a man at the bar of the Collecting Ring. "You waiting for anything?"

"I'm going," said Velvet quietly. "He just wants to look round."

Mi saw them come down the grass, the piebald trotting with a sort of hesitation.

"He's in two minds whether he'll bolt," thought Mi.

"Showy horse . . ." said a spectator.

"Butcher's girl . . ." said another. "The youngest. Got a seat, 'ant she?"

The piebald's best eye was towards the crowd, his white eye to the center of the field.

The trot broke hesitatingly into a canter, but the horse had no concentration in him. He looked childishly from side to side, hardly glancing at the jump ahead.

"He'll refuse," said Mally, who had arrived at Mi's side. But Mi made no answer.

Sir Pericles had jumped like a trained horse. The piebald's jumping was a joke. Arrived at the jump in another two paces, he appeared to be astonished, planted his forelegs for a second, looked down, trembled, then leapt the little bush and rail with all four legs stiff in the air together. Dropping his hindquarters badly he came down on the rail and broke it in two.

"Two faults," said Mi.

"Only two for breaking that?"

"Hind feet. Only two."

Again the piebald trotted, flashing, his grass-fed belly rounded, and his shoulders working under the peculiar color of his hide.

"Why don't she canter 'im?" said a voice.

Mi turned on the voice. "First time he's seen anything but his own grazing. It's a miracle if she gets him round."

"The In-and-Out'll finish him," said Mally under her breath.

The piebald jumped willingly into the In-and-Out, then paused, and remained inside.

A shout of laughter went up from the crowd.

"Oh . . . poor Velvet . . ." murmured Malvolia, agonized.

The piebald attempted to graze, as though he were in a sheep pen, and again the crowd laughed.

"She's handling him gentle," said Mi. "She's trying to keep him thinking he's a winner. She's backin' him, see. . . . I don't believe he's ever backed a pace before." The piebald had backed two paces till his quarters lay against the first jump of the In-and-Out. With a light heart he responded to his rider, and with a spring he was out again and cantering on.

"Do they count that as a fault?"

"I don't know," said Mi. "Watch out . . . now. . . . It's the Gate."

The piebald broke the gate. He would have liked a stout, stone wall, but this flimsy thing that stood up before him puzzled him and he did his goat-jump. All four legs in the air at once and landed back upon the laths and broke them.

"That horse is breaking up the field," said a voice.

Mi glared. "He's knocking his hock," said Mi; "that'll learn him." For the piebald limped a pace or two. It "learned" him. Unlettered as he was he had no thought of refusing. He saw the friendly wall ahead, and taking it to be enduring flint he went for it with a glare of interest, ears pricked and eyes bright. The wall was three foot six. He leapt five. For a second it seemed to the crowd as though the horse had nothing to do with the wall but was away up in the air. A little cheer went up and hands clapped in a burst.

"Don't she ride him!" said the voice. "It's that Velvet girl. The ugly one."

"What, that kid with the teeth?"

"That's who it is."

Mi knew that Mally's beauty stood beside him and he resented it. He half turned his shoulder on her. While Velvet sat the piebald he thought her the loveliest thing on earth. Like Dan, his father, he hardly saw the faces of women.

"Hullo, she's missed the stile!"

"Did he refuse?" asked Mi, keenly.

"I don't think she saw it," said Mally. "She simply rode on."

The judge waved his stick and called to a Starter. Velvet cantered, glowing, radiant, to the exit gate. The man who held the exit spoke to her and pointed. Velvet looked behind her, paused, then shook her head.

"Not coming . . ." shouted the man to the Steward.

After a brief pause . . .

"The last Competitor," announced the Broadcaster, "did not complete the round."

"Why ever didn't she!" said Mally, as she and Mi left the rope to fight their way round to the tree. They scrambled out from the crowd and ran.

Velvet was standing looking at the piebald as though bemused. Merry, her face happy with pride, was holding the horses.

"Marvelous, Velvet, to get him round!" said Mally, coming up. "Why didn't you jump the last jump?"

Velvet turned and looked, and Mi could see how her face was shining.

"I thought I'd better not," she said gently.

"Why?"

"He did the wall so beautifully I thought he'd better end on that."

In a flash Mi felt again what she was made of. That she could take a decision for her horse's good and throw away her own honors.

"It was the right thing to do," said Mi.

Edwina arrived. "What made you miss the stile?"

Velvet said nothing.

"People near me thought you'd funked it," said Edwina half indignantly. "You must have bin asleep to go and miss it."

"She's no more asleep 'n my eye," said Mi. And Mi's little eye, like an angry sapphire, raked Edwina till she shuffled her shoulder and itched.

"It's you, Edwina, now!" said Mally, looking at the torn program. "On Mrs. James. Bending."

"A lot of chance I have!" said Edwina. "Mrs. James'll break every pole."

"She gets rough and excited," said Velvet.

"But it's Adults!" said Merry. "They won't have nippy ponies. It'll be easier."

But the Adults were seated on the smallest ponies they could ride. They looked like giants on dogs. Every grown-up was riding his sister's pony, and Mrs. James, galloping like a wild animal, nostrils blowing and eyes rolling, broke all the poles she could break. Edwina led her back without a word, disgusted and silent.

It began to rain. Merry put a sack round her shoulders and pulled out the *Canary Breeder's Annual*. Edwina left them and went towards the tent.

"She got any money?" said Mally, looking after her keenly.

"Can't have," said Velvet. "She was broke yesterday."

130 ～

"P'raps she's got twopence for an Idris. Wish I had a crunchie," muttered Mally.

"Kandy Korner's got a stall here," said Merry, reading. "What's happened now?"

"It's the tea interval," said Velvet gloomily. They had won nothing. They had made not a penny. They owed Mi thirty bob.

The rain slid, tapping, through the branches, and swept in windy puffs across the field.

It made a prison for them, it pressed them into a corner of life, a corner of the heart. They were hung up. Velvet was hung up in life. Where was she? A butcher's daughter, without money, in debt, under suzerainty, an amateur at her first trial of skill, destined that night to a bed of disappointment among the sleeping canaries. She did not think like that. But cared only that the piebald had jumped one jump as she had dreamt he might jump, with power, with crashing confidence. He was ignorant but he had no stage nerves. Of her own powers she had no thought.

Staring out into the lines of rain, lightly she lifted her hands and placed them together in front of her, as though she held the leathers. So acute was the sensation of the piebald beneath her that she turned with surprise to see him standing under the dripping branches. A look of simplicity and adoration passed into her face, like the look of the mother of a child who has won honors. She had for him a future.

The rain came down in long knitting needles. Backwards and forwards blew the needles, as the wind puffed. Wet horses, wet mackintoshes, wet dogs, wet flapping of tents, and then as the storm was rent a lovely flushing of light in the raindrops. Wind blew the sky into hollows and rents.

"That Violet that Mi met, she's at Kandy Korner," said Merry. "Serving with them for a week on approval."

"We can't borrow from her if she's only an approval. She'll get into trouble."

"Mi," said Velvet, looking round the tree, "you round there? Is it dryer there?"

"No."

"Your Violet's with Kandy Korner. Got a stall down here."

Silence. Displeasure.

"You couldn't touch her for another twopence."

"Not till I see daylight with that thirty bob."

Edwina had gone off with one of the mackintoshes. The saddles were heaped under the other. Merry, Mally and Velvet flattened themselves, shivering, against the tree-trunk.

"There's Mother!" said Velvet suddenly.

Across the field, swaying like a ship at sea, came the red and yellow meat van.

"She's brought tea!" said Merry.

"She'll thread my needle!" said Velvet.

Mally ran out into the open and waved. The van nosed and swayed towards them.

"Father's driving! If he stops . . . He'll never let you race, Velvet!"

"Stop him buying the program if you can! Here, tear ours . . . give him the wrong half! Then he won't buy another."

Velvet snatched up the program and tore a little piece out with her thumbnail. The van drew up under the tree. Mi opened the door and the giant bulk of Mrs. Brown descended backwards.

"We've done nothing, Mother! Nothing at all!" said Mally.

"That's bad," said Mrs. Brown. "Here's your tea."

"I'm not stopping," said Mr. Brown, from the wheel. "There's a sugar box in the back. Pull it out for your mother to sit on. You're wet through, the lot of you. You ought to come home."

"Coats is soppy," said Mrs. Brown. "How's your vests?"

"Dry," said Velvet, edging away. "Dry's a bone."

"You stay for one more race or whatever you call it," said Mr. Brown, "an' then you'll take them hosses home. I'll be back to fetch Mother."

"But we've PAID . . ." began Velvet in horror. The self-starter whirred and he was gone.

"Does he mean it, Mother?"

"You're dripping," said Mrs. Brown, cutting up a Madeira cake. "Mi, come round here an' get some food."

The cake grew wet even as they ate it.

"What's the next?" said Mother. "Gimme the list." She studied it for a moment.

"That's next, Mother," said Velvet, pointing.

"Was your name in it?" asked Mrs. Brown, looking at the hole.

"Yes . . . it was. 'Tis."

There was a long pause and Mrs. Brown slowly stroked her chin. Mi looked down on her old felt hat in which a pool of rain was settling. Velvet ran one nail under the other and shot out a piece of earth.

"I'll thread your needle," said Mrs. Brown at last.

Velvet looked into the heavy eyes and smiled. The eyes blinked with the violence and worship of the glance.

The voice of the broadcaster came roughly through the wind and rain.

"Event Number Five," said the Voice . . . "Competitors for Event Number Five . . . go to the Collecting Ring."

Sir Pericles was saddled in a moment, and Mrs. Brown rose to her feet.

"Where'd I stand?" she asked.

"Mi'll take you. Mi! It's right far up there."

Mrs. Brown walked like a great soldier up the field.

In Velvet's heat she was the only child. She rode out of the gate of the Collecting Ring with four others—two livery-stablemen from Worthing, a grizzled woman with short hair and a hanging underlip, and a young man in checks on a hired horse with poverty streaks.

"I've plenty of chance," she thought. "I'm lighter than any of them." All the horses were dripping and began to steam with excitement.

"Be slippery at the corner there," said one of the livery-stablemen.

They reached the starting post, and the sodden starter came down towards them.

The faces, shining in the rain, looked back at him. The young man in the check suit lay up on the inside against the rail. The woman with the hanging lip scowled at him and edged her horse nearer. Velvet came next, and on the outside the two stablemen. The flag was raised. Before it could fall the young man made a false start. While he was getting back into position the grizzled woman took his place.

"Don't shove!" said the young man, but the woman made no reply. Up went the flag again and the bounding of Velvet's heart swept Sir Pericles forward.

"Get back . . . that child!" shouted the starter.

Velvet swung Sir Pericles back behind the line and brought him up. The flag fell again neatly as she got him square. She drove for the center of the first hurdle. Out of the corner of her eye she saw the grizzled woman's horse run out. The young man in the checks she never saw again. Perhaps he never started. As she landed she saw a horse and man on the ground beside her. The heat was between Velvet and one livery-stableman.

Sir Pericles, the little creature, brilliant and honest, never looked to right or left but stayed where Velvet drove him, straight at the middle of each hurdle. He fled along the grass, jumping as neatly as a cat, swung round the sharp, uphill corner towards the table where the sewers stood, Velvet kicking the stirrups free, neck and neck with the livery-man on a blue roan. The roan drew ahead. The sewers' table neared. Velvet flung herself off as they drew up; her feet ran in the air, then met the ground and ran beside the horse.

"What have you got off for?" said Mrs. Brown calmly, as she began to sew.

Velvet glanced with horror at her rival, leaning from his saddle while a tall girl sewed at his sleeve. "Oh . . ." she breathed. She had forgotten the instructions. She had had no need to dismount.

But Mrs. Brown's needle flashed in and out, while the blue roan fidgeted and danced, and the tall girl pivoted on her feet.

It was an easy win for Velvet. She was in the saddle, off, and had time to glance behind, before the roan had started. She heard his galloping feet behind her but he never caught her up and Sir Pericles went steadily down the grassy slope, jumping his hurdles with willing care.

A burst of clapping and cheers went up.

"Stay in the field!" said a steward. "Wait for the other heats to be run." Velvet sat alone in the rain, in a cloud of steam from the excited horse. One by one the winners of the three heats joined her.

The first was a boy of about nineteen, with a crooked jaw. Steaming and shining and smiling he rode up to her on a brown horse with a hunter build, long tail and mane.

"You did a good one!" he said to her.

"I'd only one to beat," she said, "and even then it was the button that did it."

"That's a beautiful little horse," said the boy. "He's *neat*."

They turned to watch the finish of the next heat.

They were joined by a fat little man in a bowler hat, a dark grey riding coat and soaking white breeches. He took off his bowler as he rode towards them and mopped his shining bald head. His horse was a grey.

"What a horse . . ." he said as he rode up. "I hired him. Couldn't hold him fer a minute. Just went slap round as though he'd got a feed at the winning post. I'll never pull it off a second time, not unless he chooses to! Lands on his head too, every time. Not a bit of shoulder."

"The saddle looks too big for him," said the boy. "It's right up his neck. But he's a grand goer."

"It's right up his neck, an' so'm I," said the little man, dismounting. "It's the way he jumps. Next round I'll be down and off and rolling out of your light! Here's the last! It's Flora Banks!"

"Who's she?" said the boy.

"Tough nut from Bognor," said the little man under his breath.

Flora Banks wore a yellow waistcoat, had a face like

a wet apple and dripping grey hair. She rode astride on a bay horse that looked like a racer, lean and powerful and fully sixteen hands. Velvet's heart sank.

"My poor Flora," said the little man calmly, bringing out a match, "you've got an overreach. You're out of it!"

The Tough Nut was off her bay in a second, flung her cigarette into the grass and knelt and took the bleeding forefoot tenderly in her hands. The big bay hung his head like a disappointed child. He was out of it. She led him, limping, away.

"Makes us three," said the little man, mopping his head. "Two really. I can't last another round. You go it, little girl, an' get the fiver. Hi, they're calling us."

Down went the three horses to the starting posts, reins slipping in cold fingers, rain whirling in puffs. Velvet's breath would not sink evenly on the downward stroke. She shuddered as she breathed.

"Lay up against the rails, little girl," said the bowler hat. "I'm so fast you can't beat me whatever you do, but I'm coming off. Where's that Starter? Goin' to keep our hearts beating while he drinks his coffee? Hi, where's that Starter? The blighter's drinkin' coffee!"

The Starter burst out of a little tent wiping his mouth and ran through the raindrops that suddenly grew less. The miraculous sun broke all over the soaking field. The freshness was like a shout. Velvet shaded her eyes, for the start was into the west. Water, filled with light, shone down the grass. The flag was raised and fell.

The boy on the brown horse got a bad start. Velvet and the little man rose together at the first hurdle. Velvet had the inside and the grey lay behind her. At the second hurdle she heard him breathe, then lost him. At the slight curve before the third hurdle he had drawn up on her inside, between her and the rail. She had lost her advantage.

Suddenly the boy on the brown appeared on her left. Both the grey and the brown drew ahead and Velvet strung out a near third. Like hounds over a wall they rose, one, two, three over the fourth hurdle and went sweeping round the uphill curve to the table.

Mrs. Brown stood like an oak tree. Velvet galloped and drew up in a stagger beside her, throwing the single rein loose on Sir Pericles' neck. She stooped and hung over him, kicking both feet free from the stirrups to steady him. Trembling, panting, his sides heaving in and out he stood, his four feet still upon the ground, like a bush blown by a gale but rooted. Mrs. Brown's needle flashed.

Velvet was off, stirrups flying, down the grass hill, the blazing light no longer in her eyes, going east. First the grey, then the brown, were after her. At the fifth hurdle the grey passed her, but the brown never drew near. The grey was wound up to go. Its hindquarters opened and shut like springs in front of her. She saw it rise at the sixth hurdle just ahead of her, and come down almost upon its head. It slowed. As she drew up she saw the little man was done, stretched up unnaturally on its neck. He took a year falling. She passed him while he was still at it—jumped the seventh and eight hurdles and whispered to herself as the noise went up behind the ropes, "A fiver . . ." And the piebald's glistening future spread like a river before her, the gates of the world all open. She pulled up, flung herself off Sir Pericles and glanced down at his feet.

He was all right. And the Steward was examining her button . . . That was all right too! Here came the sisters . . . The little man in the bowler, unhurt, was leading his horse down the track. Mrs. Brown . . . Where was Mother? Mi was by her side.

"Lead him off! Don't stand there! You look daft," said Mi lovingly, and his little blue eyes winked and shone. "Good girl, Velvet!" said Mr. Croom as she neared the exit. And hands patted her and voices called.

The ruthless voice of the Broadcaster was gathering competitors for the next event.

"Thirty shillings is yours, Mi."

"You'll have to give me forty. I want ten to get me teeth out of pawn."

"You put them in again?"

"I had to. Hadn't nothing."

"How is it they're so valuable, Mi?"

"Mass o' gold. My old dad got 'em done. He said, 'You always got money on you if you got gold in your mouth.' I can raise ten shillings on them most towns."

"You whistle better without them."

"Yes, I do," said Mi. "Where's that Jacob?"

It was the evening, before supper. They had turned the horses into the field after a good meal, and the piebald in with them. He had shown no sign of kicking. He trotted happily about among the new companions, his tail raised in an arch and his nostrils blown out with excitement. Velvet leaned on the gate and Mi stood beside her. The others had gone home before them down the road, clinking the buckets.

"Sir Pericles was lovely," said Velvet for the twentieth time. Mi was tired of grunting assent. The reddest sun that ever sank after a wet day went down behind them and sent streams of light through rushes and branches. Mi shaded his eyes to look for Jacob, that thorn in his side.

"Was The Lamb really only fourteen-two?" asked Velvet casually.

"Some say fourteen-two. Some say fifteen."

"Smallest horse ever won the National, wasn't he?"

"Won it twice."

"You ever bin round there?"

"The course? Know every stick. Been on it hundreds a times."

"What's the highest jump?"

Mi gazed into the field. He stuck his chin towards the piebald. "He jumped as high as any today."

"I thought he did," said Velvet, low and happy.

There was a long silence. The fields rolled uphill. The hedge at the top of the field was indigo. Sir Pericles was cropping, like a tawny shadow against it. The piebald, disturbed and excited, cantered the length of the hedge, neighing. Sir Pericles looked up, kicked gaily at the empty air, and cantered too. Mrs. James rolled an eye and laid her ears back.

Evenings, after triumphs, are full of slack and fluid ecstasy. The air swims with motes, visions dip into reach like mild birds willing to be caught. Things are heavenly difficult, but nothing is impossible. Here stood gazing into the field in the sunset the Inspirer, the Inspired and, within the field, the Medium.

Under his boil of red hair Mi's thoughts were chattering "Why not?"

And beside him Velvet looked, throbbing with belief, at her horse.

"Pity *you* don't ride," said Velvet at last.

"The rider's all right," said Mi mystically.

"What rider?"

"You."

A pause.

"There's jockeys from Belgium," said Mi, following the insane thread of thought, "no one's ever seen before. Who's to know?"

"You think he could do it?"

"The two of you could do it."

"Mi . . . oh, Mi . . ."

Pause.

"Who'd you write to? Fer entries."

"Weatherby's."

"Where are they?"

"Telephone book. London somewhere."

"Weatherby's."

There are evenings, full of oxygen and soft air, evenings after rain (and triumph) when mist curls out of the mind, when reason is asleep, stretched out on a low beach at the bottom of the heart, when something sings like a cock at dawn, a long-drawn, wild note.

Velvet and Mi dreamed a boldness bordering on madness.

The race was being run in stage light, under the lamps of the mind. The incandescent grass streamed before Velvet's eyes. There was an unearthly light around the horses, their rumps shone. The white of the painted rails was blue-white like ice. The grass snaked in green water under the horses' feet. There was a thunder rolling in the piebald like a drum. His heart, beating for the great day of his life.

"Weatherby's," said Velvet again. The word was a gateway to a great park. You could touch it, crisp, crested, full of carving . . . *Weatherby's.* Green grass, white rails, silk jackets. Through the arch of Weatherby's.

"Who's to know I'm a girl?" said Velvet, very, very far along the road.

Mi was not far behind her.

"Just wants thinking out," he said. His belly felt hollow with the night air. "Supper, Velvet." Slowly they left the gate and walked towards the village.

"Once I caught a dove," said Donald, sitting up to supper on the gymkhana night.

"Oh, no," said Mrs. Brown absently.

"I did," said Donald. "It was in . . . July. When you was in France."

"Never bin to France but once," said Mrs. Brown. And suddenly the soles of her feet tingled with the sting of Calais cobbles, slipping, slipping under her tired weight. Memories surged up. In the air tonight, this gymkhana night, when little Velvet had touched the tail of glory, there was something abroad.

"It was on the roof," said Donald.

(Coming up out of the water in the early dawn after a gale . . .)

"I put a ladder up. A man gave it to me. I caught it in my hand."

Silence . . .

"I EAT it," said Donald quietly, and looked round.

"Poor dove," said Velvet kindly, as nobody said anything.

"It said I could eat it," said Donald.

(The water had been kinder than the beach. She had been exposed in front of thousands, dripping, huge, shapeless, tired. She had been held up by her soaking legs and chaired to the hotel. The battle with the water had been pure and dark, but in the morning she began to wonder why she had done it. Dan had been pleased. It was for Dan that she had done it. He had made a warfare between the water and her strength and courage.

She had never thought of the crowds on the beach, the cameras, and newspapers. She had a sense of honor and chastity as sharp as a needle, and she had been outraged. Great burning virgin as close as an oyster and dark as the water at night. Stupid, fierce, honorable, strong and courageous. She and Dan could have opened a new world together, he directing, she enduring. She could have been a great mare whom a jockey rode to victory. Dimly behind the hooded eyes of the innocent and savage mother those aspirations washed.)

"It was that dove that made me sick . . ." said Donald.

"Shut up with that dove," said Mr. Brown, reading his paper.

~ NINE ~

After three days of gale the sea's surface lay in an oily, molded condition, yellow as clay, folds thick as treacle and casting shadows. Gulls tipped in the dun valleys and rose on the crests. No water broke. The clouds tumbled and heaved, subsiding, and shadows like the shadows of creatures streaked the sea.

After imprisonment of wind and rain the washing flew in banners down the gardens. Velvet mooched about the village, basking, her clothes and face dappled with sun. Little boys carried tires to the yellow sea and floated in them. The village stank of seaweed.

By the head of the shore stood a singing mendicant, mouth yapping aimlessly, a thread of aged sound coming from him.

Edwina walked lightly down the street with Teddy. Teddy carried his beach gramophone and Edwina's bathing dress. They waved to Velvet leaning on the cobbled wall and went down the gap to the beach. They did not want her and she did not want them. There was nothing sad about that.

There are pleasures earlier than love. A may tree, a cat's back will evoke them. Earlier than love, nearer heaven. As Velvet leaned on the wall and heard the cries of Teddy's gramophone she would not have changed her bliss for theirs.

She turned and saw Meredith coming towards her and the two watched the gulls idly, side by side.

"I could eat," said Meredith, yawning.

"M'm," said Velvet. She held the money bags.

After she had given Mi the forty shillings she had put three pounds in the Post Office Savings Bank. But Mr. Brown, pleased with the performance at the gymkhana, had given her five shillings. She had wanted to bank this too but there had been outcry among the sisters.

"Come on, Velvet," urged Meredith. Velvet pulled out two shillings, and laid them in a crack on the top of the wall. One of the shillings she put back again.

"We'll have one between us."

"Doughnuts?"

"We can't eat six doughnuts each."

"We'll have," said Merry, "one doughnut each, one candle-grease bun, one crunchie, one Mars . . ."

"I should be sick," said Velvet decidedly.

"Perhaps sixpence between us is enough. One doughnut each, and one crunchie."

"You go an' get them then. An' bring me back the sixpence."

Velvet lolled happily on the hot wall, just tickled and touched awake by the idea of approaching food. The juices in her mouth got ready. An airplane flew over her head, spewing advertisements in smoke. She turned on her back with her shoulders over the wall to read what it wrote.

"Buy Nougat Nobs" she read, written across the pale blue seat of God.

"Did you see the airplane?" said Merry suddenly beside her. "I got Nougat Nobs instead of crunchies."

"Well, you can have 'em," said Velvet. "It'll bust my blessed band."

"Thanks," said Merry contentedly, not protesting.

Meredith somnolent, loved her food, lived in dreams, loved her canaries, was inaccurate, incurable, and never quarreled.

Standing against the sunny wall, she had soon overeaten, and undid the ends of her hard leather belt. The screaming of the canaries never really ceased for Meredith. As she ate slowly her head was full of yellow wings. Dreadnoughts and Rollers and Hartz Mountain and mating. Mating was her preoccupation. If you mated a Hartz Mountain to a Roller . . . or a Yorkshire Dreadnought—what about the green streaks on the wings? Would they be increased if Mountain Jim were mated to Arabella? She leaned back against the wall to ease her stomach and dreamed on. A child, when it has overeaten, does not get a clouded brain.

In her mind the mating always took place safe and sure and certain, and with instant results, She saw a long line of descendants almost simultaneously created. She felt the power of the Patriarch; looking down her family line, and rambling, slow and vague she told a story to herself. Her memory tracks were scored by the noise of their songs wherever she walked. Constantly she was eased by dreams and sensations of flight. Some day she would construct a real aviary, real trees inside the wire netting, and she herself would walk inside the birdhouse and call the birds off the branches onto her shoulders.

146 ⬤

"Where's that sixpence?" said Velvet suddenly.

Meredith handed her fourpence.

"I got an extra two doughnuts," she said. "I was simply frightfully . . ."

"What?" said Velvet.

"Hungry," said Merry.

There was a long, sun-warmed, friendly silence.

"I wish I could eat like that," said Velvet with a sigh.

"You're nearly the youngest. You're weak," said Merry, fallacious tags of breeding in her mind. "You can breed a hen right out."

"Mother's not bred out. Just look at her!" said Velvet, irking. "And Donald's not weak!"

"I shouldn't think strength matters," said Merry, yawning. "It's guts."

"Mother says I'll get over being sick," said Velvet. How often had she had assurance from the calm and rocklike eyes. Above the paunchy cheeks, eyes that held neither anxiety nor alarm. Mrs. Brown watched the growth of Velvet as God might watch a sapling's growth: without concern, with unheeding conviction. She would grow, she would cease to be sick. Like Merry, if Mrs. Brown had been asked what her hope and expectancy in life was for Velvet she in her wordless way would have answered "guts." It was what Dan Taylor had required of her, endlessly, all through the night. Against the tide too. Father must see to the fallals and the gold bands. She, Dan's Araminty, only wanted staying power.

"You weren't sick at the gymkhana," said Merry. "I forgot to expect you to be."

"I prayed an' prayed," said Velvet.

"D'you think that's any good?"

"Not much. Because I always do it. But I don't dare leave it out."

Merry flicked a grain of flint down towards Edwina's head. It missed. Edwina stretched herself in the sun below the wall and put her arms behind her head.

"Don't," said Velvet. "She'll make a row. We're so comfy."

"Pity she's getting a sort of enemy," said Merry.

"It's because she's in love."

"But why . . ."

"It just turns you. Like drink."

In happy silence they watched the silver enemy below them, her ash hair pillowed on her coffee arms. Teddy looked at her like a gooby. She flung a word to him now and then, and the gramophone, pushed into a hollow in the cobbles, sang on. "It's lovely, that noise," said Velvet dreamily, and licked the last stub of crunchie.

There was a sound of hoofs behind them and three horses came round the corner from the livery stables, setting out for the Hullocks.

Merry and Velvet swung round and leaned, backs to the sea, on the wall to watch.

"What's the matter with people who can't ride?" said Merry.

"Dunno," said Velvet.

They watched the riders intently.

"Nothing's right," said Velvet.

"Look as though they were kneeling," said Merry. "Their knees are forward and their feet are back . . ."

"You can see miles away on the Hullocks," said Velvet, half shutting her eyes. "They heave as the horse heaves. They have enormous legs, all loose."

"It must be awful," said Meredith, "to ride like that."

The horses disappeared and sun and sparrows took their place.

"Must be awful," said Velvet after a while, "to be a livery horse."

Merry slid her feet further into the sunny dust. It rose in a roll round the toes of her shoes and she said nothing.

"It's not what they're born for."

"What are they born for?"

"They're simply born," said Velvet rather suddenly, "to try to get to know what one person thinks. Their backs and their mouths are like ears and eyes. That's why those horses move like that and hang their heads down from the wither like a steep hill."

"What horses?"

"The livery ones. They've got broken hearts."

"How d'you know?"

"Oh," said Velvet, "I can see. It's like seeing the dead go by."

"You once said you'd go in a livery stable when you grew up."

"I could never go in a livery stable," said Velvet.

The sun shone and warmed her, and Velvet was in a state of abeyance, of waiting. She was a pond which stood empty but was certain of the mysterious, condensing dew.

"I'm going home," said Velvet, after a pause.

"I'm waiting here," said Meredith.

Velvet left Meredith and slouched up the street. She looked in the shoe shop with an urge of heart. "Butcher's Velvet," thought Mr. Ede, and crossed the street to speak to her.

"Piebald didn' do too bad at the Pendean," he said, stopping and looking at the shoes. He was hardly prepared for the beaming eyes that turned on him. "He's beautiful, Mr. Ede," said Velvet earnestly. "I hope you'll never feel bad you let him go."

"Rough animal," said Mr. Ede, embarrassed. "Bit mad p'r'aps. You done wonders to him. Wouldn't stay in any field of mine."

"He's settled down nicely," said Velvet. "He's a very boyish horse."

Mr. Ede passed this over as fanciful. He thought she looked queer too. Delicate and spiny. And all them teeth. In truth Velvet could look like a fairy wolf gone blond. She had this look as she turned back upon the shoes. Ede left her and Mi touched her on the shoulder.

"Looked up Weatherby's?"

" 'Tisn't in the telephone book."

"Just write 'Weatherby's. Racin' experts. London,' " said Mi. "Just ask for the rules of entry."

"What'll I say?"

But Mi was in a hurry. He didn't know.

Her mind began its letter across tan and silver heels, plaid bedroom slippers and sea-shoes of canvas. She moved homeward, carrying disjointed words like broken crockery in a napkin.

The spaniels were sitting, sunning, round the door, Wednesday's joint disturbing them already. The female laid her nose from time to time to the bottom door-line and drew long breaths and rolled her yellow eyes. The chained house dog flew out silently, choked on the end of his chain and fell back.

The sitting room was empty, mother in the kitchen. Velvet pulled her lesson books from the dresser drawer and found a sheet of foreign writing paper that had laid in the grammar book for months. The ink bottle was on the cactus shelf, the pen beside it.

She sat down and wrote swiftly for fear of being disturbed:

Dear Sirs,

I am an Owner of a Horse. Please could you send me the Rules of entering for the Grand National Race?

I am, Sirs, Your obedient Servant,

V. Brown.

There was a bit of blotting paper in the meat ledger, an envelope in the dresser drawer. In five minutes she was going back down the street with the letter and a penny for the stamp machine, the letter addressed according to Mi's advice.

She and Mi met at the midday joint. She whispered: "I've done it."

"Written it?"

"An' posted it."

He seemed surprised. She could not eat.

"I don't like cabbage," said Donald.

He was not answered.

"I don't like it but I eat it," he said, looking at Velvet.

"You're a marvel," said Mally.

"Yes, I am a marvel," said Donald. "I don't like cabbage, I don't like food, but I eat it. Velvet doesn't."

This provocation blew over.

"Eat your food, Velvet," said Mr. Brown after a suitable interval. "That band sitting softer?"

"Much," said Velvet. "But I'm not hungry."

"I'm not hungry either," said Donald, "but I eat my food. I eat it all up, even when I'm not hungry."

"I don't like to see a great slice of English leg left

like that," said Mr. Brown. "If you can't eat it lift it back." The slice was returned to the dish. Velvet thought, as she chopped up her cabbage and hid it round her baked potato, that the box at the Post Office had just been cleared.

"You girls bin eating snacks?" said Mr. Brown, looking at Meredith's plate.

"I got gristle," said Merry hurriedly, pushing with her fork, and dividing plot from plot.

"Doughnuts," said Mrs. Brown placidly. "They look like it."

"Pay for 'em or put 'em down?"

"Pay for 'em!" said Merry indignantly.

"I'll have no putting down," said Mr. Brown. "Hand me that plate, Merry. You're behaving like a customer."

Meredith got up and carried her plate to him.

"That's not gristle, that's fat," said Mr. Brown. "You just carry that back and eat it up. If snacks in the midmorning's going to spoil a leg for you, you better have no more of 'em. Ten sheep coming at four, Mi."

"Right," said Mi.

"To be killed?" said Donald.

"Yes," said Mi.

"Why killed?" said Donald.

"To make meat for you."

"For me?"

"I said so."

"I want to see 'em be killed," said Donald.

"Well, you can't," said his father.

"Do they break an' fall down and die?"

No answer.

"Who dies them?"

"I do," said Mr. Brown. "And Mi."

Donald looked at his father without the slightest disfavor but with added respect.

"If there's a sheep's head for tonight give it me while it's warm, Mi," said Mrs. Brown. "You can't cook it so tender once it's chilled down."

~ TEN ~

When the answer from Weatherby's came it contained terrible difficulties. Velvet took it to Mi.

"Oh, well," said Mi when he looked at the blue entry form. "I oughta known. It brings it all back." Mi's wicked knowledge of the North came over him in floods. "There's this to be done . . . an' that . . . and this and that. . . . See if we can't get round it. You'll be disqualified in the end in any case, my girl. Might as well be disqualified all round. All you want is the chance to do it. I wonder if we're dotty."

"Who could you ask?"

"Ask!" said Mi. "Ask the churchwardens. You leave it to me. It's Lewes races tomorrow. I'll be over there and have a talk. You get on with the animal. Leave a lot to me. An' don't talk!"

"I never!"

Mi glanced at her a moment. He had been absorbed in his thought.

"No, you don't," he said. "But 'Dwina'd hand it on to Teddy, and Merry'd forget she wasn't to speak . . .

154 ~

An' it may never happen. You'd best just get on with the animal if you think such a crack of it.''

"Don't you?''

Mi heaved a big breath, first in, then out of his lungs. "I think more of you,'' he said in the end.

"I'm nothing without him,'' said Velvet.

"Get on now,'' said Mi. "An' don't keep asking me how I'm getting on. What's more, there's another thing. You might have a shot at the Tindles jumps in the mushroom valley.''

"They're all wired up.''

"Yes; well, I'd unwire 'em. Take some pliers. They're a lazy lot over there now the horses are gone. There's no one in the valley before seven.''

September passed and October came. Velvet by now had grown bolder. She no longer rose in the dawn to fetch the piebald to the mushroom valley but took him in the red-haired autumn under cold afternoon moons of October on dew-drenched grass. The mushroom pickers cleaned the valley before dawn. No one came down from Tindles, the hill village of the Derby winner. The old man was old, old. His horses gone, his men lazy. He warmed his toes and looked at his Derby cup but kept indoors between the sideboard and the fire.

Velvet grew so bold she ceased to replace the barbed wire over the jumps. The great brushwork barriers stood up free and clean and twice a week the piebald leapt them from end to end of the field. Sometimes Mi came with a bamboo rod and caught him a flick on his belly or his hock as he flew over.

One day when his work was over he came in the evening with a spade and dug a pit before one of the jumps and dragged logs to lie at the lip of the pit to make The Pie take off earlier. He came back with Velvet in the morning early and she and the horse leapt the contraption. After which Mi filled it in again and threw sods on it.

"They'll think we've buried someone," said Velvet. "You do take a lot of trouble, Mi."

"Know what he's just jumped?" said Mi, straightening his back.

"What?"

"Jumped the third on the National. Third jump's a ditch an' fence. Same as this one. I wrote to a chap on the railway up there for the measurements."

"Railway?"

"Truckline. Runs on the raised embankment alongside the course. You on'y got to run down and measure."

Now the piebald jumped as he had jumped the five-foot wall when they had first seen him, hitching his quarters up behind him and leaving inches to spare. Not a twig on the jumps moved except from the wind of his passage. Velvet lay on his neck like the shadow of an ape and breathed her faith into him.

One evening before supper, Mi and Velvet alone under the lamp, Velvet read the accounts of races. The Cesare-witch. Prophecies about it beforehand.

". . . the conditions will be ideal for all except the mudlarkers," she read aloud. "What's that, Mi?"

"Dud talk o' mutts," said Mi.

" 'Munition started so slowly he was always tailed'?"

"The same," said Mi.

"And 'he galloped the opposition down in grand style.' "

"And the same," said Mi.

"Oh, no!" said Velvet. "I like that! It's what I'll do. I'll gallop the opposition down. It's grand."

"If you like," said Mi.

"I do," said Velvet.

Silence.

"We gotta call him something," said Mi.

"What? The piebald? Can't we call him The Pie?"

"If you like. It's a mutt name."

"I'll always call him The Pie. But if he's got to have something grand . . ."

"We gotta choose the name and choose racing colors and send up and ask Weatherby's if they'll pass 'em. Sooner the better. They'll print 'em in the Calendar."

"I'll have black and pink," said Velvet.

"You'll look awful."

"Could we call him Unicorn?" said Velvet slowly.

"That's the sort," said Mi. "Longish. Historical."

"Is Unicorn historical?"

"Seems to me."

"He could just be Unicorn for the race?"

"Yes, he could. But he'll be put down Unicorn for ever in the history books."

"On'y if he wins, Mi . . ."

"Win or no, he goes down. Some of those books put every runner that ever ran. Starting with the 'Lottery' year, with Jem Mason up. That was eighteen thirty-nine. Seventeen starters."

"You know a heap."

"Any chap knows anything knows the first Grand National."

"Lamp's smoking, Mi."

Mi turned it down.

"An', Mi."

"M'm."

"I don't like Unicorn."

"Well, think of something else."

"I'll never like anything but The Piebald. It's his name. He's got to go in the books like that."

Mi looked up. The thin face opposite him had grief in it.

"They weren't all so grand," he said at last. "There was Jerry M. and Shady Girl. An' Old Joe won it in eighteen eighty-six. An' there was Hunter an' Seaman and Miss Lizzie, an' the Doctor, an' The Colonel . . . Why, there was The Colonel! He won it twice. You call him The Piebald an' it won't hurt. It'll do fine."

Velvet gave him a look of love. "Thank you, Mi," she murmured.

"Here, take the papers," said Mi, "an' look at 'em."

"Gotta enter his sire and his dam," said Velvet, poring over the Rules.

"Well, that's that," said Mi, yawning.

"Whad'you mean, that's that?" said Velvet. "He's got a sire and a dam somewhere, hasn't he?"

"Orphan. Horse is an orphan. Here, hand me the Rules!"

Mi drew the lamp nearer and leaned his face deeply upon the little page. " 'In entering' . . . m'm . . . m'm . . . 'he shall be described by stating a name.' . . . We gotta name. Settled. 'The age he will be at the time of the race.' . . . Blacksmith says he's six. Might be more. We'll put 'aged.' "

"That's a horrid word."

"It's fine. It means grown up. No more o' them silly years. We'll put 'aged.' "

"What's next?"

" 'The color' . . . (they'll cough a bit when they read he's a piebald) 'and whether a horse, mare or gelding, and the Calendar or Stud-Book names of his sire and dam.' That's where they get us!''

"Oh, Mi . . .''

"What a bit! 'If the sire or dam has no name in the Calendar' . . . wait a minute, wait a minute . . . 'or if the pedigree of the sire or dam be unknown, such further particulars as to where, when, and from whom the horse was purchased or obtained must be given as will identify him.' That's us all right.''

"What'll you put? You can't put about the shilling an' the raffle.''

"Make 'em sit up.''

"Too much. They'll sit up and see me!''

"You're right, yes. Pity though. Been a bit of fun. We'll put 'Bought from Thomas Ede, Farmer,' an' the date. Previous bought in Lewes Market. . . .''

"That reads odd.''

"You aren't asked to state all the buys. We'll leave it at Ede.''

"Anything else?''

"Not that I can see.''

"S'sh! Here's the others!''

Donald had out his jigsaws. He was doing a map of the world in big simple pieces. He could not get it started because two bits of the margin were missing. He begged and pleaded and nagged, "Will you help me? WILL you help me?''

Merry helped him most. Mally stuck in a piece or two, Edwina bent over him and played the mother till she got bored.

"There's India!'' said Edwina, skipping from mother to teacher.

"All the pink bits, Donald, belong to England.''

"What's England?"

"Us."

"There's a pink bit and there's . . . LOOK, Donald . . . there's a . . ."

"D'you know," said Donald, looking at her with his earnest charm, "in my black socks I've got HOLES!"

"Goo!" said Edwina, laughing suddenly. "An' you haven't any black socks either . . ." And looking up she saw Teddy's face under the light of the lamp outside. She was gone with the swoop of a moth through the door.

"Will you help me?" began Donald again, leaning towards Mally. Mally flicked a slice of wood towards him. "There's England and France in that bit."

"What's France?"

"Over the water," said Mally, chucking her thumb over her shoulder. "Over the sea."

"I seen France once," said Donald.

"No!"

"I seen France once an' all the houses were slipping down in the water."

"Huh!" said Mi. "He doesn't know it's land. Thinks it's built on the Channel!"

"Bed, Donald," said Mrs. Brown in the doorway.

"I'm busy," said Donald. "We're all busy."

"Get on, Donald," urged Mi.

"Why do they have supper'n not me?" said Donald, feverishly searching for a piece of wood.

Lewes races had long gone by, Mi had made his arrangements. He had met a friend here and a friend there and had a talk or two and borrowed a bit, had his week's wages in advance from Mr. Brown, and finally had paid a visit to Croydon. Edwina didn't notice, Merry didn't ask, and Mally, her nose twitching, didn't know enough to go upon, though sometimes she prodded like a person prodding with a stick in mud who thinks a treasure can be seen.

One day Mi came to Velvet after supper. He whistled her out of the living room with a suck of his tooth and a cock of his eye. "Sign this," he said in Miss Ada's stall, the private sitting room of their lives. Miss Ada ate her bedding undisturbed.

"What is it?" said Velvet.

"It's a Clearance," said Mi. "You put 'James Tasky' here."

He had his pen in his hand and a glass bottle of ink.

"Who's James Tasky?"

"He's you. He will be you in a post or two. Just ask me nothing. Sign what I say."

Velvet wrote at the bottom of the paper "James Tasky," balancing the paper on the lip of the manger. Mi produced three inches of blotting paper from his pocket.

"Now . . ." he said with satisfaction. "Now we post it . . . see? An' we get a license . . . see? An' the real Mr. Tasky's not even in England. What a catch!"

"Where is he?"

"Being sick on the Baltic, I shouldn't wonder. He told me all about it. Horrible sea, the Baltic. Water's shallow and bumps on the bottom an' comes up again. How people can go in ships beats me."

"We gotta have the name in by the second Tuesday in January," said Velvet.

"Say that on the form?"

"Yes."

"Well, we'll have it in. We've put our backs in this

now, and our shirts an' all. What d'you call it? About that horse? Putting it what?"

"Putting The Piebald in history," said Velvet. "I think of that whenever I feel giddy and it stops."

"Well, I'm putting you in history. See? Like my old Dan put Araminty Potter. It's a foreseen thing. Like God might a thought of. Come along now and get a stamp out of your mother for me. I'm done this week to a penny."

Christmas came and went. The Piebald's muscles grew tauter. One evening in the first days of January, Mr. Brown took Edwina and Mally and Meredith to the pictures. Velvet would have gone but she felt shivery after tea. When they had left the house Velvet and her mother and Mi sat alone. Mrs. Brown did a patience, Mi cut a piece of cork to fit a bottle, Velvet did nothing, the wind howled round them, the carpet rose against the door. The spaniels lay heaped in Miss Ada's stall.

"Bus'll be near blown over," said Mi. "They'll catch it going in."

Mrs. Brown laid out another card. Jacob shivered and recrossed his delicate forefeet.

Mi looked at Mrs. Brown as he cut his cork and knew the moment had come to include her. When he looked at her he saw a pillar of fire. He put aside the great dun-colored coating, the enormous thighs, the shoulders which bore a pack of muscle like a yoke across them. He saw instead those mysterious qualities that made him say of any uncouth, unwieldy, unmanageable horse, "He's got heart." By heart he meant a heart that would stay.

"There's a horse," he said, feeling his way to break the silence, "over at Pendean would carry you."

"Never bin on a horse," said Mrs. Brown.

162 ⬤

"Makes no odds," said Mi indifferently—but he would not let the silence close again.

"Should tell yer ma 'f I were you, Velvet," he said in an odd voice. "Now's your minute."

Velvet looked up. Mrs. Brown laid out her cards unmoved.

Velvet watched her own feet. "Piebald's fit," she mumbled, "to run in the National."

Mrs. Brown ruminated, laid down her cards. Said: "What about it?"

"Thought of runnin' it," said Velvet.

"You did?"

"M'm . . ."

"The Grand National with them jumps?"

"M'm. . . . Thirty jumps."

"Stiff," said Mrs. Brown.

Nobody spoke. Mi cut his cork. His fingers stuck and slipped. Velvet would never disobey her mother.

"What'll it cost?" said Mrs. Brown.

"A hundred pounds to enter. And money for a horse-box. An' me night's lodging. (I gotta see it.)"

"What do you win if you win?"

"Oh," said Velvet vaguely, "thousands and a cup. But it's not that, it's for the horse. Besides, if they find out they'll disqualify me. It's only for the horse."

"What makes you think it can win?"

"It can."

"Can it, Mi?"

"Shouldn't wonder."

"Well," said Mrs. Brown, and gathered up the cards into a neat pack. Her peasant's eye, half shrewd, half visionary, insected the idea, and the features of her big face not stirring she moved her head with elephantine majesty. Then she rose and going to the sideboard took out a key from a drawer. She left the room and was heard above walking in her own.

Velvet closed her eyes. Her feet were cold.

"My feet are cold, Mi."

"Keep still. Lie still."

Mrs. Brown came back with a box, her lips moving as though she were talking to herself. Unlocking the box on the table she counted out money, old-fashioned money, gold—gold sovereigns.

Mi leant forward. Velvet sat up. Mi knew what they were.

"Your prize? What you won?" said Mi, quiet.

"Kept it," said Mrs. Brown. "Thought I might. Thought I would."

"Look at it," said Mi. "Never seen such a thing since I was a lad."

Mrs. Brown's thick fingers built castle with the coins.

"There's a hundred. Twenty fer expenses." She looked straight at Velvet. "I gotta fancy, Velvet, that you pay your entry in this." She tapped the castles.

"Pay in the gold itself?" said Mi.

"It'll bring you luck," said Mrs. Brown.

"Weatherby'll think it odd," said Mi.

"You got a thing you sign?" said Mrs. Brown.

"Yes," said Mi, and fumbled in his coat pocket.

Mrs. Brown took the blue form and read it.

"Not there," said Mi, "that's the Grand Military. Next page. Top o' page seventeen. 'Liverpool—continued,' it says."

Mrs. Brown read in silence.

"Queer," she said at last. "Queer thing. I had a feeling."

"What?" said Mi.

"An' see there," said Mrs. Brown, handing him the

form and plunging her finger on it. "See what it says. 'Sov. Ten sov. each. Fifty sov. extra.' There's the wording clear. They can't go back on it. You use them sovereigns. I had a fancy they'd come in."

Velvet hung softly against her mother, putting her arms round her shoulders. Mrs. Brown took her suddenly on her lap. Mi was so affected he called Jacob into the yard. But before he went he hit his lips three times with his index finger at Velvet behind her mother's back. She stared at him vacantly and he shook his head and closed the door.

"Who'll tell Father?" whispered Velvet.

"I'll tell your Father," said Mrs. Brown, rocking her.

Of this discussion Velvet heard nothing. When the battle was over she was given no more than the result. But in the deep of the night forces were involved that stirred Araminty Potter to love and to fury, and finally to love again. In meeting a hard, but as it turned out a brittle, opposition from her husband, Araminty rose like a sea monster from its home. After her years of silence she grunted with astonishing anger, and William, powerless and exasperated, stung like a gnat upon a knotted hide. That something which was obstinate and visionary and childish bound Mi and Velvet and her mother together, and in the night Araminty, in doing battle for their dreams, fought too for her own inarticulate honor.

The difference ran to its end, they were shaken profoundly, and slept in friendship at dawn. Mr. Brown rose next morning, spiritually bruised, feeling that he was going to be made ridiculous, but acquiescent.

The first effect of this discussion was that The Piebald stood in Miss Ada's stall and Miss Ada found herself once more among the tools (which she shared at night with the spaniels). Velvet took her gymkhana money out of the bank to buy oats, and what she could not buy her mother saved from the housekeeping.

The horse was walked endlessly uphill. There was not a steep hill-surface for miles around that Velvet had not sought out and ascended. The faulty, pear-shaped quarters of The Piebald swelled with muscle. Clipped out, he shone blacker and whiter than ever, his long tail and mane washed in the vinegar suds from Edwina's hair-rinsings, his pink albino hooves scrubbed with a nail brush and polished. He grew to look like a newly-painted rocking horse, freshly delivered.

On the first Monday in January Mi took the whole entry money of a hundred pounds in gold sovereigns in a bag up to London. He went to Messrs. Weatherby in Cavendish Square, walked up the stone steps, pushed the doors, and stood at a wooden counter not unlike a bank. A tall man asked him offhandedly what he wanted.

"Entry. Fer the Gran' National," said Mi, pulling out the completed form, dumping the heavy bag on the counter, and pushing it towards the man.

"What's that?"

"Th'entry money," said Mi.

"Ten pounds. Have you brought it in silver?" said the man superciliously, touching the neck of the bag with his fingers.

"Ten? I've brought a hundred. In gold."

The man drew the bag towards him and opened it. He peered inside with astonishment. "What's this? Sovereigns?"

"A hundred sovereigns," said Mi.

The man looked at Mi consideringly. He indicated a stool. "Will you wait?" he said. He was away a moment, then returned with a companion whose air was even more exalted and critical.

"Do I understand," said the second man, "that you have brought a hundred sovereigns in pre-war gold to pay for an entry for the Grand National . . . Race?" He brought out the word "race" as though it were the crime which Mi had committed.

"Yes, sir," said Mi cheerfully and simply and shifted his feet and leaned on the counter. "It's quite simple, sir. I thought you'd like it best jus' as it was. I didn't know where best to change it into paper an' as this is as good's a bank (the man's eyes lightened just a shade) I thought I'd bring it here."

"To what horse does this refer?"

"It's a piebald horse. Property of Miss V. Brown. She owns it. Her father's a butcher down . . . The address is here." He smoothed out the form.

"Who is the trainer?"

"Privately trained, sir."

"Not by the owner?"

"Well, yes, by the owner. Yes, sir, trained by her since she's had it."

"How do you come to bring up this money?"

Mi paused a moment and sucked his tooth.

"It's a fancy of Miss Brown's mother, sir. She had the sovereigns tucked away for years. Kind of store, sir. She had a fancy it would bring the horse luck if she paid the entry money with the sovereigns."

"I'm afraid we can't do deals in gold. This is worth more than a hundred pounds."

"You mean I get some change back?"

"You would if we took it. But we can't have anything to do with the price of gold at the present rate. That is not our business."

"I don't think," said Mi slowly, "that Mrs. Brown wants any change. A hundred sovereigns is a hundred pounds to her. She's old-fashioned. She's set on paying the entry with this hundred pounds here in this bag, sir."

"There's another thing," said the man. "You don't need to pay a hundred now. It's ten sovereigns now, fifty sovereigns extra if left in after January 30th, with an additional forty sovereigns if left in after March 13th."

"Sovereigns," murmured Mi. "It says 'sovereigns,' and these are sovereigns."

"Well, that's the . . ." (the gentleman looked acid), "the wording dating from the original . . . er . . . inception of this form."

"Clear enough," said Mi. "Sovereigns it says. I don't want to make difficulties, sir, but I've brought you sovereigns, haven't I?"

"I think you had better wait," said the gentleman, and he and his companion disappeared. Mi sat on the stool again and eyed his bag. He read the antique sporting notices. There was a ginger and green notice, stiff with discolored varnish, about paying for the weights in the weighing room. He frowned at it. He had never heard of such a thing. Then he saw that it was dated a hundred years ago.

After a long interval the gentleman returned, alone.

"The sovereigns will be accepted," he said curtly, "but there is no need to deposit more than ten as yet."

"I'd sooner leave the lot," said Mi obstinately.

"The reason for the division of the entry amounts," said the gentleman, disliking Mi more and more, "is in case the horse becomes by a later date unable to run."

"This horse'll run," said Mi.

"You cannot foresee," said the gentleman, "acts of God."

"M'm, I can," said Mi, "m'm, I can. You take the lot an' stack it for me. Safer here. I might get it lifted off me on the way home. You got a fine big place here. You got room for ninety sovereigns stacked away. You can give me a paper for it. They need me at the butcher's down there. 'Tisn't easy to keep making journeys. You'll need the lot before we're done."

Again the gentleman disappeared and a very exalted head was put round the lintel of an inner cubicle and two very shrewd and dwelling eyes inspected Mi.

Finally a receipt was handed to him, the bag and form taken from him and Mi was ready to depart.

"Who's your rider?" said the gentleman, almost sociably at last.

"Foreign chap," said Mi instantly. "Comin' over later."

"He'll have to get his Clearance, you know," said the gentleman, "from his own accredited Jockey Club."

"Yes, sir," said Mi quickly. "Yes, thank you, sir."

"What's his name? Do you know him?"

"Tasky. James Tasky."

"English?"

"Mother's English. Chap's half Russian."

"From which country then does he get his Clearance? There is racing of course still in Russia."

"Mr. Brown's working it all out," said Mi. "I'm just the hand down there. I know what I hear them say, that's about all."

"Well, good-day then. Just a minute. You'll notice on that receipt 'Received one hundred sovereigns in gold sovereigns, value to be decided by Coult's Bank when the final payment is due.' That means you get an amount returned. You'll explain that to the owner, please."

"Right, sir. Good-day, sir."

Mi was out in the airy light of Cavendish Square and he ran his hand across his brow.

"Mother nearly ruined it with 'er whimsies," he said.

It was March. The days of March creeping gustily on like something that man couldn't hinder and God wouldn't hurry.

"What about me jacket?" said Velvet in her whisper, somewhat hoarse, again and again.

"*Leave* yer jacket!" said Mi testily. "I keep telling you. Leave me thinking of it."

"I can't sew, remember," said Velvet warningly.

"Think I don't know that! My sister's sewing it."

"Your SISTER! You gotta sister!" Velvet sat bolt upright.

"I gotta sister. I got two."

"You never told us!"

"I'm no family man," said Mi shortly.

"Your old Dan . . . your old father's dead?"

"He's dead!"

"You gotta mother?"

"Dead too. But where I sprung from an' what I left behind's my business."

"But your sister's my business. She's sewing my coat."

"And well she can do that for me," said Mi, reflecting. "I never asked her for a penny. I got her her job. Bin there years."

"Where?"

"Sews for a tailor at Newmarket. Does the tailored shirts. I sent her that top of yours yer ma said was past darning."

"The top of that cotton dress what mother used the bottom for knickers?"

"That's the one."

"Well, it was too small, anyway. I hope she makes it bigger. What about the stuff?"

"Black an' pink I told her. She's in the way of getting the stuff up there. She'll get the cap made, too."

"And the breeches and the boots?"

"You leave it to me up at Aintree. That'll sort itself up at Aintree. Overnight. The valets go round with spares in their cases."

"Valets?"

"Fellows that look after the jockeys. Press up their clothes an' do their boots. There's a gang of them go round the race meetings."

"Now," said Velvet at last, as low as low, "there's another thing."

"M'm?"

"Mother," said Velvet. And the spinning air seemed to stop round them in anxiety.

"It's a thing I'm thinking of too," said Mi. "Worries me."

"Yes," said Velvet. "D'you know, Mi?"

"What?"

"I couldn't do it 'f I didn't tell her."

The telling was done at the shop at night. Mi arranged it when Mrs. Brown was totting up. She spared the electric and totted by candlelight.

"You gotta pretend I'm not your child," said Velvet, long after bedtime. She dragged up her words as though the roots were deep.

"You was nineteen when you swum the Channel," said Velvet. "I'm fourteen but my chances come early. You mustn't think I'm your child. I'm a girl with a Chance."

Her mother's throat clicked. She blazed into fire without moving an eyelash.

"Mi's in the street, waitin'," said Velvet. "It's him an' me." (She paused at the gasp her mother gave.)

"We're out on it together," went on Velvet, not knowing the terror that cooled her mother's fire. "We think . . . I think . . ." (coming up closer and speaking very low) "I kin *ride* the horse."

"Almighty God," said Mrs. Brown, mild and reverent. She was thanking Him that her child was her shining Velvet. Not all messed up with love. Not all messed up with love an' such. That Mi was to Velvet what Dan had been to her, that stuff grander and tougher than a lover. Now what was this suggestion that was like a wild dream?

"In the race, Velvet?"

Velvet described the machinery, Mi's plans, Mi's devices.

"If I'm found out then they'll send me home. Father'll be angry. Just as likely I won't be found out. Well, then, we'll do our best. The horse is great. He's like a Bible horse."

The interview was over, except the silence and the thinking.

"I don't want to speak to Mi about it," said Mrs. Brown at last. "Tell him not to speak to me about it. Not a word. It's a weight on me. It's a terrible . . . I can't be but your mother, Velvet. . . . To think Mi shoulda lent himself to this."

Then at 'the very end . . . "I'm all ashake. Let there be no whisperin' an' talkin'. I must put it from me an' pray to God."

Velvet left her. The candle guttered but the totting did not continue. Later the heavy woman walked home.

~ELEVEN~

March ran two thirds of its days.

Mr. Larke, the chemist, called in to fetch his meat book. "I'm hair-washing," called Mrs. Brown from the scullery. Mr. Larke stood in the scullery door critically.

"Two drops a' camomile is what you ought to add," he said.

"Bleach 'em?"

"Bleach 'em."

"Bleached enough already."

"When I say 'bleach' I should say 'bring out the color.' "

"Vinegar's what I use," said Mrs. Brown.

"So I can smell," said Mr. Larke.

"I got your last week's book made up," said Mrs. Brown, rinsing Edwina; "it's on the sideboard by the apples. Now Velvet. Edwina, you go and rub your head an' Mally'll give you a hand."

Edwina came staggering back into the living room, her head and face blindly wrapped in the bath towel

Mrs. Brown had popped over her. "My back aches," she grumbled. "I wish I could wash my own."

"Velvet!" called Mrs. Brown.

"I'm coming . . ."

When Velvet reached the scullery Mrs. Brown looked at her. "I won't risk it," she said. "Might make you squeamish, bending. I'll brush it through with a wet brush an' you can sit by the fire an' comb it."

"I'm taking the book then," called Mr. Larke loudly. "It's a great day for you all. Anxious. I'm not a racing man myself but we've all got our eyes on you, Velvet. There's a bit of money on you in the village."

"Thank you," said Velvet, through the brushing.

"Say it louder," said Mrs. Brown.

"Thank YOU," shouted Velvet.

"Right," said Mr. Larke. "Where you stopping?"

"Hotel," shouted Mrs. Brown. "She's doing it slip-slap. (Why don't he go? Makes you testy all this popping in an' good-wishing.) . . ."

("There he goes," said Velvet. "I can feel the draught on my legs.")

"I'm dry!" shouted Edwina. "Can I go?"

"You can't be dry. Come here an' let me feel."

Edwina came in.

"Damp all roun' your glands," said Mrs. Brown, feeling. "You don't go down the street like that."

"Teddy's just . . ."

"Teddy kin wait."

"He can't."

"Anybody kin wait, Edwina," said Mrs. Brown, brushing hard, "for a pretty girl."

Edwina suddenly smiled all over her light-built face. She went back to the living room.

"Isn't she getting grown-up," said Velvet.

"You're all on the edge of it."

"Not me."

"There you are!" said Mrs. Brown, laying down the brush. "You fluff up with a bit of water."

"It'll all be down again flat in an hour."

"Greasy scalp," said Mrs. Brown. "Get Meredith down for me. She's with the birds."

It was the last evening before the start at dawn. Velvet and Mi were traveling to Aintree in the horse-box. The last evening meal. Donald was allowed to sit up. Taps came on the door as they ate and friendly voices called in. The whole village had of course long known that the piebald horse, won for a shilling, was going to be run in the Grand National. Velvet's Grand National. "Gran' National Velvet," Mr. Croom called out to her in the street. "Good morning, Gran' National Velvet!" and two boys outside the sweet-shop had clapped their hands. "Got any tips for the National?" called the postman.

"The Piebald!" said Velvet with her shy look.

"Yes, they're going up to Liverpool tomorrow," said Mrs. Brown at the door twenty times. "Mi an' Velvet are going in the horse-box." She filled the doorway with her body and behind her shadow Velvet sat. It was a soft March night between a pair of howling gales, a black, cold trough of peace, pierced with stars. Stars that above her mother's head as she stood in the open street doorway seemed like Christmas trees, slender, growing into the sky. The lamp on Edwina's hair, her father's folded neck, her mother majesty and silence, Donald's film face and dear, disgusting habits, the sideboard, heavy, loaded, bottles of ink, dish-covers, salmon tins, apples, vinegar bottles, Merry's bird-absorbed face,

Mally's loyal and sharp eyes, Mi's grin, Mi's slouch. Mi's way of coming through the door, Mi's shadow, the lying Jacob, the pleasure-loving, self-indulgent Jacob, agreeable dog, sensitive, agreeable dog . . . these things (not in words, but in the burning warmth of the present) swelled her leave-taking heart. She had a wordless premonition that this was an egg into which it was impossible to re-enter. When the shell had burst, it was burst for ever. She felt this only as a dog howls for packing, mournful and simple and going, going, gone.

Going, going, gone, full of stars and cacti, and yellow canaries screaming in the morning.

"What d'you want, Velvet?"

"I'm getting my shell-box."

In silence they watched her fetch her box and put it beside her plate.

Edwina laughed suddenly.

"Coo lummy, Velvet! Paper horses just before the Grand National!"

"Beastly pair o' words," muttered father. "Get 'em from Teddy . . ."

"H'm . . . Teddy uses better words 'an that!"

(Warm bickering of family life. Fathers and daughters. . . .)

"Can I see wot's inside that box?" said Donald.

Velvet's face lightened. Donald should look at them tonight. He had never set his fingers on them before.

"Have you finished, Donald? Come an' sit on my lap."

"I kin climb up. Don' you help me." He walked up the bars of her chair like a ladder and bumped himself down onto her lap from the arm.

She opened the lid and a little shell fell off.

"You've dropped a shell!" (burstingly).

176 ▬

"I must stick it back."

"Let me look!"

"Ssh, wait . . ." Velvet put her thin finger inside and hooked up a race-horse.

"Hullo! This is Grakle!" she said. "Who's been changing them round? Who's touched my box?"

"I did," said Merry in a small voice, "I did, Velvet. I'm sorry."

Velvet looked astonished. "I don't mind, Merry," she said. "I didn't think you ever cared about them."

"It was yesterday afternoon," said Merry. "The canaries were so alive. You can't *do* anything with them. I took your horses out to exercise. I just took out the National winners and jumped a bush behind Peg's Farm."

"Show me, show me," hammered Donald, leaning over the box and poking his fingers inside.

Velvet put her hand over his fingers. "(In a second, Donald . . .) But I'm glad, Merry. I'd love you to take them out. Which ones did you take?"

"Tipperary Tim an' Sergeant Murphy and Manifesto. Doesn't Manifesto look lovely with his ears forward and the shine on his shoulder? He's a right-facing one. Where'd you cut him from?"

But Velvet bent her head suddenly over Donald. She had cut him from a library book down at the schoolhouse.

"*Now* pull them out!" said Donald.

"All the National Winners are on top," said Velvet, groping. "The ponies are underneath. There's a tiny . . . there's a Shetland. . . . Here it is. Look, Donald! Isn't he fat and like a kitten!"

"I like real horses," said Donald, unmoved.

"Good, good boy," said Mally.

"Oh, there's my darling Chestnut Fourteen-Two!"
said Velvet, half mourning over them. "Oh, why
haven't I looked at them for so long?"

"Can't do everything, Velvet," said her father, twisting his chair round so that he could read better under
the lamp. "You got your things packed up?"

"They're ready," said mother, clearing away the
last dish.

"I'm going to bed," said Mi. "We're off at five.
Won't do her no good to sit up."

"She won't," said Mrs. Brown. "She'll go in half
an hour."

"On top o' my food!" said Velvet indignantly.

"Food or no," said mother.

"Band all right?" said father.

"Sitting fine," said Velvet, who knew this was a
gesture of love.

"Let me see that Manifesto," said Mi, standing in
the doorway. Velvet picked the horse out.

"Won twice," said Mi. "97 . . . an' 99."

"How'd you know all that, Mi?" said Mr. Brown
from his lamp and paper.

"Dunno," said Mi. "There it is. What a shoulder . . .
eh? What a horse . . . eh? Looks too clever to win."

"Shouldn't they be clever?" said Edwina.

"Jumpin' thirty jumps when they can stan'
still . . . !" said Mi. "He did that course eight times.
Greatest National horse ever was. Why he won it
twice."

"I can't understand you, Mi," said Edwina. "You
just said he wasn't clever."

" 'Tisn't everything to be clever," said Mi, and disappeared to bed.

178

"How come Mi never to ride?" said Mr. Brown into his newspaper.

"Tell me some more," said Donald.

"I wish we could all go to Liverpool," said Mally.

"Cost too much," said Mr. Brown. "Yer mother plumpin' her prize-money on Velvet, that's one thing! We can't spend no more—just in the air."

"Bed for you, Donald," said Mother.

"Tell me one more horse 'fore I go."

"There was once a horse called Moifaa," gabbled Velvet, looking at her mother.

Mrs. Brown nodded. "Just tonight. Just a quick one."

Donald swung round his eyes and hooked them upon Velvet's lips.

"Moifaa was sent from New Zealand in a ship."

"Where's that?"

Velvet pointed to the floor with her finger. "Same as Australia. Down there. Th'other side."

"M'm . . . m'm . . ." said Donald greedily, waiting.

"The horse was sent right round the world and the ship went down near Ireland."

"How d'you know?" said Mally, listening like Donald.

"Mi told me. An' the ship went down an' the horse swam to an island off the coast, and the island had salt grass an' there was nothing to eat an' the horse walked up an' down the seashore looking out to sea an' neighing."

"An' what?"

"Screaming for help."

"The horse did?"

"Yes. An' fishermen were fishing an' they rowed near an' saw him. A horse standing neighing on an island where there'd never bin a horse. Never bin a cow. Never bin anything. It gave 'em the creeps an' they went home."

"Did they leave him there?"

"Left him there all night with all that grass an' all of it salt an' all that water an' all of it salt, and him used to a good stable and lots of men. He musta bin scared stiff. He was a great big ugly horse, seventeen hands high, an' I bet he was a brave horse."

"Did he die?" said Donald, his eyes blazing.

"No, he didn't die."

"Yes, he did. I KNOW he did."

"You can't know because he didn't. He was fetched by a steamer or something . . ."

"He DIED," said Donald with a blazing, inner look.

"He didn't, he didn't. He won the National."

"He died on that island," said Donald like a fanatic. "I was there."

"You weren't. What a story. You weren't born."

"I was born, I was born . . ."

"You were a star," said Edwina annoyingly.

"I wasn' a star. I was born an' I was there an' that horse died. He died on that salty place an' I saw 'im die and he lay down an' his eyes . . ."

"Hysterics," said Mrs. Brown calmly and whisked him up. "He's never any good when he's missed his hour." Donald went to bed weeping and was asleep in ten minutes.

"You didn't wash him, mother!" said Mally, scandalized, on her mother's return.

"Wants sleep, no washin'," said Mrs. Brown. "Now, Velvet!"

"Just after Donald? Not NOW?"

"This minute."

"I must put my shell-box away."

180 ━━

"Put it away."

"I'll put the race-horses in at the bottom."

In went Manifesto, Tipperary Tim, Sergeant Murphy, Ally Sloper, Why Not, and Shannon Lass—five right-handers and one left. Then the Shetland, then the four ponies, and on the very top of all the prize among her findings (another theft from the Free Library book) the little grey stallion, the Lamb (by Zouave—dam by Arthur).

"There they are," she said with a sigh, and shut the lid.

"Cheer up, Velvet," said Mr. Brown.

"Feels mixed up," said Mrs. Brown. "Get on, Velvet, don't hang about."

Slowly Velvet climbed the wooden stairs to bed. Her head seemed hardly to have touched the pillow when mother, dressed in her pink dressing gown, shook her in her bed. Dizzy, she rose, and, shivering, dressed, then swallowed the hot cocoa, and holding a piece of cold sausage in her fingers climbed into the van of the horse-box which had arrived in the dark before dawn. Her suitcase was stuffed in after her, Mi arrived, carrying another through the dark yard, a spaniel yelped from Miss Ada's tool shed, and the box was off, The Piebald already housed by Mi twenty minutes earlier.

"We're off, we're off!" whispered Velvet.

"Tscht!" said Mi. "You stow it till it gets light," and he settled himself on the straw to finish his night's sleep.

Endless journey in the horse-box till the South gave way to the North, bit by bit, and the day was broken by fresh packets of sandwiches.

"Don't we stop *anywhere,* Mi?" said Velvet as the hours crawled on.

But Mi was full of thought. There was a frown on

his forehead and an edge to his tongue, and now and again he glanced at his large suitcase.

The horse-box driver, hired from Worthing, was a stranger, a glum fellow who seemed to have no interest in horses, the Grand National, the countryside, or the passengers he carried. His eye was glazed on the road ahead of him, and his mind was mesmerized by hours on the clock and miles to be covered, and the relation of these to each other.

Five miles outside Aintree they paused and broke the journey for a pot of tea. Mi glanced at Velvet and rose.

"You off?" said the driver, half asleep over his cup.

"Girl got an aunt here," said Mi gruffly. "Takin' her to her aunt."

The driver slipped his legs out and lay back deeply in his chair. His eyes closed.

It took Mi twenty minutes to get Velvet's hair chopped perfunctorily in the van of the horse-box. It was the back by the nape of the neck that took the time. He bent down and crushed the sweepings in among the straw with the horse.

"Whiter'n straw," he muttered. "Looks like stubble."

"Won't he come any minute?" said Velvet anxiously.

"Any minute," said Mi. "Can't be helped. Got no-where else to do it. Pull up them trousers and give me yer skirt." The aged little skirt, the width of a school-boy's pants, was stuffed into the suitcase.

"Where'd you get 'em all?"

"Don't talk. Hurry. Slip your arm in the braces, they're all ready."

A hard white collar, slightly soiled, and a spotted tie hung on a nail.

"Can you manage 'em?"

"Yes, I expect. Is there a stud?"

Mi took his own from his neck, and tied his handkerchief in its place.

"You manage 'em an' I'll go an' talk to him if he wakes."

"What'll I do when I'm finished?"

"Slope round the back an' wait about. When we've gone get some tea and ginger an' sit in there. Here's a shilling. I'll be back in a couple of hours, near. Then we'll take the tram into Liverpool an' go an' have a look at the Adelphi. Look sharp now."

The little man who emerged from the back of the horse-van was very much thrown together. As he walked he seemed to settle down; he turned up his coat collar to hide the badly-tied tie, and jammed his greasy hat more confidently over his brow.

Mi and the driver emerged, the engine started, the horse-box moved away.

The skies, which had held off, now lowered and broke. Rain fell and the little man stirred his cold tea endlessly, fencing the occasional questions from the landlady.

The landlady had no sort of doubt.

"It's a girl," she said to her husband in the kitchen.

"No business of ours," said her husband.

"None," she agreed.

The inn was empty, the rain thudded, the white-faced clock tocked on, no customer came in. When Mi pushed the door open and dropped down upon the mat Velvet woke with a jerk from a cold half-sleep.

They started up the road, Mi carrying the heavy suitcase, Velvet the small papier-mâché one she had brought. The trams began half a mile away, but by the time they reached them rain was entering their collars and wallowing in their shoes.

Climbing onto the hard seats they jolted off, huddling close together for warmth, the little sturdy man with the red hair and the lad with the greasy Homburg hat.

"What's the Adelphi?" said the lad, low.

"Toff's place," said the other. "Maybe it's too toff. I've forgot. There's the Stork too. We'll walk round and see."

"Be wet. Walking round."

"Couldn't be wetter."

"Funny, that chap driving off with my hair."

"Turn your head round this way and let's look." Mi inspected the nape of the neck under the Homburg hat. "I'll have to trim it better," he said, "s'choppy."

~ TWELVE ~

Drenched with rain they stood at the portals of the Adelphi. Mi laid his hand on the little man's shoulder. "Mind the porter!" he said in a whisper. "Stand back here behind the concrete. I gone an' forgot. This place is too swell."

"Feet are sopped," said the little man.

"This rain's like ink. It's a bad start off. Stop a minute . . ."

"Ah," said the little man and looked hungrily through the revolving doors. "Coo lummy," he whispered, "aren't they gay in there! It's all looking-glass!"

They were on the arrival terrace of the Adelphi above the dripping Square, rustling with the noise of falling rain and overflowing pipes. The trams nosed by, the wet lamps flashed, "Ovaltine" went in and out, the grey buildings were polished with water.

"See the toffs go in," said Mi as the taxis drew up. "There's Lord Derby!"

"Where?"

"Crossing the hall, see? Why . . . he's got Tommy Weston with him.

"The big man?"

"No, his Lordship's the big one. Let's go to the Stork."

They trudged away in the rain, Mi carrying the bigger suitcase, which seemed to be melting at one corner.

"S'chap wantsa room," said Mi. "He's a foreign. Name Tasky. I'm not looking for one for myself. I'm lodged."

The Stork took them in.

Velvet stared at him.

They went up the stairs to a small room at the back.

"How'd you mean you're lodged?"

"Tsch! Talk quiet."

They reached number seven, went in, and Mi shut the door. It was a bare room with a small bed and a sixty-volt electric light.

"I don't need a room. See? I got to do some nosing round. There's chaps I'll see an' chaps I'll listen to. I might go round to th' Adelphi."

"The Adelphi!"

"Why not? Place is full o' chaps like me. Not on the top level. Round the pantries. You can see things if you cross the hall purposeful from time to time. Nobody asks. There's the telephone lobbies. Head lads doing a bit of telephoning. Michael Beary'll be chatting about I daresay."

"Who's he?"

"Good gosh, Velvet!"

"Eh . . . I'll never get my feet warm," said Velvet, sighing.

"Get undressed an' I'll poke round an' get you a hot bottle."

"But . . . Me being a lad . . ."

"Yepp. Beat your feet with a brush, then. I'll do it."

"Rub 'em."

"Beat's better. Where's the brush?"

Velvet knelt down and undid her suitcase. "I didn't bring a brush," she said, desisting suddenly. "I thought my hair, now it's off . . ."

"I done it not so bad," said Mi with pride. "It's white skin where the hair used to hang. I'll snip it cleaner in the morning."

"Can't we get something? It's the one place that shows when I've got that cap on. How much money you got left?"

"Precious little," said Mi. "Enough fer your room an' gettin' out there. You get into bed an' I'll come back in ten minutes."

Velvet lay shivering in bed, too tired to turn out the devouring light which blanched her under its beams. The bones of her forehead were sore when she pressed her head in her hands.

Mi returned. He carried a tiny glass full of a brilliant green liquid, placed it carefully on the mantlepiece and took out from under his coat a gin bottle which he had filled with boiling water.

"There goes one an' six," he said. "We gotta be careful."

Velvet opened her eyes.

"Got this in the yard at the back," said Mi, shoving the gin bottle under the bedclothes and near her feet. "Filled it myself. That's peppermint drink on the mantlepiece. Alcohol. It'll keep till the morning. It's mint an' spirits. Now you go to sleep an' I'll look in some time in the night."

He went out and shut the door, leaving the light still

187

on. Velvet slept fitfully beneath its glare, unaware of what was amiss. At three Mi looked in but she was still and he closed the door. At five he came in and found her awake. It was yet deep night, the light on and the windowpane black.

"Streaming outside," he said. He looked white and tired. Then, turning to the mantlepiece, "You've *drank that stuff!*"

"I thought I was going to die," said Velvet, sitting up and looking bright, "'n'hour ago. The room was going round. I got up an' drank it off. S'marvelous. Have you got another one an' six case I feel worse?"

"I might have," said Mi, sitting down on the one hard chair. "Don't you go taking to drink."

"Drink? Is it drink?"

"Told you it was spirits."

"Well, I forgot. I was bad. It's saved me. Just look at that black rain on the glass. They won't put the race off, will they?"

"The going'll be heavy as lead. Now see, Velvet. You ready to listen to a lot o' things?"

"Yes, Mi."

"Well an' ready? Cos I got a lot to say."

"Yes, Mi."

"Well, first here's a map of the course. I got it from a chap. You oughta walked round with me this morning but it's so wet an' if I get you tired you'll be no use. Besides it's best you do without seeing what the other side o' Becher's is like."

"When did you see it?"

"When did I see it? Didn't I tell you I know it all up here like my thumb? One time I used to shift coal on trucks on the line alongside Becher's. You can't see much on the National, there's such a crowd, but the

188 ～

Liverpool Autumn Meeting in November you got all to yourself. You can stand up there an' see the ambulance come an' see the men standing there with ropes ready an' all.''

"Ooh, Mi, ready for what?''

"Ready to lug the horses out of the drop.''

"Ooh—Mi.''

"Huh! It's not going to happen to you! You got The Piebald jumping under you. Don't you forget that. All I mean is don't be surprised when you ride at Becher's, an' don't think you've jumped over the lip of a quarry, 'cos it isn't a quarry and you'll stop dropping in the end an' if you're not surprised the horse won't be.''

"Yes, Mi.''

"Now. We'll take the jumps all round. Same as if you were walking round, which you should be.''

Mi pulled his chair up to Velvet's bed and flattened the thin paper map on her sheet.

"Plan of the Liverpool Racecourse,'' it said. "Distance of Grand National Course about four miles 856 yards.''

"Now then,'' said Mi. "Just listen. You start . . . *here* at the corner. It says 'Paddock' just behind.''

"Yes, Mi.''

"(An' don' keep saying, 'Yes, Mi.') Don't fuss too much about your start. It's no odds getting off in a tearaway. What you got to do is to jump round and jump clean and go as fast as you can when you know what you're doing. But wait till you know what you're doing before you hurry. Mind you, he doesn't know nothing about racing. He won't be hard to hold. I know you got him under your thumb. Now . . . First you cross a road. On tan. The tan'll fly up in your eye. Keep 'em shut across the road. Then the first fence. Plain fence. Then the next. Plain fence. You done just as big in the mushroom valley. There's nothing in them, but don't you despise 'em. Many's come down in the first two. There won't be much tailing there. You'll be all clustered up.

"Then comes a rail, ditch, and fence. I'm not saying it isn't an awful whopper for them as stands at the sides an' looks. It looks awful from the truckway. But it won't look so bad to you, you won't know it. You'll see a yellow-looking log lying low on the ground and you must take off in time before it. It's on the lip of the ditch. It's not the landing so much there as the take-off.

"Then there's two more thorn fences. Then there's Becher's.

"Now *there's no need to fall at Becher's*. No need at all. I watched it an' I know. If I was sitting below you on the far side I wouldn't want to see the eyes popping out of your head as you came down. Just sit back. If you lie back you'll only be upright to the ground. Don't jerk his head whatever you do. It's a long way down but he'll land steady. Just keep as still as if you were a dummy, and put confidence into him."

"What's the drop, Mi?"

"I don' know but it looks twenty. On account of the ditch at the bottom. But you clear the ditch. That's nothing to do with you. You land on uphill grass an' gallop on. Then there's a . . . (I can't read that one! It's printed on the black. It's a plain jump anyway.) Then there's the Canal Turn . . ."

"Mi, I can't remember it all!"

"Put yer mind to it. The Canal Turn's a teaser. You got to put yer mind to it. There's a chance of horses running out there. They got a screen up to stop it but they seem to want to run out to the left. There's the canal shinin' right ahead. Perhaps that's it. They don't want to swim.

"You want to make for the middle of the jump at the Canal Turn. Don't you go skidding in to the left and saving ground. If you get on the inside as they turn an' you've just landed, God help you. Even if you can't remember anything else remember to keep to the middle at the Canal Turn. You can't go wrong. There's the canal shinin' just in front of you. A pack of seagulls'll rise most likely as you come up. They always do."

"Mi, I swear I can't remember any more."

"But I gotta tell you about Valentine's."

"I'm getting sick again. You're making me sick again."

"You're a nice one. Wish I'd got you a double!"

"That mint stuff?"

"M'm. Gotta get all this into you. Even if I drop the rest of the jumps I gotta tell you it's twice round the course."

"Well, I know that! Is it too early to get the mint?"

"It's not six yet. It's dark. Gosh a'mighty look at the rain!" Mi walked to the window.

"Well, go on. But not about the jumps. Yes . . . tell me about the water jump."

"The water jump's pink," said Mi despondently.

"How d'you mean?"

"You got to say to yourself. ''It's pink. I gotta jump all of the pink.' ''

"Why's it pink?"

"Everything else is grey," said Mi, dully. "The water's puddled on pink clay. It looks meaty. It's opposite the Grand Stand. The people'll be yelling."

"Go on, Mi! Tell me some more!" Velvet sat up straighter seeing that her supporter was flagging.

"M'murdering you, Velvet? V'I brought you up here to kill you . . . ?"

"No fear. No you aren't! You're tired. You're soppy! It's no more'n a day's hunting."

"Oh, yes, it is! An' you never done a day's hunting."

"Come on, Mi. Piebald an' me'll go round like crickets. Tell me some more."

"I wish yer mother was here, Velvet."

"She *is* here! She's inside me. Ain't you always telling me that if she hadn't swum the Channel I shouldn't be up here?"

"Tha's true. But you get so sick an' all. It's an awful drawback, this vomiting."

"I'll grow out of it."

"I'll get you some more mint when it's daylight."

"Where's the money coming from?"

"I got that much. On'y we gotta be careful. It don' matter f'we land at the end of the race without a bean but we gotta have enough to get there."

"How we going out?"

Mi looked at her. "Taxi," he said. "That's what I bin having up for. Chap'll do it fer three and six."

"Gosh!" said Velvet.

"I gotta get you out there fresh . . . see?"

"Well then, come on then, tell me some more."

"Look here now, I talked to a lotta chaps. This is how it is. Them jumps in the valley you gather yer horse up, don't you?"

"Yes."

"Well, you can't go on doing that twice roun' the National. Or if you do you gotta do it like silk. Cos when a horse gets as done as that he can't stand being gathered up, not like you would at the beginning. You gotta haul him in. You remember that! You gotta haul

192 ⟨⟩

him in s'though he . . . s'though he was a big fish that was on'y half hooked. When he gets onto the Racecourse . . .''

"At the beginning?''

"No . . . that's what they call the end. The Racecourse. It means getting onto the straight after the jumps. It's when you get off the National Course an' come galloping up on the Gold Cup Course just before the Grand Stand. They call it 'coming onto the Racecourse.' ''

"Yes, Mi. Yes . . . well, I mean?''

"What was I saying? Oh, yes. When the horses get onto the second round, or a bit after (some don't do it till the second time Becher's), they begin to get their necks stickin' out so far you wouldn't know 'em. They can't jump like that. On the other hand if you pull 'em in with a jerk you throw 'em down. You want to haul. You want to take a pull an' a pull, s'gentle s'though you got 'em on a piece of silk an' it'll break. You gotta judge yourself how much you'll hustle after you've landed an' how soon before the next you'll take a little swig at the hauling.''

Quite suddenly Mi dozed. Velvet sat and looked at him and tried to remember the order of the jumps. The map had fallen out of his hand on to the floor but she did not like to disturb him to reach for it. The rain slashed and dribbled on the whitening pane. The electric light flickered once or twice as though the power stations were swimming up into daylight and meeting the morning shift. Mi woke again with a start.

"Th' Adelphi's full o' chaps,'' he said at once, brightly. "They say 'Yellow Messenger's' your trouble. He's a bay. Seventeen hands. Yellow jacket, crimson sleeves. And the Yank horse too. 'Bluebottle.' I shouldn't bother though. Just go round s'though you was alone."

"You bin about all night?"

"Won't hurt this one night in the year. It's nearly six. I'm going to get you some breakfast. Everyone's about already."

"Shall I get up?"

"No, you stop there. You'll be warmer. No point taking you about till I've got to. I'm going to get some stuff somewhere to tan up your neck."

Mi left her with the map to study and went out. Velvet looked idly at the map but she seemed to learn nothing from it. The rain and the blackness and the night had beaten everything flat in her. "I wish Mi hadn't told me so much," she thought. "I like it to come to me while I'm doing it." And she pushed the map slightly to one side and shut her mind against it. Mi came in with some coffee and slices of white bread and a square of butter.

"Mi," she said at once, "don't tell me a thing more. I want just to slide along till it's time thinking of nothing at all."

"Huh!" said Mi, putting the tray on the one chair. "Think a race like this is won by luck?"

"Everyone riding today," said Velvet, "knows more'n I do. I can't win that way."

"What's your way, then?"

"Jus' knowin' The Piebald can do it, an' tellin' him so," said Velvet, buttering her bread.

"Easy with that butter," said Mi. "Spread it thin. You've no stomach for grease. Here's the stuff for your neck. It's iodine. I borrowed it."

"Won't it smell that blood-smell?"

194 ⬤

"It'll wear off. We'll put a drop of water to it so it won't look so yellow. Bend your head down, let's try."

Mi had mixed a drop or two in the tooth glass, and painted it on below the white cropped hair. "It's that queer hair of yours is the trouble," said Mi. "Look like an albino."

"What's that?"

"Soft chaps. Soft-shell chaps, like eggs."

"Gimme the cap an' le's look."

Mi dived into the suitcase and pulled out a black silk cap. Velvet drew it over her cropped hair and well over her eyes.

"It's not too bad," said Mi. "Not much hair shows. The brown of your neck's much better, but where'll I end it off?"

"Wash it round weaker an' weaker with water."

Mi did his best.

Slowly the morning drew into wet daylight.

"Now I'm going out to the horse," said Mi. "I got him locked in an' I got the key. I'll pay the bill here. Don't you move till twelve."

"All that time?"

"You'll give yourself away if you put your nose out. At twelve jus' walk down with the bag an' walk out an' pop into the taxi."

"What taxi?"

"He'll be waiting. He don' know nothing about you but he's a chap I used to know. He'll be here at twelve sharp waiting to pick you up. Ferret-faced chap, but he's all right."

"Where'll I find you?"

"He'll bring you to where I want you, near the course. I'll have your dinner waiting for you."

"Don' give me anything to eat, Mi. Not jus' before like that. I'll never stand it."

"Not a ham sandwich?" said Mi, arrested at the door.

"Oh . . ." said Velvet.

The morning drifted by. Velvet rose and became the little man. At twelve to the tick he walked sharply down the stairs carrying his suitcase. He had padded shoulders, a common suit, a dingy white shirt and pale blue tie, a brownish overcoat with a half belt and Mi's old Homburg hat spotted with oil.

The taxi was there, the little man nodded and stepped inside. Under his coat he had an empty heart. He was crushed by delay and the rain.

The taxi took him through the mean streets for twenty minutes. It seemed impossible that so great a racecourse could lie buried in so mean a place. Suddenly there was a clearing on the right, and gates. Like the clearing and the gates of a cemetery lying in the surf of a metropolis. The taxi stopped and the little man leaned out of the window. Mi walked toward him from the corner of a fence.

~ THIRTEEN ~

This was the North with its everlasting white railings.
The stands were filling already. The Union Jack,
Stars and Stripes, and Tricolor flew over the grandstand.
The minor bookies under their stand-umbrellas had been
in position since eleven. Their fantastic names were
chalked on boards so that they looked like a fresh haul
of fish in a market. "Special this Day! Bream . . . Ernie
Bream . . . Alfy Haddock . . . Mossie Halibut . . . Duke
Cod!" They were shouting and clattering and taking
turns in gangs at the snack bar. Everything else was
more or less awaiting the glory of the day. "Champagne
bar . . . champagne only." This was empty. Inside the dining room the white tables were spread and the knowing
old waiters hung like old flies swarming in doorways.

The police had marched out in a dark stream an hour
before and had taken up positions round the course.
There was a constable at every jump with a folded
stretcher laid beside him, its rug within its folds. Each
man had a red flag and a yellow flag with which to call
his neighbor.

The public was flowing in like a river.

The whole course was blackening on the rim like a lake that has thrown up seaweed upon its banks. It had been black since daylight, but the seaweed was deepening and deepening, the truckway was solid with life, the ten shilling stand at the Canal Turn was groaning, the Melling Road, which crossed the course, from being an ivory band across the green became an ebony. Great passenger airplanes hummed over the stands and made their descent. A foreign king and queen arrived in Lord Sefton's box.

Tattersalls was like a thawed ice-rink. Pools had long appeared over the course. Thousands and thousands of people were wet, but not yet to the skin. And they hardly felt it.

The changing room for jockeys was warm and gay like a busy nursery. Jockeys' valets, with the air of slightly derelict family butlers, had been ironing in their shirtsleeves since seven in the morning. Two large coal fires behind nursery wire-guards were burning briskly, and over the guards hung strips of color. Gypsy silks were all across the long tables stretched down the middle, and the valets ironed and pressed and swore and grunted and cleaned soft boots and hunted for odds and ends in their enormous suitcases, the traveling houses of their livelihood. Down one side of the room hung little saddles, touching little saddles. Below them saddle cloths, numnahs, girths. Below them on the boot boxes countless little boots. Brown boots with black tops so soft you could hardly walk in them. Boots like gloves that are drawn on to a child's ankle, and filled out with a child's toes. Boots as touching as the saddles.

Outside in the weighing room the hooded scales had been uncloaked and the clerk of the scales was already at his desk. The declaration counter had its pens and inks and its stacks of empty forms waiting to be filled.

In the hospital room the nurse put a few more coals, delicately with her coal pincers, onto the bright fire.

While the second race was being run Mi signed "Michael Taylor" at the foot of his declaration card, and paused a second higher up on the card. "James Tasky" he wrote firmly. Then filled in the horse's name. He blotted the card and passed it into the box.

Then he went back to a little haunt of his.

"Now . . ." he said, half an hour later, crooking his finger in the doorway, and the little man picked up his suitcase and followed him.

"I'll take that," said Mi huskily.

Mi hustled the little man in past the unsaddling enclosure to the holy stillness of the weighing room, and, through the swing door into a corner of the changing room, pushing him down on a boot-box overshadowed by hanging garments.

"They're nak . . ." gasped the little man, sitting down.

"Tscht!" muttered Mi, standing over him.

The jockeys' valets bustled here and there, grumbled, stumbled, fell over boots. Two of their charges with hard red faces and snowy bodies were standing naked by the nursery fireguard. Mi looked grimly down at the little man.

"Keep yer eyes on yer knees," he muttered fiercely. And knelt to hold up the white breeches he had fished out of the suitcase.

"Who's your lady friend?" said one of the naked midgets, turning round to warm his other buttock.

"Miss Tasky. From Russia," said Mi without a flicker.

"Speak English?" said the midget, turning again like a chicken on a spit.

"No use wasting any dope on him," said Mi. "Can't speak a bloody word. He's a Bolshie they've sent over. To pick the winnings!"

"You sim to be doing the lady friend to the lady friend all right?"

"Doin' what I'm paid for," said Mi. "Times are ugly down South. I on'y jus' come up."

"Well, of all the muck-rakin' cheek," said the other naked midget, scratching his stomach . . . "that's that Tasky's riding that out-a-condition, pot-bellied whisky horse I saw brought in last night. Turnin' the Gran' National into a bloody circus!" and he cracked the end bone of his index finger like a pistol shot.

"Come on, Bibby, get dressed, do," begged an austere butler. "Going to ride the National in your pink skin?"

As Bibby turned away Tasky stood up gently, black, pink sleeves, black cap, white breeches, little black boots, brown tops, Mi pulled the saddle, saddle cloth and numnah, off the iron bracket. "Sit down an' wait," he said loudly as to a foreigner, pushed him back on the boot-box and stood over him.

Then, on the door opening. "They want you for the chair," he said.

"Thought he didn't understand English," said a voice.

"No reason why 'e shouldn't begin," said Mi. "CHAIR, I said," he yelled into Tasky's ear. "Come on!"

Outside in the weighing room all was quiet and regulated. "That's a toff," thought Mi, seeing a tall man get off the chair. He was obviously a gentleman rider, a "bumper."

"Weight?" said the clerk of the scales.

"Ten seven, near enough," said Mi. "He don't speak no English, sir. Russian."

Mi pushed the little man towards the scales. "Sit, can't you," he said in a hoarse whisper. "Double up!"

Tasky sat in the chair and nursed his saddle.

"Ten six and eleven," said the clerk's assistant.

"Penny piece," said the clerk quietly, and dropped a small piece of lead into the weight flap.

"An' a half," said the clerk. In went another piece. The Clerk wrote carefully in his book.

"Get off," hissed Mi. Tasky never budged.

Mi gave him a pull. "Job, sir, this is," he said. "Seems more a nitwit than . . ." He bustled the little man out of the room, throwing his brown overcoat round his shoulders.

"Who's that?" said someone, opening the door of the stewards' room.

"The Russian, sir," said the clerk of the scales, looking up at the clerk of the course.

The heavy, streaming daylight broke on them. The worst for Mi was over, the worst for Velvet to come.

"Keep in the crowd," said Mi. "I got to go for the horse. Keep movin'. Don't come out into the open. Don't rush at the horse when you see me lead him out. I got to go roun' and roun'. Wait till you see the others walk into the paddock . . ."

"Paddock?"

"Rails. There. Walk straight up to near me and stand by the bushes in the middle. I'll lead him up to you. I'll jump you up."

"Jump me up?"

"Jump you. I gotta take her knee an' jump you. Like the horse was too high fer you to get on. I'll take yer coat and I'll lead you out an' that's all I can do for you."

"You going now?" said Velvet, small, small in voice.

"I'm going. An' I got togs. You'll see. White leading rein an' all. Borrowed 'em off a head lad, friend o' mine."

Mi was gone and Velvet drifted through the crowd.

But suddenly Mi was back again. "Keep your eyes skinned an' keep AWAY from everyone who'll talk!" he hissed, and was gone again.

The crowd buzzed round the Tote, and many looked curiously at Velvet's black cap and bony childish face. She was not unlike an apprentice lad.

The horses were parading in the paddock. There came The Piebald. Velvet stared at him in shivering appreciation. He wore borrowed clothes with a knotted yellow rope bumping on his quarters. Mi led him with a white leading rein, wide like a tape. The number . . . 4 . . . was tied on Mi's left arm. As he came into the Paddock a buzz came from the crowd and here and there laughter. Round and round went the horses, and the rain down Velvet's neck.

Suddenly she saw the little men go in. Wide shoulders, gay caps and little feet. She walked forward, entered the paddock, and went straight to the bushes. There was a pause. The horses circled. Every jockey went up to his owner. She alone had no one. She stood firm and looked around her, conscious that this was her worst moment today.

Then up came Mi with The Piebald. She stripped her coat off and he held it on his arm, pulled the rugs off the horse onto his shoulder, stooped to her left leg and flung her up into the saddle. Almost at once the horses moved away, Mi walking beside her to the gate.

She was quite definite, quite easy. Now it was over, the creeping like a thief, the doubts, the waiting. No one would stop her now. The worst moments had come and gone, and there could be no doubt at all that now she and The Piebald were in together for the Grand National.

"There . . . I never told you," said Mi, low and hoarse, walking beside her. "Don't lie up on his neck! But it's too late now . . ."

"Ssh," said Velvet, looking straight ahead of her at something that seemed like a crane upon a raised embankment.

"I'll not 'ssh'!" said Mi, his heart bursting. "I'll say, "Think of yer ma!"

He snipped off the leading rein by its chromium hook and The Piebald swung through the gate.

"Coo . . . lummy . . ." said Mi, struck short. "I never told her to ride down in front of the Stands before going to the post . . ."

But for Velvet it was only follow-my-leader. She went down easily with the other horses, turned, stood slightly in her saddle, and galloped back. Mi started running for the truckway. "I'll never make Becher's . . . not in this crowd. Not unless there's a muck-up at the post."

Just ahead of him, turning out from the stable road-way, came the black motor ambulance, with the doctor sitting sideways in the back, looking at a paper. Behind the ambulance, from the same turning, crawled out a sinister, square-bottomed coffin, a knacker's cart, drawn by an enormous pigeon-chested shire-horse. Ahead of the ambulance, and blocking the way, went the horse ambulance, with its crane, drawn by two shire-horses in tandem. All made their way to Becher's. Another knacker's cart was trundling along far away by Valentine's, and yet another pushed its way in Melling Road.

"Black slugs . . ." said Mi, running, panting, pushing.

At the post the twenty horses were swaying like the sea. Forward. . . . No good! Back again. Forward. . . . No good! Back again.

The line formed . . . and rebroke. Waves of the sea. Drawing a breath . . . breaking. Velvet fifth from the rail, between a bay and a brown. The starter had long finished his instructions. Nothing more was said aloud, but low oaths flew, the cursing and grumbling flashed like a storm. An eye glanced at her with a look of hate. The breaking of movement was too close to movement to be borne. It was like water clinging to the tilted rim of the glass, like the sound of the dreaded explosion after the great shell has fallen. The will to surge forward overlaid by something delicate and terrible and strong, human obedience at bursting point, but not broken. Horses' eyes gleamed openly, men's eyes set like chips of steel. Rough man, checked in violence, barely master of himself, barely master of his horse. The Piebald ominously quiet, and nothing coming from him . . . up went the tape.

The green course poured in a river before her as she lay forward, and with the plunge of movement sat in the stream.

"Black slugs . . ." said Mi, cursing under his breath, running, dodging, suffocated with the crowd. It was the one thing he had overlooked, that the crowd was too dense ever to allow him to reach Becher's in the time. Away up above him was the truck-line, his once-glorious free seat, separated from him by a fence. "Coo, lummy . . ." he mumbled, his throat gone cold, and stumbled into an old fool in a mackintosh. "Are they off?" he yelled at the heavy crowd as he ran, but no one bothered with him.

He was cursed if he was heeded at all. He ran, gauging his position by the cranes on the embankment. Velvet coming over Becher's in a minute and he not there to see her. "They're off." All around him a sea of throats offered up the gasp.

He was opposite Becher's but could see nothing: the crowd thirty deep between him and the course. All around fell the terrible silence of expectancy. Mi stood like a rock. If he could not see then he must use his ears, hear. Enclosed in the dense, silent, dripping pack he heard the thunder coming. It roared up on the wet turf like the single approach of a multiple-footed animal. There were stifled exclamations, grunts, thuds. Something in the air flashed and descended. The first over Becher's! A roar went up from the crowd, then silence. The things flashing in the air were indistinguishable. The tip of a cap exposed for the briefest of seconds. The race went by like an express train, and was gone. Could Velvet be alive in that?

Sweat ran off Mi's forehead and into his eyes. But it was not sweat that turned the air grey and blotted out the faces before him. The ground on all sides seemed to be smoking. An extraordinary mist like a low prairie fire was formed in the air. It had dwelt heavily all day behind the Canal, but the whole of the course had remained clear till now. And now, before you could turn to look at your neighbor, his face was gone. The mist blew in shreds, drifted, left the crowd clear again but hid the whole of the Canal Corner, fences, stand and horses.

There was a struggle going on at Becher's; a horse had fallen and was being got out with ropes. Mi's legs turned to water and he asked his neighbor gruffly, "Who's fallen?" But the neighbor, straining to the tip of his toes, and glued to his glasses, was deaf as lead.

Suddenly Mi lashed round him in a frenzy. "Who's fallen, I say? Who's hurt!"

"Steady on," said a little man whom he had prodded in the stomach.

"Who's fallen?" said Mi desperately. "I gotta brother in this . . ."

"It's his brother!" said the crowd all around him. "Let him through."

Mi was pushed and pummeled to the front and remained embedded two from the front line. The horse that had fallen was a black horse, its neck unnaturally stretched by the ropes that were hauling it from the ditch.

There was a shout and a horse, not riderless, but ridden by a tugging, cursing man, came galloping back through the curling fumes of the mist, rolled its wild eye at the wrong side of Becher's and disappeared away out of the course. An uproar began along the fringes of the crowd and rolled back to where Mi stood. Two more horses came back out of the mist, one riderless. The shades of others could be discerned in the fog. Curses rapped out from unseen mouths.

"What's happened at the Canal Turn? What's wrong down at the Turn?"

"The whole field!" shouted a man. The crowd took it up.

"The field's out. The whole field's come back.

There's no race!'' It was unearthly. Something a hundred yards down there in the fog had risen up and destroyed the greatest steeplechase in the world.

Nineteen horses had streamed down to the Canal Turn, and suddenly, there across the course, at the boundary of the fog, four horses appeared beyond Valentine's, and among them, fourth was The Piebald.

"Yer little lovely, yer little lovely," yelled Mi, wringing his hands and hitting his knees. "It's her, it's him, it's me brother!"

No one took any notice. The scene immediately before them occupied all the attention. Horses that had fallen galloped by riderless, stirrups flying from their saddles, jockeys returned on foot, covered with mud, limping, holding their sides, some running slowly and miserably over the soggy course, trying to catch and sort the horses.

"It's 'Yellow Messenger,' " said a jockey savagely, who had just seized his horse. "Stuck on the fence down there and kicking." And he mounted.

"And wouldn't they jump over him?" called a girl shrilly.

"They didn't wanter hurt the pore thing, lady," said the jockey, grinning through his mud, and rode off.

"Whole lot piled up and refused," said a man who came up the line. "Get the course clear now, quick!"

"They're coming again!" yelled Mi, watching the galloping four. "Get the course clear! They'll be coming!"

They were out of his vision now, stuck down under Becher's high fence as he was. Once past Becher's on the second round would he have time to extricate himself and get back to the post before they were home? He stood indecisively and a minute went by. The course

207

in front of him was clear. Horses and men had melted. The hush of anticipation began to fall. "They're on the tan again," said a single voice. Mi flashed to a decision. He could not afford the minutes to be at Becher's. He must get back for the finish and it would take him all his time. He backed and plunged and ducked, got cursed afresh. The thunder was coming again as he reached the road and turned to face the far-off stands. This time he could see nothing at all, not even a cap in the air. "What's leading? What's leading?"

"Big brown. Tantibus, Tantibus. Tantibus leading."

"Where's The Piebald?"

"See that! Leonara coming up . . ."

They were deaf to his frantic questions. He could not wait, but ran. The mist was ahead of him again, driving in frills and wafting sedgily about. Could Velvet have survived Becher's twice? In any case no good wondering. He couldn't get at her to help her. If she fell he would find her more quickly at the hospital door than struggle through the crowd and be forbidden the now empty course.

Then a yell. "There's one down!"

"It's the Yank mare!"

The horse ambulance was trundling back with Yellow Messenger from the Canal Turn. Mi leapt for a second on to the turning hub of the wheel and saw in a flash, across the momentarily mist-clear course, the pride of Baltimore in the mud underneath Valentine's. The Piebald was lying third. The wheel turned and he could see no more. Five fences from the finish; he would not allow himself to hope, but ran and ran. How far away the stands in the gaps of the mist as he pushed, gasping, through the people. Would she fall now? What had he done, bringing her up here? But would she fall now? He ran and ran.

"They're coming onto the Racecourse . . . coming onto the Racecourse . . ."

"How many?"

"Rain, rain, can't see a thing."

"How many?"

Down sank the fog again, as a puff of wind blew and gathered it together. There was a steady roaring from stands, then silence, then a hubbub. No one could see the telegraph.

Mi, running, gasped, "Who's won?"

But everyone was asking the same question. Men were running, pushing, running, just as he. He came up to the gates of Melling Road, crossed the road on the fringe of the tan, and suddenly, out of the mist, The Piebald galloped riderless, lolloping unsteadily along, reins hanging, stirrups dangling. Mi burst through onto the course, his heart wrung.

"Get back there!" shouted a policeman. "Loose horse!"

"Hullo, Old Pie there!" shouted Mi. The animal, soaked, panting, spent, staggered, slipped and drew up.

"What've you done with 'er?" said Mi, weeping, and bent down to lift the hoof back through the rein. "You let 'er down, Pie? What in . . . ? He led the horse down the course, running, his breath catching, his heart thumping, tears and rain on his face.

Two men came towards him out of the mist.

"You got him?" shouted one. "Good fer you. Gimme!"

"You want him?" said Mi, in a stupor, giving up the rein.

"Raised an objection. Want him for the enclosure. Chap come queer."

"Chap did? What chap?"

"This here's the winner! Where you bin all day, Percy?"

"Foggy," said Mi. "Very foggy. Oh, my God."

Back in the fog a voice had spoken into a telephone. It had need only to say one word. All else had been written out beforehand. And in that very second in the offices of the Associated Press in New York men had taken off the message.

"Urgent Associated New York Flash Piebald Wins." The one word the voice had said into the fog was "Piebald."

Up went the red flag. The crowd buzzed. "What is it?" "Did he fall?"

"Must've hurt hisself jumping . . ."

"Fainted."

"Jus' dismounted, the silly . . ."

Dismounted before reaching the unsaddling enclosure. Objection. Up went the red flag. There was tenseness along the line of private bookies, pandemonium in the bookies' stand under the umbrellas, tight knots gathered round the opening to the weighing room, behind which was the stewards' room. Glasses were leveled from everywhere upon the board. If a white flag went up the objection was overruled. If a green it was sustained. But the red remained unwaveringly.

"Taken him round to the hospital."

"Stretcher, was it?"

"Jus' gone through where all those people are . . ."

The doctor had got back from his tour of the course

in his ambulance. Two riders had already been brought in and the nurse had prepared them in readiness for his examination. Now the winner himself coming in on a stretcher. Busy thirty minutes ahead.

"Get him ready, nurse."

The winner lay unconscious wrapped in a horse blanket, his face mottled with the mud that had leaped up from flying hoofs.

"Looks sixteen," said the doctor curiously, and knelt to turn the gas a little lower under the forceps.

"Bin boiling for twenty minutes," said the nurse.

"Place full of steam," said the doctor. "Been watching . . . ?" and he passed to the end cubicle.

"No," said the nurse shortly to his back. She disliked the Grand National, and had waited behind the stands to patch up the damage.

The constables with the stretcher placed the winner on the bed by the door, leaving him still wrapped in his blanket. They retired and closed the door. The nurse slipped a towel under the muddy head, and turning back the blanket started to undo the soaking jacket of black silk.

"Nurse," roared the doctor from another cubicle . . . "No, stay where you are! I've got it!"

"Could you come here a minute?" said the nurse, at his side a few minutes later.

The doctor straightened his back. He had a touch of lumbago. "I'll be back, Jem," he said. "You're not much hurt. Cover up. Yes?"

"Just a minute . . . over here."

She whispered to him quietly. He slapped his raincoated cheek and went to the bed by the door. "Put your screens round." She planted them. "Constable," he said, poking his head out of the door, "get one of the stewards here, will you." (The roar of the crowd came in at the door.) "One of the stewards! Quick's you can. Here, I'll let you in this side door. You can get through." The crowd seethed, seizing upon every sign.

Mi crouched by the door without daring to ask after his child. He heard the doctor call. He saw the steward go in. "Anyway," he thought, "they've found out at once. They would. What's it matter if she's all right. She's won, the little beggar, the little beggar."

The sergeant of police was by the stables. "Message from up there," he said briefly to his second. "Squad to go up to the hospital door. Row round the door. Something up with the winner."

The police marched up in a black snake. The people fell back. An ambulance came in from the Ormskirk Road and backed down the line of police. The red flag remained for a moment, then slowly the green flag mounted on the board. Objection sustained. A frightful clamor burst out in the grand stand.

In the stewards' room the glittering manifesto looked down out of his frame and heard the low talk of his appalling desecration. A butcher's girl on a piebald horse had pounced up beside him into history.

"Got her off?" said one of the stewards in a low voice.

"Just about. There was a bit of a rush for a second. She called out something as the stretcher was being shoved in. Called out she was all right . . . to somebody in the crowd. I'm glad we got her off quick. The crowd's boiling with excitement."

"How'd it get out so quick?"

"I dunno. Swell row this'll be. It'll have to be referred back to Weatherby's.'' The clerk of the course came in. "Crowd's bubbling like kettles out there, Lord Henry. By Jove, it's the biggest ramp. How'd she pull it over!''

"Who's gone with her?''

"The doctor couldn't go. He's got two other men, one a baddish crash at Valentine's.''

"Well, somebody ought to 'a' gone. Find out who's gone, will you?''

The clerk of the course disappeared.

"Tim's Chance wins, of course.''

"Yes, that's been announced. There's no question. The objection is sustained definitely here on the course, and the rest must be referred to London. There'll be a special of the N.H.C., I should think it might be a case for legal proceedings. Well . . .'' (As the door opened) "did you find out who went with her?''

"A second doctor, Lord Henry. A young man who's here very often. Friend of Doctor Bodie's. And a constable.''

"There should have been an official. Of course there should have been an official. What's the hospital?''

"Liverpool Central . . .''

"Isn't there a friend or relation with her?''

"Nobody.''

"Well, she called out to somebody!''

"The somebody's hidden himself all right. Well for him! She's quite alone s'far as we can make out.''

"D'she say anything?''

"Won't speak. Except that one shout she gave.''

"If my daughter'd done it,'' said Lord Henry Vile, "I'd be . . .'' He paused and stroked his lip with his finger.

"Pretty upset, I should think . . .''

"I wasn't going to say that,'' said Lord Henry. "No.''

⟶ FOURTEEN ⟵

Almost as soon as the ambulance was off the ground
little breezes began to blow hither and thither bearing the fact. Without the name. A girl had won the
Grand National.

A girl had won the Grand National. By the look of
the stretcher "a slip of a girl." By the memory of the
crouching black and pink ant on The Piebald, again "a
slip of a girl." The news began to crack like gunpowder
trailed to percussion caps. At each percussion cap an
explosion. At each explosion men flung, hurled about
their business.

The U.P. man on the roof of the grandstand went on
with his telephoning (at two pounds a minute). He had
laid his field glasses down now and was talking feverishly. "Urgent bulletin," he said violently, "astounding
rumors circulating track. Is winning jockey girl? We
upchecking." And a little later, in his shorthand Chinese, "Stewards' decision. Quiz moved London."

As the ambulance turned into the Ormskirk Road the
news had broken. It was flashing to London in waves

214 ⟶

of light, in waves of air. It was "breaking" on London. At first the smaller men flashed it, unscrupulous, out for speed at all costs. The graver men hung back. Verify, verify! It *couldn't* be. The serious sporting reporters, associated for a lifetime with the turf, felt it couldn't be. Almost . . . it had better not be. Such frivolity, but . . . what news! NEWS, sparkling, rainbow NEWS. London was disturbed, tickled, a few seconds before the graver men felt they could spring for it. Then they sprang. And the full blast swept down the lines and the airways. Like a whiff . . . the miraculous transmission of accurate, verified, imagination-shaking news. It could hardly be a scoop because before one could close the telephone box everyone knew it. But details . . . where was the girl? In a second, having delivered their blast on London, they turned like hounds after the girl. The ambulance was gone. Where? The Liverpool Central . . . Ah . . . The taxi rank was in the Ormskirk Road.

But once before the Liverpool Central had housed a fame-shaker. And the resident medical officer was a grim fellow with yellow hair, blue eyes and set mouth. He had been through the war and he had been through that strange medical upbringing in a good Scottish hospital which gets into a man's bones and transmutes him forever from common humanity. He was steady and wily and fine, and he could act as quick as news could flash. And for reasons of his own connected with his attitude and their attitude towards truth and scientific thought he had a cold impatience of the press.

The murmurs surrounding Velvet came with her like raindrops on the ambulance. She had not long been wheeled into the Women's Accident Ward, and the nurse in charge had hardly propped screens round her bed, before the resident medical officer had mopped up the rumors, his curiously flat ears very wide awake.

"Be down from Aintree," he thought, "in a jiffy."

He found, actually, that they were already drawing up at the gates.

The resident M.O. closed the ward doors and placed the constable who had come with the ambulance on duty.

The constable was not sure it was the right duty . . .

"Just a minute, officer . . ." said the resident M.O. swiftly, increasing the constable's rank and giving him a cold-water flash out of the blue eyes. "Not more than a second while we wheel her into a private ward. Can't have the press in round the bed. I think you'll find that's why you were asked to whip out of Aintree. Right ahead, nurse. 'Nother blanket over her . . . (*right* over her) when you get her on the trolley."

Two white-coated men sped down the ward with a trolley.

"Over your face, girl, too, for a minute," said the resident M.O., leaving the constable at the door and going down the ward to meet the trolley. "It's all right. Want to get you into another ward. Quiet."

A nurse sprang to push the double doors back onto their catches for the trolley to pass.

A Press Association man approached the M.O.

"Let the trolley pass," said the M.O. abruptly. "Stand back. Operation case."

The trolley passed swiftly out of view under the nose of bowler-hatted men who were arriving.

But the balloon of notoriety wasn't going to stay on the ground just because of the principal M.O. The press bellows had now begun to blow and the balloon to lift.

Yet the little creature still lay snug like a kernel in

the private ward of the Liverpool Central, with the door locked and a nurse giving her a blanket bath. Then in came tea on a tray, two meat sandwiches cut in triangles, a chocolate bun in a paper, a rice bun, a piece of plum cake and two slices of white bread and butter. Velvet snuggled down and began to wonder what next and what next and when the heavens were going to fall. And, above all, where was Mi?

Mi, rubbing down the piebald horse in the stables at Aintree, was bearing the brunt of everything. He was knee-deep in the press, he was wanted in the stewards' room, he was wanted by everybody. Even the bookmakers would have liked to get at him.

"This horse won the National, ain't it? This horse 'as got to be rubbed down. I don't know a thing 'cept that I was hired to do over the horse. Hired at the last minute. Well . . . what? Well, if I'm wanted in the stewards' room I'll have to go. But this horse wants rubbin' and rubbin'. Who's going to do it for me?"

There were plenty of offers. There were even men who had a nodding knowledge of him.

"Why, Mi, you old tout . . . who's your lady friend? D'you mean to say you didn't know? What about the changing room?"

"How was I to know? She got pants on, ha'n't she? I on'y know she couldn't speak a word a' King's English, an' was s'flat's a pancake and as dumb's an oyster . . . Comin', sir . . . Rub him well . . . Give his backline a massage . . . under the saddle. Makes the blood flow . . . I'll be back in a minute. I got nothing to say to 'em. Stewards . . . My hat! . . . Comin', sir!"

In the stewards' room nothing could be got out of Mi. He was heavy-minded, obstinate and repetitive. Lord Henry Vile did not look as though he believed him, and finally it was decided to take his address and refer the inquest to London, at a special meeting of the National Hunt Committee. Mi gave his address as Post Restante, Lewes.

"Fishy sort of address," said Colonel "Ruby" Allbrow, looking at him straight.

"I can't hide, sir," said Mi, suddenly looking as straight back. "I'm known here to lots, an' I'm known there. The police'd lay their hands on me in a day 'f I was to monkey up."

"And the horse?"

"Horse goes back to the owner, sir. Horse-box is coming for it tonight."

"And not you?"

"Not me, sir."

"And the owner's address . . . We have the owner's address, Mr. Gray?"

"Yes, we have the address," said the official. "The owner must be behind it all, m'lord, if you'll excuse me interrupting."

"Yes . . . that'll be looked into. Letter must be sent and so on. Who's going down to the hospital?"

A spasm crossed Mi's face. He opened his mouth but said nothing. Velvet alone in that hospital. 'S sick as a cat. But there were doctors an' all that. It'd soon be in the papers how she was.

Velvet lay in the hospital refusing her name. She and Mi had no plan beyond the winning of the Grand National. How should they? They had bitten off a piece of dream together, and like winged children accomplished it. Beyond, all was an uncharted sea. They had not had one glance at life after the winning.

Still by instinct she refused her name. The heavens were going to fall. Father was going to know, the village was going to know, Edwina was going to say sarcastic things because Teddy didn't like all the fuss. There was going to be trouble for her and Mi, though pure white glory for The Piebald. And the longer she kept her name secret the slower the trouble would be in coming. She lay and smiled wanly, and shook her clipped white head.

Indeed she wasn't pressed enormously to tell. The M.O. didn't care a rap about her name, and the nurse in charge of her simply washed her and fed her and choked back her curiosity because she too had had a cold-water flash from the blue eyes of the hospital's despot. The young doctor who had brought Velvet down had disappeared, but he came back later accompanied by Dr. Bodie from Aintree and the clerk of the course himself.

The M.O. stared at them with his curious look and told them quietly that they must not stay more than five minutes with the patient. The nurse was present at the interview. The clerk of the course asked formally for Velvet's name and address. Dr. Bodie blustered a little when Velvet sighed and said shyly she couldn't give it. The young doctor said nothing. He was more than thrilled whichever way the situation turned. At the end of five minutes the M.O. came himself to say it was time.

"Shock," said the M.O. with a grudging apology in the corridor. "Very young."

After they had gone the M.O. came back. "Sorry, I must have your name for hospital purposes," he said, and he pulled the silver pencil out of his notebook.

Velvet looked up with confidence into the ledger of that secure face, and said at once "Velvet Brown," and spelled the address clearly for him.

"Age?" he said.

"Fourteen. Nearly fifteen."

"There'll be a doctor up to go over you in a few minutes. Dr. Bodie tells me there's nothing broken."

"I didn't fall off," said Velvet. "I slid off. After the post. I couldn't feel my knees."

"Feel any pain anywhere?"

"No, thank you. I could have got up, only my legs . . ."

"All right. Right. Enjoyed your tea?"

And the M.O. went, like an iron ghost, and the door closed invisibly behind him.

At five-thirty she had a drink of bromide and chloral, and twenty minutes later the gates of the world closed down on her while the second batch of posters in London and Liverpool and all the great cities of England, France, Germany, Italy . . . fell sloppily off the printing machines, were baled up, dispatched, and, drying, fluttered at street corners and receded on the backs of newspaper cars. "Drama of winner of National this afternoon." "Unknown girl wins National." (This paper thought the fact so first-rate that there was no need to attract by mystery.)

"Extraordinary affair at Aintree."

"Piebald wins but disqualified. Rider found to be woman."

Ten minutes later more posters . . .

"Girl winner in Liverpool Central Hospital."

In the great cities of America the boys were calling "Extra!" and the stop press of all the papers shone in green, red, and blue ink. From France the *Intransigeant* and the *Paris Soir* sent two men over in airplanes to Aintree. The Associated Press of America got an all-clear interview with the clerk of the course. In Shanghai the first 3.30 flash had just caught the last editions of the morning *North China Daily News.* Rome and Berlin did not trouble themselves profoundly. The thing grew and grew and grew, and turned over on itself, and heaped itself up. People walked in the streets not knowing that the air quivered with question marks. The common air, not seeing or tasting or breathing any different, was heavy with one idea, one burden, an incoming wave of query into England. This questioning air, sweeping through impediment in a silvery attack, poured round flesh, wood, and stone till it found the wireless masts and there, settling and transmuting itself into something more possible to human understanding, became the word of man.

There was a pause. The queries massed like birds and waited. "We must know more!" cried every foreign agency and every newspaper.

"You shall know more," soothed the deep voice of Reuter, sedate and cautious, before it ringed the world with its answer.

The reporters had been baffled at the Liverpool Central but Dr. Bodie was got at. Eager, in fact, to be got at.

He could not tell the rider's name but he described this and that, and after a while, the information having been looked over and binged up here and toned down there, and written almost all in most expensive plain language (that there should be no delay anywhere in decoding) Reuter sent round the world the following message . . . "61610 Lead all stop Girl has won and lost Grand National stop Most sensational incident in Aintree history occurred today when discovered winning jockey mounted Piebald was young girl stop Since women jockeys unallowed compete National Piebald disqualified by stewards stop Girl fainted after passing post carried ambulance room on stretcher where sex discovered by doctor who states age between 14-16 years stop Faint due fatigue unserious injuries stop Girl who refused reveal identity rode under Russian jockey Tasky's name stop Stewards National Hunt Committee ordered fullest investigation stop For woman to complete National course regarded as one most extraordinary feats in annals British racing stop Drama mystery associated this amazing affair whipped up excitement feverpitch countrywide stop Result race now reads . . ." (and the names of the first three horses were given).

As this message left London it flashed in a few seconds along the trunk lines that were being held open for it, through Egypt, to India, South Africa, Australia, and to Singapore and the Far East. From the arteries ran the veins. Men in Shanghai, Sydney, Capetown became disseminators almost at the same moment that they had been receivers. And in a steady spreading belt round the world ran the reply to the frantic queries.

In each country there was a smaller proper machinery to receive it and its redistribution was carried out in eddies from the main encircling belt. In each country the smaller proper machinery distributed it to the newspapers, and newspapers set it up in print, printed it, issued it, sold it, and it was read by white, brown, yellow, red and black men who exclaimed in their tongues—"Whew!"

Heads of news agencies, heads of syndicates, heads of newspapers said in their various languages, "This is a press ballyhoo. Spread all out on this. This is front-page stuff."

"We gotta splurge," said a great man in New York. "Get the dope from that dame. She's swell!" And he cabled, "Ten thousand dollars for exclusive rights of personal story." A girl in London got into a fast car and drove rapidly down to the coast.

It was the great bellows of the glory machine starting to blow. But it had not nearly got its wind up yet. The pink balloon of notoriety had hardly done more than shake loose its ropes and fill out. And the little creature whose name it bore lay very slight, very sheltered, under the deep and fumy blanket.

"It's Velvet. Sure's fate it's Velvet," said Mr. Brown, standing in the street doorway. "Come in, gentlemen!"

"Mother! Hi! Come on in here!" he called. "Here's our Velvet gone . . . I feel hot in the stomach, gentlemen. She ain't hurt herself? (I gotta sit down.) She safe?"

Mrs. Brown filled the inner doorway.

"Mother," said Mr. Brown, looking white and shaken, "our Velvet gone an' won the Grand National. Ridden it herself . . ."

Certainly Mrs. Brown's eyes changed their color in some way. They did not gleam. They were too high in their shallows for that, but a curious light seemed to shift in them.

"She's not one for words, sir," said Mr. Brown, taking out his handkerchief and wiping his hands. "(Fingers gone all sticky. Takes me that way.) I can't take it in what she done. Where is she, then?"

"She's in the Liverpool Central Hospital . . ." began one of the reporters.

"Why?" said Mrs. Brown like a pistol shot.

"Just fatigue, so we understand," said the reporter.

"They're from the newspapers, Mother," said Mr. Brown.

"She slipped off her horse, Mrs. Brown," said the reporter. "Fainted after she had passed the winning post. No bones broken, no harm done. Is this the first you have heard of it?"

"Papers don't get here till seven," said Mr. Brown. "On the Tilling's bus." He looked at his watch. "It's a quarter of now."

"Then you have no doubt," said another reporter, "that the rider is also the owner, your daughter Velvet?"

"He don't even know," said Mrs. Brown suddenly. "Don't you tell him nothing, William. I know them."

"Why ever not?" said Mr. Brown. "She's got a bit of a down on newspaper gentlemen, sir," said he apologetically. "Haven't you, Mother? She had a bit of a bad time with 'em once."

"Tell 'em what you like. You've begun," said Mrs. Brown, shutting the door. She crossed the room in majesty and went up to her room.

Mr. Brown gave a lengthy interview only interrupted by the gentlemen's desire to get away and to the telephone to catch the last edition of the evening papers.

The reporters were shown the paper horses in the shell-box.

One of them thought the shell-box touching, but did not say so.

"Fresh, fresh, fresh an' hot!" said another as they sped down the street.

"Old lady's bin in the news," said another. "Wonder how?"

"Bloody old cathedral!" said the first.

In the morning at the Liverpool Central Mother sat by Velvet's bed (Mother, carrying her washing things in her old "Art" bag).

"I've come to take you home, dearie," she said.

Velvet, dazed with her sleep still, and brilliantly happy, smiled through her dreams.

"Nice kettle of fish," said Mrs. Brown.

"Traveled up through the night," said Mother. "You done well, Velvet."

This was the summit, and Velvet felt the beating of glory.

Before coming in Mother had had a talk to the resident medical office and they discovered in their wordless way that they felt alike on certain subjects. It was found that Velvet could be taken out by the laundry entrance.

"She's ser little she could go in a laundry basket," said Mother.

"No need for that," objected the M.O. who was against exaggeration.

And Velvet (and Mrs. Brown with her, for her bulk had not yet become as famous as it did a few days later) went in the laundry van, its rear backed up against the Laundry Entrance.

They reached the station in safety, for though the film of the Grand National had already been on the screens of thousands of cinema houses the night before, and the morning papers were alive with Mr. Brown's interview, there were no pictures as yet (Mr. Brown had not dared to ask for the one off Mrs. Brown's dressing-table), and the crouching black ant flashing by on the film bore no relation to the peaky young man walking beside the big woman to a third-class carriage on the "Merseyside" as its engines got up steam.

"Better you kep' 'em on," Mrs. Brown had said in the van. "N'anyway I never thought to bring your others. Look the proper boy!"

The carriage was full, but no one's attention was caught. Velvet behaved like the obscure child she thought herself to be.

They reached London, crossed it on the Underground, and took the local train.

A taxi stood in a dark corner of the station yard. As Velvet was pushed into its gloom by her mother she was caught by the eager hands of her sisters. "Velvet, Velvet . . . Oh, Velvet. . . . What you got on? Coo lummy, she's dressed like a boy!"

"Ssh!" said mother. "Don' talk so . . ." The taxi started off.

"Velvet, it's glorious! All the afternoon, ever since yesterday, everybody comin' to ask. We knew it was you las' night when the newspapermen came. All the papers got pictures of us in, but it's you they're waiting to get! American girl come in a car, an' the things she asked father said it made him hot to hear her. She said she gotta get your story."

"What story?" said Velvet.

"Don' talk ser much," said mother. "She don' know about all that yet."

When the celebrated child returned home that night she was able to walk under the triumphal arch which the villagers had built with haste in the morning.

(And this arch and this street opening were the gateway to a village whose roofs and whose faces were the same but whose nature was changed to her. From now on she walked, fastened to that glory, whose teeth were sharp and held well, but whose things were golden. She walked with an eagle on her back, observed by all.)

As the station taxi turned into the narrow lane of the village, shouts and dangling lights brought it to a halt.

226

There was a rope across the street, hung with lanterns, and by its light the glossy flutter of the leafy arch could be seen. Mr. Croom was at the taxi door, a bouquet of lit faces behind his shoulder, and Velvet was lifted out and walked under the arch and was carried home, rockily, on many shoulders. Mrs. Brown paid off the taxi, and strode with her face glum. She was reminded of Calais.

In the living room at home there was not room for everybody, and the villagers hung in the doorway and shuffled in a tail in the street. The bottle of port came out but there was not much in it, and Mr. Brown sent Mally out for more. It was not long before Mrs. Brown bore Velvet, like a child of paper, to her bedroom. "You'll lay there," she said, "an' I'll bring you your supper."

Greatest wonder, it was Edwina who brought her a hot-water bottle, who stayed to talk in marveling whispers, and listened with Velvet to the clamor down below. Mother brought the tray up, cold salt beef and chopped beetroot and a cup of cocoa. Velvet nibbled gently, changed feet on her hot-water bottle, watched the dark sky through the undrawn curtains.

"No one's to come up," said Mrs. Brown. And Velvet finished her supper and lay and waited for Mally and Merry, who came when the visitors had melted.

Mi turned up, having mysteriously come by a later train for nothing. Velvet slipped on her clothes again.

"You got up?" said Mrs. Brown as Velvet walked into the living room.

"It's dark now. Pitch," said Velvet. "I mus' just go up the field an' fetch him in." She turned and took her shell-box of paper horses off the sideboard.

"They seen that, Velvet."

"Who did?"

"The newspapermen," said Mrs. Brown. But Velvet did not seem to understand.

Mrs. Brown expanded her breast in an unusual and vigorous sigh.

"She won't pass no one now, though the whole village's bin hanging round the horse from what I hear. Better let her go. She won't pass no one ser late. Heigho . . . I bin a darn donkey once in my life an' it seems I bin it twice."

Velvet, dressed in her own clothes, went up the road between the ditches with Mally. The cats' eyes gleamed and shifted and went out. Nettles and cats' eyes and stars and stillness and not a soul about. The Piebald was flashing his colors under stars by the gate. The other horses hearing her step cantered down the slope whinnying. They greeted her with little jealous screams and lashings.

"D'you know what you've done?" said Velvet to The Piebald, but he shook his head suddenly as though a night gnat was on it.

"Wasa matter, Pie old darling? Hasn' he gone in at the haunches terrible, Mally? Just in one day."

". . . An' what a day!" said Mally.

Velvet, her cheek on the top of the gate. Sir Pericles' breath blew her hair. "The worse was I got my mouth open an' couldn't shut it because the wind dried it. What was *your* worse, Pie old darling?"

Velvet turned solemnly to Mally. "He'll be in every book, Mally. He'll be the horse of this year, that won it this year. Though they disqualify us they'll never dare to drop him out altogether. He won't be on the Aintree Roll of Honor . . ."

"What's that?"

"A brown board with gold letters. But he'll be in the books the writers write. The first piebald horse that ever won the National. By what I've heard about it they'll try to buy him, but I'll never sell him. SELL you, Piebald!"

"The poor others!" said Mally. "Do they mind?"

"No, no . . . Pericles! Little sweetie . . . Mrs. James! You're squealing, you jealous old woman. She's tried to kick George, Mally. Get away . . . there . . ."

"George deserves all he gets," said Mally. "He pokes his nose in everywhere and it's food he wants, not love. He and Mrs. James thought you'd come with a bucket."

"Come on, Piebald," called Velvet, searching for the old halter they kept behind the wall. But The Piebald was cropping the cool night grass away with a layer of dark air between them, as though horses that had won the Grand National were turned out to grass in the early spring every night. Unceremonious and incredibly enduring, he moved away.

"Come on," said Mally, "I should leave him. It's warm. He won't hurt. Mother said not to let you stay long. You're dead tired."

"I gotta see Donald before I sleep," said Velvet.

"Donald?"

"I thought about him the night I was going to ride. In that hotel bedroom. I was sick as anything . . ."

"Oh, poor Velvet! An' all alone!"

"No, Mi kep' comin' in an' out. I thought about if I was killed an' never saw Donald again. On'y for a flash, but I thought it."

"Funny thing to think. Why Donald?"

"It was funny. But I thought it anyway," said Velvet doggedly. "I mus' jus' see him when I go in."

They entered the house.

"Velvet wants to see Donald," said Mally, some-what aggrieved.

"I wanter kiss him in his bed," said Velvet.

"She's overstrung," said Mrs. Brown. "Go on up, he's dead asleep."

Donald lay flung out in an abandoned and charming attitude. His eyelashes were tender, bronze and shad-owy; his hair a touch damp. The strangeness of his youth and exposed face, his battle for power by day and his abdication by night were something that Velvet had hardly expected. A gateway drew open within her and the misery and wild alarm of life rushed in.

"Velvet's crying over Donald!" said Mally aghast, running down to the living room.

"Carry her to her bed, Father," said Mrs. Brown calmly. "It's to be expected."

⤐ FIFTEEN ⤎

Next morning the Browns rose as usual. Edwina came down to take in the milk and the greeting of the milkman was a little long because it contained moderate congratulations. The milkman was a steady fellow.

From then on, however nothing else was as usual. The crowd began to collect upon the Green in knots about nine, and by ten it was definitely clotted and pooling in the street. Mally, with her twitching nose, went out towards it early and scented radiations. The crowd, which was small and scattered at the time, definitely stirred as the front door opened, and something in the white faces and black eyes all looking one way made Mally shut the door again.

"I believe it's about Velvet," she said with a gasp into the scullery. "Ther's people outside."

"People?" said Mrs. Brown. "Someone want her?"

"Just people," said Molly. "Standing about."

Mrs. Brown went to look. She pulled the front blinds down over the cinerarias. So on a sunny morning at the end of March Velvet started her first day of glory as though someone had died in the house.

The crowd grew denser during the morning and none of the Browns put a nose out of doors. Mrs. Brown set the four girls at little jobs in their bedrooms and told them to keep the yard end by the canary cages. The crowd made a great deal of noise in the street as it drifted about, and the house seemed very small.

"Are you sure it is only about Velvet?" said Meredith. "It isn't a revolution?"

Mr. Brown finally decided that this wouldn't do and he must go down to his shop. He went out the back way and was not definitely recognized, except by the local man on the Worthing *Witness and Echo*. This man walked beside him and asked him questions as he went towards his shop. Mr. Brown was not at all unwilling. "She was always a one for horses," he said, and gave a lot of details.

"I kin do without me shopping," said Mrs. Brown in the gloom at home. "There's enough of that cold salt beef."

"Jolly!" said Edwina. "Winning the Grand National an' living with the blinds down an' eating cold salt beef. I don't know that Velvet's done us much of a turn."

The first gloomy morning of fame went by, blinds down, salt beef, and everyone immured in the house. In the one local paper which they took there was a lot about Velvet, but no one thought of sending out for all the other papers.

"The ink don't print up Velvet's face too good," said Mrs. Brown with distaste. It was only what she expected.

The picture was called "The Gate-Crasher at the Grand National."

"Darn silly title," said Mally. "She didn't knock a thing."

Velvet was suffering from reaction and sat about limp. She did not bother about the newspaper except to glance at her picture. "I'd like to go out an' look at The Pie."

"You don't no one leave this house," said Mrs. Brown. They yawned and moped and grumbled.

"We'll have to go to a hotel if this goes on," said Edwina, who had once been to a hotel.

"That's what we'll do," said Mrs. Brown surprisingly, "if it don't blow over in a day or two. It's not but what I'm not proud of you, Velvet. But what's the good of you standing up for them gaping loonies to look at. They can't get no more out of you than they have done. You done your best up at Aintree and that ought to be enough. But what gets me is this gaping an' gaping an' handshaking an' behaving unfriendly an' curious as though you were a black savage they'd caught on the beach."

"Did they do it to you, mother, too? When you swum it?" Velvet jerked her head to the sea.

"They'd no modesty," said Mrs. Brown shortly, and said no more.

"Mother'd like to go out with a broom," said Meredith, after Mrs. Brown had left the room, "an' sweep 'em away."

"Mother's a one," said Mally, pulling a chair up for her feet.

But the middle-day post consoled Edwina and gave them all something to do. The door bell had been rung incessantly by the representatives of newspapers, but Mrs. Brown had the big bar-arm down and stuffed a duster in the bell. She knew the postman's knock, however, and he had had the sense to go round to the back.

There was an enormous box of chocolates for Velvet from an unknown admirer, and almost at the same moment a florist's man appeared groaning under a silver wicker basket loaded with pots of ferns and pink azaleas, and draped from head to foot in pink ribbon. This was from two of the aldermen on the Worthing Corporation.

But in the post itself there was something incredible. Among seven letters for Velvet, six were love letters, and again among them two were proposals of marriage. Edwina and Mally read them aloud with yelps of delight.

But the seventh, addressed to Miss V. Brown in a clerkly hand, was a different affair. It was written on paper like cardboard, its heading was neat and in fine scrollwork, and it explained to her that the stewards at Aintree, not being satisfied with explanations given on March 23rd, the matter was referred to the stewards of the National Hunt Committee, and the enquiry into the running of The Piebald by an unqualified rider would be held at 15 Cavendish Square on the following Tuesday, at which meeting Miss V. Brown, owner, was requested to appear.

"Trouble's got to come," said Mr. Brown, when he had heard the letter too. He had by degrees, and through the day, night, and morning, become a father who walked on air. "Trouble's got to come, Velvet, but nothing can take away what you done, my girl."

In the early afternoon the crowds grew denser.

"Brown family totally surrounded," read the headlines in the London papers. "Extra police drafted in." This brought more crowds. Worthing made hurried arrangements for a special bus-line, that people might see the crowds and become part of them.

Mrs. Brown closed the door upon reporters. And closed her lips. And closed her eyes and thought. To her the house seemed threatened. Edwina, Mally, Meredith . . . even the canaries seemed threatened. And Velvet most of all. The warmth, the cosiness, the privacy of life were blown with draught. Her house had a side taken out of it and she could not close it four-square.

How long would it take to live it down? It was like a gale. It was like staying indoors in a gale. She let the spaniels into the living room, as one calls in a yard animal in a dangerous hurricane.

"I gotta get some air," said Velvet feverishly at three o'clock, and stepped out of the back door to the orchard.

"Good day, Miss Velvet," said a slim lady instantly.

"Good day, Miss," said Velvet.

"I just wanted to ask you," said the lady—

"I've got a car here," said the lady. "Let's sit in it."

Velvet hesitated. It was not in her to refuse. She crossed to the lane, looking back at the cactus window.

The lady opened the door of the car and Velvet got in.

"Now," said the lady, settling down with Velvet beside her, "you're a great girl. Why, you're not as much as fourteen!"

"Fourteen," said Velvet shyly.

"Got any boy friends?"

"Oh . . . Mi. Mi Taylor."

"Who's he?"

"Dad's help. Father's help. In the slaughterhouse."

Velvet was without defenses. Her innocent and murmured sentences were like poppy seeds in a corn field. The field went scarlet and smelt narcotic and bloomed. But mercifully this was in America, and Velvet never knew what was written and said.

They had not got far (but far enough) with the interview when Mrs. Brown intervened. She called from the back doorway and Velvet, breathing relief, sprang from the car and went to her. The lady followed. "One moment . . ." she said, crossing the road too.

"No!" said Mrs. Brown sharply, and sent Velvet in behind her bulk.

"Excuse me," began the lady, "it's for the American press."

"In England we got rights," said Mrs. Brown, and shut the door in her face.

A big Daimler pushed its way up the street at three-thirty. Out of it got a little man with a big head and a garden of rich fur on his coat collar. He had a talk with Mr. Brown, whom by luck he saw going in at the street door. He sat in the living room for half an hour and as he rose to go he was heard to say that he would send his Daimler for both of them.

"Both who?" said Mrs. Brown, coming in when he had gone.

"Gentleman from the pictures," said father. "An actor. Well, an actor-manager. Come from Elstree in Essex. Come all the way to ask if Velvet could go an' pose for them."

"She going?"

"Says he's sending fer her tomorrow."

"Well," said Mrs. Brown, coming further into the room, "had she ought?"

Mr. Brown looked at her uneasily. "Hear that, Velvet?" he said to Velvet, who was sticking pictures of The Piebald into an album. "What do you feel about it yourself?"

"Think it might be fun," said Velvet carelessly.

"There y'are," said Mr. Brown irritably. "An' I don'

see any harm. He wants the horse too. He's sending down a horse-box . . .''

"Wants the horse?" said Velvet, looking up.

"Says he's made for a film, that horse."

"Can't have the horse," said Velvet swiftly, and went on pasting.

"What's that?"

"Piebald on the films!" said Velvet with a light firmness that had never been there before. "He seems to forget."

"What's he forget?"

"That *that's* the horse that won the National."

"That's why he wants him, Velvet," said father with unaccustomed patience.

"*I'll* go," said Velvet, getting up. "It won't be half bad for us all to go and see me doing things on the curtain an' the band playing and us sitting looking. But The Piebald! He doesn't know, he wouldn't know. He's out there in that field steady and safe. He believes in me. I wouldn't let him in for a thing that he couldn't understand. He's not like a human. He doesn't know how to be funny, and he shan't learn!" And the tears of her unwonted defiance streamed down her face.

"Well!" said Mr. Brown.

"An' what's more," sobbed Velvet, "an' what's more . . .''

"Well?" said Mr. Brown.

"I've read about horses . . . horses that has won . . . an' they write about them n-nobly's though they were statues. How can you write about a horse nobly if it goes on the films!"

"But what'll they be writing about your horse more'n they have done?"

"Not in the papers," said Velvet, now fairly howling,

"not in the p-papers. That's nothing. Mother—Mother—Mother l-lights the fire with that! In books! Big books. Roll-of-honor books where they put down the winners an' call them the Immortal Manifesto."

"The Immortal what?" said Mr. Brown.

"Manifesto. 'N' how can they call him the Immortal Piebald if he goes on the . . ."

"More like call you the Immortal Velvet!" growled Mr. Brown, thoroughly taken aback.

"Me! That's nothing. I'm nothing. If you could see what he did for me. He burst himself for me. 'N' when I asked him he burst himself more. 'N' when I asked him again he—he—doubled it. He tried near to death, he did. I'd sooner have that horse happy than go to heaven!"

"Behave yourself, Velvet!" said Mrs. Brown sharply. "Get upstairs. Merry's in an awful mess. She's upset the canary cage, water an' sand 'n' all on your bed. Get on up and help her."

As the door shut—"That child's got something that you don't value, William! That child's more mine than all the rest."

"I valued you all right once, didn't I, Araminty?"

"You did, William. Or maybe was it the pop an' squeak roun' me?"

"Now, Araminty," said Mr. Brown, rising, "don't you go an' cut queer with me over this. I'm bound to say I don't know whether I'm on my head or my heels sometime. It's like having a gunfire of bouquets thrown on you all at once n'you hardly know where it's coming from. It's like them sweepstakes that we all read break up the home, but we won't let all this to-do break up this home, will we?"

"You always was a nice chap," said Mrs. Brown. "On'y I'm so buried under me fat I feel half ashamed to tell you so. Love don't seem dainty on a fat woman. Nothin's going to break up this home not even if you lose yer head, but it'll make it easier if you keep it. On'y leave that child to me. She's got more to come. You think the Grand National's the end of all things, but a child that can do that can do more when she's grown. On'y keep her level, keep her going quiet. We'll live this down presently an' you'll see.''

After this, the longest speech Mrs. Brown had made for years, she went out into the yard to look for Donald.

She found, as she had hardly expected, that Donald was talking to a reporter.

There had been a pause. The reporter had not before tackled a mind which answered when it chose, on what lines it chose, or not at all.

Donald's interest in him was flickering, subterranean, critical. He was as usual torn by the suspicion that there might be something better to do.

''But she's a nice girl, your sister?'' said the reporter desperately.

''She wasn't a nice girl larse . . . July,'' said Donald. ''She didn't pull the plug after her bath. Mother said she wasn't nice.''

''Oh, well!'' said the reporter almost gaily. ''That's nothing! I've got a Gertrude that does that. She gets smacked for it.''

''Older'n me?''

''Much older than you.''

''I like pulling the plug but I'm not allowed to.''

The reporter's notebook remained blank.

''Yes, but . . . all that's no good to me.''

''Velvet tried to pull it,'' went on Donald. ''She broke it. It wouldn't pull. Father said it was a trashy plug.''

''Tell me something more about her.''

"She doesn't wash her neck sometimes."

"Tell me something different," said the reporter. "When your sister, Velvet, was a little girl . . ."

"I wasn't here," said Donald quickly.

"No, of course," said the reporter. "You were . . ."

"I wasn't a star either," said Donald. "I was somewhere. Doing things. Where do you smack your Gertrude?"

"Tell me, like a nice little chap . . ." (contempt surged over Donald and his lashes half veiled his eyes) "what sort of things does your sister play with?"

"My sister Velvet?"

"Your sister Velvet."

Donald considered. The reporter waited.

"See where I cut my ankle?" said Donald, holding up his leg. "I arsed fer the iodine myself."

"Yes, said the reporter dully, "it looks a bad cut."

Donald, like Jacob, could do a thousand things at once. He could hear, feel, see, gauge, forecast, decide, act. He was a twinkling surface, giving off and taking in. He was an incredible telephone exchange run by motes and atoms and impulsions. He had heard Velvet crying, he knew it was nearly dinner time, he knew there was a broccoli stump blocking the water gutter, he knew at last that this fellow was as empty as a bladder, and his mind went white towards him and turned red and blue and yellow towards everything else.

"Velvet's bin crying," he remarked, practically to himself.

"Why's that?" said the reporter keenly.

"I gotta go," said Donald, seeing his mother coming and walked away.

~ SIXTEEN ~

Velvet Brown, at a tender age and of a tender sex, won the Grand National. The mind of the public was at once stormed, irradiated and convulsed with a new surprise, fresh, keen, voracious. The fact crashed in the papers like a set of bells. The Mind of the public swung like bells too, pealing, pealing. As newspaper edition after edition came out the peals were set going in waves one after the other. The Mind could only swing and swing and ask to be pushed again. And the pushers flocked to push. The bell ringers pealed and hauled. The music of news broke and poured over the land. Portions of the Mind began almost at once to rebel. There are people who prefer wonder to arc through the sky, fall with its own curve, and cease on its fall. But the professional bell pealers and wonder mongers were not going to allow much of that. Bells must be handled again as their sound dies; wonder must be propped up and carry on in a straight line through the sky; the gaping Mind which had come alive like a young chicken must be stuffed with details and choked with news.

The enormous and delicate and intricate machinery which hangs on the fringe of news was set going. Men hammered tin because piebald horses must prance on the heads of tiepins, women painted little mugs and teacups in Staffordshire, Velvet galloped across nearly a mile of white cardboard, stamped out in diamond shapes and bent to hold a pound of chocolate creams. It was for the second impossible to be more notorious.

For a time Velvet and the sisters wandered in Arcady. They became princesses in Eden. People gave them sweets, adored their horses, took their photographs. What was so piquant in the papers was that in a row of beauties "it was the plain one that did it." This was somehow full of salt.

Only when the portraits of the paper horses, surreptitiously lent by Mr. Brown, appeared below a picture of the shell-box in a Sunday paper did Velvet say slowly, "Who gave them that?"

"What?"

"My shell-box."

But this blew over, and the shell-box was safe again on the sideboard, and Velvet hardly remembered that she had felt little scratches on her youth.

"Coo lummy . . ." began Edwina one day.

"You will please . . ." said Mr. Brown, "remember that you are now in the public eye."

"It's Velvet's public eye," said Edwina rather rudely. She was getting out of hand. But except for Edwina's rudeness, and that was always latent in the poor, up-growing, beautiful child, and except for Mrs. Brown's not unusual silence, and for little plumes of unhelpful vanity in Mr. Brown, there was no real deterioration in the Brown household.

Mally and Meredith adored the fuss and the sweets

and the visits from newspapers, and the marvel of the cinemas, and took delight in spotting "Velvet Novelties"; that piebald horse which now definitely galloped on the head of a tiepin at Woolworth's, and postcards with Velvet crouching in a black shirt tearing past a winning post.

"Let's collect them!" said Mally. And they began to make a collection.

When Velvet saw her face for the first time on the cinema she felt a little strange. It was an enlargement face, done thin on the canvas in black and white. It seemed like her. She could not say it wasn't.

"I look like that," she thought. And took it for granted that she did.

The same face, transplanted onto postcards, became almost a code sign. She could not have said what she felt but it was queer. However, she shook it off. "If you want something for your collection," said Edwina one day, "there's a brown silk in the window at Tinkler's called 'Velvet Brown.' "

"Tinkler's?"

"In Worthing."

"Is it expensive? Could we get a yard?"

"Ask them to give you a sample bit with the label pinned to it."

"Will they?"

"Get Velvet to ask them."

"Oh, yes, of course."

That was one of Velvet's very little burdens. The sisters always pushed her forward to ask for anything they wanted. Nobody refused Velvet anything. She became aware of this and grew delicate and obstinate.

When she went out she felt an insistent desire on the part of other people to get in touch with her. And once in touch it was quite literal—they touched her. They shook or held her hand, since the hand is not private, but only the body.

They came with a rush, with eagerness, as though they could get virtue, as though they could draw meat and drink. And when the "touching" was over and the child's hand had been shaken they hovered a second with baffled hunger, and murmuring "It was fine," retired. It crossed Velvet's mind occasionally to think they wanted something more of her.

Mally kept the "collection" with energy. It was in a box in the bedroom and was beginning to look like a rag-bag. There was a powder-puff called "The Velvet," in gold letters on printed voile, and a mechanical piebald horse that wound up and hopped across the floor. There was a cartoon in one of the evening papers of Velvet coming over Becher's sitting between the wings of Pegasus, and all the other horses looking scared. It was called "The Unseen Adversary." There were marvelous love letters from strangers, and boys at school, and workmen. One of the best began "Divine Equestrian"— but they all got very crumpled up and difficult to find.

There may be wonder in money, but there is money in wonder. And nothing is so cheap as a newspaper, where, when true news is truly breaking it starts up under the feet like a hare on the downs, and prince and poor man come in on the equal and swing along for their pennies while the news runs. And now the news was running hot and strong and pouring from it, as it ran, the true authentic scent. No basket hare this, let out and egged on to trot tamely by its keeper, and while Velvet lasted there was no need to bring carted news to the meet.

While the day approached for the sitting of the National Hunt Committee, the whole world was made to believe it was waiting for details.

"Coo lummy . . ." said Velvet, late on Monday night. And Mr. Brown found this excusable.

"Can't eat you," said Mrs. Brown, and glanced at Mi. It was Mi they could eat, she felt.

"We'll get away an' up to London early," said Mi. "We don' want to be messed up with hand-shaking tomorrow."

~ SEVENTEEN ~

In an upper room in 15 Cavendish Square, round a board table, the board had assembled. It was a distinguished company, mainly of robust and kindly men. They had as their spokesman, Messrs. Weatherby's lawyer, Mr. Simkin, and as their chairman, Lord Tunmarsh. The others were Colonel "Ruby" Allbrow, a man with an extraordinarily scarlet forehead, which turned his name into a better joke than it already was, Mits Schreiber, who had ridden in the National three times, Lord Henry Vile, Mr. Little (a descendant of Captain Joseph Lockhart Little), and Mr. Thomas, who was no descendant of "Mr. Thomas" (since the famous bearer rode under a pseudonym) but liked to think he was, Mr. Seckham, Mr. Coleman, Sir Harry Hall, and others. The clerk, Cotton, was in attendance.

"Sickening, this Velvet uproar," said Mr. Little, as they met.

"I've read none of it," said the chairman, taking his seat, "or as little as I could help. I'm in a position to judge the case on its merit. I only read *The Times*."

"What about the evening papers?"

"The evening papers," said Lord Tunmarsh, "are for the servants' hall. Is the girl here?"

"She's downstairs, waiting."

"Very well, Mr. Simkin! Will you tell us our position? Is it a case for prosecution? Is it a case coming under our own laws, how we stand, in fact?"

Mr. Simkin delivered a small oration on the laws of impersonation, standing as a black silhouette against the windows facing on Cavendish Square. He sat down. "It's beyond my imagination," he finished—"that is why I find it so difficult to give you, gentlemen, a crisp ruling—it's beyond my imagination to suppose that a female should have done such a thing. Should have so deceived US."

"But a female *has* done it, you ass!" (muttered Mits Schreiber). "Very much done it."

Simkin rose and went to a row of yellow calf volumes on the shelf.

He took down one. Over clapped the pages, flying under his dusty thumb. His long upper lip closed over his teeth.

"Attempting to defraud," he muttered. He looked sharply over his shoulder. "It's understood that we judge the case entirely—" There was an irritable and suspicious note in his voice.

The chairman looked up sharply. "You're not referring to the newspaper hurly-burly, I hope, are you, Mr. Simkin?"

"No, well, I hardly imagined, Mr. Chairman, no. And this a case of—(if I'm not mistaken) of fraud. I have it here. 'Attempting to obtain money under' . . . 'Obtaining money under' . . . no, she hasn't 'obtained.'

Attempting to obtain. That's it. Attempting to obtain. It's very clear.'' He looked up. "We can prosecute.''

"Legal, is it?''

Lord Tunmarsh looked uncomfortable. "Let's see the girl first. She's waiting?''

"Downstairs.''

"Let's see her,'' said Colonel "Ruby'' Allbrow. "Have her up. After all it was a good show. A first-class show she put up. What's her age?''

"Her age,'' broke in Mr. Simkin, looking at the Chairman, "is said to be fourteen. This I should say was a romantic understatement on the part of the Press. Might I say, Mr. Chairman, before the . . . young woman . . . comes into the room that I think that it would be a pity if any note of admiration be acknowledged during the interview. If indeed any is felt.''

The chairman nodded. "I think, Mr. Simkin, you can leave that to me. No admiration can be felt for what is practically a criminal proceeding. Involving forgery very probably. We'll have to look into that question of the faked clearance.''

Mits Schreiber addressed the Chairman.

"But if she's fourteen, can we prosecute a child of fourteen? Who put her up to do it?''

"Apparently nobody.''

"Impossible! Are we prepared as to what . . .''

"Have her up,'' said the chairman. "We shall know better when we see her. I'm not prepared, any more than Mr. Simkin is, to take it from her that she is fourteen. We have been loaded with more or less inaccurate (I daresay) descriptions of this young woman morning after morning. I need hardly say that—Not that we've any of us read 'em all, but—''

"Every bally word, Mr. Chairman!" broke in Mits Schreiber. "I'm a Velvet fan."

Lord Tunmarsh did not smile.

"Well, keep it to yourself, Mits. This is a meeting of the National Hunt Committee, and for myself I feel that we have been extremely offended by a piece of vulgarity. Mr. Simkin feels the same on behalf of Messrs. Weatherby. Please ask her to come up."

"Call her up, Cotton."

Velvet was shown up to the committee room of the National Hunt Committee.

The dusty stairs were dark. The door opened. The room was light.

All the men sitting round the table rose. Lord Tunmarsh drew a chair out for her. Velvet sank, sat on the edge, folded her hands. Fourteen men saw a featherweight plain child in a red jersey, dark blue wool skirt, blue wool coat with brass buttons and childish brown shoes with stub toes. They drew a breath.

"Good afternoon," said Lord Tunmarsh at last. "You are Miss Velvet Brown?"

"Yes," Velvet nodded gently. (Oh, God, don't let me be sick . . .)

"I really . . ." said Lord Tunmarsh, after a pause, but stopped himself.

"Well, was it you all right riding that piebald? It was you, wasn't it, Miss Brown?" broke in Colonel "Ruby" Allbrow on the silence.

"Me."

"What put it into your head, girl, to do a frivolous thing like that?"

Velvet slowly spread out her thin hands and counted the fan of muscles. She breathed something about the horse.

"What's that?"

"I knew the horse could do it," she said again.

"But why *you* riding? What d'you want to ride him *yourself*? Why not get a professional?"

"He . . ."

"Yes?" said Lord Tunmarsh, leaning a little towards her.

"He goes very well for me."

There was a pause.

Like an explosion, "He DID do that!" from a red-faced gentleman in checks.

"I think we shall have," said Lord Tunmarsh, "to ask Mr. Simkin to explain to her . . . just what . . . what we feel about the matter."

Mr. Simkin rose with alacrity. Rustled his papers. Blew out and drew down his upper lip.

Velvet looked up at him with her docile look. The fine bone round her white temple was blue with shadow, her newly-cropped pale hair hung close and uneven round her ears, she raised her head, and watched him with mild, intelligent eyes. Her lips parted slowly over the gold band and white teeth. Lord Tunmarsh whispered to his neighbor "hard to believe" and the neighbor whispered and shook his head.

Mr. Simkin read his clause from the yellow volume, under the heading, "Attempting to obtain money under false pretenses."

"You being a female," said Mr. Simkin . . . "and not an accredited male rider . . . come under this heading. It was a . . . for the time being . . . successful deception. Upon . . . ah . . . US. Upon Messrs. Weatherby (and the committee of the National Hunt). It was done to obtain a prize of . . ."

"No, no, it wasn't!" said Velvet.

"Eh . . . what . . . why not? You stood to get the prize?"

"Yes, sir. Yes, I did. But it wasn't done for that reason. It was done because . . ."

"And why was it done? We should like to know that?"

"Because," said Velvet, looking out of the window into the chimney pots of Cavendish Square, "the horse jumps lovely and I wanted him to be famous. I didn't think of the money when I planned it all."

"Ah, and now we come to that!" said Mr. Simkin. "You say you planned it all. That, Miss Brown, is hard to believe. You are, I understand, a child. You have obtained a false certificate from my . . . er . . . people. From US. From Messrs. Weatherby. You posted an Esthonian clearance to us and in exchange we forwarded to you the usual license. It was a monstrous imposture. How was it done?"

Velvet looked at him, her eyes full of light.

"There was so much to be done," she said at length.

"You mean that I am choosing only one of the grave impostures which you and your friends have . . . er . . . practiced. It is precisely the name of those friends which we wish to have laid before us. This is . . . Miss Brown . . . a very SERIOUS OFFENSE. A grave deceit has been practiced not on . . . upon US . . . but upon the public. The money of the public is in our trusteeship. We guarantee to the public that this great and famous race . . . into which you have entered so lightly, so frivolously, so mockingly, is a race which is run in such a way that they can put their money on it . . . er . . . safely."

" 'Safely's' a bit strong, Simkin," said Lord Tunmarsh.

" 'Safely', m'lord," said Simkin with obstinate pride. "Weatherby's prides themselves that they make racing safe up to the limits of the usual chances."

Lord Tunmarsh bit a piece of nail off his thumb. Mits Schreiber laughed.

"How old are you?" said Lord Tunmarsh suddenly.

"Fourteen, sir. Fifteen next month." This no longer seemed doubtful. Mr. Simkin resumed.

"Who has helped you in this?" he said startlingly to Velvet. "We want the names of your friends!"

"Mother knew. At the end," said Velvet.

"Your mother knew. That is important. Your mother is Mrs. Brown."

"My mother was Araminty Potter. She swam the Channel once."

"Her mother was Araminty Potter!" said Sir Harry Hall, whistling. "Swam the Channel breast-stroke twenty years ago. She downstairs?"

"No, sir."

"Your father's a . . ."

"Butcher, sir. A slaughterer-butcher."

"He knew?"

"No, he didn't know. Only afterwards. When I got my fall."

"So Araminty Potter married a butcher and got you?" said Sir Harry Hall. "And you've gone and swindled the almighty Weatherby's and won the Grand National . . ."

"Sir Harry," intervened Mr. Simkin, "I don't think this conduces to her understanding of the situation. Doesn't help. Doesn't help at all. If your father didn't know, Miss Brown (supposing this to be exact), and only your mother knew, then we must look for *other*

252 ━

supporters. I should like to begin with the Esthonian clearance? How was that got? And who procured it?"

Velvet looked at them, halting. Gazed at them. The light filled her face and she seemed to rest and wait. It was not a question of deciding. She and Mi had decided already. Both had known that they would have to pay for The Piebald's fame. In Mi's case he was praying for Velvet's.

"Mi's downstairs," she said at length. "Mi will tell you. We knew he would have to."

"And Mi is . . . ?" said Mr. Simkin, still standing against the windows in silhouette.

"Mi is Mi Taylor. He helps my father in the slaughterhouse," and even to her child's ears it seemed a rummy description of the glory of Mi.

"This Mi Taylor . . ." said Mr. Simkin, and stooped to whisper to his neighbor. The neighbor sent a paper round to the Chairman. Lord Tunmarsh nodded.

"Will you wait downstairs, Miss Brown?" he said. "We should like to speak to Mr. Taylor."

Velvet disappeared and Mi was before them. His cap in his hand, his hair already rising from the damp comb he had run through it on the stairs (having spat on the comb).

"Mi Taylor," he said, nodding.

"Mi . . . ?" said Mr. Simkin, writing.

"Michael," corrected Mi.

"And you are Mr. Brown's assistant in the business?"

"I landed up there," said Mi, "to do anything. Clean the slaughterhouse, buy sheep, help their ma, and so on. The boy's a handful."

"A boy?"

"Just a small one. No account yet."

"Well now, Taylor," said Mr. Simkin, clearing his throat, "I don't need to tell you that a frivolous and monstrous outrage had been committed. An impertinence and also, I imagine, a legally punishable fraud."

"Yes, sir."

"This fraud has ostensibly been committed by a child, the young lady we have just seen, Miss Velvet Brown. Obviously she could neither have planned it nor carried it through. Without help. Without the direction of another mind. What part did you play in all this, Taylor? We have got to know and we are going to know and I warn you to make no trouble over speaking the truth." Mr. Simkin sat down abruptly and gave the table a pencil tap. Everyone looked at Mi.

"I knew a boy," said Mi very simply, and he paused and sucked the hollow beside his tooth. "This boy knew a boy. . . . It was at Lewes races. Well, it was at Brighton races first and then I saw the other boy at Lewes races . . ."

"Their names?" said Mr. Simkin, writing.

"No," said Mi. "I ain't going to give you their names. You kin judge fer yourself when I've done. There was a whole trail o' boys. All talkin'. You know what they are, these races. Ain't got nothing to do. Lean up against each other an' jabber. More an' more kept coming in. No good to give you their names. I don't know 'em all. But the upshot was there was someone knew a fellow coming over that had a clearance from Esthonia. Going to ride a horse that come by air and dropped dead at Croydon. Then he hadn't any horse, see? So I met him. 'Long of these fellows I'm telling you about. They didn't do anything but jabber, so it's no good giving you the names. All they did was to say they knew a fellow had a clearance and didn't want his clearance. I oiled up the fellow an' got his clearance. Didn't want it so I got it. He didn't think any more about it. He's a half-Russian boy's bin riding out there for some count. He's gone back now. Never thought no more about it. Then I just posted in the clearance and got a license. See?"

"And this boy from Esthonia? Where is he now? He is, I suppose, the boy whose name is on the license? Tasky?"

"That's him. Where's he now? He's in Russia, s'far as I know. He got orders to cut off the hoof o' the dead horse an' take it back to the count. Fer an inkstand, I daresay. They make them into stands. Told me he was going straight to Esthonia, and then on to Russia where the count's got a winter job as a sort of a riding master with the Bolsheviks. Tasky and he, they go together most winters, so he said."

"Not much chance," whispered the Chairman to Colonel Allbrow, "of getting at Tasky. ('Less he ever comes again.) Looks to me as though the only culprit's here, in the room."

"So it seems to me, Taylor," said Mr. Simkin, "that the whole of this monstrous affair has been engineered by you and by you alone, if we are to believe you?"

Mi chuckled. Or the shade of a chuckle brushed him. He flicked it away and answered, "No."

"No, sir," he said. "There's Velvet. Velvet thought out the thing. It come to her. It come to her like the horse did, out of the sky."

"How did the horse come to her?" asked Captain Little, leaning forward.

"Why, she got it fer a shilling in a raffle in the village! There were yards about it in the *Express!*" said Mits.

Mr. Simkin frowned.

"Is that so, Taylor?" he said sharply.

"Yes, sir. You can go down to the village an' see. Anybody'd tell you. The horse belonged to Farmer Ede an' it made a filthy nuisance of itself, getting over walls and tearing down the village street. Nearly killed a child and nearly had a pushcart over twice. Ede couldn't do anything with it. He stuck it up for a raffle at the village fair in the summer. Didn't do badly: got nine pounds six shillings. Velvet took a ticket and won it. Then things went on an' on and she got moony about the horse, religious. She's a queer child. An' one day . . . when I see it jump a five foot wall by itself an' make away . . . I said . . . just kind of careless . . . just said . . ." (Mi waved his hand.) " 'Make a Grand National jumper, that would!" Then Velvet never said anything but she never let up on that. She just went on."

"It seems not possible . . ." said Lord Tunmarsh. "I never heard such a tale!"

"It's no tale," said Mi earnestly. "It's just Velvet. I know what's in her blood because my old father . . ." He paused.

"Your father?" said Mr. Simkin dryly. He did not like the eager, little-boy interest the committee was taking in the tale.

"My father was old Dan Taylor," said Mi, "an' he was a Channel trainer. He trained Araminty (Velvet's mother) to swim the Channel. *An'* she swum it. Against the tide in a terrible dirty morning in a storm . . ."

"I remember!" said Sir Harry Hall. "It was a bigger thing than anything that's bin done since. It was done breast-stroke. It seemed incredible."

"Well, then, that's her mother. It's in her blood. If you'd see her mother now you'd never believe it. Great old woman she is, all muscled up an' tight. An' silent. An' plucky's fire still. The father, he's not added nothing. It's the mare that's done it. An' Velvet, fer all she's such a sickly bit, she's like her. She'll sit on a horse like a shadow and breathe her soul into it. An' her hands. . . . She's got little hands like piano wires. I never seen such a creature on a horse."

"What are you by trade, Taylor? A professional rider?"

"I can't ride," said Mi slowly.

Sensation in the room.

"You can't ride, Taylor?" said the Chairman, after a pause.

"Never bin on a horse," said Mi, and it seemed to come home to him. He looked out of the window at the chimney pots.

"What's your history, then?"

"I couldn't swim," said Mi. "An' my old man carried on terrible. I went inland. I couldn't bear the sea. I wouldn't stick the sea down there at the coast now if it wasn't for Velvet. I went up North and I did this an' that. Got in with this lot an' got in with that lot. I was all round the racecourses and the livery stables. Doesn't take me much to live. I walked from here an' there an' landed up at Lewes at the races an' did a job fer Mr. Brown—Velvet's father. He asked me to help fer a day with some sheep in the slaughterhouse and then I saw that Mrs. Brown was my old man's Araminty. So I stayed."

"Well, gentlemen," said Mr. Simkin, looking more sour than ever, "we've heard the history of how it was done, and on the face of it, and *for the time being* it seems as though this deception *might* have been carried through in this way and by this one man. I say 'might.'"

We shall have to verify. It remains now of course to decide on our course of action. The man can be proceeded against legally, I should suppose, for attempting to obtain money under false pretenses. There is no doubt in my mind that had this fall of the rider's not taken place and had the prize money of £7,560 (not to speak of a cup worth two hundred pounds) been awarded, as it would have been if no objection had been lodged, then this man Taylor stood to gain, either the whole sum (the child being obviously under his influence) or in the case of the family being in the plan then no doubt the money would have been divided. It is not there . . ."

"Here!" said Mi. "What are you getting at!"

". . . it is not therefore . . ."

"I'm no thief!" said Mi. "The money'd 'a' bin Velvet's. She's the owner, isn't she? I did no more'n believe in her an' talk to her an' get her the clearance. She's the little wonder 'at's done it all. It would 'a' bin her money an' I'd 'a' seen that she kep' it. Her mother knew about it. She's no soft chicken. As for the money. . . . Why, we were so busy pulling it off we hadn't begun to think about what Velvet would do with the money. It was the horse she was thinking of. 'Putting the horse in history' she called it. She'd got that out of somewhere an' she kept thinking it and saying it too, sometimes. She'd think it at her dinner and at her tea. You could see her, with her eyes shining and her stomach heaving too, pretty often. She's got a terrible stomach, and when she gets excited she's an awful vomiter. *Me* the money. What's the use of seven thousand pounds to me?"

"Seven thousand pounds, Taylor, is always useful."

"I shouldn't know what to do with it! What'd I do? I don't want to live any better'n I live. It suits me. I don't want to be cluttered up. I wouldn't know the first thing what to do with seven thousand pounds. It would give me the itch. Maybe I'd bury it.''

"The whole story," intervened Lord Tunmarsh, "is so strange that I think we should like to discuss it alone. Will you wait downstairs, Taylor? There seems to be a commotion outside, Allbrow.'' The Chairman turned towards the window. "Is it a fire?''

Mr. Simkin looked outside into the Square.

"Crowds of people," he said. "Thick on the pavement.''

The door was knocked upon and hurriedly opened. A clerk came swiftly in and looked enquiringly at Mr. Simkin. Mr. Simkin pointed to the chairman. The clerk whispered.

"Good heavens!" said Lord Tunmarsh. "Open the window, Simkin.''

Mr. Simkin struggled with the dusty catch. Mr. Seckham helped him and the ancient window flew up. A roar flooded in on the air. The committee listened.

"They want the child," said the chairman. "Taylor, go down and look after her. Bolt the doors, Simkin! Get down and see everything's shut. What's your back way out?''

"The bar's down across the street door, m'lord," said the clerk. "But they're all up over the window sills. They seem to think Miss Brown is getting . . .''

"Getting what?''

"Two men, m'lord, shouted through the doorway as I was shutting it, 'You tick her off an' we'll cut your livers out!' m'lord.''

" 'Ticking her off,' they think! Well, so we are. Come on, young Mits! You get her out the back way!''

"The crowd's gone round there like water flowing, m'lord."

"I suppose there's a roof exit?" said the chairman, looking at the ceiling. "These old massive roofs. . . . Where's your fire exit? Here she is!"

"I brought her up," said Mi. "Such a din and faces at the windows. You better up here, an't you, Velvet?"

"What do they want?" said Velvet, looking white.

"To save you from us," said the Chairman. "It looks to me as though you're going to get a Lindbergh-Amy-Johnson week. I suggest we suspend the committee and that Captain Schreiber take the victim out over the roof. Here y'are, Mits! Take my card as chairman."

"The police are coming," said Mr. Simkin, looking down. "Mounted police."

"Oh, let me look!" said Velvet.

She hung out of the window and the crowd caught sight of her. A roar went up.

"Now you've done it!" said the chairman.

It took the police an hour to disperse the crowd. Meanwhile Mits Schreiber, Velvet, Mi and a clerk crossed the roofs of Cavendish Square and descended by J. Denvers' "Cotton House." They knocked at the glass window of the fire escape and were let in by a typist.

"Fire down the Square!" said the typist.

"Yes, we're from it," said Mits briefly. "Is this the way down?"

They went down into the street by the iron staircase and were met by the manager of the Cotton Works at the bottom.

"Card," said Mits Schreiber. "Thank you very much. Thank that girl of yours for letting us through."

"Fire, m'lord?" said the manager.

"Kind of fire," said Mits. "There's a taxi. Come on while the crowd's busy down there."

They left the clerk behind and bundled into a taxi. Velvet and Mits sat together and Mi on the strap seat.

"Where d'you want to go?" said Mits to Mi.

"Victoria Station, sir," said Mi. "But I'd like to take her to the pictures first."

"I shouldn't," said Mits Schreiber. "Not today. You'll be mobbed. They're still running the film of the National. But you'll be mobbed if you put your nose inside. The place is simply feverish today."

"Victoria Station," said Mits, "and drop me off at Brook Street." The taxi started. "I've got to get to Scotland tonight."

"What'll you all do to us?" said Velvet timidly.

"Drop the whole thing of course," said Mits absently. "But you won't get your money or your cup, you know."

"That bay'll get it," said Velvet. "He was a good bay."

"I'm not sure you won't be officially warned off, too. No Newmarket Plate for you now."

"Oh . . . THAT . . ." said Velvet.

"Yes, I forgot. It's not much after winning the Grand National. What are you going to do now?"

"Oh, jes' go home," said Velvet. "I expect I'll go out an' have a look at the horse tonight."

"Look here . . ." said Mits Schreiber earnestly. "We're getting to Brook Street. I've bin all over the world with horses an' I want to say this. You try to keep life just the same for you from now on. The public's been after you, but they're flogged tired, and they'll drop it soon. There'll be a tale about our flight tomorrow in the press, and that clerk Cotton'll go an' give away what we dare. You've been having a queer kind of hot air puffing round you. You've bin blown up like a pink pig in the air fit to burst, and maybe now they'll let you die away with a squeak like a pink pig does. Don't let me find you one day with a hard face an' a dirty bit of cigarette and nerves all gone to blazes, looking for this hot hair again! It's bad stuff. Mi—what's yer name, look after her! Here I am. Stop, man, stop! Blast! he's overshot the house. I bin some funny crowds an' I know! That child's bin written across the sky like somebody's pills. You see she gets over it! Good-by, both of you. Off you go. Victoria Station, Brighton line.''

"Oh, isn't he nice!" said Velvet. "So they're going to let us off! Aren't they sweet, Mi? I say, Mi, have you got money for the taxi?''

"No, I haven't," said Mi. "I got the tickets an' a shilling. I knew I hadn't.''

"It's two and nine," said Velvet, leaning forward. "Here's the station, too."

The taxi drew up and Mi opened the door and got out. As Velvet stood in the door there was a soft fluttering noise, like veiled pistols being shot into blankets. Velvet was snapped and snapped again from every angle. The black hoods of the cameras were turned on her in a set circle. She saw hooded men kneeling, squatting, standing. Mi clutched Velvet by the arm and swung her towards the taxi-man. "I'm short," he said. "Ain't got it, Percy. Give you a shilling an' . . .''

"It's all right. I can lend it to you," said a nice-looking boy in a blue suit.

("Gentleman!" thought Mi.)

"Here y'are, taxi," said the boy. "Look here, Miss Brown, I've got a car here. I'll drive you . . . both . . .

262 ⬤

down to Brighton. Drive you home, see? Sports Bently.''

"You the press?" said Mi shortly.

"You come in my car and see," said the boy. "I won't publish a thing you don't . . ."

"Come on, Velvet," said Mi. "Run for it!"

It was too late. They couldn't run in a heavy sea. The crowd pressed in from behind to see what was happening. "What'sa matter? Accident? No, that girl that won the National. They're photographing her. Where? What? National Velvet!"

"National Velvet!" shouted the crowd as Mi and Velvet pressed slowly forward.

"Won't you let me pass!" said Velvet in a small voice. She had her foot trodden on. Several shook her hands. Left hand, right hand. She lost her purse.

"No fun about this," muttered Mi. "This is awful."

"My purse has dropped. Now I've no ticket," she called to Mi.

"Leave it. Don't stoop down. You'll be trodden on," said Mi, getting his arm round her.

They surged past the fruit shop and the telephone boxes and a door opened in the great ticket office and a man swept them inside. Velvet dropped onto a chair panting.

Half an hour later the police got them into their train. An hour later the red Buicks were tearing up the Embankment from Carmelite Street . . . "National Velvet at Victoria Station."

"National Velvet had up before the Hunt Committee," "Great Crowds in Cavendish Square. Flight with Lord Tunmarsh over the roofs." (This was an error, owing to the card.)

*　　*　　*

The fever about her raged until the findings of the National Hunt Committee came out in the evening papers. *They had decided to drop the whole thing.*

Again the news machinery was set in motion. Cleared lines gulped that which sped along them. But by the morning the story was dead. The public had been overwhipped. It could stand no more. Dead news like dead love was no phoenix in its ashes.

"Velvet Brown," said the man in New York, whipping out his orders. "Cut her out. Old stuff. That Jane only rates a couple of sticks."

Chrysanthemums, roses in winter, glacéd sweets, love letters, interviews, satin pillow-dolls—the house had flowed with gifts, Edwina, Mally and Merry had eaten themselves sick, but Velvet, who did not care for flowers, could not stomach many sweets, did not read the love letters, never played with dolls, remained with her real desires sharp and intact, the ascending spirit with which she was threaded unquenched by surfeit.

While the glory had sedged and seethed about her she had been aware that as she moved so had the public rippled. That she had been like a boat that made a wake, that waves on either side had clapped and sparkled.

But no one had learned anything about her. No one had formed the slightest picture of her, and she had gathered an impression of isolation as she moved, was touched, hemmed in. Her thin face on the sheet of the cinema was not more strange than her portrait had been in the minds of those who had surrounded her. Her name, which had blazed in the sky, now hung there in a quiet corner with the letters unlit. The arch at the opening of the street first withered, then blew down.

The village took her back. If people called her "National Velvet" it was in fun and affection, and like a dig in the ribs. It meant "What next, you little blighter! Get on with your growing."

Mrs. Brown found an old trunk for the chocolate boxes and the flower ribbons and Mally's collection. It was April. The gymkhana summer was all before them.

Thus Velvet was not fifteen when the thing left her and passed on, the alienating substance, the glory wine. She was like a child who is offered wine too young and does not really drink. She put her lips to the goblet while thinking of other things. She got off. She glanced the most acute and heady danger and got off. The press blew, the public stared, hands flew out like a million little fishes after bread. Velvet had shone, a wonder, a glory, a miracle child.

And now, finished with that puzzling mixture of insane intimacy and isolation which is notoriety, Velvet was able to get on quietly to her next adventures. For obviously she was a person to whom things happened, since in a year she had become an heiress, got a horse for a shilling, and won the Grand National.